THE CADUCEUS CODES

THE CADUCEUS CODES

JR RAY

HealersLetters

Cover and interior design by Bea Reis Custodio
@beareiscustodio
London

Cover images: Cdc and The National Cancer Institute, Unsplash

ISBN 979-8-9898784-1-3 (Paperback)
ISBN 979-8-9898784-0-6 (eBook)

CONTENTS

LIST OF CHARACTERS
Ages given in 2030

Manny Garcia — Thirty-five-year-old scientist originally from Argentina whose wife died of cancer

George Garcia — Manny Garcia's fourteen-year-old son

Michael Kochanski — Forty-five-year-old Polish American businessman who lives in Chicago and invested in a startup that was sold to Drukker, an AI computing corporation in the San Francisco Bay area

David Campbell — Thirty-five-year-old MIT trained scientist originally from Texas who completed high school at StarHall, a boarding school in the Northeastern United States. He works with Michael Kochanski as a scientific consultant.

Elise Sheraton — American MD PhD divorced and in her late forties, a pediatrician. She moves to Saburia for temporary employment by Soria Medical Clinics, an international medical chain

Pandolf, Northern California

Shelly Sharma — Twenty-nine-year-old MD, resident in Ob/Gyn at Pandolf Medical Center, her father is originally from India

Julia "Lucky" Malone — Twenty-nine-year-old MD, resident in Internal Medicine, Pandolf Medical Center

Charlie Malone — Lucky's fifteen-year-old brother

Michaela — Charlie's off and on girlfriend

Dean Baluyn — CEO of Pandolf Medical Center in his mid-forties who also completed high school at StarHall. He is part of the elite Mather family

Chicago, Illinois

Alex Marion	Thirty-four-year-old artist who also does forgeries
Callie Marion	Alex's twenty-eight-year-old wife and mother of their two children
Jim Sichet	Forty-four-year-old Chicago lawyer and politician who also attended boarding school at StarHall with Dean Baluyn
Oscar Sanchez	Twenty-four-year-old runner for Kochanski in Chicago, undocumented immigrant originally from Latin America

New York City, New York

Mary	Seventy-year-old real estate tycoon, widow, and grandmother who lives in Manhattan and develops cancer

Saburia (a small fictional nation in East Africa with a coastal border on the Red Sea)

Red Sea coast location has a military base with a medical clinic that is staffed by Soria Medical Clinics

Arjun Bhattacharya	Late forties, an Indian American physician who is the military base's Medical Officer and a friend of Dr. Elise Sheraton

Ramses, the capital of Saburia

King Mohammed Saburi	Forty-four-year-old monarch of Saburia who also attended StarHall with Dean Baluyn and Jim Sichet
Queen Salma	King Mohammed's forty-four-year-old first wife
Queen Noru	King Mohammed's nineteen-year-old third wife
Syed Malik	King Mohammed and Queen Salma's twenty-three-year-old son

PROLOGUE

March 2030, the day started at 7 a.m. for one of New York City's largest hospitals. Cold outside, staff streamed from the dark into brightly lit buildings. Among the early patients, Mary also arrived. Seventy, petite, she said nothing while a tech drew her blood and helped to thread her through a scanner. By 9 a.m., she waited at the hospital's renowned cancer center to see her oncologist.

Having Dr. Bains as her physician meant paying extra for health insurance, and then arguing that she wanted to see him and not the other "providers." Those strangers knew little about her except for what they gleaned from the computer. Her refusal to see anyone but Dr. Bains made the medical staff impatient. But she was persistent. *I may look easy to push around, but guess what, guys, I have plenty of time to wait.*

This time, they took her in right away, to a small, windowless exam room.

Dr. Bains strode in, a tall man in his fifties, for once no fellows and residents lockstep behind him. "I'm sorry, Mary," he said. "There are new spots in the liver."

He explained that her cancer had returned.

But I feel fine. After a shocked silence, she asked, "What's next?"

"In the United States, we've exhausted all reasonable options—"

"You mean this is terminal?" she exclaimed, feeling chilled.

"No," he said gently. On his computer, he pulled up a website. "I can't officially recommend their approach, but I've been looking around for you. The Chinese are at the frontiers of this war. I think this is one of their initiatives. Still experimental."

Dr. Bains scrolled through a blur of screens on the wall monitor. "Your insurance won't cover this. But you can afford it."

She muttered, "Time is like land—you can't make more of it. Both are more valuable than money."

"Spoken as someone who's done well in real estate," he said.

She noticed that his scribe was also missing today. In blueberry scrubs, one was usually there, intruding on their privacy, clicking everything into the computer, ringing up all the incomprehensible charges that would appear on her next medical bill.

He did not enter his "unofficial" recommendation into the work computer. He saw her looking at his idling workstation, then at his hands in his lap. He glanced at the closed door.

"Mary, I don't always put everything into your file. When I send patients outside the system . . . ." He looked down again.

"If it were you in my situation, would you sign up?" She felt her eyes wet, her voice tremble.

"Yes." He offered her tissues.

"I trust your guidance. And I want to live." She dabbed her eyes.

Before she left, he gently touched her hand with his blue-gloved one. "Good luck. Keep me in the loop about what you decide to do?"

• • •

After her appointment, she clicked on the link Dr. Bains gave her. After making herself "sleep on it" for one night, she enrolled in Soria Clinics' experimental trial. That Friday, she slit open the thick envelope that arrived in the mail. The printed heading of the cover letter said: Soria International Medical Clinics. Below, there was a note from a "Manny Garcia PhD." She felt confused. That was not a typical Chinese name. Could Dr. Bains have been incorrect about the nationality of this clinic, she wondered? Garcia welcomed her to the trial—"grateful for your participation."

She and Dr. Bains had decided to start more chemotherapy just in case she changed her mind about entering Soria's experimental trial. Getting her first home infusion, she told the masked nurse how she wanted to be outside, sharing not just this season but many more with her grandchildren.

Actually, I want to bawl! My life's melting too, like that ice outside, like my snowball piles long ago when the purple crocuses started to bloom on Gramma's old farm.

The nurse propped up Mary's pillows. "You really don't want to be outside around all those people, carrying germs like fleas."

"Being sick makes me feel ninety-five," she grumbled.

Brilliant sunlight flooded her room, reflecting off the snow draping Central Park. The winter season was melting into spring, and slush dropped from the trees. Far below, merry pedestrians shielded themselves with their hoods.

After the nurse left, Mary clicked the clinic's link on her laptop, deciding the clinic's true nationality did not matter, really, because she was *not* going to change her mind. She typed in her login details and password. The image of a sun filled the screen, yellow with a tie-dyed halo radiating outward. The next screen announced:

OUR SERVER IS DOWN
PLEASE CHECK BACK LATER
LEAVE YOUR MESSAGE HERE

It was always like that. She left her note and signed it off—"MARY."

Except for the biblical Mary, her name was common. She was another in an infinite procession of Marys through time. "BEELZEBUB" would have been a less boring account ID.

She poured herself a glass of icy Chardonnay. They had told her not to mix her chemotherapy with alcohol, one poison with another. Really? Her future might be just a quick fatal drink anyway.

The wine bottle's label showed a watercolor of a castle above a frozen ocean. Crumbling stones in the wall met sand and water with shards of ice.

She had given Dr. Bains a case of the wine. Later, he said, "My wife also thanks you. She likes the poem on the back."

She read it again:

Always, those who love me will feel you, hear the song of our bond until the roar of war and water break us down to ghosts and stones.

The wine had a seawater tang. She drank, drowning in memories, recalling herself as a girl who loved pink hydrangea, then a woman who kissed the father of her children and rested her cheek against his muscled shoulder.

Bare branches had pierced the skies when they carried his body away, that winter her husband died. In her memories she saw him again; and then again, echoing in their daughter and grandchildren, she heard his voice and even his quiet sense of humor. How did people die and not disappear?

Mary's eyes returned to her bedroom's picture windows. Though she had paid a steep price to repurchase and renovate her childhood flat, her investment had beat the stock market over the years. Into the dimming city skies above, she murmured her remembrance, her response to the poem on the bottle:

"In the whisper of the wind, listen. In a flash of color in the woods, I see you. In our songs, I am with you. You love me all over again when I dream of you . . . until I fade away, too."

She closed her magazine, a bound volume of glossy pictures, luxury properties for sale, and fell asleep. Her laptop turned off from inactivity. Dusk crept in, the windows glowing gold. She was dreaming again, traveling on the Silk Road to a faraway town of colored tents that flowered on desert sand under a silver and blue sky. Since Dr. Bains thought her new treatments were from China, her mind now journeyed east. Dropping below the horizon's sunrise, her sick body entered a half floor in the kingdom of medicine into the lab of a modern alchemist named Manny Garcia PhD—its healer.

CHAPTER ONE

The next day, Mary's digital message traveled not east but west, westward across the continental United States, not at the speed of Lewis and Clark in the 1800s but of an electromagnetic wave more than two centuries later. It landed in a Soria company phone in Pandolf, California, about two hours from San Francisco.

The phone broke the silence with a merry alert. Its owner, Manny Garcia, thirty-five, originally from Argentina, was alone in a lab on a Friday evening. In the steel cockpit of a confessional-sized AI machine, he hummed *G*, *C*, *A*, and *T*, the nucleic acids of DNA, stringing them into long chains of letters and then breaking with *A*—the only letter in Pia's name within the DNA code—in memory of his wife. Pia had passed from cancer. Her birthday was this month, and what a party he would have given her—fireworks, colored balloons, and kisses.

The Drukker console before him flashed a spectrum of lights. Sounds spoke a language only a trained operator understood. An avatar lounged on one screen, "The Frog Den," the nerve center of a make-believe galaxy. On the arcade-style Toccata Touch keyboard, named by a fellow music lover at Drukker, he clicked a "TEST" red dot that opened windows of theories and flashing algorithms. Pursuing them through dense woods of numbers and patterns, minutes and years, disease and disaster, he ordered the chaos of information in a patient's file by biochemical motifs across an entire sequence of medical metamorphoses.

When the computer suggested a break, he tapped the screen to pause working on Mary's medical file and open the secure message on his Soria Clinics phone.

March 15, 2030
Hello, I am one of the patients in your cancer trial and a grandma

who would like to have more time with her grandkids. Thank you so much for your help! What can be more precious than hope?

Gratefully, Mary

The message was written yesterday. Soria Clinics must have held it overnight for review before releasing it to him. Strictly speaking, Pandolf Medical Center had not authorized him to work on his secret side project for Soria. His contract specified that anything "an employee created with company time or resources was (their) intellectual property." Still, what was the harm? During these off times like tonight, no one else was on the Drukker computer, and he was making tremendous progress using its latest AI to run biological programs.

Soria was an international clinic chain that had sent him terminally ill cancer patients' digital records, de-identified for privacy. For them, he was tallying treatment recommendations. Soria, like Garcia, had not asked Pandolf for permission to use their equipment for their project. He had not pointed out their breach of normal protocol, either.

It was time. *Tap.* A thin glass bar, the first disk, ejected near his knee. *Tap again.* Another bar. Three more followed.

The Drukker asked, "Do you wish to run this file?"

Tap, yes.

"Your data will no longer be retrievable. Do you still wish to run this file?" A sympathetic synthetic woman's voice.

Garcia hit the "ENTER" key. Pages of code scrolled down the monitor, raining many colors before the screen went black. Then the trademark sun dawned its 3D security logo.

He scrawled in black marker on the five glass disks the names that Soria had given him for the research subjects, all pseudonyms except for Mary. There were four other files besides Mary's, terminal cancer patients who were wealthy enough to pay but had not yet signed up for the trial. On their disks, he wrote their aliases: "MARK," "MATTHEW," "LUKE," and "JOHN." As for Soria's use of biblical figures for the other name choices, he figured that plenty of rich people with savior complexes dabbled in the medical field.

Mary was his first patient for his new AI cancer vaccine design. His job, ignoring religious superstition, was to make recommendations to

Soria's machine learning and artificial intelligence team—to help her immune system combat the dynamic genetics of cancer. Feeding medical data into the computer, from digitalized blood and biopsy results to imaging, he sleuthed how each patient's tumor had evolved. The ingenious metamorphoses of cancer, from a single cell to changing hide-and-seek colonies of millions within the victim's body, then became targets for the Drukker's AI. His aim: precision medicine for Mary and other terminally ill patients to have remission, even a cure, and then die one day of something besides cancer.

Heart pounding, breathing shallow, he slipped the five disks into cases that he dropped into his backpack. He was a scientist, not a thief, he told himself. He had never bent the knee to anyone else's moral code; instead, he had become an unbeliever in the church of American academic medicine and would pay the worldly price. To seize this chance to pursue his research ideas, after working all his life for other (dull) people on their projects, it was the right thing to do.

Next to the supercomputer housing, a frayed notebook swung like a hanged man from a nail. In it, his fellow scientists scribbled their times for reservations to use the Drukker, their illegible writing often causing feuds about schedules. Shared by many labs, the powerful machine was worked on simultaneously, but the scientists soon discovered that the greater the number of users at any time, the slower the processing of their experiments. After one team "accidentally" terminated Garcia's experiment, perhaps to speed up theirs, Garcia now sat in the console for hours, vigilant for interruptions, while the computer worked on *his projects*! When he briefly left, it was for a bite from the vending machine or oatmeal in hot water mixed with dry milk from his research supplies. For a dash to the restroom, he threw his backpack, coat, and papers onto the seat to prevent anyone else from occupying it.

Garcia himself was the Pandolf campus Drukker expert who had led the team that brought the supercomputer to Pandolf. One would have thought that gave him seniority and his work priority, he thought. *No, Garcia, what gave you that stupid idea?*

What is today? he then wondered. After he checked his phone to find out, he jotted his name into blank spaces for next week's schedule. Luckily for his unauthorized research, he was able to get time for it on the AI machine because no one else used the machine during the graveyard hours he worked on Soria's project. Those midnight hours also made getting caught less likely.

Time, its inexorable order in clocks, calendars, and schedules—then an alarm beeped on his watch. Time to scramble that last record in the printer. Mary was his first and only patient so far. Her treatment files *had* to get to Saburia in time—or they would not work. The personalized vaccines he had designed had an expiration date because her cancer was not only growing but changing, evolving to where his antidotes would have to be updated to treat her. He tapped instructions into the blinking console.

On his personal phone, he checked the home camera. Yesterday, it had showed someone inside his apartment, a masked shadow that disappeared through his door. *Who? Why?* The building super had said that it wasn't him or the building handyman and suggested he change the locks. Instead, panicked about someone spying on his forbidden experiments, Garcia accelerated his work schedule to complete Mary's treatment file for Soria and then destroy all of Soria's data on the Pandolf computer.

His task to destroy the data on the computer required a hardware intervention. With his toolbox, he lay back down on the floor and slid under the printer. Engrossed in delicate electronics by the light of his headlamp, he heard the laboratory door open and close. *Who could be entering the lab now?* Sweating but cold with fear of getting caught, he slid back out from under the printer and turned toward the sound of footsteps.

"Dr. Garcia!" A young woman's voice.

Relieved it was only Shelly Sharma, he exhaled and sat up.

Seeing her surprised face, his relief turned into annoyance, then resignation. Sharma often slowed him down as they worked together in the lab, interrupting a complicated algorithm or a time-sensitive experiment with questions or just conversation. At those times, trying not to lose his stream of thought, he would patiently stare at the screen and murmur brief responses as needed until she returned to her goggles and pipette.

In the medical hierarchy, she had to call him Dr. Garcia for his PhD. But he could call her by her first name. Though she was an MD, she was lower than him in the laboratory hierarchy as an Ob/Gyn resident in training. And both called their boss, an MD-PhD, Dr. Nepski. And Nepski called her "Shelly" and him, "Manny." *All quite silly to keep track of.*

"What are you doing?" she asked.

"Just checking patterns!" He stood up quickly. "The company rep said it'll be a while before they can finish our updates. I just started a minor patch."

Leaving cables and tools still under the printer, he returned to his desk, trying to divert her attention away from his sabotage of the printer's records. "Come, I want to show you how I do laser testing—"

"Sorry to interrupt you, Dr. Garcia, but I'm here for my experiment."

How could she not be interested in chaos analysis? he wondered. Across the room, the AI printer hummed. He walked back to the machine to confirm that the destruction of his files was complete. Relieved, his job finished, he returned to quickly pick up his backpack to leave.

Why was she still standing there, looking at him expectantly? he wondered.

He thought hard. "Shelly," he finally ventured, "have you organized the backup data drives?"

Her face turned stony.

"All lined up and labeled," Sharma said brusquely, gesturing at the storage cabinet. "Sorry I'm late today. I was working on the Pandolf fundraiser with Dr. Nepski."

"What fundraiser?"

"We had on our green armbands. Didn't you see?" She pointed to a flyer on the wall.

He remembered that no one showed up for their weekly lab meeting that morning. To get into the building, he had plowed through a green-clad crowd starting a 5K run, cameras, banners, and the distant thud of music. "Oh, yes, the Green Martian Microbe-athon."

"What'd you say?"

He shook his head. "You know what I think. Pandolf is part of this grand medical-academic-pharmaceutical government system that feeds itself. They don't even pay taxes by being nonprofits. But you know how much our CEO was paid last year?"

She looked away, not answering, clearly disinterested.

At least the kids at the Dock enjoy my rants, he thought. The Dock was headquarters of the Drukker AI corporation in the San Francisco Bay Area. There, they saw him as an old sixties type of guy and had even taken his vegan idea to Manufacturing—for all the Drukker seat covers to be synthetic instead of animal leather.

He had accepted this job at Pandolf only after he found out that they were going to buy the Drukker AI technology. His medical research for Soria Clinics required its multidimensional modeling and big data analysis. Now he could load an experiment file and sit at the control board, forgetting even to eat or drink. Over hours, data spewed onto his monitors as endless as the dust in the universe. Perhaps he could not compose the classical music he loved, but as *this* type of composer, he found the right tunes to turn noise into music.

He liked technology more and people less as time went by. But he liked Shelly Sharma. About thirty, mixed South Asian and White, she was a resident doctor who worked with him on research to strengthen her applications for advanced surgery fellowships, part of the army of resident doctors in Pandolf who floated through its labs. Sharma lived in her miniature world, like a mouse in a storybook, a young woman who spent hours pipetting placenta extract into endless wells in plates to slide into the analyzer. Back at the Dock, only two hours away in San Francisco, they had robots to do that type of repetitive work.

Some days ago, they had discussed his ideas for her new experiment over dinner. Walking to Palatine Hill, Pandolf's Italian restaurant, he matched his long stride to her shorter steps. Palatine Hill overlooked an expanse of sloping lawn down to the central lake of the medical center. At night, the silver lake mirrored the lights and traffic of the medical campus, glittering within the darkening valley. A distant ambulance whined and threaded its flashing way into the hospital campus from the highway.

Inside, plaster walls displayed a painting of low Roman hills, the buildings half ruined and half vegetated, reflecting a dawn sky flushed red and streaked with gold.

"Palatine Hill in Rome actually looks a bit like this, just more dilapidated," he told her as a waiter led them back outside to the patio, warmed by heat lamps and a firepit, past another painted panorama, this one of ancient gods and battles, framed by exposed brick.

At dinner, he sipped Chianti and explained his idea. "Drukker has a pipetting robot so you can scale up your experiment. But Dr. Nepski says he wants to see preliminary results before he budgets it."

The candle flickered in its glass globe between them. Their eyes met, hers a liquid brown with the candlelight flickering in their lucid centers. He reminded himself that he was her mentor, a duty that precluded romance—even if the god of love didn't care. Anyway, any romantic spark within him was a distraction right now. The gaps in their ages, pasts . . . and futures put a thick pane between them.

She jotted notes into her phone. Then she scrutinized the lower crescent of his glasses. *I forgot to remove my Drukker prototype eyes!* he remembered. Wary of questions she might now ask, he removed his glasses. Her face was blurry now.

Quickly throwing in a question to distract her from his experimental vision augmenters—he asked about an advance in remote surgery. Excited, she explained how robots had recently performed a series of transplants—controlled by a surgeon hundreds of miles away.

She had seen his Drukker prototype glasses, he thought, now deep in his jacket pocket. She indeed had the sharp eyes, he thought, of the surgeon she was training to become. Working on lab equipment beside her, he had also noticed the length of her fingers and the dexterity in how they moved. Surgeons, originally butchers in the history of medicine, saw but often didn't see—he was glad that she didn't ask him for a closer look at the Drukker vision analyzer. But Sharma had both smarts and stamina—she ran marathons—she might ask later, he thought, to look. By then, he should make up some lie to evade her.

For dessert, they shared a tiramisu, a generous American portion. When Garcia's wife was alive, they used to share dessert too. "Like a kiss," Pia would say. After one bite, his eyes grew wet, and his throat tightened.

He and the Italian head waiter then discussed the Old World, before pandemics and across oceans of water and time, a favorite opera, remote towns.

"I love his cute accent and tux, even if he makes me feel kind of scruffy," said Sharma.

"You always look great."

They parted amid the lavender scent of jumbles of flowers in the restaurant's lobby. He walked out into the chilly breeze. Under the night sky, at the valley's edge, he took a shortcut home.

• • •

That was some days ago. Now, looking at Sharma in the lab, Garcia understood. "I'm sorry, I just remembered. We were going to discuss your project today."

"Yes, you totally forgot, didn't you?" she accused.

"I'm sorry. And I totally get why you were late."

She was quiet.

"Still, about your cancer fundraiser, do you really think that if a cure came along, these folks at Pandolf would be any better than the Romans with Jesus or the Church that almost burned Galileo on the stake? What would happen to their careers, money, buildings, the porphyry marble, their fountains . . . ?"

He knew she had heard the bitter edge to his voice. Then he thought he heard a sound and looked behind him. No hidden colleague had jumped into "his" machine. Trying to relax, he inhaled, pressing shoulder blades together, then exhaled, arching his back up like a cat and stretching his arms.

I have to get out of here. Time is short.

"All that sitting, hard on the body. I'm not as young as you," he said, changing the subject. "I have to go to the airport right now to pick up my son. But let's reschedule for a time next week to go over your experiment?"

Now she smiled. "All this time, I didn't know you had a son."

Embarrassed, he looked away. People saw that he spent most of his time in the lab, and when he came to social events, he was alone. What did they think he was: divorced, single, gay, lone wolf . . . ?

He explained, "Yes, my wife passed away seven years ago. Jorge is fourteen now. Because my previous work situation wasn't stable, he lived with other family. But he's finally moving here with me." He hesitated. "He wants to be called George now."

"George," Sharma said thoughtfully, "like my original name was Sushila, an Indian name, my dad's Indian American, but I go by Shelly. Maybe your son likes 'George' because it makes him feel more at home in the United States instead of 'Jorge.'" She said 'Jorge' with a heavy American accent.

"Papa did not come to the United States until he was an adult," she continued. "Then he shortened his name so people could pronounce it. When I was growing up in Texas, my father worked very hard as a country doctor. It's a treat when he tells us stories about his childhood in India. I remember once how he explained that the word *blue*, in English, resonates in a sad way. But in Hindi, his native language, the same word makes him think of the bright blue of a peacock feather or a woman's sari."

Unexpected memories of Pia drifted before Garcia—he willed away her aura and the sadness that would follow.

Distantly he heard Sharma say, "Or as my dad said about *pink*, 'In American English, it is hot pink, cotton candy, or a pop star's lipstick. But in Hindi, it's the color of desserts you share with your family or festive powder that you toss at friends during Holi, the Indian spring celebration.' He misses India, always very cheerful when we go back to his hometown for visits, chattering with all his relatives in Hindi and revisiting all his old haunts."

He let her trail off, then said, "I'm sorry I didn't go to your fundraiser. I thought we had a meeting this morning, all us lab rats, foreign postdocs."

"You want your own lab?"

"Yes. But I'm grateful for all the latest technology here." He moved away from her, signaling that he had to leave.

He pictured George at SFO, fourteen years old, waiting alone, the airport growing deserted late into the night, as human predators creeped in — who prey on abandoned looking teenagers — like in the trafficking stories when he turned on the news. His fears as a father were warranted.

"You better go, don't be late for George."

"Thanks for understanding," he said, his sense of urgency building. "Just text me for another time to talk about your project." He walked out quickly. Shadowed glass doors slid open into the dark corridor. His back bowed with the weight of the backpack. Outside, he saw lighted hospital buildings and heard faint music from distant homes. He wondered how it was night already. He had just seen the blurred sun out of a lab window as it set over the tall buildings of Pandolf Medical Center.

Alone, he remembered his phone call to George in Chicago. The call had disconnected, then reconnected after rapid clicks. *Was someone listening? Why?*

They talked in Spanish. "Dad, why do people not trust science?" asked George.

"That's unfortunate," he had said, pulling his hair away from his forehead.

How could he tell the boy that his father's scientific world was crushing bureaucracy, that his bosses only saw him as a tool? About his disappointment with himself and his self-doubt about breaking the rules? He could not tell Jorge that from inside the system, he, too, had lost his faith.

His second phone, the Soria company phone, beeped a new notification from David Campbell. Campbell, a scientist from Texas in his mid-thirties, was going to transport Mary's files and the rest of his data storage disks to Saburia.

Saburia was a small country on the Western coast of the Red Sea, a desert state newly created in hopes of peace after waves of violence on a historical strip of the East African coast. There, Soria Clinics had just built a new facility.

Garcia texted Campbell back to say that he was about to place the drives in a hiding place in the Pandolf hospital complex and leave him a hand-drawn paper map with directions to find them.

"Look forward to going to the Red Sea coast myself one day," Garcia now dictated into his phone as he walked quickly.

"Saburia is fiery hot," Campbell texted back. "Nothing to do but work, but you would like that. Thanks to your encouraging preliminary results, Soria is buying the Drukker. Investing in your terminator T-cells. You could continue your work there! Whenever the machines land in Saburia."

"Wish I could go, away from the little minds who rule my life here."

"Why not?"

"Nope. My son is visiting soon. I mean, he's not just visiting anymore—he's moving in. Permanently."

"Wow! Jorge?"

"He wants to be called George now."

"When was the last time you saw him?"

"We video chat all the time."

"I mean in person?"

"Two weeks ago in Chicago, when I saw Michael."

"Michael's in Saburia now, waiting on me."

Michael Kochanski was a Polish American businessman in his mid-forties who had connected Garcia to Soria Clinics. Speaking accented English on a video call, Kochanski once told Garcia, "I like the idea of cancer as a disease to live with, not fatal, so patients become regular customers. more glamorous than selling disposable razor blades."

When Garcia had frowned, Kochanski explained, "A joke. The business principle: I lose money when I sell you the razor holder but make it back every time you buy more blades from me."

"I know what you mean. But this isn't that simple. A lot of work goes into proving scientific theories. And most of the time, they have no merit."

"Stop fussing," said Kochanski. "Time runs out for everyone. Those dying patients have nothing to lose except for worthless relatives waiting to inherit money. Soria Clinics makes sure patients understand that their treatments may not be successful."

Garcia suppressed his exasperation. "Well, thank you for this opportunity with Soria."

"Oh, don't thank me too much. Soria pays me well for consulting, and your work so far is free for them."

"I meant that otherwise, my research ideas wouldn't be going anywhere. But doing this research on the side, using Pandolf's equipment without telling them, is not ideal."

"Why would Pandolf care? The computer is not used for anything else when you're on it. You're not hurting anyone or getting paid."

"If they find out, there may be trouble," Garcia said. "But then I have no loyalty to Pandolf or any respect for their authority. Just another flawed system."

"You will break the system open." Noticing that Garcia easily lost track of time, Kochanski then suggested that Garcia's Soria watch-phone do it for him. Now as Garcia walked to Pandolf's main hospital campus, the watch beeped that he was back on schedule with that inscrutable god, Time.

Time, he thought, had stolen his wife and morphed their baby into a hairy adolescent named George. Time had dissolved his hopes and plans after his excited arrival alone to the US nine years ago, to work at the National Institutes of Health (NIH) in Bethesda, Maryland, planning to bring his family from Argentina once he was settled.

A brisk wind swirled the night air outside the hospital complex. People walked or sat at tables. Many still wore masks, prepared for another pandemic. Some were shadows among the glows of cigarettes and phone screens between sculptures and trees. His vague fear increased— he knew many of those shadows were armed—a response to increasing crime everywhere. Garcia entered a tall, lighted building and flashed his badge to bypass the security checkpoints, relieved to be safely inside.

He, too, had finally purchased a pistol seven years ago, after his wife had been diagnosed with cancer.

"It's for self-defense," he reassured Pia as his range instructor had advised. "Rates of violence keep rising. But don't worry, you won't see me in a crazy internet crime story."

Unshaven and grim-faced—he was in a hurry that day—he thought his driver's license picture would be perfect to parade on streets online—for hawking everything from hateful politics to chips and booze.

Inside the hospital lobby, the floors were marble, and the fountain glittered many colors. The gift store beckoned through its glass walls. On its shelves, crystal pieces gleamed, and porcelain statues dreamed—among silk flowers, stuffed animals, and a palette of face coverings on mannequin heads, shades of green from the recent fundraiser.

Medical fundraisers, he thought, were a feeding trough for the health care establishment, giving public funding to crooks and cronies at palaces like Pandolf. Then there was the media, telling sensational stories about so-called medical cures to sell advertising.

Garcia opened his notepad, in which he doodled during Nepski's lab meetings. One page had a hospital campus map where he had marked his route. Moving quickly—but not so fast as to draw attention—into more remote areas of the building, he clipped his ID badge onto his jacket. His paper map, hand-drawn to bypass possible electronic hackers, led him through endless corridors, on bridges over streets, past the last signs of a cafeteria and the pediatric emergency room and farther back, into the oldest sections of the complex under renovation.

Finally, past construction signs, he entered a room. Carefully, he placed his laptop, the five glass drives, and a purple case into a steel locker, one of several in rows against a wall. On its door, he pasted a name sticker that read: "Dr. Arjun Jagdishwar Bhattacharya." He had used a gas flame in the lab to darken the label so it looked as old as the others around it, just as faded by time, as to not catch attention. He still needed to get the map to Campbell, to guide him here for the pickup. He tore the map out of the pad, folded it, stuck it in his jeans pocket—where he felt his phone and pulled it out.

Text messages from Jorge had streamed in: "Landed," "K waiting," "Still waiting... DAAA... AAD!!!"

He had forgotten about Jorge. His chest tightened. Jorge had already been waiting over an hour. He wasn't the typical kid waiting at SFO, picked up within minutes, nice clothes, fine luggage, talking to his fancy Ear Dot. No! Traffickers and gangs at bus stations, train stations, and airports targeted vulnerable kids like Jorge, who looked lost and hungry as they sat alone—indefinitely.

He texted Jorge—George back: "OMW!"—on my way. He walked quickly through the hospital corridors but again not so fast as to draw attention. Once outside, he ran. Early tomorrow morning, he would hide the map for Campbell and return to the lab to put away the hidden tools.

A guilty random thought: *I forgot to buy Jorge's ketchup!*

He took shortcuts in the woods to his car. Clouds hid the moon. *Hospital complexes leak opioids,* he thought. Pandolf really needed to clean up the gang activity near the campus. Emerging from the trees, he saw that the parking lot was deserted—until red and blue flashes glowed over his right shoulder.

Why don't I hear ambulance sirens? He turned around. Someone grabbed his elbow.

"ICE, Immigration and Customs Enforcement, Mr. Garcia."

Panting, shocked by this incomprehensible turn of events, he checked their IDs to be sure they were who they said and then followed their instructions. Then he rode in the back of an unmarked car on a black highway, leaving behind the lights of Pandolf.

Cold logic took control. Of all the things he had imagined, corporate spies, Pandolf security, he had never expected ICE. *Why? My visa is in perfect order.*

"My son's waiting for me at the airport," he said. "Over an hour. Please. We must get him first."

"Why?" snapped an agent.

"Please, sir. He's only fourteen. He has no one else here."

Silence, then, "Okay. We just rescued a bunch of kids his age from some... filth."

"Thank you. Thank you." Garcia said, almost in tears.

CHAPTER TWO

After Garcia abruptly left the lab, Sharma tried to work. She felt dispirited. *Dr. Garcia forgot about my new project. Maybe he doesn't think it's that great.*

Then she remembered her mentor in medical school, now retired, one of the first women of color to become a robotic pelvic surgeon. She would have told her to "forge on."

She did not notice the night guard at the lab who waved goodbye as she walked out, absorbed by thoughts about her last shift at Hunterview Hospital. She had assisted in seven back-to-back Cesareans: a blur of blood, screaming infants, cold operating rooms, tired parents, and hurried staff and doctors.

Hunterview was a rural hospital, where she worked with busy community doctors. Dr. Brickstone came to mind, square jawed and handsome, robust frame sculpted by dawn workouts. He discussed sports with anyone anytime. He had a worshipful gaggle of women, patients, nurses, and even administrators. After every Cesarean, Brickstone would admire the newborn in the warmer and give the same speech, then turn to the waiting computer while she painstakingly sewed the mother's skin back together.

"That thin scar is all the patient will ever see of her pregnancy journey," he said.

SuperDoc Brickstone will deliver your baby, fix your sink, change your tire—but never a poopy diaper.

But at least with Dr. Brickstone, that was surgery, not the endless days she spent parked at the women's outpatient clinic: crowded waiting area, cramped exam rooms, and assembly line of "jiffy" Pap smears, talking and talking to patients, then clicking through encyclopedic templates in their electronic health records.

Her father, a doctor, complained that he had "no time anymore to talk to my patients, beta. Instead, I click on the computer. Yesterday, I had compliance training before I could learn about this new implant for depression."

"Yes, Papa, but you'll retire soon."

Finally, to compete for a surgery fellowship, she also did research. For that, thankfully, she had Dr. Samuel Nepski for a mentor. In his forties, tall, with dark eyes and copper-colored curly hair, he had assigned her to his own lab team at Pandolf.

Sleep deprivation was frequent. One evening, she fell asleep driving and rear-ended a Pandolf shuttle bus. Undisturbed, the large bus moved on, thanks to physics' laws of momentum, bus riders unaware that there had even been an accident.

She didn't tell her parents in their weekend video call, annoyed when her father teased her about his "glory days" of medical training before reforms set limits on residency hours: "Back-to-back thirty-six-hour shifts awake in the hospital, only one night of sleep in between."

She walked back to her apartment that she shared with Julia Malone, who went by Lucky. They met two years ago on Pandolf social media. About her age, Lucky was an internal medicine resident from a wealthy family in Maine. Lucky would not have been "slumming" with Sharma in their apartment if it hadn't been for the convenience of living on campus.

Their apartment was walking distance to the medical center campus, in an old building for temporary residents like them. The main entry was a heavy and tall wooden door, and steep stairs led up to the floors. The water was never more than lukewarm, making showers quick.

On Lucky's side of the bathroom counter, around a magnifying mirror, makeup colors spilled like an art set— pencils, tubes, and palettes of rouge and eyeshadow, with perfume bottles and stands of jewelry. Lucky's encyclopedic wardrobe hung in plastic sheets in two closets with long mirrors, next to shelves lined with designer shoe confections. Sharma's own side of the bathroom counter was rebelliously bare.

But now in residency, Lucky mostly sported scrubs and clogs, her makeup basic. Outdoors, she wore wraparound sunglasses and a wide-brimmed hat. When they first moved in together, Lucky said, "Everyone in my family gets cataracts and skin cancer, being so white. I wish I had a touch of your dark coloring."

Sharma stiffened. *Really, this is awkward.*

"You don't mind me saying that?"

"Not at all," she lied.

But now Sharma talked back. The other day, Lucky said, "You should stop straightening your hair. It's pretty—natural."

Lucky had corn silk hair straight out of a shampoo ad.

"I may cut mine short," Sharma told her. "Quick wash and dry. You should talk. People spend fortunes to have their hair look like yours. You roll out of bed with it."

Lucky pushed her to come to parties, loud music and swarms of people acting like the waves of pandemics would never return. Lucky turned on her firefly sparkle, drawing people to her, while Sharma waited for Lucky to be ready to leave and made polite conversation mostly with strangers. Then Sharma became the designated driver for a carful of drunk people.

Lucky's long-distance boyfriend, Harry, also their age, used to play ice hockey as she played lacrosse in their prep school in Maine. She saw pictures of people like them, usually in the "Style" sections of the *New York Times* and *Vanity Fair*, partying in penthouses of skyscrapers. The couple lived in a world of trust funds, no student loans, and families who not only paid the full ticket but even donated money to their schools.

"My test scores weren't great in medical school, so here I landed at Pandolf," Lucky told her. "The long distance with Harry is just temporary."

Lucky drained her glass of wine, "Another reason I came to Pandolf was to get some space from Harry because he's the only person I've ever dated. Maybe I need to break it off . . ."

"Why? In cultures like my dad's, people might be with only one partner their entire life."

In a video call, her mother observed, "Well, proximity is important for relationships—"

"You learned that from my culture," her father interrupted off-screen. He was an Indian immigrant; her mother was White.

"I meant that now that Lucky and Harry are living in different cities, they may grow apart," her mother said. "I moved to Texas for to be with your dad after we started dating."

Her father's grinning face then popped onto the screen. "You were right about moving to Texas for me. And about most things since then. But at least I still get to handle the 'big picture.'"

Neither Sharma nor her mother responded to his dig. Her father's too-old joke was that her mother handled all the "small things" for the family, from the grocery list to the budget, while he handled the "big things" like world politics.

On Lucky's rare vacations, the couple traveled internationally, sailed, skied, and scuba-dove. Lucky suggested that Sharma could join them. "Sometimes we go with groups."

"No thanks. Why do people want to inhale salty water and then sit on a hot beach? Or ski in frozen cold—only to break a leg on a black run? Don't they know what vacation means?"

Lucky did not smile.

"Joking, sorry, thanks for inviting me. But . . ."

"But . . . ?"

"For one thing, I don't ski. And I don't need to go to Rome. I've family in India, a more ancient civilization."

Growing up in Texas, when her father wasn't working marathon hours, vacations were to see family and friends, traveling to Disneyland or India, where older relatives were tagged with the proper Hindi descriptions of their place in the family, cousins had many names based on relationships, and everyone else was usually just "Uncle" and "Aunty."

"You get your thrills in your career, I get that," said Lucky.

One day Sharma complained to Lucky, "This nurse took *forever* to come and help me with a huge patient who needed a pelvic exam. While I waited, I watched a doctor on TV tell an obese man to 'zip your mouth, get off the couch, and start starving.'"

"The world keeps getting meaner."

"I was afraid I might laugh—"

"It was kind of you to not laugh," said Lucky, her voice flat, judgmental.

"Sometimes I want to tell those patients who no longer want sex to 'just fake it if you don't feel it.' People are dying of cancer, and they are wasting my time with their sex life."

"It's a good thing you're going into surgery. Operating on people who will be asleep and won't hear you say things like that. Entering their chemo orders for a nurse who is compassionate."

Lucky sighed. "But you're the smartest person I know."

"There's more than numbers. The person with the best GPA and test score may not be the best surgeon, or thinker, or leader. Anyway, talking and talking in that women's clinic is *not* my skill set."

"Shelly, it's hard to feel compassionate when you're always stressed out and sleep deprived. You just do too much—residency, research, fundraisers . . . a recipe for burnout."

Sharma tried to be more empathetic about things she had never experienced. To put brakes on older patients' monologues, she said in her kindest voice, "Oh, menopause is a bear, but we can't stop the clock."

Or: "We have a great service for libido issues here at Pandolf." Point-click-done, she electronically transmitted the order: "Ambulatory Referral Sexual Health."

As for the expectant moms, they worried about everything. She listened, adrenaline levels rising to meet theirs, asked questions, and put their answers into the computer with matching anxiety.

The HatchPal software was her soothing AI partner that translated her notes into elegant grids of AI suggested problems, assessments, and treatment plans for her to edit and approve. Doffing her gloves, then rubbing in sanitizer, she moved from one patient room to the next. Speedily, she filled vials with specimen swabs and tissue, for which the label machine spat out barcoded stickers.

Always on time, she forgot patients' names but not the case details. They knew her as "the little Indian lady" or "the quiet Mexican doctor." Or a recent customer service comment from an expectant mom that said, "It's hard to tell what Dr. Sharma is thinking about when she's with me—with her mask up to her eyeballs."

• • •

Lucky owned a cat, Livingstone, a large orange tabby with green eyes. Fighting their efforts to keep him inside, he would protest loudly at the back door. When they opened it, he "escaped from Al-CAT-traz," across the neighboring balconies, down the black iron fire escape into the dense woods behind them. Lucky had adopted him, one of a feral litter, at a bed and breakfast near a lighthouse on the rocky coast of Maine. She said that his ancestors arrived with hers, on ships from the Old World to the East Coast, earning their passage by eating mice and fish scraps.

After getting into bed, soft paw-falls on her comforter meant Livingstone. She briefly lifted the window a crack to let in fresh air. Then a spitting irrigation spout splattered her forehead. Little chips of paint hit the floor as she slammed the window back down.

She rested against the fur, purr, and pillow, feeling herself relax, replay the sweet memories of the one person she thought about the most: her mentor, Dr. Samuel Nepski. She remembered a recent visitor at the lab, Dr. Nepski's father. Deep forehead furrows spoke of his advanced age. Tailed by his proud son, he had whizzed around and asked questions.

"Exciting theory," he said about her new experiment. He praised her father's "service in an underserved community. Sam is pushing Pandolf to expand outreach to more local, rural hospitals."

"Like how our residents — like you, Shelly — and specialists go to Hunterview Hospital," said her mentor.

Dean Baluyn, Pandolf's CEO, had invited the whole lab team to dinner at The Provençale, a French restaurant, tucked into the forest edge of the hospital campus. She walked the mile from her apartment toward the darkening rows of woods. The sunset flamed the tall buildings orange, the same sun that dripped gold that morning on the red brick sprawl of Hunterview Hospital where she had traveled for work earlier that morning.

The pricey Provençale was popular among senior faculty and affluent visitors. Local members of the Mather family had donated their art collection to Pandolf, now housed here. Inside the marble entry of the restaurant, fresh-cut flowers and exotic plants spilled colors and perfume. On the wall, a grand painting from centuries ago showed an aristocratic French couple in silks and frills, flirting in a swirl of forest and cloud.

After a security check—security was intensive, from hidden cameras to discreet guards—the tuxedoed host led her into the main dining area.

An unseen piano played. She passed tables draped with creamy linens in a spectrum of pastels, jeweled circlets holding rolled napkins, sky-blue fine china—almost transparent—with pink and gilt edging, and crystal glassware with matching rims. Past lighted fountains and under massive chandeliers, recognizing no one, she followed the hostess into a private banquet room. French oils also hung on the walls of this room, ornately framed, featuring sturdy peasants in pastoral landscapes.

Crowning their long table, flanking the Baluyns, was the Nepski family. Sharma sat down next to Manny Garcia.

"To the spirits!" Baluyn, in his forties, raised his glass. With bubbly Champagne and wines, ruby reds and golden whites, from Bordeaux to Burgundy, the guests joined in. Some dissenters had beers and cocktails. An abstainer, Sharma nursed a fizzy "limonade" and searched for vegetarian entrées in the menu.

Today's special was steak tartare. The menu described the raw beef and egg dish: "Tartare is named after horsemeat eaten by the warrior Mongolians, legendary cavalry who conquered their empire under the cunning leadership of Genghis Khan."

Garcia murmured to her, "I'm vegetarian. But I bet tartare tasted better to a skinny, hungry young warrior back then than to us sitting most of the day."

She watched the subtle changes on Sam Nepski's mother's face as the lab team introduced themselves — people of various shades of color and permutations of features to accents reflecting foreign countries of origin — and how she became expressionless when Sharma took her turn. Then the senior Mrs. Nepski gave Garcia the same vacant look. If Garcia noticed or cared, he didn't show it.

Like she doesn't even see us, a couple of worker bees in her son's hive. But I bet she would see me if I looked and talked like Lucky, a Midwestern vision of blue eyes, milky skin, and yellow hair.

Sharma remembered some of the patients during her dermatology rotation in medical school, trying to be as White and young as money could buy. Taut skin, hair a daylight blond that did not match their brown eyes — faces like Sam Nepski's mother's—they became a guessing game for the medical students, looking for clues to the magic of Botox, laser abrasions, and skin fillers. One fellow multiracial student, Karen, had never even deigned to speak to her. Sporting large diamonds, two in her ears and one on her left ring finger, Karen had also scored a spot in one of the nation's most competitive dermatology residencies.

"Well on her way to buffing the looks of her rich clients," Sharma grumbled to her mother. "A waste of medical training!"

Still, Sam Nepski had his mother's good looks. At lab meetings, which she diligently attended, Dr. Nepski sat at the head of the table, slim, tall, impressive in his knowledge, and aggressive with his questions. And on television, Sharma watched her mentor, a sharp dresser, blink modestly into the camera as he explained complex medical concepts. The mother–baby dyad was his world. In suit and tie, he lectured the public about preeclampsia, which could affect pregnant women at the end of their pregnancies, causing strokes, seizures, and even death. Videos of swollen women, masked doctors, blinking equipment, and endless tubes played.

Thirty years ago, his father, the senior Nepski, had done groundbreaking research into this pregnancy complication, and his son now readily found friends, mentors, and opportunities. He had millions in grants, dozens of publications, and multiple awards, as well as appointments to prestigious committees and boards that determined certifications of specialists, approval of research funds, and safety clearances for new medications for pregnant women.

Garcia once complained, "Nepski is handsome, yes, with just the right touch of gruff and long hair to be the picture of a doctor who finds cures for all ills. A star salesman. I think his ideas are recycled—just new names for the old disease, toxemia. Sure, you learn the changed terminology—eclampsia, gestational hypertension, XYZ—"

Another rant, she thought and inwardly rolled her eyes.

He went on that day: "But youth should be about igniting a fire, burning the old and creating the new. Instead, you doctors memorize and regurgitate to pass marathon tests. So, they bully you, chain you with debt, don't allow you to stop working long enough to wonder. Or to question. Just another generation of robots well trained to work their machine—never 'the captain of your soul or the master of your fate.'"

"Enough, you're depressing this Doctor Zombie."

She found Garcia irritating in so many ways: his rants, his frequent negativity about the world, and his blinders on about anything besides his own work—like forgetting their meeting to discuss her experiment. Then what kind of father, she thought, would not mention his son after all the time they had spent together?

No, she was going to think about Dr. Nepski instead. She fell asleep in bed, cheek against cat, into a dream where she and her mentor were alone together in a cozy nook of the Provençale. Burning candles and soft lighting allowed for hushed conversation. Like the Cheshire cat in timeless space, Livingstone watched from a shelf above.

"You and Dr. Garcia are two sides of the same coin," she said to the dream Nepski.

He looked grave. "As with our world, it's nothing and everything, death and life—we are on the other side of the unknown. Even here: smoky mirrors, low notes by Ravel for a left-handed pianist . . ."

Amid buzzing, their profound exchange shuffled into nonsense. She awoke, reflexively grabbing for her ringing phone in folds of bedding.

An emergency at the hospital? Upright now, her body tensed.

Bright digits—"1:04 AM"—glowed on her phone screen with a DNA helix twirling the letters D R G A R C I A in the background.

Garcia's voice crackled with static. "Shelly, sorry to wake you up. I need your help."

"It's okay," she said, slumping. "I was only finally asleep, a lovely dream. How's George?"

"He's fine. But I have a problem with my visa, going with some people now to straighten it out. George is here with me. He can stay with you for a few hours?"

"Um . . ."

"You're a friend, thanks!" Garcia hung up.

No wonder he had no friends, she thought. It was just like him to assume she would help, like all the times he had mansplained to her about the medical research establishment. Weird, she then wondered; who addressed visa issues after midnight? Didn't Pandolf track that, given their international workers and patients?

"Mom," she said, instructing her phone to connect, but instead the Genie displayed her parents' latest pictures—white beaches, topaz ocean, and clear skies, a beach rental in Goa—with the message: "No connection."

She left a message. "Hey, need some advice . . ."

To buzz Garcia in, she had to go to the living room. Groaning, finger-combing her hair, yawning, cat following, she checked her phone's call history as she walked, hoping that Garcia's call had been part of her dream. No, this was real.

Lying on the common room couch, she pushed away the cat's insistent paws and sharp claws. Then she set the phone ringer to a particularly obnoxious Indian party jingle for calls from Garcia in the future. Next, she tapped ride requests into her phone for Hunterview Hospital the next day, expensive, but best not to drive sleep deprived and have another accident.

• • •

She had been driving home in a rainstorm after dark, peering through her windshield, her wipers on their fastest setting, when she felt a frightening thud and stopped. A black shape rose in front of her bumper. She jumped out of her car to find a man in a long, dark overcoat, thankfully uninjured.

He listened to her flustered apologies, then said politely in a British accent, "My black coat made it hard for you to see me. I understand. Could you please give me a ride home?"

Remembering crime stories, she hesitated, then agreed. His wife was upset but curtly served hot milky tea with sugar cubes. They said they were researchers from England. She told them that she had visited London and that her father had studied in the UK, not mentioning the racism he said he had experienced. "He loves aphorisms: says getting into America was like winning the lottery, how great opportunities are fearsome and that prizes go to those who run the race."

Their response was a polite smile. When she left, they did not ask her for any contact information, and she did not offer hers, either. They reminded her of some of the other international researchers she met in labs, quiet, closed off in insular bubbles, ironic for the fact that they were part of the global scientific community.

Like her, others at Pandolf had accidents, too. Last summer, while rushing to 6 a.m. rounds, a pediatrician forgot his toddler in the car. Fortunately for the child in the heating car, a passerby broke open the window. Dean Baluyn lauded the rescuer for paying attention while walking "instead of looking at their phone."

Lucky had a different perspective. "As health care workers, we can't take care of ourselves, leaving our children in hot cars, or like you, Shelly— having accidents. Instead of Baluyn lecturing us, we should be asking what he's doing about *that*."

Lying on the couch, waiting for Garcia to arrive, Sharma fell into another dream where she was nibbling on biscuits with tea in the Britishers' living room—in their home in London. They invited her to stay, become part of their world. She became their cat, resting in front of the fireplace where chestnuts roasted in crackling logs.

Foreboding shadows on the walls became a monkey that demanded, "Take the chestnuts out, and share them with me."

Catching her stealing them, her hosts became angry and told her to leave. With burned hands, she found herself alone in front of a darkening theater. The drama was moving outside, where the skies roared cold rain, water gushed into gutters, and crowds rushed away.

"All this isn't real," the couple shouted, now standing before her, twins except for their clothes, one dressed as a man and the other as a woman, They filled the doorway of a London Underground stop, surrounded by a frigid moat.

Shaken, she awoke and looked with relief at her uninjured hands. Feeling chilled, she got up and made herself a hot mug of cardamom chai—like her father made it—to sip with his favorite British biscuits.

"Don't tell me how they're British," he told her. "After they appropriated my culture. I just return the favor. At least we got our Kohinoor back." In 2029, the British government returned many Indian jewels to India, including the infamous Kohinoor diamond.

Awake, she now wondered why Garcia had been doing his own repairs on the Drukker AI printer. He traveled often to Drukker headquarters, the Dock. Once, he told her, "People there are young like you—smart, enthusiastic . . . but it's not conservative like it is here. There you see tattoos, piercings, kilts, rainbow colors, flip-flops! One of these days, would you like to come with me to visit the Dock?"

"Sorry, I'm too busy here."

"I understand. Still, the Dock's a cool place—there's always food, even a conveyor belt going twenty-four seven with hot pizza you can order on a touch screen. Machines mix you any drink you want. I like the mango kiwi seltzer. You should see the organic gardens you can walk through, fresh-pressed juices from what they grow right there. And the architecture is world class—international classic in some places, modern and playful in others . . ."

Garcia had rambled on that evening at dinner, complaining about how men like Dr. Nepski were too powerful, and could permanently derail anyone who crossed them or competed with them.

"Why just *men?*" she interrupted. "A woman can do that too."

Then she explained that as far as *she* was concerned, her career plans were going well. Pandolf had good benefits: insurance, pension, and a 403(b). Dr. Nepski deserved praise for Pandolf expanding outreach to rural patients. Dean Baluyn deserved to be paid well as CEO.

That evening, the patterns of scratches in Garcia's glasses caught her eyes. *Why just their lower half?* Was she watching too many surgery videos, the designs of veins and arteries branching, lymph channels and nerves knitting?

Garcia's grumbles were a distraction. Successes that he could never even dream of awaited her. In a few years, she would finish her fellowship and be working at a top research institution, curing ovarian cancer.

No, she thought, her future would not be tedious pandering to privileged women in rich suburbs, like Karen, finishing her Dermatology residency, or becoming another Brickstone in a nowhere place like Hunterview Hospital, or toiling in someone else's lab on *their* ideas like Garcia. Someday she would be *(literally)* a cutting-edge surgeon like her former medical school professor and be doing groundbreaking research on her own ideas in her own lab like Dr. Nepski.

At the lab, when Garcia had stepped out for lunch, she had overheard Nepski tell his father: "Garcia doesn't catch fire about our work."

"He doesn't belong here—"

"Maybe I don't connect with him because I'm not like him."

"As his boss, you have a lot of power over him. But even I can't do more than just begin to understand where he comes from and what he wants."

"I care about Pandolf and what we stand for."

"Of course," his father said. "Still, remember that we're here because our family was going to follow the crowd in Poland, and then my crazy uncle killed our Nazi guards. It's the *only* admirable thing my uncle ever did. The Puritans left England to put an ocean between themselves and their lunatic king. Yet here we are, centuries later, reverting to that Old World of rulers and serfs, where Dean Baluyn, your CEO, is a descendant of the Mathers, an original Puritan family."

"Meaning?"

"Meaning I'm the son of an immigrant who saw other worlds. Sam, you are one more generation removed, even. Garcia is from another world."

"I try to understand him."

"I know. We raised you well, to be kind, cultured, well-traveled. But sometimes people are too far apart. It's times like these when I feel a wind blowing, change-a-coming, like my father said he felt as a boy in Poland a long time ago."

"Meaning? What's the harbinger?"

"Meaning maybe a misfit like Garcia might bring us some unexpected good—in the midst of big changes possibly ahead."

"How?"

"Only time will tell."

She wondered how the father, Dr. Nepski, like her also a child of an immigrant, saw potential in Garcia when she didn't? Her own Indian father's world was half a globe and decades in time in the past from hers. She spoke to him in a different language from his mother tongue.

She thought her mentor was one of the kindest men she had ever met, especially to try so hard with Garcia. Even if he was not just one, but two generations, thousands of miles, and a different language removed from his Jewish immigrant forefather from Poland,

Livingstone jumped back onto the couch with her, his sharp claws retracted this time. She scratched his head and belly, thinking about her Indian father and White mother. "You and me are mutts—weeds with flowers pretty enough that people keep us around."

She dozed off again and woke around 4:30 a.m. when the doorbell jangled inside the apartment. In the fog between sleep and wakefulness, a revelation broke open. At the Palatine Hill dinner, when the candle's flame had flickered in the crystal of its holder, the refracted light filled the lower half of Garcia's glasses with the trademark Drukker sunburst. Then Garcia had taken his glasses off when he saw her paying attention to them without explanation. And he didn't put them back on all evening? *Why is he so secretive sometimes?*

The doorbell rang again. She pressed the old button to unlock the main entry and heard the massive doors creak open. Then she heard loud footsteps on the landing, followed by dragging and banging until the racket stopped in front of her apartment—silence—and then a tentative knock.

She opened her door. In the dim light of the stairway, she looked up at a slender teenager, mid-teens, with long hair, almost a unibrow, and glasses specked with waterdrops. A large suitcase sagged against his right leg. In his left hand, he carried a trademark red plastic bag from the new luxury brand, Salome. Through a tear in its bulging side, there poked a yellow pencil.

Smiling, this tall boy—*he's Dr. Garcia all over again*—stuck out one bony hand with long fingers. "Hi, Dr. Sharma, I am George Garcia. So sorry to keep ringing the bell."

• • •

Sharma ignored the outstretched hand. Who knew where it had been and what germs it carried? Chaos knocked.

She forced a smile. "Hi, George, come on in."

"Thank you," he said, hardly audible.

Keeping her voice welcoming, she asked, "Is your dad on his way up, too? Take this towel to dry yourself. The irrigation in California does get crazy. Here you go, hand sanitizer. And put all your wet stuff—yes, the bag, too—there on top of that mat. The floors are hardwood. We don't want them getting wet."

He nodded, warm brown eyes like his father.

"Oh, no, we don't wear our shoes inside the apartment," she said. "They go on the mat, too. But keep your socks on or your feet will get cold." He slid his feet out of his large sneakers and carefully placed them next to her small pairs, then waited expectantly.

"Where's your dad? Isn't he coming up?"

The cat slipped out into the stairwell, and she rushed to scoop him up.

"Livingstone," she said. "He was a feral kitten. Still runs off outside. But you can't let him out. He belongs to Lucky, my housemate."

George touched a finger to the cat's nose.

"So, where's your dad?" she repeated.

Wiping his face and glasses carefully with the washcloth, George replied, "Dad says hello, but he couldn't come up because he had to go with the other men. He'll call you."

"Okay." *Other men. What does that mean?* "Sounds like you had a long night. Have you eaten?"

"They had crackers on the plane, um, and pop." Shyly, he didn't say anything more, just gave her the look of a hungry teenager.

"There's a twenty-four-hour pancake place around the corner," she said. His face brightened. "Leave your coat on, put shoes back on, tie your shoelaces this time— double knots surgical style. Just a sec."

She returned to her bedroom, closed the door, and tried to call Garcia one more time. Again, the call went to voice mail.

When they went outside, the horizon's edge was blinking a new day's dawn. They crossed the lawn, dodging sprinklers, to the sidewalk that led to the Golden Griddle. There, she sipped lukewarm green tea and picked at a house salad: wilted lettuce and nonfat dressing with a chemical aftertaste.

George had stacks of pancakes and liver and onions, then downed a giant chocolate shake and many glasses of ice water. He demolished a mountain of onion rings under a downpour of ketchup. Putting down his empty ketchup bottle after its final exhalation of splatter, he reached over—long arm—to the next table for more ketchup. Watching George finish, then poke his fork at the crumbs, she insisted he order more food. He protested, surrendered, and doubled his meal.

Over their "brinner"—last night's dinner plus breakfast—they discussed the school he had attended in Chicago and his life with his uncle, "a famous artist," and his "beautiful" aunt, the original owner of the ripped Salome bag. George pulled out a picture of them on his phone: a suited older man with a pensive-looking young wife.

"Second marriage?" Sharma guessed.

George nodded. "He has a son in New York City with his first wife."

"So, you're here to stay, your father told me. Will you miss Chicago?"

"Nah, I'm used to moving around. I left Argentina after Mom passed and moved to Paris with my grandmother, then to Chicago. Now I'll start Pandolf High School. Hopefully, Dad and I can go back for a visit soon to—" and here he said a name of a place in Spanish she could not catch.

"I don't speak Spanish well. How many languages do you know?"

"English, Spanish, French, Italian. Dad wants me to take Mandarin and genetics at Pandolf High. He says the science classes are amazing because we're next to the medical center."

When they returned to her apartment, she set him up on the living room couch and texted Lucky to let her know. She should understand, she thought, since Lucky's brother, also in high school, had spent many nights on that very couch.

Charlie was a charmer, with his gelled blond hair, silver laptop, and musical phone. Lucky was supposed to supervise him, but he just came and went, Ear Dots stuck behind his ears except for when he peeled one off to talk. Helping her in the kitchen, Charlie discussed Indian food with her, and he would ask about her day at the hospital while telling her jokes with his flirty "I know I'm adorable but don't trust me for a minute" smile.

Now George sat solemnly on the same couch, his tired eyes like a stray animal's.

"Bathroom's that door there," she said, briskly moving back and forth between the couch and the hall closet. "Here you go—fresh towels, sheets, blanket. Change into your pajamas, brush your teeth, and go to bed. Lucky, Dr. Malone, is my housemate and will be walking through this morning."

She made a mental list for Garcia: *your son needs a shave, haircut, comb, and reminders to fix his bad posture and untied shoelaces.*

Then her phone rang, her ringtone for unknown callers, the band Stargod. She didn't usually answer but hoped this was about Garcia coming to get George.

"Hello?"

"Hello, Dr. Shelly Sharma?" said a man with a Texan accent, her home state.

"Yes?"

"Dr. Sharma, this is David Campbell. I'm a scientist friend of Manny Garcia. He can't talk to you right now, I'm sorry."

"Why?"

"ICE has detained him indefinitely."

She was silent. *Detained indefinitely!* Aware that George was listening, she was careful now not to say anything aloud that could upset him.

• • •

She remembered one night, as a child, when an immigration agent had called her father's phone. She answered it. The woman only identified herself with a serial number. Her father took the phone from her and went to another room and closed the door. "You blow hot. They're ICE cold!" her father joked later.

"How do you know?" she asked Campbell.

"Manny called me. Now his phone is off. And ICE? You can't talk to a human being, just their AI."

"But—"

"He asked me to take care of George until he returned. Dr. Sharma, there is an empty apartment in your building—available for subletting online, 252. I'm clicking 'ACCEPT' right now. I'll grab it this morning and move him out. Your building is close to the school George will go to. He can walk there and back. I'll make all the arrangements. Is it okay if I swing by later today? We can meet at the Ivy Drip across the street from you."

He spoke fast, she thought, pressured speech like someone with bipolar disorder.

"Dr. Sharma." He was pleading now. "I know you're busy. You need to keep him at your place just for a few hours. Please help. You don't know me, but George does. Ask him!"

"George, do you know this Mr. Campbell?" she asked.

George brightened. "Yes, Mr. Campbell is a great friend of my dad."

She worked out details for a tentative meeting after work. Soon, she thought, she could close the door on this strange twist in her carefully planned life.

But her father's voice teased her otherwise: "The best laid plans of mice and men . . ."

And her mom would say, "But Shelly always lands on her feet like a cat."

Feeling uneasy now, she remembered her own burned hands in her dream in the Britishers' living room, her as the monkey in one of Aesop's Fables, a warning to not be a cat's paw.

She turned to George and told him to get some sleep.

CHAPTER THREE

David Campbell, a tall man with light brown hair in his mid-thirties, waited outside the Ivy Drip, a casual dining spot on the Pandolf campus. Sunday evening, he was supposed to meet Dr. Sharma and Garcia's son, George. When he spotted a petite woman and a lanky teen approaching, he quickly closed the distance between them.

Smiling, he introduced himself to the woman. She did not smile back. Stiffly, she said, "Hello, I'm Shelly Sharma."

Then he turned to George. "And look at you, you're now a foot taller than when I saw you last in Chicago."

In the restaurant, Sharma asked Campbell to show her his passport and driver's license, taking photos of them with her phone.

"Security," she said.

"Of course."

"So, how do you know Dr. Garcia and George?"

"I met Manny at the NIH four years ago as a scientific consultant. I'm a doctor too—like you— but a PhD in Biomedical Engineering. Then I met George in Chicago when I visited, right, George?"

George smiled happily.

"Whom do you consult for?" she asked.

"Many clients. Have you heard of Soria International Clinics? Chain of medical clinics around the world. The original founder was Indian. Your last name is Indian."

"Yes, but that doesn't mean I've heard of Soria."

"Fair enough. Few have. The original owner was bought out moons ago anyway. Now, it has become one of those international corporations, nebulous, fluid, faceless players on changing boards—"

She interrupted: "So, you live around here?"

"No, just happened to be in the Bay Area for work when Manny called me to help." A lie. He had come here only to collect Garcia's Soria laptop and disks. "Now I'm going to stay at Pandolf Hotel for a few days to help get George situated. I mostly work remotely."

"That was a lucky coincidence you were around." Her tone was guarded.

They ordered food. Garcia had told him that Sharma was in training—busy, independent, not tethered to a partner or convention, determinedly focused on her path, her head to the ground. Campbell did some online research, then decided that she might just be perfect, unlikely to have the time or interest to question his plans. His meal fit his edgy mood: a beer and some chicken wings.

He watched her trying to coax George to switch from soda to healthier selections of milk and juice. Dinner lasted long enough for George to down the signature steak sandwich, the enchilada special, slices of strawberry cheesecake, and several glasses of "pop, what they call soda in Chicago," he said.

Sharma drank a kale smoothie, neatly dabbing her mouth between sips, taking tidy bites of her "healthy" burger—open-faced bean patty—using a fork and knife, like a surgeon.

Over the loud music, her voice was firm. "Did you get that sublet in my building for George?"

"Yeah." Campbell looked at George. "I have a place for you to stay in Dr. Sharma's building, close to your school. You can't stay at your dad's . . . there's been some misunderstanding. Right now, ICE is watching his apartment."

"So, the men in the car with us were ICE?" said George, staring at him.

"Yes."

They looked at him like they were expecting him to say more.

"I don't know more yet."

George asked, "I don't have to go back to Chicago?"

"Do you want to?" asked Campbell.

"No."

After a silence, Sharma said, "It seems like Chicago would make sense until your father returns."

"I'll be fine," George said quickly.

• • •

David Campbell had first met Manny Garcia at the NIH four years ago. Michael Kochanski had asked him to recruit a scientist for Soria Clinics to develop new projects based on the latest AI technology. Kochanski's email read:

> "Hey, hey, your business colleague here. Baby we gave to Drukker is growing up; it's inspiring to go to Drukker Board meetings. Soria Clinics is building a facility on the Red Sea coast.
>
> I just met a Doctor B (Indian name too long, too many consonants like my Polish name before I changed it)."

Then Kochanski cut/pasted B.'s email to him: "… *slow progress in treating some cancers, despite daily media feed of miracles, from our modern gods of governments, academic centers, and corporations.*

I say fundamental drivers of the human quest are the thirst for knowledge, adventure, glory, power, riches, about the individual. It is personal, always has been. As for the greater good of humanity, that's a retirement project for elderly people. Many young scientists see few rewards for their labors, neither credit nor profit. Old minds—blind, obsolete—trample the bloom of the young genius, the disrupter.

Michael, start-ups like the one you sold to Drukker give me hope. Yes, we can make breakthrough progress in medicine, too. Human ingenuity shines brightest in the darkest times. The interest from the new Saburian king is also encouraging. He wants to make Saburia the alternate destination for groundbreaking research that doesn't have a home.

That Michael, you're on the board of Drukker is key—Soria is interested in acquiring your machine to process their research but stopping short of purchasing it. Want preliminary results first. Can you help?"

Then in Kochanski's email, there was a vague job description—for Campbell to recruit a scientist to develop a new Soria Clinics project.

Campbell first saw Manny Garcia in the audience of a pixelated online presentation, when he asked a sharp question. Campbell called a private investigator for a background check, then travelled to the NIH to find Garcia.

July 2026, the sprawling campus was still deserted from the latest pandemic. Garcia was eating alone in the mostly empty cafeteria, where only vending machines dispensed food.

"Hi," Campbell said, standing in front of Garcia. "I liked your question the other day about the receptor B-071. Okay if I sit down?"

Garcia looked up, shadows under his eyes, a mask dangling from one ear. "Sure."

"I used to be a postdoc in Dr. Jansen's lab," he told Garcia. "Down the hall from Kelly, who presented the data on B-071."

Dr. Kelly Ho was an established scientist. But using only her first name, and speaking in his natural Texan drawl, he wanted to appear informal and relaxed.

"I'm Manny Garcia, a postdoc in Dr. Ernst Dietrich's lab." Garcia admitted that he was job hunting. "My grant ran out," he said, looking around as if expecting the world to stop.

"I remember working here, Manny, just how stressful the grant application process is . . ."

"Yeah, I had a couple of new applications. One didn't even get scored." With his fork, Garcia picked at the icing on a sagging slice of carrot cake, still in its vending machine box, and sipped cold coffee. "My other application failed eventually, too. But two other proposals out of our group were funded. So, Dietrich's lab will go on. That's how the game is played. But for me, no money, no funding, no job."

"Tell me about your unscored application."

Brightening, Garcia answered, "It's a novel approach, using AI to analyze the immortalization of cancer cells and how they evolve to defeat the body's defenses." Garcia looked down again. "But Dietrich's research is on premature labor. Still, on this big campus, I thought I could pull together the resources and equipment for my idea. Dietrich resented that, said I was here to work on his research on premature births, how his lab was already hit by budget cuts when all the NIH money was shunted into research on how this last epidemic happened."

A thin, young man pushed a vacuum around the empty cafeteria chairs and approached them.

Campbell waved to him. "Sorry, give us a few more minutes."

Swiveling away in a dance move, the masked janitor said nothing, listening to music from Ear Dots like Mickey Mouse in "The Sorcerer's Apprentice."

Looking down shamefaced, Garcia said, "When none of my applications were funded, Dietrich brought down the hammer on me and my 'bizarre' theories. So, here I am, searching for another slot for foreign scientists like me, to drop into the soul-shredder of the bureaucracy."

"Manny, do you have a family to support?" Campbell knew the answer from Soria's investigator.

"My wife died from cancer. Her name was Pia." He examined the uneven edges of his fingernails. "We looked at many treatment programs. That's what motivated me to write this grant."

Campbell watched Sorcerer's Apprentice in a far corner, fast dance moves in his footwork, before turning around to head back toward them.

"We have to go, Manny—that guy wants to sweep us out. Email me that grant request they rejected."

After he drove back to Washington, DC, Garcia's email kept him up late, intrigued him in a way he had not felt for some time. Then messages bounced between them—his questions and Garcia's answers.

To meet Garcia again, he decided to not return to the NIH. His visit had stirred bad memories of working there years ago, after he had graduated with his PhD from MIT, his longtime home. When he left Cambridge for Bethesda, Maryland, he also left behind Susan, black-eyed Susan. Keeping their breakup friendly, they had dinner together. Both teared up. He gifted her a bottle of her favorite Napa port. For a while, he called her to ask after Max, her dog, then stopped when Max passed away. She was married now with kids. He saw her name in the author lists of scientific journals.

At the NIH, his mentor was an MD-PhD whose research was in a rut, and who stubbornly ignored his suggestions. Disappointed, he left and joined a medical school as junior faculty doing research in one of their labs. Feeling like a tour guide, he also guided students in their lab projects.

Then he was invited to receive a lab skill teaching award at their Faculty Club. A building on the National Register of Historic Places, portraits of distinguished school leaders hung on the walls. At the dinner, a school dean sat at the table next to him. Face flushed pink, she beamed with authority as she told the woman next to her, "These MD-PhDs, they try to do two different things well: practice medicine and research. Like trying to be a great Navy captain *and* Air Force pilot? Ridiculous."

Later, he told the head of his lab about her rant. He laughed. "She's unhappy about the university budget. Her share versus our share. Then there's her . . . lack of credentials. David, stay in your own lane around here, or medical school politics will drive you crazy."

To add to his disillusionment, one of his grant applications to the NIH — the one he was most excited about —fell through. Then he left the medical school lab to start his own consulting business and connected online with Kochanski.

The owner of a property management company in Chicago, Kochanski had hopped on the tech bandwagon and invested in a biocomputing start-up. The start-up attracted a venture capital group and then Drukker, a midsize California company. For the buyout offer, Kochanski asked Campbell to value the technology. The successful sale included a slot for Kochanski on Drukker's board.

Next, Kochanski was asking Campbell to help him again, this time for Soria International Clinics. The network of clinics had originally started in Mumbai, India. But now, after multiple ownership changes and going global, the new Soria—in name only— planned to open a hospital in the new Saburia on the Red Sea.

After he and Susan had broken up, the single life meant an obsession with the gym and looking good—now a habit for him. After his workout, he and Garcia met again the next evening at a bar in DC. Over beers, Campbell asked, "So, your wife's passing motivated you to do this?"

"Yes, Pia was in Argentina when she got sick. I was here in the US. I was going to relocate her and our son. Then one day she went to the hospital in Buenos Aires. Appendicitis, we thought. But when the surgeons operated, they said it was ovarian cancer, spread everywhere. After she passed the next year"—he drew a sharp breath—"my son went to live with my mother in France. But my sister lives closer to me in Chicago. Her husband is an artist there. Jorge will move to Chicago to live with them until my job situation is settled."

"I'm sorry."

"Thanks, yeah, not ideal, my family . . . I mean." Garcia's eyes were moist. "I had to watch my castle burn." He leaned back and put his hands behind his head. "Then for the grant, I wasn't asking for a lot of money . . ."

"The NIH has a flat-lined budget," said Campbell, "and it's all being fed into the bugs right now. With what's left over, they must take care of their own first. Those crooks and cronies are a waste of my taxpayer dollars."

Garcia frowned. "The government certainly managed to support Dietrich's lab well for decades."

Frustrated scientists, thought Campbell, made low-hanging fruit for private ventures. Pleased about angering Garcia, he went on. "The government tells the taxpayer that their bureaucratic meddling with science will translate into results, blah blah blah. But then, commercial research is just for shortsighted profits, for the next year or two, so there are not many major breakthroughs there, either."

Garcia nodded. "Totally agree. You know, the data out in the universe is infinite. One could make fascinating discoveries for a lifetime that will make no difference in anyone's life. Dietrich has published lots of papers, some quite interesting, but despite that, our neonatal ICUs are fuller than ever with premature babies."

Campbell raised his beer. "Big breakthroughs come from the young like us, not old-timers like Dietrich. Never trust a scientist over thirty, right, or maybe forty in our case? I question all the millions that Americans give our cancer research nonprofits, and their ads with the cute bald kid and a movie star."

Garcia's eyes met Campbell's cautiously. They looked around quickly to see who else was within earshot.

"I have a proposal for you," said Campbell, lowering his voice. "One that, I hope, will give you a cancer breakthrough by thinking out of the box. I assume you've heard of the Drukker?"

"The new AI machines. That was the other thing I needed from the NIH to conduct my research. They don't have it yet . . . still in committee."

"Well, you may like what I have to say."

After leaving his job at Dietrich's lab, Garcia accepted a speedy offer from Drukker to train at the Dock.

Garcia wrote to Campbell, "Such youthful excitement here! I wish I could work on my cancer research at the Dock."

"They don't have the kind of tissue lab you need," observed Campbell. "They're just a medium-sized company. And they don't have an institutional review board to approve human experiments."

"You're right, I would need that IRB approval for even analysis of de-identified patient cancer data."

Then when Nepski's lab at Pandolf Medical Center requested to buy the Drukker AI, Drukker board members, specifically one Michael Kochanski, facilitated a discount on the condition that they bring over a Drukker-trained scientist. They recommended Garcia as best qualified for further training, already with NIH experience in pregnancy complications.

At Pandolf, Garcia grudgingly admitted to Campbell that "things are okay," even if he wished he had found work at a cancer lab.

They were on a video call. Garcia then said, "I've been meaning to talk to you about Texas."

"What do you mean?"

"That you're not just Texas, like you were when you put on the accent back in the NIH cafeteria."

"That's my natural accent, growing up near Dallas. Usually, I do tone it down, but you got the real me that day."

"But later, I heard your Boston flavor. You were in Boston for MIT. People change the way they talk depending on where they are and who they're with, sometimes not even realizing it. Maybe I notice because I come from another country, the 'stranger in a strange land.'"

"Ah, I understand. As long as you know I never mean to be disrespectful."

"I know," said Garcia.

• • •

The empty apartment below Sharma's was "well-lit, airy, 2-bedroom and furnished"—at least so boasted the online ad. The balcony led to the iron fire escape on the side of the building, where the cat soon discovered the route from one apartment to the other after George gave him snacks.

A week after Garcia's detention, George and Campbell were setting up his computer in the apartment.

"ICE called me," said George.

"What they say?"

"Just making sure I'm okay. I told them I was staying with Dr. Sharma for now. But they didn't say anything about Dad. My aunt wants an update about us getting a lawyer?"

"I'm working on it. Also, George, ICE isn't your friend. Tell them only what you must, and don't lie. They'll find out. Do you know what it means to only give people information on a 'need to know' basis?"

"Self-explanatory. But . . . maybe they do care that I'm okay? The man sounded nice."

"Maybe the person you talked to cares but not the system. And all your visa papers are in order. Your dad gave your school copies."

The screen before them now lighted up. Many smiling faces, shades of colors, ages, dresses, and sizes—Pandolf High School's website.

"Many students look like me here, a racial mix," observed George. "Not like the school in Chicago. How's Dad, you think? I mean, when will I be able to talk to him or see him?"

The boy looked anxious. Campbell said reassuringly, "Your dad will be fine. They'll fix their mistake." *I hope so.*

Back in his room at Pandolf Hotel, Campbell emailed Michael Kochanski in Saburia. "How exactly are we helping Manny? I haven't heard anything from you except that his sister in Chicago has no money for a good lawyer. And you can't pay George's bills forever."

Ten days later, Kochanski called. He frowned on the screen. "Problem fixed for Manny, not for me. Soria Clinics wants *me* to get deeper into this mess. Manny's pilot research showed promise. They want him well taken care of. Soria will pay all Manny's legal expenses. And George's bills. How's George?"

"Just fine. Jumped right into school. His level of math and science is great even for a school that teaches the kids of Pandolf's doctors and scientists. Speaks four languages, says 'sir' and 'ma'am,' and opens doors for women. The teachers love him!"

"We're already in April, almost the end of the school year," said Kochanski, "but sounds like you got him enrolled smoothly enough."

"Surprisingly easy. Forms signed by Manny, George's vaccination record from his aunt, all came over the school fax. And I needed another emergency contact for George besides me. So, I asked Sharma."

"She said yes?"

"After I made her feel guilty. And only as a last resort."

"Great." Kochanski smiled broadly. "And keep sending me all of George's expenses for reimbursement— *from Soria.*"

"Emailing now," said Campbell. "This hodgepodge of people helping George out is like that African proverb, 'It takes a village.' I had a laissez-faire upbringing myself and turned out just fine. And me helping him out feels like paying it forward—to another kid."

"Feels good, huh?"

"Yup."

Meanwhile, the school counselor had been unfazed by Campbell's vagueness about Garcia's whereabouts or return and said, "Many of our families are complicated here in Pandolf. International. Temporary residents. We'll make sure George gets all the support he needs, as we do for all our children."

Perhaps she gave the same bland assurance frequently.

He asked Sharma, "Is Pandolf not working on Manny's detention? They may be able to get him released."

"I called Dr. Nepski, our lab head, the very morning George appeared. But he can't discuss it with me. Honestly, Mr. Campbell, I think Dr. Garcia has been fired. They're interviewing scientists to take his place."

"Not good."

"Also, Dr. Garcia was fixing something under the printer the last time I saw him. When I told Dr. Nepski about it, thinking maybe it still needed repairs, he looked surprised."

"Why? Manny is the Drukker expert, trained to do minor fixes on that machine."

"Well, that's all I know."

"Please don't tell George any of this."

"I won't."

"I don't understand why George doesn't seem as upset as I would have expected about his dad's detention," Campbell said.

"Well, he hasn't lived with Dr. Garcia for years. Probably doesn't feel much different. I can't imagine growing up without my parents. It's sad."

• • •

George soon found a housemate in Charlie, Lucky's younger brother, again in trouble at his private school in Maine. He had come to Pandolf for another "visit" and now refused to go back.

Lucky told Sharma, "My parents are fighting a lot. Charlie wants to transfer to Pandolf High, probably to get away. My parents are appalled, you know—public schools, wild parties, police visits, no social connections with other important families, weak academic preparation for college."

Borrowing Lucky's sleeping bag, Charlie settled into George's apartment.

"Charlie's stubborn," said Lucky to whoever would listen, this time Campbell. After Sharma introduced them to each other, Lucky and Campbell often ran into each other in the apartment building stairwell or the boys' apartment.

"Dr. Sharma mentioned that your parents were concerned about Pandolf High School."

"A great school. But my parents don't listen to me, either."

Campbell offered, "This might sound strange, but would you like me to talk to your parents?"

She looked startled. Perhaps he had been too forward, he thought. After some hesitation, she said, "You don't mind? Thank you!"

Campbell had a video chat with Charlie's parents, who seemed like nice people, just like their daughter. He described attending StarHall, the elite boarding school in New England, then his degree from MIT. Like Sharma, Charlie's father asked to see his passport and driver's license.

"Nice zip code," he said, noticing his Texas address. "You have a ranch there?"

"Yes. And I'm a business scientific consultant. You may have heard of Drukker, one of my clients?"

"I saw Zoser just bought them out."

"Indeed. Now, back to your son." Campbell clicked open a popup of public-school rankings. "See, Pandolf High School is ranked near the top. Charlie will be there with the kids of doctors and scientists here at the medical center. Tech is the latest. With all the international students, Charlie will learn to deal with other backgrounds and cultures, like I did at StarHall. It's an international business world out there now. His housemate, George, already speaks four languages."

"You'll keep an eye out for Charlie?"

"Yes, sir."

"But it's April, school's almost over, isn't it?

"California schools go into June."

Campbell stopped. Pandolf had special programs for itinerant kids, usually foreign ones like George—month-long "transition" modules. He wasn't sure what Dr. Malone (the father) would think of his son around non-English speakers and poor, migrant children?

Dr. Malone considered. "He was already asked to leave one private school, and this other one isn't working out well either. I think he's just a normal boy with growing pains. And our public school here is terrible! And I'm not a fan of boarding schools like StarHall even if you went there. One needs family around. At Pandolf, Lucky will be right there at least. His mother's on board."

Dr. Malone then looked around and whispered, "Truth is, Charlie's little friends growing up are now getting into drugs and drinking. At this rate he'll go into rehab before he graduates high school. He needs a fresh start."

After Charlie's parents agreed to let him stay in Pandolf, a new bed and computer arrived at the sublet for the second bedroom. Charlie also received the latest Genie smart device—"the One"—that his parents had withheld as punishment.

Then Kochanski wanted Campbell to access the wireless network in the boys' apartment. "We should keep an eye on things, especially for any communication from ICE."

A package from Chicago arrived a few days later: a webcam inside a framed Vermeer print. Campbell texted Kochanski, "declining" to install it in the boys' apartment. Then his phone vibrated immediately.

"I don't see a problem," shouted Kochanski on the video call, his accent growing stronger. "But I must respect your local American customs. Fine, send it back."

"I will."

On the screen, Kochanski's shoulders relaxed in defeat.

Campbell added, "I'll let George and Charlie know about the limited monitoring we are doing. They have a right to know. This is America."

Less than an hour later, Kochanski called again. "David, when are you going to find Manny's stuff to take to Saburia: the Soria laptop and the rest of the files?"

Campbell drew apart the hotel room's curtains and pointed his phone camera at the lights of the medical center.

"What we're searching for could be anywhere out there."

Kochanski's voice grew louder. "What if Manny tells ICE . . . and they find it? All that hard work and our client's money wasted. You went to MIT. Call me with an update tomorrow morning."

"I'll try."

"Also, David, at the board meeting, I learned that the Pandolf people found loose cables and tools under the lab computer, as well as chunks of time when Manny had run experiments with no records. Drukker was unable to recover the files that Manny deleted. They then upgraded the Pandolf computers with security fixes. Things would have been so much easier if Manny had run the Soria files on the AI machines at the Dock."

"Drukker did not permit it."

"I know, I know," said Kochanski, exasperated, then parroted Campbell's own words from a previous conversation back to him: "Because even if Soria says the data is de-identified, it is individual human data, ultimately impossible to truly de-identify. And even if Soria's Institutional Review Board approved Manny's work, Drukker's legal counsel did not want the risk."

"Correct."

"Lawyers, regulations." A few expletives later, Kochanski finished, "But you were right about getting Manny a lawyer. Soria better pony up."

"'Pony up,' huh?" said Campbell, trying not to smile. Kochanski's accented efforts at American idioms were often, as George said about his father, "awk," like the time Garcia had called him, elated about the first patient for the cancer trial. "Her name is Mary. How courageous! Must make 'em like that in New York City."

They were on their secure Soria phones. Garcia then told Campbell that he had drawn a paper map to show the hiding place for his laptop and drives on the hospital campus. "David, I think someone is spying on me. We should not be seen together. I'll leave you the map. Just have to figure out where?"

But before Garcia could tell Campbell where to find the map, ICE had gotten in the way. He needed the map. Using George's key that his father had given him at the airport, he had already been to Garcia's apartment. But it was clear from the disorder that searchers had already come and gone.

George had also given him Garcia's badge to the lab. Now, lying in his hotel bed in the darkness, Campbell reached out to Soria IT, and they were able to reprogram the badge. They also told him, "No worries about Dr. Garcia's Soria phone. We remotely and permanently disabled it."

• • •

Early the next morning, he visited Garcia's old lab. He told the guard, "I'm a friend of someone who works here. She asked me to pick up something for her."

He flashed the badge quickly, so the guard would not see the photo, chatting the whole time about the upcoming federal inspection by Joint Commission for Hospital Accreditation that Sharma had mentioned to him.

The guard was alarmed. "Thanks. JCAHO again so soon? Let me text my guys, make sure they know. I'm new, not sure the government inspects lab buildings, but do you know?"

"No."

The reprogrammed badge worked. In the lab, he saw a neat, white jacket with Sharma's name hung along with others in a wall rack. But Garcia's old bench and desk were empty, no clues left to guide him. A young woman in the corner looked up curiously.

"Hi," he said to her, "I'm new around here. Sorry, I'm in the wrong lab. They're all alike."

She did not smile back and returned to her notebook.

Then he had another idea. Sunday afternoon, he joined George and Charlie at the Golden Griddle. Tangled hair, still in pajamas, the teens feasted on a late brunch. Stacks of pancakes with syrup, jugs of orange juice, and plates of scrambled eggs paraded before them, served by an efficient dispenser in the wall.

"Go-to place for big appetites, huh," he said, sitting down in the booth next to George, moving a dirty tray to the conveyer belt.

"Hey, Mr. Campbell," they said in unison, then returned to a fast conversation he could not follow, due to parallel exchanges on their devices and many words he did not understand.

He interrupted them. "Guess you still haven't heard from your father, George?"

Not looking up from his screen, George shook his head.

Then Charlie said, "Your dad told you he would call soon when they dropped you off at Dr. Sharma's, right?"

"Yes, maybe, I mean, the ICE men were in the car with him the whole time."

"Ooh," said Charlie, mock shivering.

"There's something wrong with you," said George.

"Sorry, I'm just trying to get you to talk about it."

"Whatever."

The teens next discussed a movie they planned to see: a sequel in a superhero adventure series. George extolled the trailer they had watched online while Charlie interrupted him often. They shared video clips of the film on their phones.

"This is where the robot blows up the skyscraper."

"But I thought the colored smoke looked fake. And there was too much CGI in this scene, too."

"No, that's real."

"No way. I can tell."

The group returned to the apartment. Inside, Campbell saw a girl, about fifteen, round cheeks, fluffy hair the color of honey, tan skinned. She stood up and nonchalantly tossed Lucky's cat from her lap. It stalked off.

Charlie said, "Mr. Campbell, you remember Michaela?"

Oh my, he thought, noting Charlie's goofy look. Teenage *romantic* relationships had not even been on his radar. He recognized her from his first time visiting Pandolf High with George and Charlie just a while ago. Today, her style of dress was more adult, and her nails were painted an electric shade of blue to match her platform shoes.

She looked at Campbell. "Do you want to come to the movie, too, Mr. Campbell? They just renovated the DreamSix theater. It's nice. It was a dump for as long as I can remember—my mom would take me to every latest Disney movie as a kid. Now they have couches that recline. A machine that mixes the best drinks."

"And a bar," said Charlie. He added, "Michaela was born in Pandolf. Lived here all her life. She's the expert on all the places to go and everyone who lives here."

Campbell smiled at them. "Thanks, if I can catch up with all of you at the theater, I will, but don't wait for me. I'm going to stay here and update the network."

As soon as the group left, he stepped over the clutter to enter George's room, where papers, wrappers, and clothes covered the floor. The orange cat popped out from under the bed and then disappeared again. Searching the room, his hands now gloved, he pulled a suitcase out from under the bed. In the side flap, he found a folded map of the hospital with a long Indian name at the bottom.

"Hello, Dr. Arjun Jagdishwar Bhattacharya!" he said aloud. "Manny, I'm impressed." Garcia had slipped the map into George's suitcase right under the noses of those agents.

He placed the map in a plastic sleeve before refolding it to put into his pants pocket. In the remote event that the map ended up in a crime lab, his gloves and the plastic sleeve would mean there would be no fingerprints, hairs, DNA, or any other clue to identify him.

Next, he went upstairs to look for Sharma. Perhaps she would explain the hospital's layout to him. The two busy women had trusted him with a spare key to help with random things: the cat, computer repairs, furniture assembly (and disassembly and disposal) and to keep an eye on the building handyman. "I don't want to be inventorying my jewelry every time that guy leaves," said Lucky.

But no one was home. Lying on the sagging couch in their living room, he sighed about the orange and white cat hairs on his clothes these days.

• • •

Lucky woke Campbell up. "Why are *you* here?"

"I was hoping to talk to Dr. Sharma."

"About what?" Her face was expressionless, sizing him up.

"Maybe you're the right person. Charlie appears to have a girlfriend, Michaela, so I just want to make sure someone has talked to George . . . about things."

She looked suspicious. "This is really going above and beyond for Manny Garcia."

He was making it up as he went and hoped he didn't sound as nervous as he felt. "This is not scientific, but teenagers seem to just put their laundry in the same washer to get pregnant."

"No, not scientific at all," she said. "What are you saying? That Charlie will be a bad influence on George and George will get some girl pregnant?" Now she sounded defensive about her brother.

"No, no, not what I meant." He put his shoes on to leave.

She opened the door.

In the doorway, he turned around. "Are you free for dinner?"

Her eyes grew wide.

"Pregnant pause—what do you say?" he joked, trying to sound casual.

Her face lit with the faintest smile. "I guess. I'm post-call and exhausted. But if you show up like this again, I'm taking back our key."

He heard himself suggesting the Provençale, a memorable first date, and, well, even if she had a boyfriend, so what? It wasn't like she had a ring on her finger.

"I need a nap," she said. "How about 6 p.m.? I can meet you there. Would you mind making the reservation?"

"Of course, and since you're so tired, I'll come back and pick you up."

"Thanks."

That evening, he bounded up the apartment stairs, suited up, shoes gleaming. Slowing down to reach the landing, he stopped, took a breath, and knocked—even if he had the key.

She opened the door. From mascara and smoky eye shadow to the silver dress and high heels that made her still not as tall as him, his quick visual tour—top to toe—left him muttering something about how he had never seen her not wearing scrubs. She had even penciled in brown eyebrows.

In the entry hall mirror, she brushed her hair and looped it into a bun. She pulled a rose jacket off the coat hook. He followed her out, trailing her lavender scent. At the bottom of the stairs, he moved ahead and opened the heavy door.

The rain had washed the spring blossoms off the trees. Their footsteps were soft on the petals littering the sidewalk. Flowers, fragrance, twilight—*how perfect*—he watched himself lead her to his rental car and open the passenger door.

The concierge at the Provençale put them at their showcase table in the front of the restaurant.

"Wow, this is flattering," he said. "You've sat here before?"

"Yes, when Harry and I come here, they usually put us at this table. Shelly calls it 'White privilege.' I don't want to argue with her. But last time we came, they had an African American couple at this table. We sat someplace else."

He hated Harry. *Why do you bring Harry up?*

"Dr. Sharma—Shelly's got a point," he said. "Do you think a lot about the differences between people, living with her, half-Indian? And

George is from Argentina downstairs. Then Pandolf Hospital gets a lot of international patients? I think about it. I do business with this guy from Poland. Says the world economy has reverted to a Middle Eastern bazaar—now electronic—at the end of the Silk Route from China. Right now actually, he's at an old port on the coast of the Red Sea."

Lucky nodded. "I have read about the Maritime Silk Road, centuries ago, trade ships connecting East to West through the Red Sea."

"Rebuilt," he said and described the Saburian base on the Red Sea coast.

"I'd love to see it one day. Closest I've been is Egypt," she said. "Here's to now." Then she made a toast to the view outside, the clear sky, bright stars, the rippling brilliance of the waters below. And he snapshotted this California moment into memory, from the top of the grassy slope to the sidewalk winding down to the lake, edged by darkness on its far side.

She told him stories about the hospital. "Hope the gory medical details don't spoil your appetite."

Not the right time to talk about my gorier meat business at the ranch.

Then she mentioned Harry's upcoming visit. *Harry, Harry!* Surprised by how jealous he felt, he reminded himself that he was doing this to get the hospital layout from her and pivoted from romance to work. He was wining and dining an attractive woman on Soria's tab, and yes, making it worth their while.

Still, he thought, Lucky's boyfriend lived far away. *Life's a winding road. Time changes everything.* The future just could make his competition disappear.

Then Lucky agreed to show him around the Pandolf complex after dinner—"tour of my queendom," she joked.

The waiter brought two checks. Lucky took hers and waved away his protests. "I insist on paying my share."

On their way out, she said, "Oh, another story: so this woman came to my clinic for her rash. Given the disease site"—Lucky nodded vaguely downward—"she asked for a woman. She told me she didn't want to go back to 'this kid doctor from outer space' in the women's clinic. Good thing Shelly's going into research and surgery."

They drove into the well-lighted, never-sleeping hospital campus. Lucky handed him her card for the doctor's parking lot. After they parked, he removed an empty laptop bag from the trunk.

"Why do you need that?"

"I don't feel safe leaving my computer in the car," he lied. *Manny, your map better work!*

"Why're you putting on gloves?"

"Hospital germs are the worst. Antibiotic resistance, you know."

He put on a mask. *Makes face ID harder.* He offered her one.

"No thanks."

Joining a parade of people, many ages and sizes, on foot, crutches, wheelchairs, or in Pandolf mobile units, they walked across marble floors, past fountains, and the always-open gift shop. He admired the views from the top-floor picture windows and vast halls for hospital parties.

She greeted staff at various nursing stations and introduced him as "Dr. Campbell, a visiting research scientist."

Then he said, "I read an article in the hospital newsletter about the renovations. I enjoy construction. Can I see?"

"Not interesting to me, but okay."

She badged into a different corridor. The crowd thinned, and the passageways grew narrow and dim. He steered her down the paths on Garcia's hand-drawn map.

"Let's go down this hall?" He pointed to a corridor with bare bulbs hanging in cages.

She suppressed a yawn. "After this, let's turn around."

Tap, tap, went her heels on the cement floors. They were now in a dilapidated part of the hospital with construction signs, orange tape, and flimsy barriers to hard hat areas. Down another long corridor, past the dark doors of many old patient rooms, they turned into yet another hallway.

Campbell surreptitiously referred to Garcia's map again. Next, at his request, she swiped her badge, and they opened an unmarked door into an ample storage space for medical supplies. But the dented metal shelves were empty.

"Look, there's a door," he said, pointing to one in the back of the room.

"Into the tunnels, probably," she said. She explained that Pandolf dated to over a hundred years ago, "like some medieval castle." She described a maze of halls and passages and rooms and additions built on, and even underground tunnels. "My dad, a surgeon, says that many old hospitals have tunnels. But Pandolf not only maintains the tunnels, but they also even build new ones, spooky if you ask me. Let's turn around."

"Wait." Turning on his phone flashlight, he walked into the storage room and lit up a sign next to the door. "'Men only,' can I get in? I hope the plumbing works. Oh no, door's locked."

"I'll find someone," said Lucky. She left and returned with a petite tan woman in a Pandolf housekeeping uniform.

"This is my husband." Lucky showed the housekeeper her ID. "Can you let him in please?"

The woman looked blankly at Lucky, who tried again in broken Spanish. Campbell, fluent in Spanish, said nothing. The woman gave them a skeptical look but unlocked the door with a heavy key on a ring and hurried away.

"My Spanish is so bad," Lucky said.

"Maybe she knows English quite well," he wondered.

"Why would you think that?"

"Just things aren't always what they seem." *Like me right now*, he thought guiltily.

Lucky flicked on the switch. "Light works. Looks like residents used to sleep back here in the old days. My dad said that back before his time, doctors in training practically lived in dorms like this, a lifestyle of 'eat when you can, sleep when you can.'"

Using his phone flashlight, Campbell dispersed long shadows and saw a moldy shower on the left. On the right, there was a dormitory hall, cracked floors and metal bed frames, divided by curtain rods. At the far end of that hall was another door, presumably to the tunnels that Lucky had told him about.

"This looks like a military dorm," he said.

Lucky folded her arms. "I think that a system that produces good soldiers—ruthless and unemotional—shouldn't train doctors. It'll be gross in there. I'll wait out here for you."

Inside, he walked past the urinals, where the air still had the strong odor. Why? Who had painted graffiti? The wall had steel lockers with peeling labels. Curious, he tried to open one. It swung open.

Then he realized all the lockers had "3-3-3-3" keyed in to stay unlocked, except one with a browned label that faintly read: "Dr. Arj dishwar atta."

He turned the dial on the combination panel according to the numbers written on his map. The bolt slid open. Inside, he found Garcia's Soria laptop, five computer disks, and a purple case he had not been briefed about.

When he returned, Lucky asked, "Feeling better now?"

"Disgusting place, but yes, thanks. Glad they're tearing this down."

With his now heavy laptop bag in the trunk of his car, they headed back to her apartment building.

At the entryway, she said she was exhausted.

He felt disappointed. "I understand, good night. I'll drop in to check on the boys. So glad things are working out for them, especially with them jumping into ninth grade when it's almost over."

"I know, right? It's already May. They'll be tenth graders soon. Good night, David."

He listened to her footsteps fade up the stairs. Then inside the boys' apartment, he heard muffled explosions of sound. Inside, he found George and Charlie—no Michaela—at their game stations, the massive 3D screen playing *Apocalypse 2050* and their avatars dodging gunfire.

He sat on the couch, staring at the screen, watching until the teens found a good stopping point. Then they regaled him with descriptions of the movie they had seen, reenacting some of the fight scenes.

Remembering the previous iterations of the superhero series, he thought how in real life there were no superheroes or their essential antitheses—immortal villains. How many more movies would come out starring the Joker, bankrolling the movie industry with endless sequels?

Truth is chaos is entertaining, he thought, preparing people for disruption. Like the monkey that duped the cat in the children's story, or that other monkey who made mischief in Chinese folk tales—nothing new under the sun.

When the boys resumed *A'50*, he slipped into George's room, still wearing gloves, removed the map from its plastic sleeve, and replaced it in the side of the suitcase. He had decided not to destroy it. With Manny Garcia in detention, someone else might find out about his map and come looking for it. If they found it missing, they might suspect him as one of the few people with access to George's apartment.

CHAPTER FOUR

The afternoon sun lit the Red Sea outside the window. Michael Kochanski watched warplanes in training exercises dart through the skies like fighting kites. Inside, the latest episode of *Black Shadows* played. On the wall screen, a parting young couple stood, a solemn Saburian man in camouflage, carrying an automatic rifle, and the woman's face tearful, their hometown under attack from the mountain rebels. Mournful music. Other men leaving for battle while wives, mothers, children, and the old huddled.

A base manager translated the episodes to him. In her seventies, golden skinned, half-Saburian and half-British, gray hair in a neat bun, Eleanor was a last vestige of a British empire that had died a century ago. He often ate breakfast with her, scooping an egg from her porcelain cup and drinking tea.

"Eleanor is 'elegant and intelligent,'" his daughter had once said, quoting a long poem with a sad name.

"Depressing English eulogy to their dominion?"

"You mean elegy," Kasia said, frowning. "You know I love TS Eliot. And he wasn't British, he was born in America." Then she abruptly ended their video call. And he never criticized her choices in poetry again.

While he called her Kasia privately, publicly she was Katya, the Russian version of her name that meant "pure." As Katya Kochanski, adopting his changed last name, her birth identity was protected.

The phone rang in his office—Trisha Talwar again, his lawyer in Chicago.

Her voice was neutral. "Michael, Chicago police want to talk to you about Oscar Sanchez's murder. I think Detective Dodd is interested in this one. I told them you were out of the country, and they said you can call them. Do you want me to sit in on this?"

"Yes. Please set up a three-way tomorrow afternoon, Chicago time.

Anything else I should know before going in?" As his lawyer, she was his advocate. How much would she press him on his lies?

"Will do."

"I would hope the purpose of their meeting is to focus on the horrible murder." *Not those fake ID papers.* Impressed that she remained resolutely silent, he continued, "Meanwhile, I've called the super to check the storage room in the Pierre to see if anything's missing. Oscar had the key code, you know, as the security guard . . . sure hope nothing's gone. It's all insured, of course."

"Okay, Michael."

Her clipped answers sounded calculating. But she always sounded that way, a lawyer after all.

Was that it, then? Had his art fraud scheme failed? His plan had been to sell an original Vermeer to the Saburian king and replace it with a forgery. Then in the future, claiming his art had been stolen and a copy substituted, he would collect on the insurance and be paid a second time for its value.

But now the police were all over the Pierre, and his security guard had died under mysterious circumstances. If the painting was indeed missing, he could still file an insurance claim for it, but he would not make any money—*I'll probably lose money in the end.* Kochanski grimaced. It was one thing to embark on such a scheme if he were already rich; it was another to do so under his desperate financial circumstances.

Oscar Sanchez had been taking the painting to the artist, Alex Marion, at night, to forge a copy. Would Marion keep his mouth shut? He must know that otherwise, he could ruin his painting career. Still, it would be best to collect the half-completed fake and give Marion some cash. Who would do that for him? He was stuck in Saburia. All the king's men, of course.

Kochanski touched the campus phone and rang up the main office. "I need to speak to Salim," he said. He then waited by the phone.

The Pierre building's superintendent in Chicago had called him a week ago to tell him the security guard, Oscar, was missing.

Kochanski's therapist had coached him on the "7/11 rule" to manage his panic at such times: "Count to seven as you take one deep breath in, and then count to eleven while you exhale. Do it seven times." He rarely got past two times.

He had wanted to tell the super that couldn't be true? Like a child? Magical thinking was a sign of insanity, they said.

Yesterday, the super had called again that Oscar's body was found. "Floating face down in the Chicago River. I had to ID it, just saw his face, awful, and I recognized his clothes."

"Did it smell horrible?" Kochanski asked.

"Why?"

"That tells us how long Oscar was underwater."

"Lost my smell with COVID ten years ago, never came back."

Thirty minutes passed. Salim did not call back.

After leaving another message, losing hope that the arrogant Saburian officer would return his call soon—or ever—Kochanski locked his door. The therapist had diagnosed his nausea at such times as a "generalized anxiety disorder"—F41.*something* in her medical coding book—and "strongly" recommended that he see a psychiatrist for medication.

Some time back, Kochanski had given Oscar Sanchez, who was undocumented, fake ID papers, duplicating Manny Garcia's driver's license. They were meant for a one-time use—to enter a court building with maximum levels of government security and bribe a judge. Short on money and time, stretched thin between Chicago and Saburia, he knew his choice of Oscar was risky. But affordable, yes. And do-able—double yes. Except for their fifteen-year age difference, Garcia and Oscar looked fairly alike.

How could he have known that the secret police sting operation for Chicago money laundering, Loop Laundromat, would indict that judge for graft? Then ICE would arrest the shocked Manny Garcia — whose ID Oscar had used — for bribing a judge.

Luckily, Oscar's body and fabricated ID were recovered. Then, *oh thank God,* within the span of twenty-four hours, Garcia's pugnacious lawyer, Trish Talwar, on a retainer now with Soria Clinics, was pushing ICE to release Garcia as a case of mistaken identity — over a month after his arrest.

The link between her two cases—Oscar's death and Garcia's ICE detention—must not have been lost on Talwar. At the very least, surely she must know that he, Kochanski, was not a killer. Not in this life, anyway.

Would the feds trace their leads back to him, Kochanski wondered, question him about Oscar Sanchez's connection to Manny Garcia? The last thing he and Soria Clinics needed was more scrutiny on their valuable scientist. He had already prepared his answer: to tell them that Sanchez had stolen Garcia's ID papers from his office—a lie he had already fed Soria.

He remembered another time feeling so sick with anxiety. Two years ago, he and Manny Garcia had met in Chicago to talk the cancer business for Soria— and the Saburian king's request for a little something on the side. A silent server poured iced shots of his vodka. After the Dew calmed his nerves, not looking at Garcia, he slipped in the king's request for the Porphyry Project.

Garcia had taken only one polite sip of the Dew, switched to water, and asked Kochanski many questions.

Then Garcia was reluctant. "You've got a nice voice, rich, Eastern European accent. It's soothing. Maybe it helps you to coax people into proposals like this. Let me think about it."

After Garcia left that day, Kochanski drank more vodka, ate a steak, and smoked a pack of cigarettes. He never told the therapist about things that already worked well for his nausea. Americans especially had an odd disapproval of alcohol, he thought, preferring medication and morality. *Heavenly Father, I've never done drugs. I'll not start now.*

That evening with Garcia, they had also talked about the new Chicago mob and its resemblance to the old Godfather movies, or was it the Vatican's connection to the Italian mafia? As fellow Catholics, he showed Garcia pictures of the new chapel he was building in the Pierre, in memory of his mother—its baptismal font and antique crucifix. Garcia was more interested in the GFCI power outlets.

The scientist said he did not believe in the devil. But drinking made Kochanski fearful. Later that night, he walked to the Pierre's chapel in the winter wind, sat on a pew bench in the dark, and prayed before falling asleep. Dawn brought another punishing hangover to whip him with shame as he prayed, "God, I promise never to do this again . . . not for a while."

Garcia then signed on to the king's project. "Michael, porphyry is an antique marble imported from ancient Egypt to build imperial monuments. Too fancy. I'll call it 'the Purple Project.' I think I feel how Oppenheimer felt about the Manhattan Project."

"What's that?"

"Something impossible becoming real. I will do what the king asks for a good cause: my cancer research."

"What's a Manhattan project?"

"The project that produced the first nuclear weapon."

"Oh, no," said Kochanski. "The nuclear club is closed, sadly, for King Mohammed."

"What do you mean?"

"Countries that have nuclear weapons don't want others to have them—so other countries must depend on them for protection. Just like how gangs work, make people pay for security."

"I like to avoid politics," said Garcia. "But ART is artificial reproductive technology. I spend time in Pandolf's embryology lab helping a Dr. Safire to use the Drukker AI. I will have to pick his brain without telling him exactly what for."

"Like test-tube babies?"

"This technology I will use is way more advanced. Michael, human germ-line experiments are prohibited by all the major governments. Can result in criminal prosecution. Maybe your idea of a club extends to controlling that type of research too?"

Kochanski snorted. "No one will care about these closed club deals fifty years from now. Think of Saburia as a less expensive version of the Cayman Islands. You won't believe the research they do in the Caymans. Even Soria does not approve. For now, Soria's not part of the Purple Project, officially. But the king has a lot of influence. If you're successful, Soria Clinic might jump on board."

Garcia stayed silent, looking thoughtful and troubled. Then he said, "How do I know the king will keep up his end of the deal? To help my cancer research quid pro quo for working on his project?"

"You don't know. Figure out how to connect the two. Then to keep them connected. If the king wants the one, he must give you the other. Otherwise, why should he care about cancer research? Few do at our board meetings. The rest complain that's practically giving away the product when the military pays fifty percent more for our technology. And internationally, the world's queuing up, price no object, to use it for so many other purposes."

"I must connect the two, you say," Garcia muttered thoughtfully. "Like game theory, money from the king to Soria Clinics for my cancer research in exchange for me working on the Purple Project, yes, keep them connected."

I have no idea what game theory is, thought Kochanski, planning to look it up. He picked up his glass of Dew. "Okay. I know you disapprove of me drinking when we talk business. If I said anything offensive that other day, that was the vodka, my rude business partner, mouthing off. Knowing what happened to your wife, I'm sorry."

"I wasn't offended."

"You do look so much happier than the man I first met working at the NIH."

"Yes," said Garcia. "I'm happy when I circle the truth."

"Meaning?"

"Human beings like to think we're the center of the world. We also used to believe that the sun revolved around the Earth, too. But human existence revolves around the truth. I'm happy when I circle the truth."

• • •

In their online meeting, Kochanski told his therapist the "beautiful" thing Garcia had said. But he had never told her about his past, ashamed and also fearing deportation. Instead, he read self-help books and diagnosed himself with post-traumatic stress disorder, PTSD, code F43.*something* in her gigantic ICD-14 medical database for health insurance claims. A colossal ledger of the human story, ICD-14 even had an "m" modifier specific for him, for adult immigrants.

Even now, drinking and smoking, Kochanski found escape with fatherly ghosts from his gang family. Growing up in small-town Poland, he had learned to slaughter animals by day, which segued into killing people at night. Gangs used boy-men like him for executing people they did not know for bosses they had never met. A hooded crone handed out assignments and train tickets at night on a street corner. Few were as good as him at disappearing, with only a touch of a knife like a feather to the throat—their best assassin—no line between animals and people, and pride in how fast he worked. Almost painless!

The gang called him "White Rat," for his color, for the red-blond bristle on his gaunt face.

Sitting in his office chair now in Saburia, feeling strapped by the invisible bands of his anxiety, his eyes grew wet for those passengers left behind at the death stations. The executing business, murder, became distressing when he grew older. Then he couldn't cross the line from killing into torture and terror. His disappointed bosses gave him other jobs instead. Then he spent most of his time in front of computer screens.

Manny Garcia had once said another "beautiful" thing: "Faster than the speed of light, life comes and goes—train escaping even the rails of time." Garcia was talking about his dead wife, his young son growing up far away, and his failed scientific career at the time.

As a boy, Kochanski remembered all the trains he rode. After a hit, successful or not, he used to take the trains back home to his safe zone. Behind his town's local bakery, which oozed warmth and delicious smells, two dumpsters exhaled the stench of yesterday's food. Skinny enough in his mid-teens to hide between them where nobody could find him, he retreated into a gloomy daze, smoking and drinking cheap vodka with salt. Hunger drove him to eat the old pastries, bread, and cheese the shop had discarded.

In his secretive hometown, where generations had grown up connected by the local sense of community, the baker shrugged off outsiders hunting for him. The old man also had a tender spot for his single mother and childhood friend. Kochanski left what he did not eat for the stray dogs he befriended—they had saved his life more than once by growling away pursuers.

One morning, he woke up next to the warm oven in the baker's shop, his mother hovering over him, her distinct scent mingling with the lemon cleaning products she used at work.

The upset baker warned them, "Too drunk to know better. You're lucky, Michael, the alcohol is why you didn't freeze to death. Next time, I'm calling the police station."

Later, his mother said, "I know you don't worry about our local police because your friend, Jakub, is the chief's nephew. But someday when you're running from your own, not just those others in the cities you travel to, you'll need a place to hide that your friends don't know about. When your own people turn on you, no one—but me—will try to help you."

Then he found other places—only the dogs knew—and didn't go home the nights he drank; instead leaving his mother some of his increasingly thick wads of money to pay the bills. She did not ask questions and always had a loving blessing and warm meal ready for him.

Besides his mother, no one cared much about another fatherless boy. A charity kid at the town's Catholic school, he found a mentor in a physics teacher and planned to become a scientist himself. After the science teacher moved on to Warsaw, the butcher recruited him for the local gang. The paunchy meatman had relatives in the police and court who looked the other way.

At the police station, delivering sandwiches, he met sixteen-year-old Irina. Russian, round face, high cheekbones, blonde and blue-eyed, she struck him as different looking and more beautiful than any local girl.

He waited outside the police station. She emerged with Jakub. He joined them as they walked to the boarding house for girls like her. They connected phones.

She told them she had once lived with her father in Russia after her mother walked out on her father's drinking and married an American.

"But she couldn't get me out," she said.

Whenever he could, he would wait outside the boarding house for her. Walk with her where she went. Later, he would sneak up to her room by climbing the back wall of the boarding house.

She told him that when she was six years old, her father had moved her stepmother, whom she called "Evil Woman," into their home.

"Evil Woman stayed in bed and had me do extra chores in the morning," she would say angrily, face just as pretty when she frowned. "She wouldn't give me a school excuse when I was late, stole my lunch money, and if she was angry, she would even throw away my homework. Then she had a baby, and I was the babysitter, too."

Her voice lowering to a whisper, she described Natasha, a girl her age who lived upstairs. They shared everything in a secret world where they were two fairy-tale princesses in a castle turret, high above wild oceans. She said it was like how he made her feel in their warm nights together, winding their languages and bodies together. Twining her fingers with his, she said he made her feel butterflies on her eyelashes.

Irina liked fairy tales. Back home, she described a hardbound collection of fairy tales from her grandparents, with illustrations in brilliant colors:

the blue teal of peacocks, the royal purple of princes, and the soft pastel of the princesses' faces and hands.

"The pictures were covered with tissue that you peeled back, and they would come to life. Those are the stories I tell you now, Michael, like the Arabian princess Scheherazade told her king. But I don't like foreign stories as much. The Russian ones are from my heart."

He stroked her fine hair, white gold, morning light on stillest lake. She narrated tales by Tolstoy, Dostoevsky, and Chekhov, names he had not heard before.

"I have only read the children's versions. I hid my books so Evil Woman would not take them away. She explained how she did it. "I had to move this china shepherdess high up. Said that was so my little brother could not break her. Still, I cracked the statue first and blamed him. The witch beat me up for not watching him better. He was cute, my little brother. But sometimes I shut him up in the apartment to go see Natasha upstairs."

He stopped her with a kiss. "Enough chattering."

Kasia, their daughter, once took him to a London performance of Rimsky-Korsakov's *Scheherazade*. "Your mother loved stories, too," he said. "We had our own thousand and one nights."

"Dad, I don't need to know that."

Kasia only knew a sanitized version of her parents' relationship, not about her mother's eyes at their first meeting—pupils narrowed from drug use—or Irina's life before he met her. According to Irina, "This new man started visiting our house. Sasha was handsome, not much older than me, fun, taking me out for ice cream. One day he gave me drugged candy, and I fell asleep in his car. My father and stepmother sold me."

What happened next was their shared truth, the real-world school they graduated from.

"Still, I found you," she said.

"Shh," he whispered, accepting her embrace, arms as soft as the wings of a baby bird. No one had ever felt like them before.

At times he found her again, but then would wake up the next morning or the next month, and she would be gone.

Even when he met her, he knew she also belonged to others. When Number One finally tired of Irina, he gifted her to Number Two. It was so with the prettiest girls. Number One said it boosted morale even if the girls were not as valuable afterward. "Why should Arabs get the first taste?" growled Number One, who hated most people, from those who were not White to those who were not Polish. Number One distributed photos and videos, online guides to help tell Poles apart from Russians.

Number Two, in a drunken bet, passed Irina on to White Rat. Number Two also told a different story of how the gangs had taken Irina. "There was no stepmother. It was her father only. Even I don't think I could be as worthless as him. He sold her for a TV and booze."

Kochanski had questioned Number Two again, hoping, magical thinking, for a different answer. The man insisted he was telling the truth. Then Kochanski wondered about all the other things Irina had told him—lies or truth? For many years, those things became garden mazes, secret rooms, hidden passages to still chase her after she had already died. But now he was alone, lost, no longer in Poland, no longer in his twenties, no longer in a life that her ghost had kept alive for so long.

After Irina died, Kochanski took Kasia to a clinic in Warsaw for paternity testing. The good news that *yes*, he was her father, strengthened his belief in science. People were treacherous, except his own mother, whom he then moved to Warsaw with Kasia. Well hidden under a new family name, Kochanski, it was safer for the two there. As soon as she was nine and old enough, Kasia traded her Catholic school uniform for one at an even safer British boarding school.

The deep web was the only way to safely communicate with Kasia now while they were apart. But criminal elements flourished there, too. Also, he didn't want to get caught in the cyber crossfire between legal groups and governments. The king's computer crew and the local Chinese tech support had set him up with a "secure server and private network." Smiling and joking, spewing technical jargon in a mishmash of languages, and wearing blinking name tags, the techies had even come to his Chicago office. Everything could be bought, he thought, even if he was not highly educated.

Sometimes he wondered what the techies said to each other about him. Proudly claiming that in China they had "knowledge of everything wireless, lawful, and lawless," one claimed that international governments stayed omnipresent while incognito, observing and tracking the wild activities of the electronic night without interfering.

Like God, Kochanski thought, looking up at the clear, starry Saburian sky. Somewhere up there was a secure satellite where the stars and strangers heard everything that he said to Kasia, transmitted on coded electromagnetic waves through a wilderness of networks to Cambridge, England. Kasia was in school—under her changed legal name—getting an advanced degree in Russian literature. That she was fluent in English, Russian, and Polish would have amazed her mother.

Salim finally returned his call. Kochanski briefed him about the painting's disappearance. "I was getting ready to ship the art to your king," he said and asked Salim for his government's help. Kochanski also confessed his failed insurance scheme, safer for him that the king know—now rather than later. Garcia might call it game theory. Kochanski called it common sense.

Anxiety a bit better, Kochanski was able to move his thumb on the remote and turn *Black Shadows* back on. On the screen, bright explosions, dusty trenches, mangled metal, and smoldering fires could have been extracted from war footage anywhere in the world. The soundtrack was gunfire, shouts, and screams. Then a green and brown camouflaged blur of military vehicles, carrying soldiers with automatic rifles, more guns pointed skyward, stormed in.

Everyone looked alike to him and only spoke Saburian. The faces of the enemies were unseen, and their national origin was unclear. Were they only Saburian? Or were there mercenaries among the rebels, from other countries, funded by foreign powers? *Black Shadows'* story line was universal, mythic, but the details were only vaguely comprehensible. He forced himself out of his chair. He could not partake in the cure for his anxiety—alcohol, a steak, a smoke—yet. First, he had to greet the caravan arriving soon from the airport.

He opened a drawer on his bedside stand. Next to his stolen Gideons Bible were his packs of cigarettes. Saburia was good. Unlike Americans, the locals and the Chinese did not find his smoking bothersome. There would also be time tonight for that steak cooked rare, red juices, morsels dipped in kosher salt, and for smoking and vodka. Tonight, he would pass out still in his suit and socks on a comfortable bed in an air-conditioned bedroom. Like that *Macbeth* woman, he, too, would never wipe all the blood off his hands.

He rang the buzzer.

"Steak for my dinner later, make it rare," he said into the intercom. "After everyone leaves. And the bottle of wine for Dr. Sheraton's welcome. It needs to be here by 6 p.m., on ice . . . and nice crystal glasses."

Then he tapped his keyboard, searching files, the internet, and even the deep web for clues to Oscar Sanchez's murder. He had to return to Chicago but couldn't until his role in the king's project was wrapped up.

His phone showed a notification that Campbell's flight from San Francisco had landed in Ramses. Then a short email from the Dock in San Francisco: the Drukker plane had successfully negotiated a joint Drukker–Saburian secret flight experiment.

Except for Oscar's death, the last few days had been good news: hope for Garcia's release and Mary, their first patient, would be here soon. She also now had hope, sublime—all that was sacred—not profane, not like all his deals and fights, or Oscar's murder, or his looming money woes with the Pierre. Hope—the one truth from his connection with his dead wife, Irina: their daughter, Kasia.

His phone rang, an unknown number in the USA. He picked up to hear Garcia's voice.

ICE had released him. "They even apologized," Garcia said "They got the wrong man. Somebody stole my identity, Michael."

He feigned ignorance. "Terrible."

"Thank you for the lawyer and taking care of George. How's David?"

"Thank David too. He took good care of your son."

"Meaning?" Garcia's voice trailed off just in case someone was listening, like American law enforcement.

"Meaning David took care of *everything* at Pandolf that was needed. Matter of fact, he just landed in Saburia. I'll be seeing him soon about some successful business we have. The Saburian king will be pleased."

Garcia's voice relaxed as if understanding that Campbell had found his laptop, disks, and the Purple Project case. "Thank you," he said, sounding relieved.

CHAPTER FIVE

When Campbell had told Kochanski the good news that he had found the Soria computer and files Garcia had hidden, Kochanski laughed. "Some things you must hide in our real world, in your memory, paper, safes, remote places like that Pandolf locker. Or get lost in a crowd, needle in the haystack, safety in anonymity—"

"Or we were lucky," said Campbell. "By the way, what's in the purple case? Nothing problematic?"

"Just some confidential material for Manny's research. Got to jump off. Before I go, a pretty blonde even, Mr. Bond. I never doubted you." Kochanski abruptly disconnected the call.

He's lying again, Campbell thought, but it was too late in the game to press for more information than Kochanski was willing to give.

He felt tired; time to sleep, then go to the hotel gym in the morning. He still had work to finish for other clients.

Campbell's Soria phone rang in the morning. It was Kochanski again. He wanted Campbell to "jump on the plane. If I had known about these delays, I would have stayed in Chicago longer instead of boiling here on the Red Sea coast." He added mysteriously, "David, I've to fly to Chicago as soon as possible. It's dangerous to keep anyone's real identity—even for a moment—off the grid."

"Identity theft is passe—" Campbell said, frowning.

"Good to always have an avatar alibi on the grid—"

Then Campbell decided he didn't need to know more about Kochanski's sketchy dealings and told the other man it was his turn now to "hop off."

But he found it hard to work, instead daydreaming about Lucky, their dinner, the clear night, the tall windows of the high banquet halls at Pandolf with only the moon and stars above; that someday after global adventures, he just wanted to go home. He might not be a king, his inheritance had been good—but not one like Saburia, a country recently created by one of the most ruthless generals in modern history, King Mohammed's father, General Saburi. But he still had plans for his own dynasty, to return to his ranch with . . . a good woman and twinkles in his eye for their children.

Before flying out, he met Sharma the next morning. Outside the Ivy Drip, he found Sharma waiting, wearing a Pandolf T-shirt and khaki pants, not her usual scrubs.

Over breakfast, he finally told her, "I've to leave next week for my consulting job, then come back again after a month."

She frowned.

"Things are settled for George—for now," he continued, "and there's nothing more to do right now for Manny."

After the social worker had discovered that Campbell's name was on George's sublet, she told him she was "monitoring the situation in anticipation of the father's return . . . soon?" And he had reassured her. "Soon."

"Well, David, I've really thought about this," Sharma now said. "George and Charlie may not be little children, but it's still not right for fifteen-year-olds to be in this apartment with next to no adult supervision. It's been a month now, and Dr. Garcia is not back. Don't even get me started on Michaela."

"Manny does have a lawyer now . . ."

"That doesn't mean he's coming back soon," she said, frowning more. "All that time they spend online." She searched for words. "Their brains aren't biologically ready for some types of people, content online . . . don't you agree with me?"

Awkwardly, she added, "I'm talking about *adult* content."

He had not told her that a Polish American businessman in Chicago—whom George and Charlie had never met—wanted to monitor every byte of electronic activity, even install a secret webcam in the teens' apartment.

"You have a point," he said. "I have some firewalls up, but they're smart kids, so that's not perfect either, I know."

"Nothing about this situation is ideal," she said. "George has a bank account and credit card. You do monitor that. Everything *does* take money."

"Yes, I follow the money. When Manny is released, I'll give him his son's spending records."

She got up, saying mostly to herself, "Now that he's gone, I miss Manny."

After she left, he sat alone at the Ivy Drip, drinking coffee. Garcia always wanted George to be "up to date with the latest technology." Even Sharma wished she had played more video games as a kid, "to be better trained to control surgical robots." Sharma was excited that women orthopedic surgeons now had exoskeletons "to do the heavy bone work that used to be done only by men."

Despite his generous tip, the waiter stopped refilling his mug. The breakfast crowd was pouring in, there was a line, and other customers needed his table. He got up. There was a lot more to do before he could leave next week to meet Kochanski in Saburia with Garcia's delivery.

· · ·

The next morning, mid-May, Campbell boarded Pandolf's speed shuttle to San Francisco and then his flight to Saburia. The Drukker plane's wings cut away from the ground. The corporate jet flew higher and swifter than commercial aircraft, soon piercing the cloud layer, then soaring further above.

He texted George: "OMW2 back to where we came from."

"K, Icarus," replied George, "omw2 school."

Lights went off in the plane as it jetted over the Pacific Ocean. Campbell fell asleep and awoke hours later in Athens, briefly disembarking for the plane's disinfecting cycle and eating a gyro chicken sandwich. In the air again, his watch showed him flying over the Greek coast. Now cruising over the dark Mediterranean, he pictured the winged Icarus in flames, falling into this storied sea, the first incinerated astronaut. Flying so high, did Icarus have a woman he loved whom he would never see again.

Traversing spans of distance, sitting on a plane, distilled a state of reverie. Time became memories, their truth relative. First, he pictured Lucky, Julia Malone, everything beautiful. He liked her real name better—Julia, Jules, Jewel, Julius Cesar, Juliette, and her Romeo . . . they would settle down, a home, endless acreage on the ranch, kid on a horse and a plane on an airstrip nearby.

When his thoughts drifted back to the problems at hand, he thought about George. When would his father be released? Garcia now had a lawyer, found by Kochanski, paid for by Soria. And Kochanski had spoken with Garcia's sister in Chicago.

Kochanski explained that he already knew Garcia's sister. "Manny connected me to her husband, a Chicago artist, for expert advice when I opened my art gallery. "

"What do you know about art?" asked Campbell, surprised.

"Exactly. Just like with you and Drukker, just like the Medicis in the Renaissance, I don't have to know everything. I just buy experts."

He remembered the time he told Kochanski, "Michael, bending the law can be okay. But I have a conscience."

"And I, too, have an honor code," said Kochanski stiffly. "I value it in the people I work with."

Should Manny's family even trust this lawyer Michael Kochanski had found?

Campbell pulled the side lever of his wide bed, folding it back into a chair. Outside the window, Homer's rosy-fingered dawn shimmered over the turquoise sea that the Greeks had jeweled into their mythology. He pressed the call button for breakfast.

The flight attendant, head demurely covered with a yellow silk scarf dotted with roses, was prompt with his tray. Thanks to Sharma's healthy influence, he ordered oatmeal, yogurt, and bananas, in addition to his usual coffee. Greece, and now Egypt, he thought as he gazed into the Egyptian woman's molasses-colored eyes. He smiled back; he could be Antony to her Cleopatra.

Correction, he thought, *my ancestry is Northern — not Southern — European.* And hers? DNA analysis from a new excavation had just again roiled the controversy about whether the ancient Cleopatra was pure Macedonian Greek or mixed with Egyptian?

"Thanks," he told her. "It's a good thing I gave up my morning bacon given where my work takes me these days."

Her bright smile vanished on media-worthy red lips. She must be Muslim, he thought—pork forbidden—and he had made a faux pas. He had only given up bacon because his doctor had told him to cut back on "salt and saturated fat." In true Campbell family tradition, his blood pressure and cholesterol were rising. Scared by his father's early death from a heart attack, he now faithfully took two pills every day—a white disc and a blue capsule. Both brown prescription bottles, along with the Soria computer drives and laptop, were in his carry-on.

With the help of cardiologists, he planned to live a long life and rebuild his broken family line. Years ago, visiting a wintry Normandy beach and a ruined castle and stone wall overlooking rough waters, he thought that the catastrophe of his father's death had breached his own family's defenses—the proverbial gate had no lock. People—from workers and relatives to his mother's partners—walked in and out during his childhood, occupiers who treated him like a second-class citizen in his own home.

Except the Schmitts. In their home, they treated him like family, even now. Mrs. Schmitt, in the kitchen, served practical advice with baked beans. Kevin Schmitt had been the manager on the Campbell ranch in the countryside. Grilling steaks from their own livestock, bratwurst from the neighbors', and making the best venison sticks, Mr. Schmitt had also taught Campbell how to hunt and fish alongside his own children. After he grew up, on one trip back to Texas, Schmitt and Campbell shared beers, burgers, and anecdotes in the local diner, frequently interrupted by people they both knew.

He thanked Schmitt. "Kevin, without you, I'm sure we'd have lost our land."

"I did it for your dad. We grew up together. Maybe my family was not as fine as yours, and we didn't go to the same schools, but we still spent a lot of time together. You're the picture of your father, from the start. I just had to steer this thing"—he waved at the brown expanse of the land outside—"until you grew up."

Recalling "Mr. Schmitt" as a younger man, before time had written on his face in wrinkles and red patches, and the surgeon had carved cancer out of his chin, Campbell now remembered the timeless, cloudless, sun-bleached sky outside the window that day. At least Dad had been spared the journey of growing old.

Campbell retired his father's friend with a big party and a generous pension. Then he returned for Schmitt's funeral. Schmitt's daughter and her husband were now the property managers and knew a lot more than Campbell about the business. They were his tenuous link to the family ranch, ensuring that the trust binding their small-town community included him, the absentee landlord.

The Wi-Fi on the plane was slow. Clicking impatiently on his laptop, *like that will make it work faster,* Campbell reviewed the ranch's reports. Having lost acreage after his father had died—sold to support his mother and him—he wanted to purchase it back. Lately, his mother reached out to him regularly, even if in her younger days, between her men friends and his stepfather, he had ended up in boarding school.

And the ranch might get a new customer, Saburia. During his last visit to Saburia, he and Kochanski had enjoyed steaks on the hotel room balcony.

"Steaks are frozen and flown in from Texas," said the Pole, washing a bite down with his trademark vodka. "Maybe the beef from your ranch next time?"

"Sure. How do they like beef on this base?"

"I like my steak bloody and my vodka rough. But for everyone else, I'll connect you to Salim, the base manager. There's the Islamic way. He'll tell you what the Chinese like, too. Maybe he'll cut you a deal."

A bottle of Kochanski's Dew vodka had stood on the table between them. Campbell only sipped the burning liquor to be polite, finding the name misleading.

After a man left with their dishes, Campbell said, "Your guy's a lot better than the assortment my mom hired when I was growing up. My zany housekeeper picked me up from tennis lessons and made me throw out all my candy and soda before entering her car, saying, 'Chemicals.'"

"Was she the rich American version of 'help'?"

"A lot of upper-class kids are raised by help. My mom was busy with her second husband. She did have the money for him to have a good time until he ran off. But she and my dad had a prenup, so the dude didn't get anything." He explained the laws that protected his inheritance, how trust and estate lawyers thwarted predatory interlopers like his stepfather.

"The world had already planned for the same old story of a man's death, his widow's future lovers, and then her second husband," Kochanski observed.

"Our lawyer said the same thing: 'Nothing new under the sun.'"

"Lucky you. Me and Manny don't have your problem, come from nothing and nowhere."

"Many of my friends in boarding school at StarHall weren't so lucky, castoffs after a divorce. The young, new wife seals the deal with her rich old husband, first with a ring and then more kids. Maybe the US should have a legal structure like Saburia here, primogeniture, inheritance by bloodline. Oldest like me gets priority."

Kochanski shook his balding head. "Only makes things more complicated." He glanced sideways warningly. Their waiter had quietly returned.

Later, when they were alone, Kochanski told him the story of Bassam, King Mohammed's older half-brother, who had not been crowned. "The royal family is inbred, and Bassam has a rare genetic disease. A disabled man can't be king here.

"David, Saburia's no paradise," Kochanski continued. "Just a little country that General Saburi, Mohammed's father, forced on the world five years ago. Then he died suddenly, and Mohammed became king. The family has quite the story, saying they descended from the pharaohs. Saburia's Eastern coast is on the Red Sea, very strategic trade route for thousands of years. This new clinic on the military base will provide medical care. It'll also be a site for research trials—that's where Manny, you, and me come in."

Campbell had pulled up Saburia online. The official page described scenic geography, endangered species like the Iyuma cat, repopulation of other species that had been wiped out, like elephants, and its safaris and shores as a safe destination for tourists. Pictures of smiling children accompanied descriptions of public schools with free education and meals.

Skeptical of official propaganda, Campbell found a snarky online gossip thread by alumni from StarHall, the boarding school he and King Mohammed had attended. It described how General Saburi had created Saburia as an independent country in 2025. His son, Mohammed, had then transitioned from Italian suits to white robes as a denizen of a desert kingdom—but still wore Italian shoes like one former pope. After his father's unexpected death, Mohammed was crowned.

The airplane's Wi-Fi recovered full speed. The morning sun blazed onto his computer screen. He slid the blind down and continued to work. For a break, he got up to walk around the cabin. Other men had boarded in Athens. There were two East Asians. Were they Chinese, Japanese,

Korean, or something else? Their masks made it hard to tell. Another was South Asian, and another looked Mediterranean or Middle Eastern. There was a tall Nordic man who towered over the others. Meeting their eyes, exchanging polite nods, he recognized not even one.

And sitting by herself, there was a White woman in her forties, engrossed in her laptop, wearing a slate-gray suit. She had short black hair, glasses, and bright magenta lipstick.

A few minutes later, she unexpectedly walked over, now wearing a mask. "Mr. Campbell, I'm Dr. Elise Sheraton." With her accent and manner, she was clearly American, *like me*. She offered her hand, medical glove on, her fingers with no rings. He quickly put a glove on his right hand to shake hers.

"Thank you," she said. "We international passengers are vectors for disease, like mosquitos. I waited for you to wake up. I got on the plane in Athens. Michael Kochanski sent me to come with you."

"Call me David. Michael forgot to mention you, sorry."

"I moved my plans up to come today. I told him but he seems distracted lately. Do you know the others here?"

"No."

From an email from Soria Clinics, he then remembered her photo, one of the doctors to staff the new clinic, with both an MD and a PhD.

She asked about Saburia. Gesturing with his hands, he described the nights—"black and filled with stars, and the wispy, glittery Milky Way." Like a silver ribbon for Lucky's hair, he thought.

On his laptop, he showed her the location of the military base, close to the Arabian peninsula, the ocean edge where from ancient times boats and ships slipped in and out of the port sporting a variety of flags and unreadable names.

"The sea roads of the ancient world," she said softly. "They connected China and India to ancient Egypt and the Roman empire ports on the Red Sea. Imagine ships loaded with spices, textiles, jade — and now here we are. Michael said the loader will come to the airport. It took a while to get the Drukker here, didn't it?"

"Yes. There were hiccups in getting the machine out of the United States. A version of this AI has military applications. But after Zoser acquired Drukker . . . Zoser's a big corporation with government connections."

She raised her brows. "Then security clearances swiftly appeared."

He had first heard about the sale in the business news, which he followed avidly, believing that nothing explained the world better than how its tides of money flowed.

"And Dr Garcia," she said. "Michael told me you found him at the NIH and he can't come yet."

"No," he said vaguely. "He has some personal stuff going on."

She nodded. "Well, let's meet up again after we land."

After she left, Campbell slid the airplane blind back up and saw the edge of the East African continent below. Then, the plane was gliding down through cirrus clouds into the capital of Saburia, renamed Ramses by General Saburi. From his first visit, he remembered clean streets, friendly people, and musical calls to worship. Security was ubiquitous. Checkpoints, dogs, and a mixture of Saburian and Chinese military guarded schools and airports, as well as the mosques and markets.

Nibbling buttered toast dusted with cinnamon sugar, he tried to remember the name of the local pudding with honey and cinnamon. From ancient times, cinnamon was imported into Saburia from South Asia, along risky routes to the West. Traders back then, he thought, were likely Kochanski types, with runners like Garcia and himself.

Kochanski joked that Garcia was "on the Asperger's spectrum," noting, "Manny's main allegiance is to his lab projects. As for his son, what do I know? I never knew my father."

Kochanski was now waiting for him on a beach some hours' drive from Ramses. What had he and Garcia cooked up, stored in the mystery purple case? Here he was, aloft with a riddle near the home of the Sphinx. Maybe best not to know, time to move on. Drukker's parent company, Zoser, had already offered him a job. They had offices everywhere, including headquarters in Texas. Their latest product, Ear Dots, stickers behind ears to replace clunky earbuds, was a roaring success.

Garcia's purple case hinted at a royal secret, he thought. Members of the Saburian royal family had attended boarding school with him. He had not known King Mohammed, who had been at the school much earlier, but he remembered a story about a glass plaque outside the principal's office with the inscription: "Duke Wellington, mid-1800s: The Battle of Waterloo was won on the playing fields of Eton." The plaque was removed after Mohammed led a student protest against colonial legacies.

On a paper napkin, Campbell sketched Mohammed's family tree with a Sharpie, like ones he had made in his European history class at StarHall. He connected the king to his first wife and cousin, Queen Salma. Their oldest son, Syed Malik, was the crown prince. In official pictures, Malik was handsome, bearded, his head covered in traditional attire. He was studying in Silicon Valley, awing his people, lighting bright hopes for their future, posting about hobnobbing with the tech titans of a golden land.

King Mohammed had a second wife somewhere, and he had recently married for a third time, Queen Noru.

Kochanski had said earlier, "The king is deeply in love with his new soulmate, just nineteen."

"Was that an eye roll, Michael? Or jealous?"

"No more wives for me. But what I'm wondering is if he'll change the line of succession if he has a son with her. His own father broke the traditional rule—primogeniture—by putting aside his oldest, as I've told you before. Rumors are that Prince Bassam is in a wheelchair and having a good time in Rio with the family money. Exiled from the royal family—for his partying ways, is the official reason."

"Why do you care?"

"Politics, David, everything follows. But Queen Salma, the crown prince's mother, is also the king's first cousin—she's his family, powerful that way, not just an expired wife."

Through the window tilting to the east, Campbell admired the Saburian mountain ridges piercing the mist, marking the southeastern edge of the country. The snowcapped peaks had surprised him on his first trip, not knowing that mountains could be found in many parts of Africa.

Kochanski had also told him, "The most popular Saburian show, *Black Shadows*, is set in the foothills, a genius idea by our king. His people imagine the evil of the rebels based there. Even the children have nightmares."

"Sounds like propaganda."

"No more than anywhere else. The global military machine supplies the rebels, then puts money into the king's war against the rebels—a successful business for the major powers, selling weapons and tech to both sides, even giving them money to help buy it and then pitting them against each other."

"That's a sad way to look at it."

"I'm not judging, you know. I'm a humble man. It's like boxing or football, except take it up a few notches and then watch, safely on your screen, as lots of foreigners die horribly. Keeps the masses entertained. Bread and circuses. Yet, we look down on the ancient Romans and their slave-gladiators."

Kochanski then tapped his head. "Boxers, football players, they get concussions. In wars, soldiers return damaged. We send the poor, the young, the powerless to fight. Some of us are damaged before we can even grow up. Watch *Black Shadows*, David. Shows are how I learned about America and Saburia. Who knew education was so entertaining?"

Campbell clicked on *Black Shadows* on the airplane screen in front of him but could not decipher the Saburian, Arabic, and Mandarin instructions to turn on English subtitles. *No longer the days of the British empire.* At least at the Saburian base, English was still the primary language for foreigners.

He called the Egyptian to help. She was brisk and careful not to lean too close as she read aloud the Arabic instructions, her gloved index finger following the writing.

"*Black Shadows* has no English subtitles," she said. "It's a Saburian show, and many Chinese people are there these days. But here, you can watch the Chinese dubbed version that has English subtitles." Fingers flew over the touch screen, and then she placed headphones on him. "You must listen to the music, everybody's language. Beautiful even if you can't understand the words." Her fingertips brushed the sensitive skin behind his ears.

Was that accidental? He inhaled sharply. Or was it intended?

On his screen, *Black Shadows* started. Armed men in military vehicles chased a family of endangered lyumas whose young fetched high prices in other countries. Then the program abruptly stopped.

The sign came on the screen to fasten their seat belts. He looked at the time on his phone and noted a three-minute discrepancy with the time on the screen. Then his phone reset, and all the times resynchronized. Puzzled, he looked around the cabin. Some of the other men clustered next to two windows.

The airplane continued its bumpy approach to Ramses. Turbulence shook the plane, reminding him that he was falling into a foreign country that still had medieval practices like public executions.

He felt increasingly uneasy. Would Kochanski abandon him if he were arrested in Saburia? What was in Garcia's purple case, for which he was a foolish mule? And what had Kochanski said during his last visit, while pacing in front of his office window? Except for a small plant on the sill, the view outside was a shimmering desert. "For poor people, the judicial system is slow. Once arrested, you would be happier being hanged than spending years in hard labor."

"Not a place I'd want to live in."

"Not me, either. If arrested, infidels like you and me are expelled to return on penalty of death. If your country doesn't want you, then convert to Islam, enter the prisons, or . . . well . . . you can die."

Kochanski went on in a softer tone, "But, also, our king has a humanitarian side—the public welfare programs, the free schools and clinics. For money to finance them, we depend on mining and tourism—the tourists who come to our coast and national parks. And environmentalists who have their causes. Let's go for a little safari."

What did Kochanski mean by "our king" and "we"? he wondered. That day, Kochanski's car on the base was being repaired, so they brought him his daughter's lavender vehicle instead. He complained about how the color didn't fit on a military campus. It was an automatic because his daughter had refused to learn to drive a stick shift. He hated the mechanical woman's voice that nagged him about his seat belt, how all the doors automatically locked, and the sophisticated electronics that shot out arctic blasts of air-conditioning.

"I want to drive a car, not be driven inside a refrigerated computer," he said. "Fact is, I don't think she'll come back to Saburia. She went out on the beach here after grabbing a beer, wearing a bikini, and got heckled by the locals. One of the Chinese guards escorted her back. Maybe the king or one of his men will buy this car off my hands for a wife or daughter."

Kochanski kept talking while they drove around the dusty brown land outside the base.

"I want to see some lyumas," Campbell said.

"I hope so. Poachers are a problem, punished by public hanging, but usually they are shot dead. Bounty hunters don't get paid extra to bring them in alive. Our king says he hates the savaging of animals and the environment."

"He told you this personally?" asked Campbell.

"Fair enough, I've only spoken to him once briefly. That's what his minister says he says. But with all the social welfare, I think no one in Saburia needs to poach to feed their families."

"But you have no idea what the king really thinks or what games he must play to stay in power," persisted Campbell, skeptical of Kochanski's hints of familiarity with the royal.

"No, but when critics complain that the king values his wildlife more than his people, I think that's unfair. Always politics and hecklers."

The seat belt light went off. He pressed the button for the attendant to help him to resume *Black Shadows*. Thinking about the skip in time between his phone and the TV, he concluded that a pedestrian reason for the three-minute time discrepancy was likely. His cell phone had to reset after traveling halfway around the globe.

But fantastical explanations were more entertaining. Sometimes he also had prescient dreams that never predicted anything practical—like a killing in the stock market—only inchoate danger. Last night on the plane, he had dreamed he was on a beach, upside-down starry bowl of black skies spilling gloriously above him, when a rent tore the night sky, a line where all the stars fell in, disappeared, and then the orange glow of a strange sun grew huge.

The first time he had had this vivid dream was at StarHall. Dr. Skinner, the school therapist, asked him, "What does it mean to you?"

"It means, I think . . . nothing really ever dies; everything just changes." He was ten and tears sprang to his eyes. His legs quivered.

He had entered StarHall at an older age than most of the others at the boarding school, who had started as early as when they were eight years old. On the margins of cliques, he had even been bullied.

Kochanski once asked him about StarHall, "Did you know a Jim Sichet? I know all you guys were in that fancy school together. But now Jim and I are on the opposite sides of the Chicago River—lots of dead bodies have floated in there."

"What do you mean, like your offices are on the opposite sides of the river?"

"Not literally. I mean we're fighting over some property. If I'm found dead someday, it'll be him."

"I only knew Jim's younger brother, a bully just like his older brother, I've heard."

Like a tuned antenna, Kochanski filtered signals from an exponential, international, electronic bazaar, mining contacts and ideas. In Saburia, he was another businessman on the Red Sea, like the ancient spice traders from South Asia on dangerous water routes or merchant sailors from imperial China who traversed oceans guided by the stars — traveling to cutthroat seaports on the Red Sea to reach the world's markets.

Campbell flew often, now used to what he recognized as anxiety attacks in airplanes, much better since Dr. Skinner had worked her unorthodox healing on them all those years ago. The dream of a sky cracking open like an eggshell became a time to "run the wall."

One spring day, Skinner had led him up a locked stairwell to the rim of a high wall, between StarHall and the rolling countryside around the campus.

"Run," she said. "Don't look down on either side at what you fear, real as it is. Once you decide to run, only look ahead, and run, run, run."

"What if I fall?" he asked, looking twenty feet down at the grass on both sides.

But he ran, high above the places he feared, inside and outside, the one-foot-wide cement wall. His destination was not far, not when he was running so fast, only to the next stairwell. He hadn't fallen.

What would a Bermuda Triangle experience be like, he now thought, where he would disappear into a tear in the universe, ride a wave of energy that compressed and then propelled him faster than light, to alight—this morning—into some unknown destination in space-time?

Black Shadows abruptly started again on his airplane screen, showing a small town bright in the sunlight, snow on the sloped rooftops of little houses. In the background rose the signature jagged tops of the Saburian mountain chain, rank on rank, appearing to march forward toward the town.

Martial music—drums and horns—displaced the pastoral twangs that filled his earphones. Ominous dots in the distant brush became a crush of rebel warriors and vehicles, closing in on the town.

Is it too late to return and build my own castle on sand beside the waters of the world's mysteries? He heard the plane roar, wings cutting to one of the thin airstrips in the vast desert below.

CHAPTER SIX

In Pandolf, Shelly Sharma rarely saw Lucky at home, who now spent all her free time with Harry, who had moved into Pandolf Hotel in May. After finishing business school, he was working remotely for his family's business.

After Garcia disappeared, the couple invited Sharma for dinner at Palatine Hill. "This place was my old haunt with Dr. Garcia," she said sadly.

Harry looked relaxed, fair hair still damp from a shower. "How're you doing with the odd couple living downstairs?" He winked at Lucky, who teased him back with a frown.

"You mean George and Charlie?" said Sharma. "They can be amusing, I guess."

The waiter brought their takeout order for the boys. Sharma took the bag. Harry scrutinized the bill. "A note from the kitchen. Hi to Charlie, from Nancy."

"The boys get food here a lot," said Lucky. "Hey, Shelly, before I leave town, let's go shopping in SF. I need new clothes, we can do a mani-pedi, get your face done at Rucci's. My guy there will find you your look. I showed him your picture, and he called you 'pretty in a healthy way.'"

"I'll think about it."

"Perhaps someone needs to discover you first," said Lucky. "I'm surprised that hasn't happened yet."

"Thanks for inviting me for dinner." Sharma put her napkin on the table and rose.

How can she think there's anyone but one person for me—Dr. Nepski—very married. . .

Harry also rose. "Already?" He was looking at her with a mysterious look. *Why's he staring at me like that?*

But Lucky said, "Wait, I have to finish my wine."

They sat back down.

"Shelly," said Lucky, clearly in no rush, "any news about Dr. Garcia?"

"No one knows when he'll return."

Lucky smiled. "We had an old bachelor like him up in Maine when I was growing up, living by himself at the end of an old road in a cabin surrounded by woods—wannabe Thoreau in his Walden hideaway. He would swing by for a mug of coffee with my dad and then be gone again for another few weeks."

Sharma stifled a yawn. "Sorry. I need to go to bed soon. You guys didn't have a 6:30 a.m. hospital meeting." She rose again.

"Well, we'll see you *soon*, Shelly," said Harry. His eyes were boring into hers.

What? Now she felt irritated.

She walked out of the restaurant, remembering her meeting with Nepski earlier that morning. They had met in the Pandolf Doctors' Lounge, a large suite with Expressionist prints on the walls, lush green carpet, and lounging sofas next to an electric fireplace. For breakfast, fragrant pastries from a local bakery, dry cereals in colorful boxes, and seasonal fruit were aesthetically arrayed. They ate—beef sausage and eggs for him, oatmeal and fresh coffee for her.

He asked, "Dr. Minkiwitz's lab for a year or two, before you begin your fellowship, or . . . ?"

"I'm still waiting to hear back about other options, like the Fujitsu Travel Award."

"I'm curious. What about marriage, kids? I know an employer isn't supposed to ask, but I have a friendly interest."

"I plan to focus on my career," she said. *"Friendly"* stung. Even the wedding band on his finger—and everything it symbolized—did not check her feelings for him, not even meeting Mrs. Nepski last fall at a party in their home.

She had walked to their home, pillows of autumn leaves underfoot, blazing colors from yellow to red to brown, a drizzle of warm rain above, wearing her rose jacket, a birthday present from Lucky.

She stopped at EZBuy to purchase a gift bottle of wine. Pandolf's twenty-four-hour grocery paired an informed staff with an encyclopedic selection of wine, beer, and liquor. Yellow wheels of cheese were proudly displayed. Sausages, salami, olives, crackers, dips, to-go fruit, and vegetable trays; bite-size to giant desserts; angel-white to lemon to all shades of chocolate. Unable to resist the tempting displays, she always walked out having spent more than she should have. But most customers did not mind the premium prices, also grabbing overpriced toiletries and other essentials before they checked out, for the convenience of not having to leave the campus.

"Everyone knows *this* Napa Cabernet," said the suited salesman, handing her a bottle wrapped in silver foil and an autumn-orange ribbon.

In Nepski's neighborhood, where Pandolf owned homes for their tenured faculty, the sun was setting, dropping below the horizon, flaming the remaining leaves on the old trees. The sidewalk wound around the edge of a cul-de-sac to the Nepskis' address. The heavy wooden door with a wrought-iron knocker was unlocked. She walked into a large hall with a vaulted ceiling where a chandelier sparkled like a melting iceberg in the sun.

In the entryway, the Nepskis greeted her. Mrs. Nepski was petite, stylish, in her thirties, smiling graciously. Sharma smiled back, handing her the wine, flushing as jealousy flooded her. After small talk, she quickly slipped away when more guests arrived. Walking around the first floor, darting from the periphery of one knot of people to another, she nibbled crudités from trays offered by waiters. Then she moved to the basement where the caterers had set up a full dinner. The bar displayed dozens of bottles, a dispensary of different shapes, colors, and labels. Like cheerleaders, the bartenders smiled and bobbled, waving cocktail shakers in both hands.

From the long table covered with white linen, she refilled her small plate and returned to the main floor. An enameled white railing curved upstairs and disappeared into the darkness of the second floor. Wide hardwood steps rose and wound along a plaster wall with painted moldings. Displayed close to the landing, photos appeared to be family portraits, dating back to old black-and-whites of weddings, a bar or bat mitzvah, the Empire State Building, and the Statue of Liberty. More pictures climbed into the darkness of the upstairs landing, where she saw faint movement—a sentient being? A grandparent? Kids doing homework?

Behind the house, two dogs scampered on the expansive, lit-up grounds. The Nepskis' life was perfect, she thought, feeling foolish about her crush. Nepski was married, he did not appear to return her feelings, and he was her mentor. Then he was Jewish, and she was not. Who was she? One hundred percent agnostic and a halfie. While her Hindu grandparents had doted on her, she had always known that she was "different" from her Indian cousins. As a child, one day, her Indian grandfather pushed a grocery cart around some Mumbai supermarket, trailed by his grandchildren. Switching into English for her, he joked with someone they ran into, "They don't know yet what god to pray to."

Dadaji often stopped to have random discussions with people he saw, friends, neighbors, strangers, in his retired meanderings, in his world where time was measured differently than in America.

In South Dakota, she had spent childhood summers with her White, Christian maternal grandparents on their two-hundred-acre farm with no reliable internet. There, she was the brown-ish girl among her blond relatives, with her Asian pride in the mastering of multiplication tables and long division, while the other kids pulled tadpoles out of their pockets to scare her. After a few weeks, her cousins matched many of her number skills while she read a Britannica encyclopedia—yellowed pages—about frog life cycles.

On the farmhouse's bookshelves, she read classics from her mother's side, like the entire Little House on the Prairie series, a strange world of white pioneer families from centuries ago. Then her religious grandmother read the Chronicles of Narnia to the children at bedtime. Church was compulsory, a stressful Sunday morning ritual to get out of the house on time.

One day, the Sunday School teacher showed pictures of lovely Buddhist temples from Japan. The teacher's "lesson": this isn't "Christian" but pagan, the "other" to be appreciated but not embraced. She complained to her father. He lectured her "to take the good with the bad": "You can learn wisdom from every religion," and, "Make it so the next time they see someone who looks like you, they don't have a bad stereotype about Indian people."

More childhood summers in South Dakota went by. Her inner voice grew nuanced, and her unfolding mind thoughtfully filtered her speech. Leaving the Nepskis' home that fall night, walking the road of memories as her feet remembered their way home, she felt the same equanimity as she had in South Dakota and in Mumbai—to accept being an outsider looking into the Nepski world, accept another boundary to not cross, another calm relationship—this time a platonic one—with her mentor: breakfasts, research projects, and professional collaboration.

There was a time when she invited Lucky to a holiday party at the Nepskis'.

"Fun!" said Lucky, carefully drawing eyeliner at their shared bathroom counter. "Oh, wait, wait, don't tell me," her voice teased, "this is for work."

"What do you think of Dr. Nepski?"

Lucky shrugged. "I only met him once. Sounds like he's always working, traveling, and working some more."

"Yes, he's always going on work trips . . ." She heard something catch in her voice—feeling surprised and guilty about a new wave of fantasies to join him sometime: a dinner, a walk through a European city square, and maybe even calling Dr. Nepski "Sam"?

Her housemate turned and fixed gem-blue eyes on her. "Oh, Shelly."

"Okay, you know that I've got a crush on him."

For the holiday party, Lucky wore the latest style fresh out of plastic wrap, high heels, sooty mascara, pink lipstick, and sparkles on her wrists, around her neck, and in her pinned-up, braided hair with dangling wisps. Analytically observing Lucky, a red and green party magnet, from a sofa in a forgotten corner, Sharma plodded through a dull conversation with someone utterly forgettable.

Then Dr. Brickstone walked by with a younger-appearing woman, not noticing her. The previous week, when she had been on call at Hunterview, Brickstone's patient hemorrhaged during a Cesarean section. She joined in the two-hour operation to remove the woman's uterus to stop the bleeding. Tension written on his face, Brickstone had not left the hospital until dawn, after the patient was stable, telling Sharma, "Well, Pandolf hasn't yet built a robot to do what we just did."

• • •

After dinner, leaving Lucky and Harry at Palatine Hill, Sharma took a new wooded shortcut she had just learned from Michaela. She went to the boys' apartment first to deliver their food. But no one answered the door. Surprised, she unlocked it. Dark inside, she opened her phone's flashlight to find her way to the refrigerator to put away their dinner.

Curious to check on the patient she had just operated on with Dr. Brickstone, she scrolled through medical records on her phone, first in the boys' apartment for some time, then in the stairwell. By the time she returned to her apartment, Lucky was home.

"Where have you been?" Lucky asked.

"Looking at a patient chart in the boys' apartment after I put their dinner away." She told Lucky about Brickstone's patient. "Do you remember him from Dr. Nepski's party?"

"Yes, I met him and his trophy wife. How can I forget after all the stories you tell me about Hunterview?"

Lucky then flashed a large diamond on her finger. "I'm going back to meet Harry in a few. But first, I do have something serious to tell you. This happened after you left."

"It's beautiful!"

"The ring is in his family. He brought it back from his trip home after graduation. Needs to be fitted still."

"Congratulations! Well, how did he do it?"

"You know Harry, he's spontaneous, it was all kind of planned in the moment. He got on one knee next to the lake. Under the moonlight. Charlie and George were there for the surprise. Harry tried to get you to be there, sent you messages, left you a voice mail. He even made an excuse to run after you when you left, worried you hadn't checked your phone. But he couldn't find you."

"I took a shortcut through the woods, you know, so the boys' dinner would stay warm. And I still had my notifications turned off from when I was in surgery—forgot to turn them back on. *I'm now looking at Harry's messages. He really tried to reach me! I'm sorry! I'm so, so sorry!*"

Lucky sighed. "Me too. Anyway, it's not safe in the woods at this hour unless you're a local like Michaela."

"I guess I wasn't thinking . . .," she said. *But yes I was thinking, but about Dr. Nepski. Don't let my romantic failure cloud your happy sky.*

"It would have meant a lot to me for you to have been there," said Lucky. "Sometimes, it just seems you are so wrapped up in your medical world that you disconnect from reality, if you don't mind me saying so."

"I don't mind. Again, I'm sorry to have missed it. Have you set a date?"

"No date yet. Honestly, I can't wait to finish residency and go back to the East Coast. That's what Harry and I have been talking about nonstop, about where we would like to settle down. It'll likely be Maine, where his family business is based."

"Should I tell anyone else?"

"Not yet. No one at work, for sure. Harry has to tell his family. And I need to talk to the rest of my family, you know my dysfunctional parents."

• • •

Meanwhile in San Francisco, two ICE agents researched Manny Garcia. They scrolled through video feed on monitors in a windowless room. T'hodd, about thirty, clicked through media on Michaela's phone: selfies, Charlie, George, other teenagers, media personalities, web pages, animals, fashion, shopping lists, emojis, how-to videos, and homework. He stopped at a photo of a map of the Pandolf campus, marked up with black arrows.

"Garcia's handwriting. Indian name written on a paper map, 'Arjun Jagdishwar Bhattacharya,' doc who used to work at Pandolf, and six numbers. Where did she get this?"

"Who is this girl again?"

"Michaela. Some kid who grew up in Pandolf and only recently made friends with the boys."

"Girlfriend? Any criminal connections?"

"Yes, she's a girlfriend, and no, all databases are clean on her and her folks."

KaLisa, the other agent, was in her forties with short gray hair. She leaned back in her chair. "What if she was snooping around the boys' apartment—kids can be nosy—and found a map hidden somewhere and took a photo? Girl seems to be the curious type, maybe a job with us someday?"

He laughed.

She continued, "Still, we better hurry. Let's go find this place before Garcia returns. What a bungle to arrest him because they found that kid in the Chicago River."

"With a fake ID of Garcia. How? But then look at all this other fishy stuff about Garcia after we talked to Pandolf."

"Yes, like what was he doing under that printer?"

"Or why Pandolf is not letting him have his job back?"

"Or that Pandolf is pulling his work visa."

T'hodd and KaLisa were in a last rush of work. As ICE, they had to look into all possible criminal activity by aliens, and they seemed to be onto something with Manny Garcia—intellectual property theft, lab negligence that endangered the public, or—?

"Doesn't help that we're missing some of Garcia's files," said KaLisa. "It's just not plausible he would destroy all his work."

"I gave you everything the Indian medical chain said they had—"

"We don't know what we don't know, T'hodd. That's what it's our job to find out. Seriously, they send aliens to the Camp for much less than this Garcia."

"Garcia doesn't do anything but work, unless he's in a relationship with that resident doctor in his lab?" T'hodd sounded bored.

"There's nothing on any woman in Garcia's life, except that thing he wrote in his lab notebook. Sounds prettier in Spanish: 'Amber's heart finally melted with mine. Now she's back to stony and cold.'"

They munched on leftover sandwiches from an office party. T'hodd went to the water fountain to refill their Styrofoam cups. When he returned, another picture from Michaela's phone was on the screen.

"That cat does not like the girl," said T'hodd. "Love the glare."

"Weird that we're letting Garcia go," KaLisa murmured. "They don't tell me everything. But I can ask to hold him a little longer if this map guides us someplace? I think he was looking over his shoulder already. Up to something. So frustrating."

The next day, along with Pandolf security, the two agents followed the map to the abandoned hospital call rooms.

T'hodd put his mask on. "This place stinks."

"You'll get used to it. Here's the locker we're looking for."

The code worked. But the locker was empty, leaving them puzzled.

"Dead end?" said T'hodd.

One of the Pandolf officers, Bobbie, said she knew Garcia's son. "My partner and I already visited them at one of the campus apartment buildings. Another resident complained about these two kids living alone, with some girl always over."

"Let's check them out," said KaLisa.

That evening, Bobbie and Andy, her partner, visited the apartment again. The three teenagers eyed them suspiciously. After their last "safety check," social workers had arrived. Campbell had been questioned, George's aunt in Chicago had been called, and Lucky had to claim responsibility for Charlie. Michaela's mother was still talking to Family Services.

"This place always smells like pizza," said Bobbie. "How're you guys doing since the last time we saw you?"

"Fine," said Charlie.

"George," said Andy, "we're trying to get some information to get your dad released. It looks like there was a map?"

"You mean my dad could be home soon?"

"I don't know," said Andy. "But about the map?"

"A map . . . yes, he left a map of Pandolf in my suitcase," said George. "I was just showing it to Michaela the other day. She grew up around here, so I thought she might find it interesting."

"Where is it now?"

"I took a picture of it on my phone," said Michaela.

"I think I remember where we left it." George found the map under some empty Chinese takeout containers.

"George, has anyone besides the three of you seen this?" asked Andy, putting on gloves to roughly take the map and shove it into a plastic bag.

"My dad, he made it."

"How long was it in your suitcase?" Bobbie's eyes bored into George.

"I don't know. I found it when I unpacked."

"Do you know what it's for?"

The teenagers stared at them blankly.

"You didn't try to find out what your dad hid on the map? A little adventure, a treasure hunt?" pushed Bobbie to the three teenagers.

"We can't get into the employees' sections of the Pandolf complex," Charlie finally spoke up coldly. "No authorized key card."

Andy and Bobbie left with the map and barely a goodbye from the teenagers, who gave them the side-eye.

George looked upset. "I hope Dad won't get mad that I let them take the map."

"Mr. Campbell would want to know," said Charlie.

George looked thoughtful. "Neh, don't want him to worry after all the trouble the last time those two cops came—"

Glaring at the closed door, Michaela said, "I think they picked Bobbie to relate to me."

"It could just be a coincidence that she's Black," said George.

Charlie rose. "Are we going to talk about this *again*? I'm going to my room and work on my statistics project. Science, not speculation."

CHAPTER SEVEN

After ICE released Garcia, he called George first. "I'll meet you at school tomorrow afternoon. We'll take everyone who wants to come for a thank-you dinner for helping us out."

They hashed out plans. George sounded anxious. "Dad, when you come back, I'll move in with you?"

"I hope so."

Garcia hung up, looked down at scuff marks on the vinyl floor of the detention complex, so many forgotten life journeys with no one to tell what had happened, to share feelings of helplessness and humiliation with.

And Jorge, what happened to my child who once told me how everything would be fine? How will I thank David? What kind of gift will Shelly enjoy?

He called Sharma that evening from his motel room in San Francisco.

"Hi—"

"Dr. Garcia! I knew it was you from your DNA photo."

Garcia explained the mistake behind his ICE detention. "Shelly, I hope you're not angry with me. I wasn't allowed to call you."

"I was a little angry—but now I'm just relieved. I didn't know you weren't allowed to communicate at all. You've been gone a month." She added jokingly, "Thoreau returns from Walden Pond."

"And you're doing fine?" he asked.

"Another Sunday night alone, going to sleep. Now that you're back, I'll have a really good night's rest."

"Thank you for being so caring. George has told me how much you've helped him. I don't know how my son could have managed without you."

"He's a nice young man. Glad you're safe, and that it was all an awful mistake. When will you be returning to the lab?"

"I don't know. I'll meet with Dr. Nepski tomorrow, then go pick up George from school. Please join us for dinner, and then I'll update you."

• • •

Meanwhile, in Ramses, Saburia, the plane carrying David Campbell bounced on the tarmac of the international airport. Heat blurred the morning air outside, where only a few planes stood. Runways crisscrossed a desert of dirt, rock, and sand.

Standing up from his seat, Campbell turned around, looking for Sheraton, and waved. She waved back and quickly came up behind him.

"I'm a bit nervous," she said. "I don't travel much. But I've done my research to be respectful of local customs as a physician. To take the best care of my patients."

"I just watched *Black Shadows*, a popular Saburian show," he said, "to help me connect."

"I think a lot of media is propaganda. I want to see for myself."

They walked past the thick frosted window in the cockpit door. A shadow of the pilot moved across it, head large and spherical like an astronaut's helmet.

Or the head of an ant? Or how the light refracted? Or I'm dehydrated?

He swigged his water. Dismounting via a steep mobile staircase into the heat, he waited for Sheraton at the bottom. She emerged, large, dark sunglasses and an amorphous cloak now over her head and body like the local women, turning her anonymous—except he recognized the tilt of her head and how she tightly folded her arms when she reached the ground. They walked together to the main building, where they sat on a bench under the awning.

They watched a giant loader approach the jet cargo area, directed by two black-bearded Saburians. Pickup trucks carried workmen to unload the Drukker machines wrapped in foam and bungee cords, between crates of military ration meals.

Finally, he thought, *the Drukker is here*, in Saburia, having overcome a tangled mess of negotiations and delays—thanks in part to Zoser's acquisition of Drukker, and more importantly, due to Garcia's successful preliminary findings, extracted in secret in a lonely Pandolf lab and approved by an unknown Soria team.

In the early morning, the metal skin of the airplane reflected the colors of the dawn sky, rose with flecks of gold. He squinted up at the sky. *Why are the clouds not reflected on the metal, now fading into aluminum gray?* Theories germinated in his brain, one in particular related to the three-minute time gap and the pilot's helmet. He grinned and nodded.

The loader stopped. A translator came up to him with the work supervisor, asking for more instructions. Then the loader went back and forth again, between the plane and the trucks, accompanied by shouts of sweaty men. Finally, the airport grew silent. The men took a break, sat in their vehicles, smoking and eating the MREs.

He and Sheraton chatted, first about the various labs they had worked in, from exciting discoveries to steamy politics. Then she asked about his family.

"Just my mom," he said. "She's living in a condo near Houston. What about you? What brought you here?"

"Short version, divorce."

Drowning further conversation, their plane whirred, buzzed, and sailed away down the runway. The air currents dislodged her silken gray scarf, and she pulled it back over her head. From her Salome designer handbag, she removed her magenta lipstick and a compact mirror, touching up her lips over perfect white teeth. Then she adjusted stray hairs with ringed hands and replaced the elephantine sunglasses on her nose. A pistol in her bag briefly glinted. He debated whether to tell her that they would take it away at the base. That had happened to him the last time he came. A young guard marveled, "In America, you just carry these around," then added that he liked American Westerns.

He waited to see if she would say more. There was the enchanted queen in a story who fell in love with a donkey. Was he that ass now, the first creature she saw? Two strangers like them in an unfamiliar place could open up to each other in ways that they might not otherwise.

"I'm here because of unexpected turns in my personal life," she said, "and all the unplanned bills." She waved her hand around her dismissively. "Otherwise, *why* would I end up here? I suppose you've got a story, too." She did not sound interested.

"I'm sorry, I didn't mean to bring up a sensitive subject."

"No worries. I'm glad that you're here. Michael didn't want me traveling alone."

Forgot to tell me about you, he thought, annoyed.

Her face, the makeup painted over fine wrinkles, reminded him of his own mother when she had been younger, now his responsibility after all the other men had discarded her, neatly tucked away in a condo complex for her age group, precisely gridded with tennis courts, a pool, and an "exciting" new group of friends.

"What about you, are you married?" she asked.

"Not yet."

"I can tell . . . you like someone. Better do it soon. Or you'll be set in your ways."

"You know, Michael Kochanski is your age, and he has no wife, either," he teased. "Your type?"

"No way!" Mock horror. "Now you'll get me into trouble. I'm good at my job, not men. Right now, I'm paying for my kids' expensive colleges. Then I'll do the things I like."

"Maybe you need to meet the right person?"

"I thought I had met the right man with my ex. You never know," she said. "Then he cheated on me."

"I can't trust a man whose own wife doesn't," he said, musing that feelings for other women would never be strong enough for him to break trust.

"I need a little walk," she said.

An occasional breeze ruffled the heating air. *Lucky, Julia, Jules.* Left alone now, he remembered following Lucky around Pandolf, from the glitter of its newest buildings to the old call rooms with only rusted bed frames, where a lonely lock might hang idly for years before Pandolf's housekeeping would cut it.

He had told Kochanski how he found Garcia's Soria laptop, disks, and the extra purple case. "Manny was smart about the old locker idea. Long Indian name of some doctor who used to work for Pandolf was a clever touch. You changed your name. What was your old name?"

"Rather not say," Kochanski replied. "David, do you think that ICE profiled Manny as connected to a terrorist group? Like with roots in South America and the Russian mafia, and training camps in Afghanistan and Pakistan? Just speaking from some insider knowledge. He has been erratic lately. Thank god *you* are a grounded man."

Garcia was *perfectly* balanced, Campbell thought, if a little too obsessed with his work. Men like Kochanski were the ones who could not be trusted. *He dodged another question. Lots of nooses in his family tree.*

But in the thrill of scientific pursuit, he and Garcia had entered an unregulated, international zone. Still, pushing the edges of scientific exploration, is this what he and Garcia intended? Campbell looked down at the backpack between his knees and puzzled again about the mystery drive in the heavy purple case.

He heard idling motors, and then another armored truck roared in.

"Time to go," he yelled to Sheraton, on the far side of the building.

The loaded flatbed vehicles pulled up, with much shouting again among the men in languages he did not understand. To examine the cargo one last time, he walked around, frowning about the serial number on one crate. *Why did Garcia want the 4D biological time printer, RT66?* RT66 AI mimicked biological processes from DNA printing to transcription of proteins.

He climbed into the truck with Sheraton, glad to be out of the boiling sunshine. With the windows rolled open, their Chinese driver also had the air-conditioning on full blast. As they gained speed, the gritty dust bit into their eyes, their clothes, and their lungs. Sheraton popped out her contacts and changed into prescription sunglasses. Then the driver finally closed the windows.

"If I knew Chinese"—Sheraton raised her voice over the loud engine— "I would have asked her to close the windows sooner."

Campbell shrugged. "She may know English very well."

"But she hasn't said a word!"

He caught the driver's face in the rearview mirror, eyes unreadable behind wraparound sunglasses. "The driver is here to drive," he said. "Even if she does speak English, maybe all she wants to do is her job, not make loud conversation over a loud engine to a couple of foreigners like us on a rutted old road."

When in doubt, be kind. Susan had told him this when he became frustrated with some foreigners in Boston who feigned that they knew no English or even the local American customs. StarHall's international student crowd had been different. All the boarders there spoke English among each other, only speaking their native tongues privately when with others from their own countries.

Next, Sheraton complained, "Long car rides make me sick. I have to go to a local airport near the base next week to get Mary. At least that will be a shorter trip."

"That soon?"

"She's coming from New York, New York," she said, exaggerating the city's brusque accent. "For security, they won't let her fly directly to the base."

"So, they're sending you to escort her?"

"Here, women doctors usually take care of the women, one reason they recruited me. But isn't it odd that Mary's in her seventies, coming here for cancer treatments, and I'm a pediatrician by training?"

Perhaps they were just desperate to find anyone.

She continued, "My background is oncology, but pediatric. Anyway, for me, the one-year contract pays as much as working for three years back home. With the possibility of extension."

"Maybe Soria will extend to pediatric cancer patients," he said. "By the way, did you notice that three-minute time discrepancy when the plane landed?"

"Nope." She didn't say more, enthralled with the endless desert view on her side. Outside the truck windows, dust rose off the road behind them. Then she let out a scream and clapped her hand to her mouth. He leaned over to her window, then they both stared out of the rear. In the receding view of the roadside, a curtain of dust closed over the small body of a child and its shroud of flies. The driver did not slow down.

Sheraton tipped her head back and was silent now. Sometime later, their desert caravan slowed. Campbell smelled the tang of seawater and recognized the low-slung buildings of the coastal military base. Between the concrete blocks, he saw blue sparks of the sunny ocean.

From watchtowers flanking the entrance to the compound, uniformed Saburians met them at the gate. Gesturing, raising their voices, then making phone calls, their driver and one sentry talked heatedly. Another guard confiscated Sheraton's handgun.

Thick accents made everyone hard to understand even when they spoke English.

Tuning out the multilingual and accented babble, he looked around. This windblown scrap of desert beach—sand, dirt, dashes of brilliant blue sea—between gray buildings blurring in the heat—struck an emotional chord inside.

Wondrous, he thought, *maybe a primal response in me to colors on a neural spectrum wired eons ago, before humans migrated north from here?*

Next, their vehicles pulled into the base, big wheels crunching down the gravel driveway. He saw new signs of irrigation from his last visit— variegated bushes, hibiscus plants, and a feral orange cat. A twin to Lucky's tabby, he thought affectionately. More grasses and gardens, flowers and fountains, this campus now flourished like an oasis compared to his last visit.

Their truck pulled up to the glass doors of the main building. Boys rushed out to carry their luggage. Under the shadow of the colonial history that the Saburian king had protested as a fellow student at StarHall, Campbell hesitated before he let them pick up his bags.

Sheraton slipped on heels and stepped out confidently. Her feet clacked into the entryway as young boys held the doors open for them, giving them wide smiles and accented hellos.

"Hey, guys, thanks!" he said, reaching out a hand to high-five one of them.

"David," she whispered, "you are supposed to let those kids take care of you, that's how they earn their wages."

An old Saburian man stood behind the desk in a hotel uniform. "Please sit down," he said, pointing to lounging orange-red sofas.

"Thanks, Captain," she said, after looking at his name tag.

After they sat, Captain handed them laminated menus. Examining hers, even turning it upside down, she pointed to one of the items. "This, please." Campbell just asked for water.

After the Saburian left, he turned to her and said, "So, that dead kid . . ."

She closed her eyes, not replying. Captain brought her a glass tumbler of whiskey, brown on blue frozen stones. She sipped.

"Oh, I like him," she said. "Especially that he speaks English that I can *understand*. But I don't want him to hear what I think."

"Let me pull in closer, we must be careful."

She lowered her voice. "You know that Saburia's economy depends on mining and tourism, especially their parks, though they're not as big as Kenya's or South Africa's. Poaching is a problem here. Markets abroad pay top money for ivory and rhino horn. Then there's that lyuma cat, endangered. But kittens are illegally sold anyway for tens of thousands of dollars—each."

"Yes, I've heard about that," he said, looking around at the lobby, decorated by wooden carvings by local tribes.

"I read that the king hangs poachers who're not shot first. Hangs them!" she said, eyes glinting. "I also heard the king loves to fly his private plane over the parks—just to admire them. Meanwhile, gangs kill poachers for the bounty."

Her voice turned indignant. "Those criminals deserve it . . . but do you think gangs get paid to kill the whole family? And they left that poor kid by the road as a scare tactic? That would be awful. Children are not responsible for what adults do."

"No! That's a morbid theory, Elise. Everything I've read says what a safe country this is, and Mohammed's a benign autocrat, maybe the best form of government. And Western educated."

Captain returned, and Campbell ordered, pointing to the menu's photos. "Is this like a sandwich with a side of . . . um? Is that a diet soda?"

"Oh, yes," said Captain. "Goat meat on bread, the best, and zero-calorie, sugar-free soda, all made in Saburia. I'll be back with your food in a jiffy." But he pronounced it "giphy."

Their young Chinese driver entered the lobby, wheeling her suitcase, smiling brightly at them. She shook her head when they tried to talk to her. "No English. Hello. Goodbye, see you later."

Campbell's Saburian "burger" was delicious. Then they followed Captain to their rooms. Sheraton led the way, tap-tapping impossibly high heels that elevated her well above his shoulder. He had only kept his carry-on with the Drukker files and his medication with him, even if he would have liked to have carried all of his bags in himself.

But the rules of hierarchy were strict here in Saburia. In fact, his American informality was often met with suspicion or contempt abroad, reminding him to smile, ask for help, and tip well instead. Today, he was too tired to smile much. The Chinese driver had declined his tip. But Captain cheerfully took his paper dollars.

He remembered preparing for his first international trip, with his class of fellow ten-year-olds at boarding school, StarHall. They had struggled through a Paris tourism manual written in French. It advised expressing interest to the natives of any country while traveling, about *their* cuisine, *their* history, and *their* culture, ageless advice from a forgotten author. Surprised locals everywhere responded warmly.

He stayed in the same room as the last time, where a botanist's drawings of rare Saburian plants hung on the walls. The suite opened to a balcony with an ocean view. For this anticipated moment, Captain had given him a tumbler of iced whiskey on stones. After drinking leisurely sips, admiring the grand vista of infinite water, he changed and met Sheraton again in the lobby.

"You took a while," she said. They sat by a small fountain that gurgled softly to an accompaniment of Chinese flute and violin music.

"Captain gave me a to-go drink."

"I suppose I should have tipped him too. I didn't know that was an option."

"Hello," said a woman's voice behind them. He looked up to a familiar, lovely face.

"I will take you to Mr. Kochanski's office," said the Egyptian flight attendant, who also seemed to work at the base.

• • •

Entering Kochanski's office, both men shouted happy greetings. Campbell was grateful that Kochanski had learned that he felt uncomfortable with tight embraces, true even before the pandemics. Then Kochanski held his hand out to Sheraton, leaning forward. "Welcome, Dr. Sheraton, so glad you arrived safely."

"Thanks." She grazed his fingertips. They seated themselves around the table with a bottle of white wine in a chiller.

"A little bird told me you like this," Kochanski said to Sheraton.

"I had a drink already," said Campbell. The Egyptian uncorked the Loire. Sheraton swirled it in her glass, tasted, and nodded approval.

"You're right, David," said Kochanski, after Campbell waved away a proffered glass. "Sobriety is part of the American competitive edge. But we have something to celebrate. Also, this wine doesn't age well, like our scientists and some girls, but not Dr. Sheraton, of course."

Sheraton's face was stony. *Had Kochanski already started drinking?* Campbell wondered. He glanced at the Egyptian woman, whose face revealed nothing. Following Campbell's eyes, Kochanski then dismissed her with a nod. After she left, Kochanski grinned like a child.

"Our Manny is free!" he exclaimed. "He's headed back to Pandolf, David."

"Oh my god, Michael! Alright, pass me a glass. Tell me what happened."

"I don't know everything," said Kochanski, as they clinked glasses. "Manny claims to be a victim of identity theft, says ICE released him when they found out, but now he doesn't know if he still has a job at Pandolf."

"I'll send him a message right now," said Campbell, tapping on his laptop.

"Let me know what he says," said Kochanski. "So, on another note, I'm sorry about your trip. I heard about the corpse. Why near the main road? A warning to us foreigners? But when I asked General Shah, he insists not. Says the body fell off a bounty hunter's truck. And he's livid that your Chinese driver kept driving instead of stopping—but she thought it looked like some terrorist trap. Now we don't want to get in the middle of that family fight."

No one spoke or looked at each other.

"Let's get started," Campbell finally said solemnly. He projected a picture of the Drukker Dock on the wall screen. "Just social stuff. We'll go through the science tomorrow."

He showed pictures of Pandolf Medical Center, the open locker with Garcia's laptop and drives, and finally a photo of his latest recruit, a Libyan.

"Pics were all taken on my Soria Clinics phone, very secure," said Campbell. "Libyan has impressive credentials. With all the recent scares, we could not renew his American visa, so I grabbed him for Zoser, and he can now work from Dubai. For that, I got another recruitment bonus."

"Nice," said Kochanski. "The American taxpayer supports his graduate education, and then an international outfit like Zoser—with no loyalty to anyone—gets the payoff."

"No politics, okay," Campbell said. "He's willing to help with our cancer project and work within our budget. Finally, here are my Pandolf kids, George and Charlie. Elise, George is Manny Garcia's teenage son—"

Sheraton looked nervous.

"Elise? You're being rather quiet," said Campbell.

"Don't mind me."

Kochanski smiled at her. "Your first time here, please relax." He refilled her wine glass.

"Okay, Manny just responded," said Campbell, looking at his wrist-phone. "He's very grateful to me for taking care of George. Otherwise not good news. He's not sure he still has a job at Pandolf."

Kochanski smiled broadly. "Just in case, I already bought Manny tickets to Saburia, through Buenos Aires and Athens. Now that the Drukker is here, there's no reason for Manny to remain at Pandolf. And Soria Clinics will keep paying for his lawyer, and to support George and—maybe even bonus me!"

Campbell frowned suspiciously. "Why bonus you?"

"I connected Garcia to Soria, didn't I? Send him a message. Also, I bought those tix under your consulting company's name, so just add it to Soria's tab."

Campbell groaned. "Michael, you *can't* just do stuff like that under my company's name. Please don't ever again! Alright, I'll tell Manny and if there's nothing else, I need to sleep."

Back in his room, Campbell pressed the remote to shut blackout shades. Poor George, he thought, separated again from his father. And suspicious how convenient this timing was for everyone—Kochanski, Soria—that Garcia had to come to Saburia now, not long after Soria had purchased the Drukker AI and housed it in their Red Sea base clinic.

Homesick, then he smelled Lucky's lavender soap and forgot everything but his hand sliding down her arm while he followed her into the Provençale for dinner, gliding over her sweater to the skin of her wrist, then touching loosened hair down her back while listening to her funny way of describing life—her life and, he hoped, someday their life together.

CHAPTER EIGHT

Manny Garcia stood amid the disarray in his Pandolf apartment and picked up a small wooden box, Pia's old jewelry box, a mosaic of Surya, the Indian Sun God on its lid. She had loved gems. Tears in his eyes, he touched the tiny stones on the picture: amethyst, chalcedony, garnet, agate, red jasper, sodalite, turquoise, and aventurine, so many colors.

From inside, he removed one item that the searchers had luckily not taken: a string of amber beads that looked like an inexpensive necklace. More discerning eyes might connect the twenty-three spheres to a certain prime number—the twenty-three sets of chromosomes in the human genome, beads not really made of amber but of a biomatrix storage material. This was the first set he had made as he refined the RT66 4D dynamic printer technology. A prototype, he had only saved these beads for sentimental reasons. He could not count on being so lucky next time that they would escape discovery. He placed the beads under hot running water and watched them dissolve into the drain.

Next, he walked into George's room. Only a student desk and bare mattress, the sole decoration in the Spartan space was a steel Möbius strip model that George had played with as a child. Finally, he returned to his own bedroom to remake the bed and sleep.

• • •

After Campbell and Sheraton left, Kochanski lit a cigarette and inhaled with relief. Finally. Alone. Then he poured a shot of Dew from the bottle in the freezer. *Who is Campbell to scold me about drinking?* he thought. *Why are Americans so judgmental?*

His computer chimed Chopin, a message from Kasia. He smiled as he listened to her speak in Polish, not English. She said she was going to visit him in Chicago soon.

Decades ago, someplace that must still exist in God's ledger of the universe, he had helped her mother to escape her traffickers. Never tender to Irina in front of the gang, when Kochanski heard that Irina was going to market like a pig, he schemed.

"If I die, it's alright," she said, shrugging one shoulder. "Never forget me."

Then he pretended to be indifferent when the gang took her away. The public bus took her and her handler south. His buddy, Jakub, provided him with an alibi for the day. In a small town where they stopped for lunch, he punctured the bus's tires. On a remote road in the Polish hills, the bus came to a stop.

He was ready. A crowd of people emerged to get air while the driver dragged spare tires. Finally, Irina came out with the man escorting her, his arm possessively around her waist. But she kicked him hard and broke through the small group. Waiting until the two were well away from the other travelers, he shot the trafficker chasing after her. The rest of the passengers heard the gunfire, saw Irina's pursuer drop to the ground, and took cover behind the bus. His face hidden by a scarf, he then rose from behind dirt mounds as she ran to him.

A May day like today but decades ago, they first dove into a grove of pine trees and stopped to eat, drink, kiss, and laugh giddily. Then they crossed railroad tracks into an overgrown Jewish cemetery.

In the graveyard, there was a grizzled man wearing a yarmulke, examining a broken headstone in the weeds, taking notes and photos. Kochanski quickly tossed his rifle into the bushes. They then strolled forward, two young lovers. The old man looked up and greeted them in Polish. Kochanski tightened his hand around Irina's waist, proud of how much she trusted him as she relaxed against his shoulder.

The man explained that he was in Poland with his wife, both professors. They were doing research inside the old Jewish cemetery. In Russian, so the man would not understand her, Irina muttered to Kochanski that she had heard "bad" things about Jews. In weak Russian, he then told her his family secret: his grandmother had been Jewish.

"She was my mother's mother. In a way, my mother and I are Jewish, too," he said.

To their surprise, the professor disclosed that he understood Russian. During the Nazi days, Kochanski explained, his grandmother had been fostered by a Polish Catholic family as one of their own for her protection.

Delighted to hear this history, welcoming them into their home, the couple fed them dinner: hot pierogi and mushroom soup. Kochanski and Irina told the couple a limited version of their own story—"a hook of truth for them to hang their fancies on," said Irina.

But the couple did not ask questions. Now he understood how sometimes it is best not to know. Young and beautiful in the springtime, a boy-man and a girl with child, they simply made the old pair happy. He hadn't appreciated them, gentle people, thinking that their kindness and trust were signs of weakness.

He told them he needed to leave to return to work, but the couple agreed to help Irina until he returned. Even after they went back to Israel to continue their work, she stayed as their house sitter. On rare occasions, he visited Irina, swelling with pregnancy, and Jakub kept up his alibi.

Eventually, Kochanski brought Irina and their baby home to his mother, who only insisted on a small wedding, just the three of them, officiated by their small-town priest. When he was often far away, his mother and Irina took turns working and caring for Kasia as a baby. Kasia was the center of their lives.

And my own life, still.

At the age of twenty-four, he became Number One—the new head of his syndicate—no longer White Rat after he murdered the last Number One and implicated his own boss, Number Two, for the assassination. While their real names were lost in the alcohol fog of his memory, he remembered Jakub. He still employed Jakub at his Polish vodka factory. His buddy was just too trusting; even now, he did not even know his role in what happened next.

The weak link. Jakub texted a lover his secret. In another gang war, that byte of information led to Irina's revenge murder. *Would they have spared Irina if she had been Polish rather than Russian?* he always wondered. Maybe. They had left his mother hog-tied outside, the baby wailing inside. They had not even shot the barking dog. Could he have done more to save his wife's life? Maybe. But at the time, he had begun to doubt Irina.

He listened again to the voice message from his daughter: "Check your email for the Chicago Symphony tickets."

The phone in his room buzzed. "Can we bring up your dinner order, sir?"

On the terrace, he ate the big red steak. The evening was rapidly cooling. Stars then glittered in the ancient sky. He thought about dead Oscar. The number of his employees who were not "on the books" had just dropped by one—to zero—freeing him in a way.

"I'm not aging well," he had told his Chicago therapist a while ago. "Maybe it's all those things that Katya sends me—links, apps, videos, music, news, poetry, stories . . . too much. Then she wants to know what I think about it. Feeling proud of her, an advanced student, of course I've to let her know. But thinking that hard is really bad for my head, my business."

"How are things with Katya?"

"Katya is the only woman I can't fire, divorce, or break up with," he said, almost boasting.

"And what happened to JoAnn, Michael?" she asked crisply.

"You changed the subject. Okay, I broke it off. JoAnn's only a little older than Katya. The two women did not like each other. Some conflicts are wisely avoided by the most fearless of men . . . I'm making a joke."

The therapist did not smile.

He felt too embarrassed then to tell her about one of his daughter's worst rants, when Kasia had reminded him to keep his promise to her mother to not remarry, adding "As soon as your girlfriend has your ring on her finger, I will be tossed out of your life. Then JoAnn will want babies. After that, she'll tell you that I should learn to take care of myself and not be your problem anymore."

Kasia had clapped her hands and pointed to the door. "Then, boom, exit right, your daughter. If you remarry, I want your lawyer to take care of me in the prenup."

He reached for her hand—she turned away—so he pointed at the Chicago sky. "Behind the light pollution, there's Orion's belt, three stars always together—you, me, and your mother. Nothing ever, ever comes between us."

Before her death, Irina had been in a hospital room, stainless steel, starched linen, and the only color was the red blood transfusing into her arm. She asked that their baby never have a stepmother, and he tearfully promised that to her. But Irina had only been around twenty years old at the time, he thought now. An older wife would have told him to be happy after she died. Shouldn't Kasia want that for him, too?

He didn't want to be alone for the rest of his life. Just this evening, he had looked hard at Elise Sheraton's face and liked it. She was closer to his age. But then there had been another girlfriend before JoAnn, also closer to his own age, and Kasia hadn't liked her, either. "Dad, I can't think of a single friend who has a stepmother she likes."

"You're exaggerating," he said softly to the closed door she had slammed behind her as she left.

He texted her afterwards. "What about Abraham Lincoln? You sent me his biography. He loved his stepmother."

"History lies," she texted back, "whitewashes Lincoln. Think! Why did most of Lincoln's children die young?"

She was getting her PhD at Cambridge, he thought. *I never finished high school.* He tried looking up the answer to Kasia's question, search engines, AI Bots, conspiracy theory websites, and he finally gave up.

When Kasia was a year old, he had wedded Irina. In the worldview of a butcher-boy-turned-big-gear-in-the-gang, the ritual in the local church seemed superfluous. But now he was grateful to his mother for insisting on it. The ceremony made his brief time with Irina feel more fated than mated, eternal in a way he had not known before or since, elevating them above other unions of human flesh and their litters, people born for the meat trade of this corrupt world. That hour in the chapel still twinkled its star above, a memory brightest when Kasia sent him something to read, see, or hear, in English, Polish, and Russian.

His steak was now red stains on the plate. But the bottle of Dew was still almost full. He wanted to talk to someone about Oscar's death. But who? His Chicago therapist would report him to the law. She had once suggested that he switch to a Polish American psychologist. He refused, saying, "But I need a homegrown person like you to interpret America for a transplant like me."

Tonight, after crossing the threshold of another door in time, paying the karmic cover charge in meat and drink, he entered a space of unreliable memories. Strains of Arabic music carried from afar over the hum of the ocean and the smell of jasmine in pots on his balcony brought Irina back to him. She had once told him the story from *One Thousand and One Nights*, Aladdin and the Genie in the oil lamp. With a happy laugh, he now told Irina that his genie was in his Dew bottle. He raised his eyes to the bright haze of the Milky Way. From the stars, Irina smiled back, *all forgiven*. He blinked back tears.

Next, entering a decades-old world in Eastern Europe, his boyhood priest appeared, the one who had performed their wedding. A small-town leader who knew all its secrets, the priest had wiry black and white brows, forehead furrows fading into bald scalp like rippled sand drifts into sea. In Polish, where each word, syllable, and pause echoed within the deepest wells of his being, Kochanski began an inner conversation with the only earthly father he knew. As a man of business, he could be flexible in turning to the priest for wise counsel. Being now alone after losing his mother, Irina, and his homeland, the truth was that life's journey started and ended alone, and the stars were rarely seen.

He turned off the light and, staying outside, locked the door to the terrace. They could clear his dishes tomorrow. He and the unseen priest sat across from each other on the terrace, bright in the rising moon.

"On a different subject, yes, I want to discuss Chicago," he said to the priest.

"Now, Michael, don't make it too complicated like you usually do."

"I recruited a kid from South America, an Oscar Sanchez, a smart boy like me at his age. I had him running a valuable painting to an artist named Alex Marion. A talented Chicago painter who specializes in portraits. Paris trained. Online reviews said he had 'a photographic eye and a master's hand in his brushstrokes.' Not a professional forger, but technically just as good—I don't need more criminal connections—and cheaper, too. So, I hired him to do a copy of my Vermeer for an insurance fraud scheme. Oscar was taking the painting to him the night he was murdered. They found his body, and the painting is still missing."

Silence. The old priest had a habit of closing his eyes and only half listening, forgetting much of what he heard and sleeping through the rest, a convenient way to forgive, do his job, whether he cared or not.

"It's a beautiful painting," Kochanski went on, trying to wake him up. "I even framed a print copy and hid a webcam inside . . ." His voice trailed off.

The still night and cold stars offered no inspiration. He poured another shot. The talking became easier.

"I offend my base colleagues by calling them 'techies,' and then that judgmental American, Campbell, thinks I'm a drunk. He refused to hang the print in an apartment to supervise another kid that I'm responsible for."

Now the pots on the terrace and all the matter in the black universe silently waited for what the priest would say.

Nothing.

Doggedly, Kochanski continued. "Marion is married, has a wife, Callie, and two kids in a private school, but no one is buying his paintings. Where does his money come from? Hmm? So, I investigate with the techies' help. We look at his bank account. A little money from family. Public aid. Some portrait work, including for a lawyer I know, Jim Sichet. It doesn't add up to what Marion spends."

He continued, "Then I find a painting of his wife, painted by a different artist, Max Something. Ugly blocks of color for the portrait of an angel. Sichet buys it. Maybe he's having an affair with Callie, giving her cash or a credit card. And maybe she told him about the forgery."

The priest's eyes remained closed. The trick to wake him up again was silence.

After some time, the priest opened his eyes.

Kochanski continued, "But then the techies check Sichet's electronic health record, using a mole in the system, and they tell me he has a 'dysfunction.' You know what I mean?"

Father looked befuddled. *How do I discuss with him men's problems in the bedroom?*

Kochanski grunted into the intercom and unlocked the door to the terrace. The servant was prompt, bringing in one of his computers and picking up his dishes. He suspected that the Saburian had already been lurking by the locked door, listening to his murmuring, thinking he was crazy.

He sifted through his picture files on the laptop. Examining it again, Herman's portrait of the forger's wife, Callie, wasn't as ugly this time.

"When I return to Chicago, Father," he said, "I'll be a frog next to that honey girl, Callie, moving fast with my tongue to catch flies." Oscar's death was unfair, untimely. His fists clenched. Drunk punches landed in the empty night.

"Son, you're a man," the priest chimed in clearly, "not a beast. Seek absolution for your guilt from me by starting with less drink."

That was the last thing he remembered. When he awoke, he was in bed. At 2 a.m., he woke up again when his phone rang. He blinked, eyes scratchy. A Chicago caller ID flashed and then the names—Trisha Talwar, his lawyer, and Ben Dodd, the detective Talwar had mentioned.

Make trouble, watch things happen ran through his heavy head. Allergic to the police—corrupt power in his experience—he said, "Hello," in his humblest voice and thickest accent.

"Mr. Kochanski, my name is Detective Dodd. I've great news! We located a painting that belongs to you."

"Didn't know anything was missing," he lied, slurred his voice, pretended to be still drunk. That would fit their profile of him. "Which one? I've been traveling for work."

"We're investigating the possible thief. Presumably, you already know about Oscar Sanchez?"

Talwar interrupted, breaking Dodd's fast interrogatory pace, "The news about Sanchez's death has been upsetting to—"

Dodd cut her off. "He's been murdered."

"It's tragic and unnecessary," said Kochanski truthfully, grateful for the few extra seconds to think. "The man, yes, lived and worked in my building as a security guard. You must mean my Vermeer. Where was it recovered . . . and how?"

"You return to Chicago soon?" asked Dodd.

"Yes."

"We'll talk more then."

"Trisha, please work with my schedule and set it up," said Kochanski, thinking it odd that Dodd did not seem to be in a hurry to grill him right now.

After Dodd hung up, Talwar asked him some questions in her way that allowed him to be truthful but not say too much.

"No," he told her, "I didn't pay Oscar's taxes because he had his own security company, a 1099 worker." He felt his chest tighten, as it always did when money was discussed, because having grown up poor, it didn't matter whether he had money now or not. "Trisha, you're earning your retainer. Thanks for helping with Garcia's release, too."

"Thanks for Soria as a client."

After she hung up, he turned on the lights, tapped his finger on the wall control and entered his walk-in closet. Ironed clothes hung on each side with gleaming shoes on a rack. The back wall disguised a refrigerator. He drank from a jug of orange juice and made a meal of Tylenol, slices of roast beef, and leftover Chicago pizza—thick crust, congealed cheese, and smoked herring.

He sank to the carpeted floor and took the lid off the box next to him. Garcia's Drukker cases were inside, the purple one on top. Its tamper-proof electronic seal had an abstract imprint—only someone in the know would see the pharaoh image. He curiously shook it against his ear. Thicker and heavier than the others, there was no sound.

Still fully dressed, he returned to bed and fell on top of the covers.

• • •

The morning after his return to Pandolf, Garcia waited outside Dr. Nepski's office at Pandolf Medical Center. The tall door had a brass plate with an engraving that said: "Samuel Joseph Nepski, MD, Chair, Department of Obstetrics and Gynecology."

Nepski's secretary was a heavyset woman in her sixties who looked ready to retire. She barely lifted her head to acknowledge Garcia before politely asking him to be seated. A few minutes later, she nodded at him and glanced at the door to give him permission.

Inside, Nepski sat behind a long desk and motioned for him to sit.

He began abruptly, "Manny, we found things under the Drukker printer. Dr. Sharma told me she discovered you in the lab. She believed what you told her about doing 'repairs' and came to me because she was concerned about finishing them. But when the technician came, he said you were tampering with the printer."

"That's correct, sir."

Nepski shook his head, then waved his hand around the room. "Look, you can see there's no lawyer here. I know the ICE detention was an awful error, and I'm happy to see you back safely. I asked Legal if I could talk to you privately. You have a family, a young son; you've never been in trouble before. Please help me to understand what is going on, scientist to scientist. . . father to father."

Garcia glanced around at the familiar photos on the walls. The historic Hearst Castle on the Central Coast of California was in one, with the touring Nepskis and their three children in the foreground. *Jorge has also seen the world, just not in that comfort and security.*

"Dr. Nepski, I'm grateful for your trust in me. A private clinic reached out to me about purchasing the Drukker for their cancer treatment center. For a pilot study, they sent me patient data files to analyze."

"Patient data!" Nepski slammed both hands on the table in front of him. "You have been experimenting on PHI, protected health information, without approval." He sighed. "What's an Institutional Review Board for, Manny, if not designed to prevent the abuse of patients' trust? If these rules aren't something you honor, you don't belong here!"

"Dr. Nepski, the clinic is a reputable international organization with internal IRB approvals. The patient files were de-identified by AI meta-analysis."

"Then why did you—*and they*—not go through our proper procedures at Pandolf? What kind of patient data were you analyzing?"

"Many types: tumor gene sequences, molecular imaging, immuno-histochemistry, radiographs, digital pathology slides, and anything else the oncologists thought could be useful. If the pilot results were encouraging, the clinic was going to buy the Drukker technology."

"Well, where are all the records?"

"I destroyed them because I suspected somebody was spying on me."

He gazed straight into Nepski's eyes. He always did when he was lying. The truth was that his files were en route to the Soria Clinic in Africa. And fact was, by institutional rules, Nepski could not ask specifics about what Garcia had discovered in unauthorized research.

"So, after all your hard work, there's nothing saved?" Nepski asked skeptically.

"No, sir, I saved nothing, I didn't want to get deeper into anything unauthorized or dangerous. I've learned my lesson."

"You weren't paid?"

"No, sir." *That at least is true.*

"Well, I'll let Legal know," said Nepski, now expressionless. "They talked to the lawyer that your sister retained in Chicago. In America, we have a basketball term, 'No harm, no foul.' If Legal can verify everything you say, things may be okay. Please cooperate with them."

Garcia kept his eyes on the floor as he said, "I am sure Pandolf doesn't want embarrassment on my account." Kochanski had already told him that "Soria's not telling Pandolf anything. They got your back. Pandolf can get in the queue to sue them if they don't like it."

When he looked up, Nepski's face was stony. "I can't give you a reference for future employment in the academic sector. We will confirm your dates of work here only. Your work visa is also not being renewed. I wasn't going to pay you for the weeks you were absent, but now you'll be paid your salary up to today."

"I really appreciate the financial help, Dr. Nepski. But why is Pandolf going to pay me after all?"

Nepski's look was opaque. "Manny, I think your consequences should have been harsher, but I got overruled. One favor before you leave. Dr. Safire has been stuck in one of his projects using the Drukker. You helped him to turn it into a fine tool for fertility research. Please point him in the right direction before you go."

"Of course. Thank you again, Dr. Nepski."

"Manny, look out the window with me. I am proud of Pandolf, the best of the best."

"Yes, sir."

They stood side by side, gazing at the large emergency room sign with lights that dazzled even in the daylight. Proudly, Nepski said, "Pandolf's Wayne Winston Mather Emergency Department was first built during the Cold War. Dean Baluyn, our CEO, is a member of the Mather family, Puritans who came to America in the 1600s. They fund our ER in perpetuity. It also is an operational emergency shelter and part of the Pandolf mission statement. In case of a catastrophe, we can care for our local community for a long time. Supplies, medications, equipment, generator power, wells . . . we have everything."

"It's good to be prepared," said Garcia. "Life's unpredictable, for sure."

Nepski did not ask Garcia about his future plans.

Leaving, Garcia said, "I am grateful for the opportunities I have received at Pandolf. Thank you for your help."

Nepski briefly nodded.

When Garcia returned to the waiting room, Nepski's secretary looked up from her computer with a curious expression. He smiled broadly back.

Had she expected him to be downcast? Did she also think that Armageddon might be coming? Outside, he quickened his pace and merged into the anonymity of the street crowds.

Later that afternoon, Manny Garcia waited outside Pandolf High School. It was May and nearing the end of the school year. Students were leaving early. One ran up to him, tall, in blue Pandolf gym shirt and shorts.

"Hi, I'm Charlie, George's housemate. I know you from your pictures."

"Hi, oh . . ." said Garcia, looking into blue eyes fringed with almost white lashes.

Then George appeared. He turned and hugged his son. Something felt different from a month ago. George quickly disentangled himself, unlike ever before.

"Bye, George," said Charlie. "Sorry I can't join up with you guys for dinner. I have a late practice."

Garcia switched to Spanish after Charlie left, as they always did when they were alone. "That's a nice young man, Jorge."

"That's Charlie—"

"I know, he told me."

"How was your meeting?" George sounded anxious.

"Bad news."

George said nothing. Brown eyes widened behind his glasses. Thick eyebrows drew together under strands of unruly hair that fell over his forehead.

"I don't have my job here anymore," Garcia explained. "But I've worked it out so that you can stay here and finish out your school year. Come, let's walk and talk."

Finally, George asked, "But what about you?"

"I don't know yet. I've been between jobs before. I'll find something."

George looked away. "Mom's watching over us, you always say. I don't believe that anymore."

Garcia patted George's shoulder. "In life, we sail with the winds. And the truth in our dreams is more important than our broken reality."

George said nothing.

"Never give up hope. End of lecture. We'll work it out, we always do."

• • •

Later, their dinner at Palatine Hill was just him and George.

"Dr. Sharma's coming late," said George. "Everyone else has scheduling conflicts and can't make it."

"People smell trouble in our family and run the other way," Garcia muttered.

"What'd you say?"

"Never mind."

The waitress arrived. "Hi, Nancy!" said George.

"Hey, George! Want the usual?"

"Sure. Nancy, this is my dad."

By the time Sharma arrived, they were eating. Garcia rose, switching to English, and handed her a gift bag.

"This is a little token for helping George out while I was gone." Saying George, instead of Jorge, was getting easier.

"You didn't have to do anything." Sharma sat down and opened the card, read it aloud. "'Time, may its passage bring much happiness.' Thank you." She unwrapped the gift, a crystal clock. "It's beautiful! So, catch me up on what's going on with you."

Garcia told her he would no longer be working with her at Sam Nepski's lab.

After a silence, she said, "Dr. Garcia, that's so sad. I'm sorry. What are you going to do next?"

"I've a couple of opportunities, but not here in town. I can't tell you more yet. George will stay until the end of the school year. Then we'll see." Next to him, George fidgeted.

"I'll miss you, Dr. Garcia."

"Please call me Manny. Now that I'm no longer your superior in the lab, we can be on a first-name basis."

"Manny," she said, testing it out. "It sounds strange to call you that, but I'll try. Can we still meet about my research project? Get some advice from you before you go?"

"Yes," he said, not sure when that would happen.

But then her phone lit up. "Sorry, guys, I'm backup call. Okay Manny, just text me." She flagged down Nancy. "Please make my order to go."

After dinner, Garcia walked a downcast George back to his apartment building. Then George told Garcia about the map the police had taken.

"I don't need it," said Garcia, pretending nonchalance as fear bit deep. "Just a scrap of paper I was doodling on."

ICE, he imagined, was still on his tail. How soon would they find out what else he was hiding?

The plan he had been forming for the last few weeks became clearly the right one. He would leave not just Pandolf, but the USA, and accept Soria Clinics' offer to move him to their Red Sea coast clinic. Now he must move quickly before he might get arrested again.

The stability he had gained after the past few years of working in the USA, in the hopes of reuniting with George, was dissolving.

Inside George's apartment, they talked for a while about school, family, and ordered things online that George needed.

When he was leaving, George said, "Dad, I was hoping that this time we'd be together for a while."

"Jorge, I'm sorry things turned out this way. I was looking forward to you moving in, too. I hope you know I'm always there for you, even if we'll be apart for a while. Maybe you can join me for the summer? Wherever I am?"

"That sounds cool," said George. But his cautious tone belied his words. "Dad, we also need to talk about my sophomore year. I don't want to return to Chicago. This school's way better."

"Pandolf was the plan for you when I still had a job. But now"—he paused—"Who's going to care for you here? It makes the most sense for you to go back to Chicago to be with your aunt. Wait, wait"—he held up his hand to George's upset face—"nothing to do but talk more tomorrow. Let me come back for breakfast, bring some bagels. Then, we can leave early so you can show me around your school. I need to start packing, order boxes, schedule storage . . ."

His heart was hammering. *They took my map.* How soon might they arrest him again? He would not sleep again until he had left the country—hopefully even by later tomorrow—before that disaster happened.

There is only one way forward for my research dreams.

CHAPTER NINE

At 8 a.m., some days after they arrived at the Red Sea base, Campbell met Sheraton outside Kochanski's door. Owlish eyes behind glasses, no makeup, wrinkled clothes, she looked like a different person these days from the person he met on the plane.

She knocked. Kochanski opened the door slowly, looking pale and mournful.

"Sleep okay?" asked Campbell. *Hungover again?* He couldn't understand why Kochanski seemed so down lately. He should be elated after Soria Clinics told them that Garcia would be arriving soon to continue his research here at the base.

"Couldn't sleep," replied Kochanski. "Someone I work with in Chicago just died. Too young. So I sit outside at night. Listen to the waves. Even went running at the blink of dawn before it became a convection oven outside."

Campbell couldn't imagine Kochanski outside in workout clothes among the guards and dogs. "I'm sorry. Someone you were close to?"

"Yes," growled Kochanski, anger in the lines of his face. Letting them inside, he closed the door, abruptly shutting out Sheraton's guide. "That woman's a minder. You two will usually find one nearby, until you convince them that you don't wear horns."

After they sat down in Kochanski's office, Sheraton pleaded, "Michael, the sensible thing to do would be to helicopter Mary straight into the base from Ramses. Please talk to these Saburians about changing their dumb security protocols."

"I've tried, will try again."

She looked around. "And where's AJ? He's back from Ramses—"

"AJ?" interrupted Kochanski. "David, that's—"

Sheraton raised a finger. "Let me finish." Then she explained how she and this other doctor, AJ, would alternate shifts "for 24/7 immune infusions for Mary. As the tumor is destroyed, the process can be toxic to the body."

"Patients sometimes must get sicker to get well," said Kochanski, "philosophically true in other parts of life too. You and David will see AJ later today."

Then Campbell described the ongoing installation of the Drukker on the base and the processing of Mary's files. When he finished, Sheraton said she had questions. "Remember, besides my pediatric oncology medical training, I also have a PhD in biochemistry. So you can answer my questions to that level."

She went on to list all her other degrees, titles, and publications, signaling her authority in the scientific world, adding apologetically, "But I didn't get far in my scientific career, so, well . . . well, here I landed."

"Why didn't you get far?" asked Kochanski.

She hesitated.

"C'mon, I'm a blunt man," insisted Kochanski.

"As a younger woman, they said I had 'sharp edges,' probably wouldn't have mattered if I was a guy."

I had career disappointments too, thought Campbell, *and I am a guy.*

By 9:30 a.m., it was time to go to the Drukker area. "I'm not going," said Kochanski, calling for their minder to return. "Elise will explain everything to me later."

The uniformed Saburian woman, in her twenties, led the two down a long corridor with industrial lighting.

Walking beside Sheraton, Campbell said, "I may not know much about Michael back in Poland, but it sounds like he hit the streets young."

"Don't know, either. There's 'book smart,' and then there are smart people like Michael. It's my first time meeting him in person. But online, I've been tutoring him in Gyani's genetics master class for laypeople."

The Drukker area was a large open space. They chatted with technicians who were setting up the machines, a cheerful group speaking a babble of languages, still taking turns at a late breakfast. The aroma of spices filled a side room where a chalkboard sign read "Naashta: Breakfast," next to a kettle of chai. Indian dishes steamed in hot plates with Hindi descriptions on index cards with English, Chinese, Arabic, and Saburian translations. A steel tray with colorful dollops of chopped red pepper and green coriander, brown tamarind chutneys, yellow mango pickle, and a peppered white yogurt condiment lay next to the sink. The Indians chatted in Hinglish about a Bollywood movie they were going to project that night on the wall.

The minder stopped to eat. "Some Indian and Saburian dishes can be quite alike," she said. "Interchange of cuisines. From thousands of years of sea trade to Red Sea ports like ours." She looked around at the Indians. "Maybe some mixing of people too. These Indians look similar in features to some Saburians."

Then she led them to the main entry, with its fountain, string music, and stone floor. Behind the desk, instead of Captain, they saw an elegant Saburian woman, her head wrapped in black. She was chatting with the Egyptian from the plane; her white scarf was gracefully draped around her head and shoulders.

They followed the guide down a hall. She touched her finger to a brass knocker on a door for Room 728, which quietly slid open to a suite that was large and painted in cream and pastels. He heard Sheraton's intake of breath as they walked into the room and faced a giant Chinese drawing, mountains sketched with black ink, thick splashes and strokes mingling with delicate lines of trees and homes, above a calm expanse of blank ocean below.

Saburian botanical prints decorated the walls around a king-size bed. Fresh flowers in porcelain vases gave a lie to the vast desert outside. An antique bronze bell from colonial days hung over the bed, with deep red and gold embroidered silk cover and pillows. Carved and painted crown molding and baseboards, as well as a delicate Persian rug on the hardwood floor, completed a picture of international luxury.

The minder looked wistful. "Our king recently changed the decor. This room used to be the royal suite back when his father became the king when this was just a military base. His father loved to hunt, and the decorator had picked ivory sculptures and stools that were real elephant feet. The rug was the skin of a dead lion, full head and claws. But now . . . this appeals more to King Mohammed's conservation tastes and international guests."

She pressed a button. Heavy gold and purple tapestry drapes parted on a large window, letting in the sun. Smoothly, bamboo blinds dropped, and then lace gauze curtains drew over them. Now, fine patterns of light danced over the dark red Persian rug on the floor.

"Sumptuous!" said Sheraton. "And that old bell is out of a Sherlock Holmes story. The king can't mind that bit of colonial history too much if he only removed the endangered animal things."

Campbell stiffened. *Would this Saburian find Sheraton offensive?* Sheraton still had her "sharp edges."

The guide said evenly, "We call this room the 'Silk Road.'" She then tapped a steel knob on the wall. A panel slid open. "Dr. Sheraton, here's the dispensary. Syringes, needles, drugs, refrigerated medicines, blood pressure cuffs, thermometers, and more."

She tapped another button and another panel slid open. "A crash cart and an AED. See, Dr. Sheraton, this is our suite for visiting patients from all over the world when they are not in the hospital, before, after, and in between their treatments. Other people can stay here, too, like a family member."

"Very impressive," said Campbell. He looked at Sheraton, unable to say what he really thought in front of the guide—that he knew terminal cancer patients were desperate, and that he thought it was wrong to take financial advantage of that. Even if the treatments did work, they were only available to the privileged few who could afford them.

How did I get here? He and Garcia had been rebels, joking about the FDA and NIH, sharing their disdain of the Western medical research establishment and its chieftains: crooks and cronies with bottomless support, from politicians and taxpayers to a matrix of mercenary pharmaceutical, hospital, and insurance corporations.

"What's wrong?" Sheraton was watching him closely.

"Need to renew my ACLS certification," he lied.

She turned back to the guide. "We have an appointment with AJ—Dr. Bhattacharya in less than ten minutes. I don't want to be late."

Of course! Campbell realized. *Arjun Jagdishwar Bhattacharya from the Pandolf locker label.*

After they left Room 728, Campbell whispered, "Elise, I think sometimes the way you talk to our guide is a little harsh."

"Just between you and me," she whispered back, "I'm proud of my particular American tribe and that we run on time. Why not be proud of where I'm from? I know they say our American history is terrible and imperialistic. But every human society has its own brutal past and present, just as bad as ours or even worse. The big difference is how much modern technology we have as a nation to destroy. That's why everyone wants nukes and the latest weapons."

Working with Sheraton means getting along, Campbell told himself, *not debating international politics.*

"That's one way to look at it," he said blandly. She looked tense, staring straight ahead, jaw set. He analyzed her. Maybe as a minority in Saburia, she was feeling insecure, feelings of vulnerability translating into defensiveness and hostility.

"So, this AJ is Dr. Bhattacharya?" he asked. "First name Arjun?"

"Yes, we worked together a long time ago, then he moved to Pandolf. I didn't hear from him for a while. Then I ran into him at a conference and—short version—he connected me to Soria Clinics. Here I am."

They stepped out of the air-conditioned building into suffocating heat. The Saburian guide was taking them next to the new clinic building. Missing his sunglasses, he squinted in the bright sunlight and realized that the last time he had been in Saburia was in the middle of winter, not so hot in the daytime. Sweating, air swimming around him, he followed his Saburian guide down a gravel path as she soldiered ahead, not slowing down.

Sheraton opened her purse and found sunscreen, which she applied liberally over her face and arms. "Want some?"

He put a pink dollop on his face, breathing in the flowery fragrance, and returned the tube.

"You've to do more than that." She put the tube back. Out of her Salome bag, she pulled out a roll-up hat, unfolded it like origami, and stuck it on her head. Its flaps fell over her ears, and one dropped down the back of her neck.

"In the fashion world, they call my bag 'Mary Poppins,'" she said.

"Is there a sun umbrella in there, too? They need to make a bag like that for men."

She laughed. "If I have to cover up in Saburia, David, I'm at least going to do it in style."

"I think you just hide behind those gargantuan sunglasses."

Sheraton didn't reply.

A new white building with a red cross sign materialized in the haze ahead. He followed Sheraton into a crowded room filled with local families and breathed in the cold air gratefully. In the corner, a water reservoir stood, with a tray and small glasses. He drank, refilling water many times. Discreetly, the locals shot looks at him, sweaty and steaming pink, paying no attention to Sheraton, another anonymous Westerner draped in pristine white, with her tan designer hat, Salome bag, and designer sunglasses.

She whispered, "If they kill me for being with the wrong tribe, I'll go with dignity—not like you." She removed and refolded her sunglasses and hat.

They followed the minder into a small anteroom. Sheraton and the minder sat down on the couch. He took a chair. A short Indian man appeared, balancing three trays, with spreads of miniature items. One tray carried tinned biscuits and chai in steel tumblers. Another carried glasses of water with ice and lemon, a box of chocolates, and nuts besides mugs of instant coffee. The last, carefully balanced between the other two, held bowls of water for washing hands and cloth napkins. After laying the trays down carefully, he hovered to help them wash up and choose what to eat, then asked where they were from.

"Texas, I always thought that was a country," he said in a thick Indian accent. "It's not? And Connecticut. It's a 'state'?" Soon he and Sheraton engaged in an animated discussion about American geography.

"I thought our appointment was twenty minutes ago," Campbell finally grumbled.

The Indian man stiffened, smiled, nodded, and promptly left. She looked at him. "Really, David?"

"You said to be proud of my tribe. How we run on time."

Soon, a tall, gold-tanned man entered the anteroom.

"AJ," said Sheraton joyfully and stood up. They kissed on both cheeks.

Dr. Arjun Jagdishwar Bhattacharya, in his late forties, was dressed in a dark blue suit, a crisp white shirt, and a purple and gold tie. Smiling broadly, he apologized for their "waiting."

"My intern enjoyed getting to know both of you. But he loses track of time. Time's relative, the East knew that before the West. Mr. Campbell, so nice to finally meet you."

Campbell rose and noted that he was about an inch taller than Bhattacharya. They shook hands. "That man is your intern? It'll be good to have another physician here."

"No, he's a *business* intern. Don't let his Lilliputian dimensions fool you, he's smarter than me. Cold adult beverages, anyone?"

Sheraton shook her head.

"I'm still nauseous from the heat," said Campbell. "Just more water, please."

The intern returned with a bucket of colorful little bottles of juices on ice, and a carafe of water that Campbell promptly emptied. Campbell then picked up a chocolate chip cookie. The cookie tin, filled with a baker's dozen of tiny cookies on paper doilies, would barely hold three of Lucky's warm, melting chocolate chip cookies, he thought. While Sheraton and Bhattacharya talked animatedly about incomprehensible treatment protocols, acronyms, and numbers, his mind drifted to Lucky.

Lucky: clean skin that smelled like soap, somewhere, somehow with him at a barbecue with beef brisket and corn bread, drinking cold beers as the evening sun set.

"Pay attention, David," said Sheraton.

"I have sunstroke. I can't focus."

"Here, drink this," said Bhattacharya.

He finished a glass of something apple-y, icy, and sweet-salty.

"Yes, Pandolf recruited me at first," said Bhattacharya, talking to Sheraton.

"You didn't want to stay there?" asked Campbell.

"I had grander ambitions."

"AJ didn't need to stay at Pandolf," said Sheraton. "He came here, to the cutting edge."

"Pays well, too." Bhattacharya brooded into his glass as he swirled it around. "Yes, I would have toiled in the Pandolf mines and then hit the race ceiling."

"Sorry, I have heard of that," said Campbell. "Can I ask who's taking care of all those people in the waiting area?"

"Our highly trained nurses," said Bhattacharya. "Until I came here, they ran all the health care on this base. But we're gearing up to be a fully operational world-class medical center, a galactic flagship for Soria. I'm a big Star Wars guy. Maybe soon we'll even be able to relocate the clinic to the capital. By the way, before you go today, David, I do want you to meet Ali. He's ten. One night, he got through our gate from the local village outside, and the watchdogs mauled him before the guards could get there. But Michael Kochanski took the kid under his wing, as well as his widowed mother and all six siblings."

Sheraton laughed. "That's a lot of brothers and sisters. But first, take us for a quick tour. We can talk shop more—MD to MD—tomorrow."

"And then I need to return to the Drukker," said Campbell, and here, he, too, recited technical terms and acronyms they didn't know. "I don't have much time to go live with the 'Mary' Drukker plate. And Manny Garcia is coming soon."

"Great news. Good job finding Garcia," said Bhattacharya. "Amazing how his AI search-and-kill algorithms update cancer vaccines as the tumor changes and hides. It's evolution in high speed. All the while recommending different chemo and radiation options, the old poisons of my specialty."

Bhattacharya showed them around. They met Ali, a boy with one eye covered like a pirate, and scarring on his face and neck. The child pressed against his mother, who was covered in traditional dress, and they could only see her eyes. After some coaxing from Bhattacharya in Saburian, he shyly said something.

"Ali says you're very tall," Bhattacharya said to Campbell. "Until you, I was the biggest man he'd ever seen, Gulliver."

They went next to Bhattacharya's office, a spacious room with a brag wall of awards and diplomas. Two large windows overlooked an irrigated garden.

"Mary comes in a few days," said Sheraton. "We'll start her with her favorite French dinner, followed by a good night's rest. No one asked me, because, honestly, I doubt she'll feel like eating much after her long trip."

"She gets one day to rest," said Bhattacharya. "Then we'll harvest more samples of her cancer. Soria sent a radiology tech to help me. A local anesthetic should work nicely . . ." He stopped. "David, where is Manny Garcia now?"

"He had to take care of a few things in Argentina first where he's from."

"Pressure's on, David!" said Sheraton happily.

"Pedal to the metal, ma'am," said Campbell. "An army of millions: T-for-terminator cells coming your way."

"But lunch first," said Bhattacharya.

· · ·

After Sheraton and Campbell had left, Kochanski waited until people were awake in Chicago eight hours behind Saburia. Then he called the Pierre Building super to make arrangements to have his artwork returned to the storage locker with an updated lock. Their conversation was quick, all business, mourning Oscar Sanchez's unexpected death without too many questions asked by either of them.

That evening in Chicago, the lawyer Jim Sichet met with Detective Dodd. The main room was a studio for Sichet's art hobby. An empty easel stood in the corner among partly finished canvases, brushes, and paints.

On the balcony, Sichet poured whiskey into tumblers. Dodd opened his briefcase and pulled out large photos. Putting on reading glasses, Sichet examined photos of a corpse. "Wow!"

"His name is Oscar Sanchez. He's not legally here, so we aren't officially spending a lot of time on this. I guess we'll never know who killed him . . ."

Sichet sipped his drink and opened a cigar box. "Sad."

Both men smoked as they discussed local news. Then Dodd's phone buzzed. "PD is picking up the painting soon. Say, why did you want to borrow it for one day?"

"To impress a woman."

"You?"

"Just a little fun. She loves Vermeer, and she's more impressed with me now. No worries. There's no Chicago-size scandal here."

"Well, really appreciate your help with recovering this painting, Jim. I owe you a favor. Do you know who sent it to your house?"

"Can't say. What I can tell you is that Michael Kochanski won't appreciate my help locating his painting. He won't know. Did you know that he has a chapel in the Pierre building? What a waste of prime rental space! I must decide what to do with this Polish bishop on my chessboard."

Both men laughed. Faint strains of music from the nearby jazz bar announced the beginnings to the local nightlife. After an unmarked police car arrived to pick up the art, Sichet offered to call Dodd a ride home.

"Thanks," said Dodd. "You know my wife will want to know why I was out late. I'll tell her it's work, then she doesn't ask more questions. For my family's own safety, they shouldn't know much about my job. But your Frances is so understanding."

"My wife's 'compliant,' sure," said Sichet. "Divorce would be expensive for her. Prenups are the best marriage security. She also enjoys being Mrs. Sichet, maybe becoming a political wife someday."

"Good stuff," said Dodd, lifting his glass. "But you have girlfriends."

"*Mistresses,* yes. Sichet men choose carefully—we don't like talkers." He added thoughtfully, "Then if she's poor, I could have more to lose than her if things go south."

"Hell hath no fury like a woman scorned. When you move on, she could try to take you for all you're worth."

"I don't think so, Ben."

Sichet then handed him an envelope. "Here's something for your daughter and her friends—four tickets to the Shebubu concert, seats right up front with no ID scanning to get in, either."

"Thank you," said Dodd. Without the identification requirement, the paper tickets could not be traced back to the person who had bought them.

After Dodd left, Sichet puttered around his studio, cleaning brushes, tidying paint tubes and oil crayons, thinking how breaking the law, bending the rules, not for the first or last time, was a win-win for himself and Dodd.

In all those years at StarHall, wealthy himself, surrounded by other rich kids like him, he had learned to excel at many games. With money and power, rules were just lines. Smart people knew the power grid, which wires were live, and which could be snipped, rewired, or ignored. The fuse boxes were in the castles of the elite. Boundaries were artificial, between those who enforced the law like Dodd, those who created them like him—and those who crossed them like poor Oscar Sanchez.

He was a leader—enemies called him a bully—whom people feared, loved, or both. His father had been like that, too, as were his little brother and sister. By agreeing to send their children to his old boarding school, even his wife understood that their children needed to learn to *win!*

He logged in to his online class in painting, wondering how much Dodd knew about him. If the detective had checked the police files, it would show a clean record even as far back as StarHall. The school's documents regarding his leave of absence had been confidential. Would it catch Dodd's notice that there had been a strangulation death at the school when he had attended? A young teacher, a brutal assault . . . the handyman had received a life sentence and then died—*the dead famously stop talking.* That teacher once told his class that the Tiber River in Rome had seen many murdered bodies. As many as the Chicago River?

CHAPTER TEN

After another visit with Dr. Bains, Mary was back in her New York City flat, in a stately building on a thoroughfare in Manhattan. She wanted to do this next step by herself, this journey to death, or this trip to the Red Sea coast to change that final date. Wounded animals died alone, and so could she, by going down a forgotten trail in the Shenandoah Valley into the overgrowth.

But Dr. Bains was right. "You need to update your daughter. If something happens to you, best for them to not hear about it from a stranger."

Leslie was her only child, married to Bart, spelled like the California train system. They were an ambitious working couple with two kids. She didn't like to bother them and found their intense sphere of existence stressful.

She once asked Leslie to do something simple for her passing. "Big services are too much work, and besides, I'll be gone by then."

"Mom, these rituals are for the living, not for the dead. I treasure my memories of Dad's service that you worked so hard on."

Before Leslie was born, Mary used to hike the Blue Ridge Mountains with Leslie's father, Mark, a large man who called his mixed ancestry the "house special" of America. In dreams, Mary still walked with him down a forest path, feeling such joy that she would never turn back.

Leslie would be hurt to not know sooner about Mary's travel plans, then would painstakingly review all the details of her mother's trip with a youthful energy that Mary could not match. An argument had erupted recently between them over something minor, she could not even remember, during which she complained that Leslie belonged "to this judgmental younger generation."

Finally, hoping her call would go to voice mail, to postpone another exhausting discussion about her plans with her daughter, Mary called

Leslie. She pictured her daughter out for the day, with boisterous kids in the back of the family van; or perhaps she was stacking laundry or working through another item in her endless list of chores, unable to interrupt a packed schedule to pick up the phone.

But Leslie answered. "What's up?"

"Nothing major, let's meet for an early breakfast this week. You like morning coffee after your workout."

"What's going on?"

"Dr. Bains . . . wants me to talk to you."

"I'll come over now."

"Oh no . . ."

But Leslie was unstoppable. An antique wooden elevator took visitors directly to the private entryway of the flat. Soon, Mary heard her door open.

Leslie's expression turned grave upon seeing her. They sat at the kitchen table with its west-facing windows. Mary put out Leslie's favorites: Manchego cheese, rosemary crackers, grapes, and a mug of herbal tea on a wooden tray from the old farmhouse—painted chinoiserie, exotic flowers on black paint. Gazing at her child in the waning light, treasuring family resemblances, she then steeled herself for disagreement as she explained her plans.

Leslie was aghast. "You plan to travel abroad to a private clinic? For a month!"

"The Red Sea coast is on my bucket list before I go. Blackest skies, no light pollution, the stars of the Milky Way, wild animals . . . ports for millennia of swashbuckling maritime trade." She then tempered the excitement in her voice to match Leslie's practical nature and added neutrally, "Fascinating to a businesswoman like me. Honey, I've already bought the tickets for Saburia next week. I didn't want to upset you until I'd decided to do it. We can still talk — even every day. The clinic has state-of-the-art communication."

Leslie stared, searching for words. "Mom, don't go alone. I wish I could come . . ." She had the same expression as her father used to get, lips pursed, jutting her chin.

"Of course, honey, but you have other commitments."

Mary did not mention Bart, who appeared to find his mother-in-law's health issues inconvenient, like a perplexed passenger experiencing delays on his namesake train.

Mary explained that "the clinic provides personal assistance every step of the way, almost like a paid tour abroad."

Leslie had many questions as she unfolded her very large phone: What's the clinic's name? Where is it? What is the name of this "brilliant scientist."

"Well, it does say that Saburia is very safe for tourists," Leslie said, looking at her phone. "Majestic scenery. Endangered wildlife. Repopulation of other species that were wiped out, cheetahs, leopards, even lions. After the latest regime change, they renamed the capital Ramses, like the Egyptian pharaoh. For women, it's Islamic law: you should keep your head and body covered in more remote parts of the country."

"I know. By the way, do you have new pictures of the kids?"

"I just uploaded more yesterday to the shared album. Pull them up on your phone."

On her phone, Leslie doggedly researched Soria clinics, the location of their facility on the Red Sea coast, and finally Manny Garcia. "He is a reputable scientist, NIH, Pandolf, but his recent work is all in pregnancy complications."

"Cancer vaccines is his latest project," Mary explained, "under the wraps for now because it is for a private company. And I just got really exciting news! Dr. Garcia will no longer be working remotely from California. He will now actually physically come to Saburia and monitor my progress."

Before leaving, Leslie said, "You'll be happy. Bart and I signed up with your concierge practice."

For an annual retainer, Mary had a personal live doctor through a concierge service who not only diagnosed her cancer but also set up Mary with Dr. Bains.

Finally, thought Mary. Leslie had complained that her last visit with the new doctor on her insurance was "transactional, I was in and out in minutes, and now when I message her office with a problem, I get AI-sounding bot answers."

In the doorway, Leslie hugged her—as always, lightly around the shoulders.

"Bart's mom says that one of the hardest things about growing old is losing control to one's children—reversing roles with them."

Mary smiled, biting back her tart response. Bart, loyal, dull, was tolerable, but his mother was not. But compared to the melodramatic marriages among the children of others she knew, things could be worse.

A few days later, her travel arrangements started with a suited young Saburian at her door. Speaking excellent English with a hint of an accent, he loaded her luggage into a waiting car outside. Then he opened the rear door. She stepped into the dark-wine interior.

"Champagne? Coffee?" he asked.

She smiled and shook her head. Then they were on their way.

She appreciated his silence inside the humming car, hard to find in help these days. Raised with people who worked for her family, she believed in boundaries, that the help should speak only if spoken to, blending otherwise into the background, even if everyone who worked for her family knew too much of their personal business.

Outside the car window, the familiar lights of Manhattan rolled by. Mentally, she tallied the cost of everything so far for this trip. Eventually she would compare that total to how much she had paid the clinic and determine their profit margin.

There I go, like Dad. After marrying Mary's stepmother, her father had adopted an irritating tic of underlining paternal advice by flipping on the country accent of his new wife's rural relatives.

"People deserve to be paid for their hard work," he said. "But always good to know how much money they make off of ya." He also told her that "inherited money becomes a curse when it takes incentives away for people to make something of themselves." Had he been referring to her mother?

I took my inheritance and multiplied it many times.

That is why she could afford the concierge doctor and Saburia for these experimental treatments that were not available in the US. Even her properties manager was a convert and went to the Cayman Islands regularly for injections, pellets for her "chronic fatigue."

In the car, Mary called Leslie to say goodbye. "I'm proud of you, honey. You're not just another trust fund kid. You and Bart work and don't ask me for money."

Strictly, that wasn't true. Mary had made the down payment for her daughter's vacation home, bordering a park. There her grandchildren could disappear into the trees to play, like the woods she had spent her childhood summers in at her grandmother's farm in New England. She also paid for her grandchildren to attend the same New York City private school that she and Leslie had attended, making this their family's third generation.

One of the first to board the plane, Mary had an upholstered berth to herself with a privacy curtain, snacks, and a minibar. Handing her a glossy guide, the masked attendant thanked her for being a "Travel Saburia first-class club member." Grateful that the young woman had not pressed her for conversation, Mary drew the heavy drape and poured herself a cold seltzer. Behind the curtain, she could hear the muffled voices of other passengers boarding the plane. After texting Leslie that she had boarded, she looked out the window at the tarmac and New York City beyond, already feeling homesick.

As the plane took flight, she watched the receding face of Manhattan below her, its lighted skyscrapers fading under clouds. She opened her brochure to read about her upcoming journey, first to ancient Athens and then even further back in place and time to a city near the birthplace of the human species in East Africa. From there, forgotten generations had ventured forth in waves over tens of thousands of years to reach this island she now called home.

"Goodbye," she whispered to her world that now disappeared under her to the hum of the plane's jet engines. "Fairest city of all. Thanks for all the courage you stand for. Back to where it all started until I see you again."

CHAPTER ELEVEN

Back in Pandolf, Shelly Sharma leafed through mail, mostly junk that she tossed into the blue recycle bin. Above her desk, there was a Dr. Seuss globe with its oceans painted blue. Neat lines divided the countries in contrasting colors. A childhood gift from her South Dakota grandmother, her cousins used to spin it fast, to prove that all the colors on the visible spectrum "blend into white." Now it wobbled.

She called her mother. "Dr. Garcia's gone again. These kids—George, Charlie—are so lost."

"They're lucky to have good people around like you."

"They're still making As in school," said her father off-screen. "Take away their phones if that changes, just like we did with you."

"Boys are different," her mother scolded her father. "Unless you want to move to Pandolf and—"

Her father popped onto the screen. Her mother put her hand on his mouth.

"Mom, I want to hear what he has to say."

"I want to tell you myself. We're coming next weekend when you're not on call."

"Oh, that will be great! Tell Dadi to come."

But she knew that would not happen. Dadi was her widowed Indian grandmother, who lived in a "retirement community" near her parents and did not travel. Instead, she gave biting monologues on video calls to her grandchildren about the "decline of civilizations."

Always asking for "updates on downstairs," the three teenagers, Dadi analyzed "deficits in parenting" and "broken Western families." From Dadi's point of view, Manny Garcia was selfishly neglecting George, and so was Garcia's sister and her "self-centered" husband, who "left his first wife and kid and then got a young Latina to marry him by bringing her to America." When Dadi was not around, her father apologized. "Beta,

Mama means well. Maybe you'll hear some wisdom in her strange words and ways, from another time and place, in a language that's not her mother tongue."

Dadi also sent emails, formal missives with words spelled in British English like *humour*, theories about Garcia's disappearance and speculation about what the American government had done to him, warning her granddaughter to keep her distance from ICE. "They don't teach history in school anymore," she wrote once. "But let me tell you. This system started with ancient Rome two thousand years ago. If you were a citizen of the state, you were privileged. But the rules were different if you were a slave from the top of Europe all the way down to North Africa, or if you were a Jew, or any foreigner who had no protection from the government. That's what imperial powers do. But we're citizens now, and they have to treat us as citizens."

Over the years, Dadi's cheeks had sunk into bones jutting against paper-thin skin, her hair faded to wisps of white over pink scalp, all foreshadowing that one day when she would return as a vivid memory, the colorful, energetic, sari-ed woman of her childhood, with her trail of smells and sounds from a land halfway around the planet, where time ran as deep as millennia.

Despite her grandmother's misgivings, at first Sharma felt relaxed about George, who was voracious about his prized Pandolf education. After moving in, Charlie absorbed George's attitude, and she happily concluded that this was another example of how immigrants fueled America's engine. She often saw the boys and the cat on the fire escape at sunset or heard the low bass of their music late at night, now softer after a neighbor had complained. Livingstone included the boys' apartment in his nightly feline rounds of the balconies before heading to the wooded hills behind the building. At 4 a.m. when she drove away to the hospital, she looked for the faint glow of their computer screens through their windows.

"Charlie's still dating Michaela," she told Lucky, who was making a rare visit to their apartment.

"I started dating Harry at their age. You look worried?"

"I hope Charlie's being . . . careful."

"Of course, Shelly. What about George? What's he up to on that front?"

"I'll have to ask."

At the Golden Griddle with George one evening, Sharma broached "that" subject. "How's Charlie dating Michaela working out for you?"

"Fine."

"I think it's important to treat all human beings—no, to treat all living creatures with kindness and respect."

George dropped his eyes. Tensing, he picked up his fork to poke at the hill of spaghetti and meatballs before him.

Forging ahead, she continued, "There are consequences to our choices in relationships, like pregnancy, diseases, hurt feelings . . ."

"Dr. Sharma, thanks," he mumbled, dabbing tomato sauce from his lips. "Dad talked to me. Also, they have classes in school, biology, psychology . . . so, yeah . . ."

Ketchup, onion rings, and syrupy pancakes evaporated. He showered an omelet with salt, pepper, and even more ketchup. Then he stabbed his fork into the air and discussed dark energy, black matter, and the expansion of the universe.

"Is that what you're going to study someday, George? Astrophysics?"

"I dunno."

"Maybe go to a seminary and search for God?"

"Nah. See, I told Dr Campbell how our world could be an engine. Then he said he heard something like that before at his boarding school growing up, a spider metaphor. Spinning its web, growing our universe, extending it farther and farther, faster and faster." He opened one large hand wide to demonstrate. "Accelerating. There could be more spiders, other worlds, alternate dimensions . . ."

"In some religions, salvation means to escape this physical web of suffering," she said.

"In that metaphor, I could be a spark of energy—trapped in a web of sentience until I burn out."

Before Sharma could ask him to explain, the waitress gave her the check.

"Thanks for dinner, Dr. Sharma," said George. "You're also working here now, Nancy?"

Nancy smiled. "I have to pay for my new car. Say 'hi' to Charlie and his girlfriend for me, oh, what's her name?"

"Michaela."

"She's pretty."

"Indeed, she's an iteration of beauty."

"What do you mean?"

"*Iteration* means a repetition of a computational procedure to obtain closer and closer approximations to the solution of a problem."

Nancy picked up the check. "Like an incarnation. You're so right, like deities or rebirths coming back to Earth. I dabble in some mystical stuff myself."

Sharma listened to them talking, wondering at how two such different people could be smiling and connecting. With her vague smile, café au lait skin, and reddish-brown afro, she thought Michaela could be like Aphrodite emerging again, this time from a golden seashell in an American ocean, beauty to be born again, infinitely through the times and tides of humanity.

Michaela did not fit in with the other girls. Not tuned in to the White, Black, Hispanic, or other tribes and spectrums of Pandolf High, she found a niche instead with George and Charlie. With fading vestiges of embarrassment about her changing body, wearing edgy clothes too big for her frame, Michaela's concession to spring's latest fashion was her collection of lace headbands.

At Pandolf High one day, Sharma met a parent that she thought was the classic patient with gallbladder disease in medical texts, the three *f*'s, female, fat, and forty.

"So nice to meet you, Dr. Sharma," said the woman. "I'm Michaela's mother, Alicia. She really admires you."

"Thanks so much." They made polite conversation, even though Sharma really wanted to ask her why Michaela had no rules, no curfew, and no other oversight?

Besides Michaela, Carrie Mather was the only girl George mentioned by name. Carrie confidently sported as much naked skin as the school rules allowed, skort barely at the tips of her fingers on her sides, and shirts dipping so low one wanted to look away. Her boldness and looks also reminded Sharma of an old painting, a French portrait of a king's teenage mistress that used to hang in her high school library before it was removed as "inappropriate."

Dadi always had an opinion: "Girls can only be that way when they have strong social protection. What does her father do? What kind of family does this Carrie come from?"

"Her dad is a cardiac surgeon at Pandolf. The Mathers are the wealthiest family around here."

"See what I mean about social protection."

Waiting to drive George to a much-needed dentist appointment, she saw Carrie huddled outside the school doors with her gang of "popular" friends. When George came outside, he waved to Carrie, who ignored him.

George entered the car. "Carrie wears a lot of makeup," she said.

Silence.

At a school theater performance that she attended because George was in the tech crew, she stood in the back just in case the hospital called. One row ahead, Michaela sat with Charlie. Carrie played the lead of *52nd Street*, a small-town girl fresh off the bus in New York City. After the performance, Carrie glided down to her proud family and friends, slender ankles atop skyscraper stilettos. Her beaming mother greeted her, a woman of an uncertain age.

Sharma critiqued the mother, seeing Botox in her stiff, ever-delighted face, the picture of wealth—coiffed, manicured, pedicured, styled, and gym figured, a younger version of Dr. Nepski's well-preserved mother. Had she also had her big toes lopped off to fit into those pointed Italian heels?

"How was the play?" Lucky asked later.

"New update. I'm not worried about George," she said, addressing the real question. "The only girl he likes doesn't even know he's there."

"And I'm not worried about Charlie. Michaela makes him happy. My parents were also high school sweethearts. Though things aren't good between Mom and Dad right now. She's talking about divorce. You're the OB-GYN. Do you think that's because she's going through menopause, that this could be hormonal?"

"That's vaguely problematic."

"I know it sounds sexist."

"I didn't say it, Lucky, if that's what you mean," said Sharma. *Your parents and brother are a hot mess*, she thought and changed the subject. "Did you see that those feral teenagers raided our fridge?" She opened the freezer door. "Look. All my dinners are gone. Maybe we should take back their keys to our apartment."

The white shelves were bare except for colorful bags of cut vegetables and fruit.

"I didn't notice. I just eat at the hospital now. I've a free meal card for being chief resident."

"Hospital's vegetarian selection is crap. I've been so busy I haven't kept up with grocery shopping. Maybe the boys ran out of food."

Lucky's voice turned firm. "I know the boys can't drive, but they can do their own shopping and have it delivered. Why do you have to do it for them?"

"They'd just get a lot of junk food and takeout. I guess I could shop online and have it delivered to them, but I like to pick my own produce, otherwise you get the rotting fruit and . . ."

The subtext was they were arguing—again—about why Lucky did not help more with the boys, especially since Charlie was *her* brother. Sharma's mother suggested it was because "Lucky's from Maine, and people from Maine believe in self-sufficiency."

With a crisp edge to her voice, Lucky now told her, "Whatever, you do you."

For shopping for the boys, Sharma used a credit card app that she shared with Garcia and Campbell. At Mather Market (Campbell would rhyme the two words with a comic Boston accent), she loaded her cart with items that a different app suggested teenage boys would like. Guided through the aisles, Sharma tapped her way through the list: items like organic milk, free-range eggs, protein powders, nutritional yeast, whole wheat bread, cane sugar granola, and finally gold-starred items in the fresh fruit and vegetable section, where she carefully picked the best produce. A lone attendant waved her in and out.

While she and Lucky talked about the boys, a *not* well-domesticated, nonorganic, and nonvegetarian Livingstone strolled in so quietly that neither of them heard him—until he crunched his kibble. They kept a stack of "Lost Cat" flyers to post every time he disappeared. Their rules were irrational, but there were no better ones. In theory, the cat was not allowed outside. Humans were his main danger, malevolent or merely careless with fast cars, pest poisons, and traps. But when the cat howled incessantly at the back doors, decibel level escalating, both homes put him out, and on pleasant nights he just prowled the woods. No one noticed until he did not return the next day or came home bloodied with scratches and gashes, triggering a blame game: "Who let Stone out, who saw him last?" Everyone then denied guilt.

In the kitchen, golden cat eyes now took stock of Lucky. Livingstone meowed his orders to open one of his food cans.

"I'm never getting another cat," said Lucky. "I have to feed him before myself even. He'd probably not even come back if he had the choice, except for easy food."

"George was telling me that in other countries where he has lived, they wouldn't have fixed him. They think spaying and neutering is cruel."

Sharma did not add that George had also said, "Maybe we should get Stone a girl cat. Good for his psychology even if there's no biology," and that Charlie had agreed. "Lucky's birthday is coming up. I bet we can find him a girl buddy at the rescue place."

"Speaking of other countries, any news from Dr. Garcia?" asked Lucky.

"I haven't spoken to him since he left. George says he's going to work at an international clinic in some new country near Egypt, S something, doing biopharmaceutical research."

"How cool! Did David help get him that job?"

"Maybe, I'm really not sure what David does exactly."

CHAPTER TWELVE

In his office, Kochanski explained to Campbell a large transfer of funds into Campbell's account from Soria Clinics. They were alone. "Much more than just George's room and board. For you to bring George to Saburia to visit his father this summer."

Why in the hottest season? Campbell wondered. But then thinking that Kochanski might not give a straight answer, he decided to wait and see.

Next at her request, Campbell joined Sheraton to go to the local airport to pick up Mary.

She grumbled how Salim, the base manager said "no exceptions" for patients to helicopter into the base from Ramses. "I call him Shroodie for being excessively shrewd."

This time, Campbell brought sunscreen, an unscented Chinese brand from the campus store. The highest SPF block, it stung as he applied it on his burned arms, over ridges of muscle that he was now regularly buffing at the gym, in lifting dates with other Chinese men.

He also wore a hat, sunglasses, and long sleeves. "I have a new respect for the Saburian sun. Of course, the campus store does not have designer stuff like yours."

"I'm not usually so 'dressed to the teeth.' There's a reason they call makeup 'war paint.'"

"You do look good in your armor. Are you feeling more settled in?'

"No, more uncomfortable than ever. *Hate* being forced to cover up. Oh, look!"

Sheraton pointed outside to a herd of elephants and changed the topic to the "hateful ivory industry." A passionate remembrance of many extinct species of local wildlife and praise for the king's conservation and repopulation efforts followed.

Late afternoon, air blurring in the heat, their Humvee came to a grinding stop in the small local airport, followed by an armored limousine and two newer transformer military vehicles that had caravanned behind them. Sheraton walked briskly to a petite figure waiting next to a stack of matching luggage in the shelter.

The elderly woman, wearing a pink and gray checkered skirt suit, introduced herself as Mary and said no more. Two other women stood with her. Olive-skinned with dark hair in tight buns, they wore pantsuits and spoke British-accented singsong English that Campbell guessed originated in India or Pakistan. They were two doctors who worked for Soria Clinics. Soon, they were talking to Sheraton about the new Soria clinic on the base.

Saburian airport workers loaded their luggage. Water bottles were passed around, and then the groups entered their vehicles.

Before leaving to enter the tank like limo with the other women, Sheraton whispered in his ear, "Those two doctors say King Mohammed is going to visit the base next month."

"Exactly why're they here?"

"To inspect the clinic, I think, and other company business. Not sure."

Campbell rode in the lead Humvee, hoping that Sheraton would sensibly mute her lectures on endangered species because everyone had looked like they needed some peace, quiet, and heavy-duty air-conditioning.

But he needed to have a frank talk with Sheraton about what exactly was going on at the base, between the mysterious purple case, traditionally the color of royalty, the appearance of so many doctors, and now the upcoming visit by the king himself. All electronic communication appeared to be monitored, as were the long hallways with ubiquitous security cameras. To begin the dance to connect without minders, he slipped her a handwritten paper note after they returned to the base: "Drinks, conversation? Pretend romantic rendezvous, two lonely Americans? I'll get the picnic."

On paper, back and forth, they worked out a time and location. Then one evening, he led her down a corridor in the Chinese quarters. "I am allowed in this part."

They exited toward the beach under a doorway camera that blinked and turned to follow their movement. A twin camera on the outside watched as they made their way to the dark ocean.

Awkwardly, they held hands and put distance between them and the buildings until they could talk freely.

Above waves crashing nearby, she yelled, "There's something about this beach, like how easy it would be to drown, or to drown someone."

She followed his eyes as they travelled the lighted guard towers up and down the shoreline where sand met some of the most strategic waters in human history. "Those look new, probably not even manned."

Years ago, he remembered a different picnic, Southern California, on a beach that was not "a bloody knife edge for businessmen—", as Kochanski once said about the Red Sea coast. He had kissed Susan, folding back curtains of dark hair behind dangling earrings. His friends came by to cheerily wish him Happy Birthday and good night. In the morning, he took her back to her sorority house. She still sent him Christmas photo cards, showing him that she was now married and had "birthed the next generation of troublemakers LOL like myself YOLO."

But the line between theater and reality blurred inside today's alien frame, a different time, beach, and woman. Using a flashlight to analyze their distance from the threatening waves, moving back to where they could hear each other more easily, Campbell laid out a thick blanket on the sand, upon which Sheraton simply sat down.

Together, with awe, they gazed up at the glittering sky. Susan had liked to say that the stars were fluorescent bacteria, and that humans were lower even—in that cosmic order—mere sparks of awareness, trivial in existence compared to intelligent life "far beyond our abilities to comprehend, who watch us under their microscopes and pitch us into the trash when they are done."

"I've never seen the Milky Way so clearly," said Sheraton. "Can you imagine our ancestors millennia ago? Unable to read or write, they had star maps, stories about gods and goddesses, battles, and mythical beasts they believed existed."

"They were nomadic," he murmured. "The sun might have told them the time. And the winds and the seasons might have told them the way. But when clouds and storms hid the skies, they still had to navigate. So, they spread out all over our planet. Where will we go next? Traveling through space, time, and other dimensions."

"We, David? Not me. Maybe our avatars will travel even farther in space and time, the AI that might take humanity's place after we destroy most life on our planet. Still, here we are, in the cradle of human civilization, no longer even looking or acting like these Saburian folk who stayed behind. So, why should our AI avatars closely resemble us either?"

She opened the picnic basket. "How'd you get this?"

"I tip well."

"Tip?" she said, close to his ear. "It sounds more like a bribe."

Her breath felt good on his skin, and he reminded himself that they were just acting. "You're talking about Western values, but I like to say that around here it's more like trick or treat. I'd rather be giving out treats than be at the receiving end of their tricks."

"You charm people into doing things for you. I hope that this time it's not you who is condescending to the local people, like you accused me of."

She reached into the hamper, pulling out hard and soft cheeses, from French Brie to American Wisconsin, crackers, nuts, and dried fruits, then plates, cutlery, a cutting board, and a knife.

"Oh my god. If Salome made picnic baskets . . . a second dinner."

"For you, a beautiful woman."

"I like hearing that, even if I know you tell that to all the women."

"Not all," he protested, "and what's wrong with making people feel good about themselves?"

"Though there's nothing Saburian in this basket."

"Call it 'the Foreigners' Special.'"

Next, she pulled out a bottle of chilled white Loire, as well as a small bottle of Kentucky whiskey.

"Not Michael's Dew?"

"A little bottle of that is in there, too, to help you remember Michael"— he paused suggestively— "and I got the corkscrew and wine glasses from the Egyptian, Yasmin."

She raised her eyebrows. "Yasmin. You *really* have been busy since we came, not just working but also making new friends."

"And I got these shot glasses from a Chinese fighter pilot."

He rolled the shot glass between his fingers, admiring the etched calligraphy and delicate paint patterns. He had met Yi by wandering into the public section of the base's karaoke bar. The host was a courteous Chinese man in his twenties, assisted by two slender older women, their heads dyed a matching blond with pink-rose highlights. The host's girlfriend sat on a stool at the corner, a pale sprite, her hair dyed white, with a tiny, matching white poodle. Among the group, there was a black-haired child with her pencil and workbooks, sometimes helping the grown-ups or playing with the dog. No one spoke English. The music was Chinese, and the large television featured Chinese entertainment, fun to watch even without subtitles. Shut out of the private rooms, Campbell was about to leave when the pilot walked in.

Yi wanted to practice his English. He invited Campbell to follow him into a private room with a bar. Was it a stroke of sheer luck that the soldiers had let him come in, an American? Or was it only because Yi had been there, their prize pilot who wanted to practice his English? Did they not know what to do with their visitor, or did they not wish to offend him by turning him away? Bars, he thought, were places where different tribes mingled to remember their shared humanity, both profound and profane.

"David," Sheraton said, "Michael told me that a Chinese fighter pilot was caught with the wife of a senior officer. Juicy gossip for the base. Is this the same guy?"

"Michael should not be telling you these rumors."

"And it boiled down to the fact that the pilot's flying skills were more valued on the base than the pride of her husband, and the wife was booted home. Business done on male terms, as usual. When the king comes next week, we'll all be back to smiles, harmony, and international cooperation."

She took a sip of her Loire. "Anyway, let's change the subject. I mean, we're having this picnic because you wanted to talk freely. About what?"

"I'm still trying to understand Soria's plans for research here," he said, trying to direct the conversation to his questions about the purple disk. "Why two MDs, you and AJ, for just one patient so far? An advanced practice nurse could back up AJ."

"AJ connected me to Soria. I agreed because this medical research is novel. And the contract is enough for my kids' college and some left over for retirement."

"You are brave to venture this far."

"I have to. My ex is unhelpful. As for his second wife, they deserve each other. I don't love men any less for it. Like I love my son and dad—who calls me 'Hell-ise' when we fight. So, I end up making excuses for men, absolving them. Still, you seem decent."

He smiled. "And Michael can be decent even if he's rough around the edges sometimes . . . ?"

"Like how some people describe me. I guess we have that in common."

The Kentucky whiskey danced in his Chinese shot glass. He prepared to be direct. "Feels like we are in a great hall, the ocean is the band, the stars our roof."

"Hmm."

"Ever read *A Midsummer Night's Dream*?"

"Yes."

"Donkey braying here," he said, "braving a queen under the influence of magic drops. There's an extra Drukker data disk that I brought here from San Fran."

"What do you mean?"

"I brought six drives to Saburia, five with biblical names for cancer patients. And a larger, heavier one sealed in a purple case."

"I don't know." She paused. "Did you ask Michael?"

"He's evasive. And Manny flat out won't tell me. Traditionally, purple is a royal color."

"So that's what you wanted to talk about, a royal secret?"

"Yes, but don't mention what I said to anyone."

"Especially with the king coming. Michael says a big fuss is planned. Now I'm curious too. I'll also get to meet Saburian Queen Number Three during the royal visit. She's planning to get pregnant and has questions for me as a pediatrician."

"Keep your eyes peeled."

"Deal." She lay back on her elbows. "Do we make a handsome couple for those cameras?"

He put up his binoculars. Sure enough, at the exit door, that odious light was still moving and blinking.

She pulled his hand and drew him to her. "No worries. I'm not interested in you that way, but let's be convincing."

"Why do people expect us to be in pairs?" he said. "At the karaoke bar, I had to tell them that Michael is not your boyfriend."

She pulled away abruptly. "There's really no respect for women around here. This is a medieval place. These Saburian women are shrouded, subjugated creatures. What do they think of me being out here with you?"

"That you are liberated. Come hang out at the bar with me."

She made an incredulous face.

"Alright, stupid things to say."

Longer silences grew between them. Her eyes were closing. Sleep weighed on his. They packed and left.

The red eye of the door camera blinked faster as they approached, a suspicious god greeting them home.

CHAPTER THIRTEEN

Light broke in the east over the Red Sea. The base hummed with final preparations for the king's June visit. For days, workers had swarmed the grounds, weeding, pruning, raking, and throwing up ladders for painting and repairs. Rows of Saburian flags lined the roads, among new purple and gold streamers that welcomed the king in many languages and dialects. Cats darted out from bushes being trimmed. Excited guard dogs barked madly in their crates. In anticipation, playing soldiers, the local boys ran around the village next to the base, wielding sticks and toy guns while the girls stuck to hide-and-seek and hopscotch. Indoors, squads of servants swept through with brooms and dusters, placed fragrant floral arrangements, rolled out red carpet, and hung more banners with traditional tribal colors and designs.

The Saburian dog handler gave the crated Alsatians extra food to keep them quiet. After completing his morning duties, on the steps outside the kennels, he finally sat barefoot and awaited the call of the horns announcing the royal arrival.

Some time ago, the Polish man's daughter had visited in her Western clothing and uncovered yellow hair. She looked about sixteen. Through her translator, she said to him that it was cruel that the base's "German shepherds" were "semi-starved." He apologized, told her that in Saburia they were called "Alsatians." He fed the animals more while she was visiting, such a shame because that made the animals sated, sleeping instead of guarding at night. But he liked the new woman, Dr. Sheraton, even if it was scandalous that an unmarried woman, divorced, too, was spending so much time alone with Mr. Kochanski, who was also unmarried, *and they both drank alcohol.* But at least the American doctor was always covered up and minded her own business.

Then there was the titillating story about the Chinese pilot and the officer's wife. *Foreigners bring impure thoughts,* he thought. He firmly lectured his wife and children on their low morals. That sixteen-year-old girl had been half-naked. How could her father let her run around like that? What were men supposed to do? Life had enough temptations.

The Saburian way was best. If he worked hard, perhaps he could afford to marry a second time. His wife was a good woman, but after four children, her body was no longer the same. With a second wife, she would have extra help around the house, and a dowry might bring more money into their home. Unlike foreign women, whose husbands discarded them, he told her she would always be cared for by him and their sons.

Then he heard a faraway hum, and the beginnings of the drums on the base, but though he stood up and strained his neck, he could not see anything.

• • •

Running late, Manny Garcia and Michael Kochanski walked quickly by Eleanor and Yasmin, who were directing last-minute preparations for the king's arrival. Garcia had just arrived at the base and often found himself lost when he stepped outside the lab after his minder was reassigned. Today, Kochanski had to retrieve him in a corridor where all the signs were Chinese, and a Chinese guard had barred Garcia's way.

"Flowers smell good," Kochanski said to the women. "What a grand welcome. Fear, awe, wonder—keeps people loyal to their rulers."

They looked at him politely.

After a pause, Eleanor said stiffly, "The way I see it, when royalty makes their people feel proud, that is the . . . apotheosis of a culture. You better hurry now if you want to get the best view from the start."

"You're lucky to get to watch from the rooftop," said Yasmin, brown eyes shining. No longer on the airlines, Yasmin was hoping to stay on the base to be closer to her family in Egypt.

• • •

Joining the gathering on the highest point of the base, Garcia watched the royal motorcade as it appeared as a dot, then a line on the horizon. The parade of military vehicles burgeoned on the dusty road as the drumbeats on the base grew faster and louder. In traditional colorful dress, the Saburian crowds below him clustered, cheered, and waved bright flags in anticipation.

Next to him, Campbell stood as rigidly as he had ever seen him. Dr. Bhattacharya and Sheraton were on his other side. Knots of enthralled Chinese and Indians watched nearby. The Saburian base personnel scattered quickly to perform their assigned tasks before rejoining their families below, who had already begun singing behind the ceremonial ropes.

The king is coming, Garcia thought, strangely also feeling thrilled.

He spotted Ali, the boy Bhattacharya had told him the dogs had mauled, waiting below with a garland of braided purple and white flowers.

Bhattacharya told them that was his idea. "The king will have to give the kid a reward. I keep telling the health minister to send the boy abroad for plastic surgery and an artificial eye. I'll not take no for an answer."

The motorcade rumbled to welcoming gates. Ceremonial guards emerged from the leading armored cars. Carrying automatic rifles, they wore khaki uniforms decorated with glinting medals and brilliant ribbons. They marched forward to line the road three-deep. The drums stopped, and the horns blew a Saburian martial song.

Then, to deafening shouts and cheers, the king, in white robes, stepped out of the first black limousine. Garcia sensed everyone holding their breath for a fraction of a second before resuming their rapturous welcome.

Next, Queen Noru emerged, round face impassive, head wrapped in hijab and body covered in a traditional cotton, block printed with local patterns. She moved to her husband's right, her eyes focused straight ahead so as not to meet the gaze of other men.

The royal couple walked ahead. More men emerged from cars behind theirs, also white robed or wearing black Western suits, enveloped by swarms of helmeted, armed soldiers in camouflage.

To audible sighs, Ali met and garlanded King Mohammed, and the Saburians cheered proudly, a wave of sound that echoed around the base.

After the king and his entourage entered the main building, his men fanned out over the campus, distributing gifts: wooden carvings of lyumas for the men, jewelry with colored glass for the women, and for the children, treats, colorful iced drinks, and Western ice cream.

After the king made his tour, he stopped in Kochanski's office where Garcia was also waiting. Close up, the king was a stocky man of medium build, with analytical eyes that bought life to an expressionless brown face wearing heavy makeup and faint tribal markings.

Kochanski discussed the completed construction of the clinic and projected images on the wall screen. "Your Highness, with your generous support, Soria has completed our military hospital. That includes two doctors, Dr. Bhattacharya and Dr. Sheraton. We've also set up the Drukker AI for research trials. We came in below budget and on time."

The king nodded his approval at Garcia. "And finally, here's your scientist?" he said in American English.

The uniformed man on his right now spoke in Saburian accented English. "Dr. Manny Garcia, we are so delighted to have you."

"Thank you! I'm so happy to be here." And he sincerely meant it. In his new lab, he had never felt so free . *No more other people's stupid projects.*

"One more thing, Mr. Kochanski," the king said, getting up to leave. "For my wife, we need her lady doctor to be a woman of good character."

Garcia saw a flush creep up Kochanski's neck as he leaped forward to open the door for the king. Neither official flanking the king looked at Kochanski as they walked out.

Later, Kochanski asked Eleanor to come to his suite. "You were right. No more wine delivered to Dr. Sheraton's room. And there's one more thing you must do for me."

He showed her a photograph. "Do you know this woman?"

"One of the queen's attendants."

"Please deliver *this* personally to her," said Kochanski, giving her the purple Drukker case.

Eleanor hesitated.

"You gave David Campbell a picnic basket and that Loire wine. After everything I do for you, what?"

"Okay."

In the clinic, Dr. Bhattacharya told Garcia and Kochanski that Ali would "indeed be going abroad for his surgery," and that "Mary won't be able to move to the VIP patient suite yet."

"Why? She paid for Room 728," said Kochanski.

"The king said that his queen would stay there for a few days. We are refunding Mary for those dates. She made sure of it. She'll stay in a regular guest suite, no medical dispensary." Now Bhattacharya looked unhappy.

"Far from ideal for my patient, but I've assigned nurses to Mary twenty-four seven."

"He *is* the king," Garcia pointed out to the other men.

• • •

That evening, while the sky dimmed and cooler breezes flowed in, the military caravan withdrew its tentacles and crawled out of the campus, grinding hum fading as it disappeared to return along the same desert road that it had come on that morning.

In Room 728, in pajamas, Noru perched on the edge of the king-size bed. She looked over to Aisha, a spectacled woman in her seventies, her nanny when she was a child, who was stitching the hem of her cloak.

Aisha grumbled, "This repair will have to work for you until we return to the capital. I will march into that tailor's shop and give him a piece of my mind about his shoddy job."

Noru stifled a giggle. "Aisha, I put a lot of wear and tear into that one, so just order a new one. It's a long, dusty road to that shop. I don't think that stress is good for you."

"I'm not that old."

Noru smiled dreamily. "I wish our king didn't have to leave so soon. Aisha, what do you know about the American woman doctor? My husband said I'd meet her tomorrow."

"What do you think?"

"Sad. Far away from her family, no husband—he divorced her. Happens in our country too. I think of those women living alone outside our village. Widowed. Disabled. Divorced. Sick. But she's better off than them because she has practical skills. I suggested to my husband that we could train more of our women to be like her for useful work."

"Like me. I couldn't marry. No looks or dowry. It was your idea that I learn medical skills."

"You do a better job with injections than any doctor. Also, Aisha, I have some bad news."

Aisha looked up from her sewing.

"The king says you can't come to India with me."

"What?"

"He was impatient. Said I need to grow up. Since I was a baby back in our village, I've never been separated from you. And now I'll be without you for at least three months, or more . . ."

Noru's voice trembled. Aisha looked down and returned to her stitching.

Noru continued, "I'm scared. But the king said he doesn't want me to suffer like his other wives who lost their babies. He says I will have a healthy son, a younger brother to the crown prince."

"Don't worry, they'll treat you well because of who you are." Aisha's tone was brusque, wordlessly telling Noru to *toughen up*.

Noru stiffened from the unspoken rebuke and changed the subject. "Any news about the crown prince?"

"No."

"Is he still traveling? Surely you've heard something from the other servants?" pressed Noru.

Aisha bit a thread and shook her head. Noru doubted her but knew it was futile to push further. In the strict hierarchy of their world, frankness only existed between equals.

After everyone was asleep, Noru threw on the cloak Aisha had repaired, laced up her wheely sneakers, and quietly went outside to meet her childhood friend, Khepri, who had accompanied her from Ramses. They would be alone and could talk more freely than when others were around, from servants like Aisha to guards and workers.

But first, she released her Turkish Anatolian Shepherd dog from the shed. Usually walking just ahead, Kalrissian sometimes wandered away for short distances to search for threats before he returned.

Encased in voluminous garments, the two women and large dog circled the compound. Noru felt hot, and her blood pulsed hard in her temples. She told her friend, "The doctor said that the injections of fertility medicines may make me feel strange."

Noru described the doctor in Ramses, an Indian woman, speaking through a translator. "She was a little thing in a white coat over a gray sari. Inspected me like I was another species. But except for the kohl around her eyes, she didn't look that different from some Saburian women."

As they chatted and strolled, they heard the crunch of a distant military boot, the occasional wild animal, and the barks of other dogs that made Kalrissian's hackles rise.

Soft, forbidden, they chanted together to the old gods of their tribe. The traditional plea for new wives trembled the silence: "Defender, Your shadow tonight is my cloak. Your mighty wings cut the air, so I pray for a child. Egg-white rich, I wait for You, powerful with life force even many moons ago. I wait. I pray nightly—bless this drop of answering life, and do not forsake me for the next month."

Then Noru said, "You're fortunate in your new husband. My king says he is a good general."

They clasped hands tightly.

"When do you leave?" asked Khepri in tears.

"Almost immediately," Noru said. "Do you know of anything about me going to India, and my treatments there to not lose my baby?"

Khepri looked around. "They listen to what we say."

Khepri pulled Noru's hand, and they walked to the wall at the edge of the compound. Huddling together, Khepri whispered, "Please don't tell anyone I told you. I don't want to be beaten or my family to be punished. They say that because the kings only marry within their family, a disease took root. The royal babies are either never born or are deformed like the cripple, Bassam, your husband's older brother. We're lucky our crown prince is healthy, but they say he may pass the curse on to his children."

"My king's other baby with Queen Salma, remember how she used to live outside our village with her yaya?"

"Yes, deep in the brush we explored as children, no one else around. How she used to cry."

"Cute with her pretty dresses, not even crippled—just mentally weak, I hear. What does that mean exactly?"

Khepri was sobbing. "No one would talk about it more. I wonder what happened to her?"

"Her mother's a cold woman," said Noru harshly. "Makes me angry how she abandoned her only daughter. Distant with me, too. Aisha says that Queen Salma prayed that the king's second wife would not have children, and her wish came true."

Khepri said nothing, afraid to criticize a queen.

"Queen Salma's not totally horrible," Noru continued. "With her son, they say you see stars in her eyes."

"Is he as handsome as they say?"

"I haven't met him. Aisha says he's handsome."

They continued whispering. "The fertility injections hurt," said Noru, "but Aisha says that I'm doing my duty for our country. She also gave me a purple box to give to the doctors in India. But I can't open it."

"I'll pray for you."

Noru embraced her friend. "We better go back. Come to my room tomorrow for your birthday gift." She then called to the absent dog, "Kalrissian!"

They waited.

Khepri laughed. "Your dog's stupid to not listen to your commands."

Noru pulled a strip of meat from her pocket and noisily unwrapped it. When Kalrissian promptly appeared, she haughtily corrected her companion. "He's the smartest beast in the world." They might have grown up together, but things had changed. She was a queen, no longer an equal.

They returned to the buildings, mostly dark, except for the hospital where the lights were always on.

CHAPTER FOURTEEN

Mary awoke in her hospital bed, retching, and hit the call button. Her nurse hurried into her room, pushed IV medication. Then Sheraton arrived, looking tired despite makeup. "How are you?"

"Better with that medicine," said Mary.

Sheraton turned around to leave.

"But how are *you*?" asked Mary, raising her voice.

Sheraton turned around, caught off guard. "Honestly—?"

"Yes."

"Lonesome. The base is a sea of men. The culture is different, too, and I can't get used to it."

Mary gestured to the chair.

Sheraton sat down. "I don't like to cover up. Or how they treat women. The lack of privacy. They must even know when I go to the bathroom. You met Manny Garcia?"

"Different than I expected. Quiet, serious, those men have the most surprises though."

"Manny says that not minding our own business is human nature."

"True. Growing up with help in New York City, it was the same thing. And Dr. B tells me he's used to it from India, how there, one can't even close a door without someone trying to peep in or listen, their ear to the wall, wondering what you're hiding."

Sheraton sat down. "And it's now electronic and AI driven. I need to be less prickly to the Saburians, come off as unfriendly, you know."

"Well, sometimes living abroad, away from your family, means feeling like you have to take extra care to protect yourself. Don't you think it's easier for these men in a place like this?"

"I've become so jumpy. Not staying here longer than my contract, for sure." Sheraton leaned forward. "Your turn to talk about you. You remind me of my mom …"

"I have a daughter, two grandchildren."

Sheraton smiled happily. "In New York City?"

"Yes. We have sleepovers, eat cookies, watch skyscrapers light up from my windows above Central Park."

"Expensive."

"Yes." Mary laughed. "They like to hear the stories of our family in those buildings, going way back, even as they sail into . . . unknown futures. "

"Colorful stories?"

"Kid-appropriate. I transform people. An alcoholic uncle becomes a red-nosed goblin. My father's awful second wife is a troll stepmother. My own grandmother morphs into a good witch. Elevators in skyscrapers lead to half floors where doors open into fairy forests. Diamonds hang like icicles on snowy white branches."

Mary stopped to catch her breath, eyes looking far away. "Paths lead to glassy pools. Castles underneath the water. They glide into grand halls with great chandeliers. Around and around twirl entwined couples. Ballroom skirts flaring. They join the dance."

"And then?"

"And then we go on more adventures together. A troll on a bridge. Maybe a sword in a stone. Then they tell me what happens next. So we make up our world together."

"They have online games now that can do that for you."

"I suppose." Mary opened her phone to show her family pictures.

I may not even see my grandkids grow up, Mary thought as Sheraton swiped through her family album and asked questions. Mary then worried that Leslie and Bart might decide it's best to not have their children visit a dying person and all those dawns they would grow up without her. *I'm not going anytime soon.* "And what about your family?" she asked Sheraton.

"I'm divorced," said Sheraton. "My parents are in Connecticut. They help with my two college kids. Or I couldn't be here in the middle of nowhere."

An old picture on the hospital table caught Sheraton's eye—Mary explained they were her parents, a young couple with Mary as a newborn, "thankfully unaware of what lay ahead."

Sheraton picked up the picture. "Alfreda is your first name. Mary the middle name. And I see a Nantucket basket on the shelf?" She added wistfully, "I'd love one."

Sheraton picked up more framed photos.

"That's Mark, my husband," said Mary. "He died young. A bike accident."

"I'm sorry," said Sheraton.

A newer photo showed how in Mary's daughter, Mark's coffee skin grew lighter, and then even paler in her grandchildren, creamed twice over under ringlets of hair that Mary said, "change shades with the seasons. They have hazel eyes, blended olive, gold, and brown."

"I'm curious?" asked Sheraton. "Will your grandchildren figure out someday that the trolls, goblins, and witches in your stories were real people in their family?"

Mary laughed. "Maybe. Or they'll find them again in their future worlds. Nothing new under the sun."

"What were your parents like?"

"They either fought or were silent," Mary said. She went on, how she was seven when her future stepmother became a fixture in their New York City flat. Overly friendly, in her twenties, "Sarah had plump, painted cheeks like Santa."

Mary's nanny, twenty-ish too, joked that Sarah came from a half floor. "It's between two regular floors. There's a secret door in the stairwell. But you'll have to be older before I can show you."

Mary had searched for the hidden door. "There was no door, just another ruse to entertain me, have some fun herself, tease a poor rich kid. I used to run up and down those stairs and chat with everybody. I'm still in touch with two childhood friends from the building."

Mary said her mother retreated to her bedroom while Sarah "sat on the upholstered couch patterned with French garden flowers like an insect in the leaves. He eventually married the painted bug."

Formal when she emerged, Mary said her mother would converse with Mary while someone did her hair and nails. She regretted it now, she said, judging her mother with her father's critical eyes and blaming her mother for their divorce. "It had been a different time. Back then, all she had known was to blame the woman starting with Eve, or to blame the help—the butler did it."

"My mother would never have let that happen," said Sheraton. "I don't understand."

"We don't know what we will *let* happen to us until—"

"I'm sorry. I didn't mean to sound judgmental—"

"A different time, a different world."

"Like here. I tell myself not to judge," said Sheraton. "But you turned out fine."

"Because I had my grandmother."

"The good witch?" Sheraton leaned forward in the chair.

"Yes. She had a farm in New Hampshire. When I was little, I couldn't say the *r* in 'Gramma.' So, she was 'Gamma.' I became 'Alpha,' not Alfreda. Alpha and Gamma, like a sorority. Dad grew up in the little house there, where the boys slept in the attic with a ceiling so low they could not even stand. The girls had the nice second-floor bedroom with white lace curtains."

"And your dad's father?"

"I don't remember him. Just died one day, working on the farm. Gramma found his body, and after the funeral never spoke about him again."

"Why?"

"Maybe today, they would have divorced. My grandfather was a handsome man. Women liked him. He liked them. And he liked to drink."

Mary gazed out the window and continued. "But Dr. Sheraton, I want to tell you about how our family farm, an enchanted world, taught me to love the land—land that has loved me back, how I made my fortune. When my cousins visited, we were like the kids in Narnia, except there was no escape hatch in a wardrobe, just a field, pond, and woods. There were dense trees around one neck of the farm. I would find my grandmother's fabric and twig artwork in the branches and ask, 'Are you a witch, Gamma?' Silence. She would chuckle. 'No, I wish I were a witch, the good kind.'"

"Sounds like fun."

"Before Gramma died, I asked her if she worried about me when I was little, when I'd be gone for hours in the woods, even after dark. And she said 'bad things don't just happen to city kids. Alfreda, always remember that I call you Alpha, and that you take risks. No girl I raise is going to be scared of spiders, snakes, and shadows in the dark.'"

"Amen."

"When I got older, I told her I didn't believe in bad spirits. And she said, 'Don't deny evil, dear. It's always just a blink away.' Her education ended in high school, and she was excited that I planned to go to college like my dad."

"So, then you went to college?"

"An hour away from the farm. Gramma and I replicated it with LEGOs: red brick buildings, iron fences, tall pillars, and great gates. There I met and then married Mark, a Black man. Gramma said she 'prayed about it' and loved him. After she died, her kids sold everything. My dad said the money from the farm paid her estate taxes by exactly the right amount, and 'that is how the cookie crumbles' for family farms. But I repurchased that farm. By then the old house was gone with its memories. I worry Leslie will sell the farm again when I'm gone unless I convince her husband about its investment value."

"Husband," said Sheraton in a tight voice. "You know, my ex married this young thing he cheated on me with, and now my kids must be nice to her—and their new baby."

"Sounds like you have a lot bottled up. That's okay, totally okay."

"Tomorrow, I'll meet Queen Noru. I hate it that women in this country still live this medieval existence. Maybe she enjoys it, being the youngest queen and his favorite."

"Aging isn't so different for women between her culture and ours, I think," said Mary. "I once listened to a history podcast about fine art. Someone pointed out how so many male artists painted their beautiful lovers. Then replaced them in their personal lives like we do flowers after they wilt in vases."

Mary closed her eyes. Hot and cold waves of nausea returned, nausea like she had felt as a child seeing the rats scurrying between New York City subway rails, nausea like she wanted to die. At the funeral, they could say she had died here in Saburia in the past perfect. That she had not read a single English book in the one-room Saburian base library before she had died, because the books appealed to male readers, their view, their world. She had even excused that as expected in a military installation filled with mostly men.

"Dr. Sheraton," she said softly. "I'm sorry I feel sick again. Before you leave, could you please open the window? Fresh air."

"Alright. I'm also giving you stronger medication now. You need to rest."

After Mary was alone, she opened her eyes and gazed outside. Like receding notes of musical discord, the waves of nausea disappeared, thank god for the drug fix.

The moonlight blurred on the dust on the upper windowpanes. She heard an owl hoot, the distant howl of a jackal, the answering bark of a dog, and something else—scraping close by. Someone eavesdropping? Beds and windows were spaces in which she could spill open the boxes of her memories, like the first time she had heard that rustling sound—because there was nothing new under the sun, just the same patterns repeating themselves, like wallpaper.

She was ten years old at her grandparents' farm. After skipping stones across the summer sunset glow of the pond, she was returning in the twilight. In the evening breeze, on the tree branches, Gramma's artwork of thread and feathers shivered. A rustling sound—someone was behind her on the dirt path—and then, a leering man's face appeared before her. She felt her legs run into the trees to one of her dreaming spots, a large hole in a dead trunk. Inside, she waited, holding her breath as much as possible, telling herself that he could not hear her hammering heart. Late at night, after the crackles of twigs and occasional gleams of flashlight faded away, she came home.

Gramma was up.

"I got lost," she lied.

"Okay, go shower, look how dirty you are! And then go to bed."

That weekend she saw him again in his Sunday suit. In the bright daylight, he was just a scrawny twentysomething, with two other young men. She crossed the street to say something to him.

"What happened?" asked Gramma when she returned.

Her face turning hot, fighting tears, she looked at the sidewalk and told her what had happened.

"What did you say to him?"

"I told him that if he crosses our property line again, you'll curse him. If that doesn't work, you'll shoot him."

Gramma's eyes widened. "Honey, I'll ask Officer Chester to have a talk with him. Let me know if you see him, or anyone else unauthorized, on our property again. But you simply can't go around talking like that. If you were older, it could get you arrested." Then she looked away with a sly look. "I like your spirit, Mary. Sometimes, you must break eggs to make an omelet."

After that, in the woods, Mary wore a loud whistle around her neck. These days, her grandchildren had watch phones with an emergency setting and GPS.

When she first arrived in Saburia, she had asked Dr. Bhattacharya, "If I die here, what happens to my remains?"

"Don't talk like that, Mary. Positive energy is required for healing. Of course, we would fly them home."

The remains, she thought. *How impersonal, whether wilted flowers or dead bodies.* But then at least she would save Leslie the trip of coming all the way here.

Unexpected waves of joy, atavistic and primeval, flooded over her. Was this the effect of the stronger medication, driving away her nausea? With wonder, she sank deeper into the moment: the sounds of the wild in the dark; then into forever: her powerful spark, mortal, among the unconscious stars of the Milky Way.

Jumbled thoughts bubbled up, like how it had been a good, long life, even if her flame had not reached as high as she had once dreamed of, like the fame of a Gloria Vanderbilt or one of the famous Astor girls whom she used to adore as a child.

She and her husband had never retired to a houseboat on the Seine, she thought. What should she think now about their dreams as a young couple for their future? A past perfect that never actually happened. Illusions? delusions? No, like for the properties she renovated, their young dreams were necessary, scaffolding that disappeared to create again, anew.

Feeling stronger, she pressed the button on her remote, and the multilingual Saburian nurse on the night shift came in. "Better? Would you like something now to help you sleep."

Not wishing to go to bed like when she was a child, too many things fresh and wondrous to still discover, Mary shook her head. "No, could you help me back out to the patio?"

Soon we'll all sleep forever, young woman.

"The night heavens are glorious," said the nurse.

When the nurse returned to check on her later, Mary was still outside, unmoving, her face pale. Panicked, the nurse checked her vital signs—they were normal—and paged Sheraton, who arrived shortly afterward to confirm that Mary was okay.

"She really wanted me to take her outside," said the shaken nurse.

"I'm glad you called me. I put her in this medicated sleep that she really needs."

"But her skin color!"

"That's her natural skin color. She just looks even whiter under the moonlight."

CHAPTER FIFTEEN

In Pandolf, California, June 2030, George's freshman year in high school was ending. He clicked open a surprise invitation to Carrie Mather's graduation festivities. Euphoric, he blurted to his father on a video call, "Her party is not just for seniors like her. She asked the entire *52ⁿᵈ Street* cast and crew, even freshmen like me."

On the screen, Garcia nodded. "Good job."

News about the party swept through social media. Pictures showed a banquet room on the top floor of Pandolf's tallest building with sweeping views of the California countryside, promising a live band, dancing, and a photo station.

George gushed to Michaela and Charlie. "What an amazing lead Carrie was. I think we'll be seeing her on screens all over the world in the future. And she's so generous to invite a freshman like me! But now I need a suit. The only one I have is the one I got in Chicago for one of my uncle's art openings two years ago." He laughed self-consciously. "My arms and legs poke out of it now."

The threesome visited the local thrift shop, where the wealthy at Pandolf left great finds. George tried on a dark blue Italian suit with a burgundy blazer.

"Mom can tailor it for you," offered Michaela.

At her small apartment, her mother measured George for the alterations, snapping her measuring tape up and down and all around, humming an old song, "Thrift Shop." George knew the lyrics and sang along. Then he said to Charlie, "Hey, man, why so quiet?"

Charlie wore with flair a purple, green, and yellow beret from the same shop. "Honestly, I've never been inside a place that sells 'gently used' stuff before." As he waited, he walked around the room—his first visit to Michaela's apartment—and stopped to look at photos on the refrigerator door. "Michaela, look at this class photo of you in first grade—and the names, so many of these kids are still with us."

"Did Carrie Mather go to the same grade school, too?" asked George. Michaela's face flickered with annoyance.

"Yes, she did," said Michaela's mother, Alicia, when Michaela did not answer. "Remember that summer camp Carrie invited you to?"

"That I hated, except for the sailboats and horses."

"When you told me how miserable you were, I did offer to bring you home early. But no—"

"Because I didn't want you to have to take time off work. My mom takes all the freebie crumbs the rich condescend to give us."

"You gotta take the good with the bad," said Alicia patiently. "Now, you love rock climbing. You first learned how to do it at that camp. And when I'm done with this suit, it'll look like George paid thousands for it."

Friday night, one day before Carrie's party, the trio stayed up late. Videos streamed on the boys' apartment's living room screen. Accompanied by their boisterous laughter, a speaker blared the sly pop hit, Shebubu's "BrikeItUp," then an oldie, Britney Spears's "Toxic," and finally a record player dolefully sang Led Zeppelin's "Stairway to Heaven."

Papers and packaging, an empty pizza box, and single socks lay on the floor. A trash can overflowed. As midnight approached, Michaela dozed barefoot on the couch. Charlie interrupted the playlist and turned up the volume.

"Thrift Shop" soon blared: "What, what, what . . ." Charlie danced with George merrily around the room, hopping over and around the clutter on the floor.

The door swung open. In green scrubs, Sharma entered, half-awake but furious. She raised her voice above the music.

"It's midnight. The neighbor will complain again. And Marla's coming in a few hours. I don't want to hear complaints about how you can't find anything after she's done cleaning. Mr. Campbell gave her complete authority to keep up this place. I'm sure she wants her bonus."

With two clattering buckets, Marla's prompt arrival at 11 a.m. every Saturday morning was a nuisance that woke them up. She was only five feet tall and had even once threatened Charlie's Genie talking-phone with her broom.

Sharma tapped Michaela firmly on the shoulder. She sprang up, only half-awake, then laced her boots and followed Sharma out of the apartment. Charlie scooted after them. "I'll be back. I want to make sure Michaela gets home okay."

Alone now, George drew on the trackpad of his laptop to go down a solitary path he took on Friday nights that led to a travel website. His father greeted him on the screen with a message in Spanish that translated: "George, you can visit over the summer. Talk soon, same time this Sunday. Enjoy your party! Love, Dad."

Then Garcia's image faded from the DelightDoor home page that now asked for a login—that George did not have—drawing open its purple curtains with pictures of gold suns to a view of the foot of a red stairway with gold ropes. He closed his laptop.

A few days ago, he had told Sharma that he did not want to return to Chicago. He was sitting on the old couch in her apartment. She folded laundry on the table.

"Why?" she asked.

"It's a long story."

"You're not that old. And I've a lot of laundry to fold."

He explained. Seven years ago, his aunt, AnnaMaria, "Dad's half sister, she's much younger," had been living with her mother, his grandmother, in Paris. When George's mother passed away when he was eight, he moved to Paris to be with his grandmother and aunt.

The next year, after a stint as another American in Paris, the artist Max Herman returned to the United States with AnnaMaria as his new wife. At the time, she was twenty-one. Eighteen years older than her, Herman had been married before with a son in New York City.

After he turned thirteen, George followed them to Chicago to live in one of the "distant, dreary suburbs," homes and strip malls that sprawled away from Lake Michigan into endless farmland—corn rows and soybeans in Illinois. "Boring after Paris, and the school was awful."

"My father came to the US young, too," said Sharma thoughtfully. "What was it like when you first came?"

He stroked the cat, picturing the young boy who had arrived in Chicago over two years ago, when he first met Uncle Max at O'Hare Airport. His uncle held up a sign that said "Jorge Garcia," and then tried to speak Spanish during the car ride home. George found his uncle's accent terrible but politely went along.

Sharma smiled. "Maybe he was trying to connect with you?"

"Yes," George said, uncertain if that was true, watching her stack precisely folded towels. Then he pressed on with his tale, translated from Argentine Spanish, Spanglish, and French—memories already uncertain narrators, filtering out the raw bits, the chaff, the ugly with that neural network programmed in his brain that any immigrant knows, always evolving and improving—into an acceptable American English version for her.

• • •

In the car, Uncle Max had switched back to American English. "It's too late for you to start school this semester. Still, you came at a good time. Spring in Chicago is a special season after the long winter. For an artist like me, it's a magical time, a storybook beginning—crystal sunlight, colorful flower blossoms, cool breeze . . ."

Uncle Max gestured with his hands, both now off the steering wheel. His tall frame leaned forward, foot pushing the accelerator hard as they sped down the left lane. Even the self-driving vehicle seemed to vibrate with excitement as he went on to describe his persistent sense of "myopia as an artist," how he saw his paintings as "lenses into the greater world" or "ideas to share with others that he could not shape any other way."

They parked under a tall building that his aunt and uncle lived in, then entered a dingy elevator to their floor. Inside the apartment, on the table in the entry hall, a jumbled bouquet of purple and white flowers lay next to a red book, face down with a cracking spine, and a face-up hand mirror. An artist's canvas was stretched out next to the table, showing a partly finished painting of the arrangement, where the mirror reflected his aunt's sunny face and her sea-green eyes.

"I gave your aunt those flowers," said his uncle, his round face briefly reflected in the mirror. "That book's her journal. I guess she ate the grapes." He tapped his head. "Doesn't matter, the image is in here."

Outside, George heard distant voices on the main street, high notes above the muted hum of dawn traffic. Uncle Max drew open the thin curtain of the small window.

"More veils," said his uncle, pointing to the morning clouds and the cold drizzle they had just walked through. "They'll part soon for sunshine."

Through the window, George saw a twin building with many windows, many with closed blinds. Behind them, other people had stories as jumbled as the one that had led him there today. Beyond, thousands of miles away in his beloved Paris, he imagined the Eiffel Tower.

When he had first arrived in France, a vivacious AnnaMaria had taken him to a traveling circus, with trapeze artists in wild costumes and a music show. He remembered her face, a young woman's, framed by long, brown hair. Then and now in Chicago, he smelled her fragrance. Then he heard her light step.

But the fairy smoke dissolved when he saw her. Restrained, older, makeup weighted her eyes. Her lipstick was unnatural. He remembered his grandmother saying how she liked older men because "her father left us when she was young."

"George, welcome!" she said in accented English. "I'm sorry I couldn't come to the airport with Max. I don't drive in Chicago traffic"—she shuddered—"and had to wait here in the apartment for our new dryer to be delivered."

They went into the small kitchen, where AnnaMaria emptied a package of buttery croissants onto a plate. "These are all for you, George, still warm." Then she poured chocolate milk. "I remembered how much you like this. Also, the orange juice is freshly squeezed, just like in Paris."

"Thanks," said George, sitting down after washing his hands and wiping them on a Louvre gift shop hand towel.

AnnaMaria poured her husband hot coffee. Still standing, he watered it down with crushed ice from the fridge door and quickly gulped it down. "Love the smell of fresh brew, your aunt was so right about getting a burr grinder." He turned to his nephew and added, "George, I have an important meeting. Business first. To be successful, a man must take practical steps. Or I'll become another artist whose big dreams die little deaths."

His expression grew pained. AnnaMaria looked earnest, his pupil-muse, her eyes growing dark. George focused on his flaky croissants, slathering them with butter.

Uncle Max then ran about the apartment, collecting his things to leave. Finally draining his coffee, he opened an email on his phone and read it aloud. "The new gallery accepted two of my paintings." His bristly brows drew together in anger. "Nick just sent this, no mention about where they will hang . . . or why the others weren't accepted? Yes, I *am* going to your office to discuss this further, personally. I want my painting of Callie framed by the cubic angles in the back room with the low ceiling. You remember?" He turned to AnnaMaria. "And I want you—you, tall blossom of auburn hair—greeting my audience in the entry hall, next to the grand window, high, high, high, overlooking Chicago."

He raised his hands dramatically above his head. "Have to scheme my way around that exclusive contract. What would Nick do anyway if I broke our deal? I'm going to ask him who else is showing at the opening." He pulled his black cap down over his ears, retrieved his wet umbrella, and abruptly stormed out.

"Jorge." His aunt now approached him, speaking Spanish, slender arms extended. He got up. She squeezed him in a teary, too-tight, too-long hug.

Then she poured herself some coffee. "Nick's your uncle's agent. They're always fighting. This is not hot anymore. Do you want some? I can warm it up in the microwave."

"Do you have eggs?"

"Of course. How many? I know, sunny-side up. And I bought lots of ketchup for you. Your father told me to—"

He cut her off. He didn't want her getting "all emotional" about his father. "Four. Here, I left you a couple of croissants."

Hesitating, AnnaMaria tore a strip off one croissant and ate it, then uncoiled one more, and soon, strip after strip, she ate the whole thing, while she fried his eggs.

"Do you want that last croissant?" she asked.

"No, I'm waiting for my eggs."

She slid the eggs onto his plate. Then he watched her crush the last croissant into the trash can so she would not be tempted to eat it later. *What a shame.* He could have eaten it later. That's what his grandmother did in Paris, throw away perfectly good food, saying, "You should eat things fresh."

AnnaMaria then settled him into the postage-stamp-size guest room. There was a new comforter on the bed, on which lay a pamphlet about a summer school sailing camp on Lake Michigan.

"Should I sign you up?" she asked. "They have a scholarship package."

He tensed, feeling offended that anyone might think him somehow below them. "I wouldn't fit in."

"You'll fit just fine into a sailboat," she said crisply. "Anyway, shall we go for a walk so I can show you around the neighborhood? And your new school, too?"

Outside, the sun smiled just as Uncle Max had promised, driving away the swampy waters of his misgivings. On the sidewalk, two children walked ahead, their calves plump, clothes fresh and clean. Backpacks hung over their left shoulders in an unconscious symmetry. Memories of his childhood, morning freshness, excitement about new adventure, now ignited his mood. He danced a few steps down the sidewalk and then abashedly looked back at his smiling aunt.

"Jorge, those kids who just walked by, their mom is Callie, a model for your uncle. His painting of her will be in that exhibit."

"The woman with them didn't look like she was related to them."

"That was their nanny, not Callie."

"By the way, when we talk in English, like around Uncle Max, please call me George."

"Sure, why?"

"That's the English translation of my name."

"I'll try. Don't get upset if I sometimes get mixed up."

• • •

His aunt and uncle took him to the opening at the art gallery. For that, AnnaMaria bought George a suit.

His uncle said to his aunt, "I think this is an adult event, not really for kids George's age."

"George will enjoy it," she insisted. "He listens to us talking about your art world day in and out. It helps it to come alive for him."

His uncle looked at him kindly. "George, you'll meet a Michael Kochanski, a real character. Listen for his Polish accent. He owns the Pierre building with this new art gallery on the top floor. It's just a few small rooms, but they are prized for their location—the Gold Coast—and the great views."

Uncle Max then talked about a Mr. Jim Sichet, a lawyer who was a "business enemy" of Mr. Kochanski. His uncle's details of their rivalry—properties and dollar numbers—bored his aunt, except for the part where Mr. Sichet had bought his uncle's painting of Callie, a subject about which she was always pressing him for "any new news?"

George found anything connected with the Callie painting intriguing. Before it was shipped for the exhibition, he peeked under the drape over it. *What secrets hid in the delicate shadows, painted on and around her face, her shoulders, her body?* He held his fingertips close enough to the surface of the canvas to feel the electricity, inner voice warning him to not touch, to seek answers instead with his eyes. He never even dared to unveil it fully.

Then, in the car, riding to the opening on Lake Shore Drive, the Gold Coast of Chicago, he was disappointed. *No gold.* His aunt looked ethereally beautiful with mature grace, no longer the carefree and playful Paris teenager he remembered. Her hair was mirror smooth and freshly styled. Her peach dress was "one of the latest designs." They arrived punctually and displayed their invitation to the guard, who looked skeptically at George but did not turn him away.

In the gallery, George beelined to the painting of Callie to see it fully for the first time. There she stood in the bright light, bold eyes, brilliant smile, a nude in light and shadow, legs discreetly angled away from the viewer in a twist of modesty. Behind her, the energetic background synchronized colors and patterns. Inside, he felt a thrill, his future calling, heroic adventures and glorious fame. Below, he glanced at the name of the painting: *Figurehead.* Self-consciously, he quickly walked away. What did that name mean? *Like a figurehead on a ship?*

Wandering around, checking out the other exhibits, he watched as his aunt and uncle worked the crowd, excitedly talking to many people. As it turned out, George was the only person of his age there. He made many trips to the tables laden with food and tried to be discreet about sampling everything, from avocado toast to strawberry cheesecake. For entertainment, he watched the adults return again and again to the carafes of wine, which never seemed to empty, growing louder, happier, and more flushed as the evening went by.

Soon, AnnaMaria found him next to the "Sweets and Treats" sign.

"What do you think about some of the art here?"

"Pretty cool," said George, turning his head toward a bank of corner windows. "And those views are awesome." The windows looked out to tall buildings, the Chicago River, and Lake Michigan to the east.

"Which one is your favorite?"

"Oh, the chocolate brownies, for sure."

Her Paris giggle, which he hadn't heard since his arrival, tickled him. "I was asking about your favorite art piece. Maybe Max was right about there being no one else your age to hang out with."

"It's okay."

He decided to go watch Uncle Max in action. His uncle stayed close to his two paintings, smoothly answering questions and interjecting jokes. Discreetly, he looked at the Callie painting, to memorize her curves, her colors, and how she made him feel, like a teenage runaway on a spaceship to find fortune in his future.

The portrait of AnnaMaria also received an enthusiastic reception. Uncle Max said he was hoping for positive media attention in the next few weeks, then looked surprised as a well-dressed couple in their forties approached him.

"Who's this young visitor?" asked the tall, balding, tuxedoed man, looking curiously at George.

"This is my nephew," said Uncle Max. "George just arrived from Paris. George, this is Mr. and Mrs. Sichet. Wow, Jim, Michael invited you?"

"I'm not crashing his party," said the man. "Michael's my competition, so of course he's showing off his new art gallery to me."

Sichet bent his head close to the painting of Callie. "I'm going to hang this in the lobby of our office building."

George noticed the slightest grimace on his wife's face.

"Thank you, Jim," said his uncle. "My agent is around here somewhere."

Sichet smiled. "I've already transferred the funds, or Nick would charge me an exorbitant interest rate." He then nodded to AnnaMaria with approval. "Is this your wife?"

Uncle Max looked flustered. "Of course, this is indeed my wife, AnnaMaria. I'm sorry. I thought you had met."

AnnaMaria smiled brightly at Sichet. "You meet so many people, Jim."

"You're more beautiful in person than in your husband's picture. And my wife would love to hear more about what it's like to be married to Max," said Sichet.

Deliberately starting to move away as his uncle followed obsequiously, Mr. Sichet said, "Tell me, Max, I need your advice. You remember how I do a little painting myself—a hobby. I'm also interested in having a portrait done of the family . . ." The two men kept walking away.

Left behind, AnnaMaria commented lightly to Mrs. Sichet about life with Uncle Max. But the other woman gave terse responses. Feeling helpless and angry, George watched his aunt, the wife of a poor artist, for whom English was not even her native language, speaking with her thick accent to this stylish lady whose husband did not even remember who she was.

Later that evening, George saw Mrs. Sichet again, martini in hand, next to the food table, chatting away with a group of women who looked old and fancy, like her. Mrs. Sichet's step was uncertain, but her smile was one of the widest he saw that evening.

Smiles like that happened often at his grandmother's apartment in Paris, where flushed women attended her wine get-togethers. Spanish growing louder, he would hear his grandmother and her circle of expatriates in the kitchen as he silently ate dinner in his room.

His grandmother once complained to her friends, "AnnaMaria says she does not sing anymore, except to her husband. That voice of hers was made for the stage. What a loss, like some caged songbird trapped exclusively for Mr. Max Herman's pleasure, that's what my daughter has become."

Another time, he heard her sounding angry. "Her husband tells my daughter he doesn't want children. AnnaMaria, she says to me, 'Even those days I feel so empty without Max, and the day's blackness lies before me until he gets home, I love him, Mom. There is no need to fill that void with children.'"

Then his grandmother grumbled, "I think he just likes her girlish shape and her intelligence to be solely devoted to him."

Before he left Paris, his grandmother sat George down for one of her "serious" conversations. "Someday, your aunt will regret not having kids. Maybe you can say something to her? Still, Max is not much of a father to his son in New York City—that boy, what's his name?"

I'm just a kid. Why would I tell her something like that? he had thought.

After the exhibit, George sat in the back seat as his uncle and aunt drove home. AnnaMaria murmured, "I feel sad for Frances Sichet. An empty marriage like that. Her husband would be shameless to put Callie's portrait in the lobby of a corporate building!"

Uncle Max laughed. "Jim's shameless, alright—as a liar. He won't. He was just making a dig at Frances. Don't feel sorry for her. I'm sure their marriage was a good transaction for both of them." Silence followed.

That happened a lot with Uncle Max and his aunt, the way they stopped discussing some topics whenever he was there.

• • •

George had plenty of time to be bored in Chicago. "Homework took minutes," he told Sharma, "mostly clicking this and that. I already knew the math and science that they were teaching."

He said he had been teased and bullied. "But everything was better after I reported them," he added.

"You 'reported' the bullies?" asked Sharma.

"The school has 'policies' against bullying." He smiled. "You could say I 'refreshed' the school administration's memory."

He had made no friends, and had sat alone at lunch in the cafeteria, eating the same grilled cheese sandwich and barbecue chips daily.

He added that he didn't even drink the water at school, which tasted bad—"I wasn't even sure it was safe."

In English class, he had an assignment to perform poetry. He memorized a poem by William Blake that his aunt AnnaMaria had admired. In front of the class, he recited:

Tiger, tiger, burning bright,
In the forests of the night,
What immortal hand or eye
Could frame thy fearful symmetry?
. . .

Proudly, he had finished. He had recorded himself at home, practicing it to remove any Spanish accent in his American English. At the parent–teacher conference, the teacher told his aunt afterward, "This is eighth grade. That piece is just not a good fit for his age."

"I'm sorry to have suggested that poem, Jorge," AnnaMaria told him afterwards. "Your teacher recommended this contemporary poet instead."

He looked the name up on his phone. "Stupid, puerile stuff," he said in English.

"Okay, I don't know what 'poo-rile' means, but I can only guess from how you say it."

Sharma laughed. "What an awful school. I'm sorry about how that English teacher treated you. Let me think about what I can do to help you stay at Pandolf."

"Things have turned out so differently here," he said. There was Sharma, Lucky, Charlie, and Michaela, his "peeps." Even Carrie Mather had invited him to her party. He remembered the proud expression on his father's face when he had told him.

• • •

On Saturday, the day of the party, Michaela came over to bring him the pants her mother had taken in at the waist.

"George, what's bothering you?" Michaela asked. "You were so happy yesterday, going on and on about Carrie's party."

"I heard from my dad last night. He's fine, he's now in Saburia. But I'm worried again. With him, things change so quickly. What if I have to return to Chicago to live with my aunt and uncle? I don't want to leave Pandolf."

"Oh, George, we'll figure something out. It doesn't make sense for you to be anxious about things that haven't happened yet."

"Still, I've been thinking—"

"'Dangerous thing' that triggers audits in A'50"

"Okay, stop quoting General DeFut"—an A'50 game character—"and listen. Our lease here is month to month, and Mr. Campbell said he could only renew it through the end of summer school, July. I'll need to move someplace after that."

"You could move into a different apartment on campus."

"But Dad said he wasn't sure who would sign for it. I need an adult," he said.

"Sorry, George, I'm out of ideas." Michaela slumped.

Then she said he looked "fine" in his altered suit, and they took many pictures. George changed back into jeans, and they shared a bag of potato chips, sitting on the couch.

"I want to see more pictures of you this evening," she said. "Have fun. Charlie and I are going to watch a movie." She blinked away tears. "I can't believe Charlie's going home so soon, and you could also be leaving."

Their band was breaking up. Charlie's parents were putting him in a new private school in Maine in the fall.

"But you know," she added, "Charlie and I talk a lot about this. We're both very young. We can't get too serious with each other."

"That sounds like your mom talking," said George.

"Um-hum, she reminds me I'm just finishing ninth grade." Michaela put her head on his shoulder and smiled up at him.

He smiled back. "You remind me of my aunt sometimes," he said. "She used to laugh like you. I'm sorry Dr. Sharma sent you out of our place like that yesterday, so early in the morning."

"Yeah, I felt so embarrassed."

"Maybe it's practical for adults, you know, to keep their expectations of us low."

"My mom's not at all like that."

"I'll talk to Dr. Sharma. You don't vape, smoke, drink, do drugs. And you're a good student." "But not everyone's like that at our school," Michaela whispered. "Were you invited to Carrie Mather's after-party?"

"No. Didn't know there was one."

"I'm sure that will be something—Carrie staggering around her parents' pool, and that'll be just be the beginning . . ."

George pulled away angrily. "That's gossip. You don't like Carrie because she's one of the popular girls."

"I don't like her because I've known her forever. I grew up with her. She's mean. But you can't see that because you're new here . . . and a guy."

Charlie entered the room. "Okay, peeps, stop squabbling. I have Mr. Campbell here on my phone calling from the coast of the Red Sea."

"Hey!" Campbell was now projected on the wall screen.

"Hi!" they said in unison. "How's the beach?"

"Hot, hot, hot. You'll see soon, George. I'm trying to line up plane tickets for you to come visit. But your father and I had an idea. How would you and Charlie like to meet up with me in Athens and spend a few days there first?"

"Wow!" said Charlie.

"Athens, the Parthenon, I'd love to see it for real," said George. "Dad can't come?"

"Sorry, George, not this time, he just got here and is still ramping up at the lab. Did they teach you about Athens in school?"

Disappointed that his father would not come to Athens, George replied after a silence, "No, Athens is in one of the games we play, *A'50*."

"What about me?" interrupted Michaela.

Campbell shook his head on the screen. "Michaela, I'm very sorry, you're too young. I can't be responsible for you."

"You're saying that because I'm a girl. That's not fair." She folded her arms. "Besides, the travel would probably be too expensive for me anyway."

"Mr. Campbell, are you sure we can't figure out a way Michaela can come?" said Charlie. "Her mom could sign a waiver. I could loan her money."

"For girls, things are different," said Campbell. "And the rest of the world is not the United States. Michaela, you would need a woman chaperone because I couldn't go with you everywhere. I couldn't even leave you alone in a hotel room. I can't fix the world."

"She *is* pretty," said Charlie.

"That's not what I meant," said Campbell.

Michaela said nothing, her face contorted into a picture of fury.

Charlie changed the subject. "Hey, I have some news. Lucky is now engaged to Harry!"

The screen dissolved into static.

"Are we disconnected?" asked Charlie.

Campbell reappeared. "Please give the happy couple my congratulations. Charlie, check with your parents about Athens, and if it's a go, I can talk to them and book tickets. I've to jump off now."

George heard the catch in Campbell's voice. *Man, that news just broke your heart. Just like Carrie is impossible in my life.*

While Michaela was probably correct about Carrie, George didn't like Carrie any less for it. He, too, wanted to have awesome parties, if not mind-altering experiences and a chic girlfriend like Carrie Mather.

Fact was that he wasn't sure he could travel abroad. At a group meeting he attended for noncitizen students at Pandolf, the speaker had warned, "Check with your counselor before traveling abroad. Want to make sure you can return, right, guys?"

In a video call, he had asked his father about traveling outside the USA to see him. Garcia had frowned. "Jorge, you won't leave the United States until I make sure you can return. I promise. Truly I promise."

Charlie had his arm around Michaela, trying to cheer her up. Looking at them, George knew they wouldn't understand. They were American citizens. His father could lose this job and move on again. Every time he saw his father now after another long absence, he looked older and smaller, with more idiosyncrasies and flaws, like his receding hairline.

What if his father was mistaken and he would never again return to the United States, to Pandolf, to this place that felt now like home?

Michaela was looking at him. "You look so sad. Let me talk to my mom to see if you can stay with my mom and me after your lease is up in July. Now, go change back into the suit and let Charlie also see how you look. Mom's so excited about you being invited to Carrie's 'grand' party."

He turned up the music on his Ear Dots before walking to his room. A message pinged.

"Yes," said George to the Dot, starting a podcast about teenage homeless programs. George had not told anyone yet about his other plan—if all else were to fail—to run away. First, as with any project that he undertook, he had to finish his research.

CHAPTER SIXTEEN

Before leaving Saburia, Kochanski popped into Garcia's lab to say goodbye. "Just you and Elise left here now. And of course, Bhattacharya. I'm leaving you in good hands."

Before Kochanski left, Garcia said, "Thanks for David bringing George to come visit me. The lawyer says she's working out George's visa issues."

Later, Kochanski rode inside a brand-new armored Humvee to Ramses International Airport to catch his return flight to Chicago. Security had been upgraded recently after Somalian pirates attempted a kidnapping near the beach.

The teenage driver proudly demonstrated features of the vehicle to the other young troops. English words like *transmission* popped up. The AC was off. With automatic rifles poking through the roof opening, they lit forbidden cigarettes and played local music.

Before Kochanski had left the base, the Saburian Chief IT officer had told him, "Your scientist's son goes online looking into running away."

"Georgie Porgie, pudding and pie." Kochanski laughed. "Meaning that kid likes to eat. For that, running away would be a dumb move."

Then Kochanski turned serious. "We can't let Dr. Garcia have distractions from work. I'll take care of his son when I get to the States. June, school's out, fine time for young men to make trouble, no?"

Unsmiling, the officer swiveled and left. To the closed door, Kochanski muttered, "Come back next time with a sense of humor."

In the Humvee, the engine roared as they picked up speed. Seeing his longing look—trying to quit smoking *again*—the soldiers passed him a cigarette. He inhaled gratefully. Fingers no longer fidgeting, he ran through cash flow numbers mentally. His next loan repayment was due for the Pierre building, the cornerstone of his future business empire. But even with the money stream from the king—including a loan—the Pierre's mortgage was going underwater.

Luck seemed to come whenever he prayed. He joined his fingers together and reminded God that he had named his property after Saint Peter, even dedicated its chapel to his mother, all his way of thanking the Father for helping someone as broken as him.

"Remember, dear God, how that 'highly recommended' Chicago architect had been skeptical?" he murmured. "He told me, 'A chapel in a commercial building . . . hmm, I don't know.' I still built it, Father. That architect had no sense of humor, either, when I asked him why it was okay the other way around, having commerce in religious buildings. Now that's been going on forever, and no one has a problem with that."

The Humvee sped faster and louder, over bumps and around corners. The young soldiers laughed with delight. A young woman, draped in black despite the heat, was walking alone on the side of the road, and they swerved off the road to get close to her. He heard her cry out, and the rough laughs of the young men. He grabbed the handle on his side door to regain his balance. *Dear God.*

He joined his fingers together again, thanked God when the vehicle kept moving. How old had these kids been when they were recruited? Certainly older than twelve, which was when he had joined the local gang in Poland. Where was the exit door from this heavy burden of life, if not death?

In a deep funk, he boarded the Drukker plane. Then, after all his drinks onboard, he landed in Chicago in a blur, and during the car ride fell asleep in the back seat, missing his usual exhilaration at seeing the skyline fronting Lake Michigan.

After thanking the driver—*What accent was that?*—and giving him a generous 100 percent tip for bringing his suitcase up the elevator to his door, he passed out on the living room couch of his condo. A headache woke him up in the afternoon. He changed out of his suit, swallowed Tylenol and antacids, and picked up his phone.

"Fresh-squeezed orange juice, three, please. And my usual order, god, I missed it."

"Thank you, your service provider will arrive in thirty minutes," said the AI voice answering the phone. "We will bake your deep-dish pizza with all your special toppings in our mobile wood-fired oven now."

After his meal, he showered and unwrapped another suit to wear to walk outside. The summer light was now dimming for the evening. Swift winds blew off Lake Michigan and rushed down the streets between the skyscrapers.

Escaping their rough howl, Kochanski stepped into the Pierre. While his current condo's address was respectable, someday, he wished he could afford to live here, in his own property. Oscar Sanchez used to live here, in a basement room, with just a fridge and microwave, using the toilet on the main floor and the shower in a nearby homeless shelter. Oscar understood the building's policies, the Disney model of separating staff and customers that Kochanski applied to everyone who worked at the Pierre, including himself.

He headed to the chapel, now locked, so no chance of running into any customers of his building. Thanks to the sound engineer, it was quiet inside the sanctuary, just a little color from the sunset seeping through stained-glass windows. Shadows grew longer.

More time needed to pass before his hangover and jet lag could abate. He pulled a cushion under his head and fell asleep in a pew, hands folded in prayer.

When he awoke hours later, he wasn't alone. Streetlights through a window illuminated a gentle smile on a round face. He looked into the bluest eyes he knew.

Not an angel who wafted in. How did the fixer find me?

"Jim!" Kochanski sat up, staring at Jim Sichet.

"Hello, Michael." Sichet sat down next to him. "I've been waiting for you to wake up. Did you know you snore?"

"Well, what do you want? How did you get a staff key card?"

"I want to help you. Your money troubles aren't a big secret."

"What do you know?"

"What do I know? How do I get a key card? Philosophically, those are meaningless questions, but practically, I know that this building is having cash flow problems. Isn't that why you came back?"

"Jim, you're so full of it. But there's something else you do know about." He searched the lawyer's face. *You know about Oscar, how he died?*

Sichet's expression was blank. "I simply know that people are waiting for this building to go underwater and the fire sale to buy it."

Underwater like how Oscar drowned?

Kochanski raised his voice indignantly. "So, a client shared confidential information with you about my building?"

Sichet looked around. "That's one guess. Knowledge is power, Michael. Identity theft is passé. Perps can't hide anymore . . ."

So, you know that Oscar had a fake ID when he went to bribe the judge.

"Like if I were to see a therapist," Sichet continued, "I wouldn't pick one who sends electronic notes flying up into the Cloud for everyone to see."

No more therapists for me.

Sichet leaned toward him. "I can help you. You have a lovely daughter. She has a great life in London. You don't want her to default on her condo. She worries about that on her blog."

"Katya has a blog?"

"Yes, she wants to be a writer, she says in her 'About Me' section. And getting a degree in Russian literature will help. Unpronounceable names for characters make surefire bestsellers."

Sichet's eyes were sparkling, delighted with his own wit.

"My daughter's not practical," Kochanski agreed. "But kids outgrow our advice like their shoes."

In the chapel, the streetlights fell through the stained glass, just like in the old Warsaw church that his mother used to attend. At services there, still a child, Kasia had kicked up her tan boots, worn over faded leggings that had had mud and dog hair washed out dozens of times. He was so proud of her designer shoes that he had spent all his savings on, only worn at church with her favorite skirt. When the skirt's hem frayed, his mother sewed on a gauze edge. But the shoes still looked new when Kasia outgrew them, and they went into the church donation box.

"My kids don't ask me for advice, either," said Sichet. "But maybe you give Katya more choices than I do mine. Being creative in a conformist world is a good way to be poor. Still, she could find a sugar daddy if you can't support her."

Kochanski drew his knees together. He could not breathe. *You insult my daughter. Keep Kasia in the light.* Now he was the older boy in the story Kasia had told him, who protected children from falling off a cliff while they played in a field of tall American corn. *No*, he remembered, *I'm a catcher in the rye.*

"What do you want, Jim?"

"A little preface. I'm not a religious man." Sichet waved his hand around the sanctuary. "But I am aligned with a certain philosophy, that our world will come to an apocalyptic end. No, not like in the movies, burned to a nuclear crisp or frozen solid. That would be too easy. Catastrophic things can happen. An asteroid ended the dinosaur age. The oceans might avenge themselves on us. A tsunami of plastic and petroleum waste can chase us up our hills of landfill. But I think slow environmental change is more likely. Humanity will be one of the last to die after most other life has gone extinct—except for the cockroaches—and good riddance to most of us. If we're lucky, some of us will survive and will need leaders to rebuild our society, hopefully a better one with fewer people. Michael, this planet needs less than 0.1 percent of its current human population and a better balance with nature."

"What do you want?" he repeated.

"I'm going to tell you something the Saburian government has given me permission to. They are a client of my law firm. Their king—yes, your king—belongs to an ancient order with beliefs like mine. We connected as kids in boarding school."

"You know the king?" said Kochanski, stunned. "From school?" Then he remembered that Campbell had told him that the king had attended StarHall some years before him.

Game on, thought Kochanski craftily. Even hungover, part of his brain was working fine, his boozy business partner. Sichet did not need to know what he knew from Campbell or from the Saburian IT kid who hacked Sichet's medical records for him—for a little side-action bribe.

"I know about Manny Garcia too," said Sichet. "Were you drunk when you gave Garcia's identity to that poor kid to do your dirty work? That was a serious interruption of the king's plans. Glad to see that judge in jail. And good thing that Talwar took care of Garcia's release. Soria Clinics is paying Garcia's legal bills, right? And you're taking the credit."

Kochanski looked away, so Sichet could not see how guilty he felt. "I only gave Oscar Garcia's identity for that one job. Everything's worked out for the king. Garcia is now in Saburia."

"Fair enough. Now all *you* need to do is make sure Garcia's kid is okay. Because we don't want our brilliant scientist to have to worry about anything else besides his projects in Saburia. So, here's my generous proposal. I'll help you with your bank loan for this building. I'll have someone—she's the best—step in to run the place instead of you. Why should you have to worry anymore about the Pierre's day-to-day business? Beth will double the income from your property, and you'll have more free time for work–life balance."

"I'm interested, Jim." *Could Sichet mean money laundering?* What did he know about the FBI operation, Loop Laundromat, that had caught the judge?

Sichet rose to leave. "Do you need a ride? Have you thought about AA? You look groggy. Grog is what sailors called rum diluted with water."

"That's my business. I'll walk home, thanks. What should I do about my meeting with the bank tomorrow morning?"

"Cancel it. Beth's your woman now. She'll talk to them."

"I haven't said 'yes.'"

"Your other choice is that the bank will foreclose. Fine, before you agree on anything, I'll send my proposal to Talwar."

"Yes,."

"She's a good lawyer. I offered her a job once. But she turned me down. Sad."

Sichet raised one palm skyward. "One thing they don't make more of is land. On our overcrowded planet, you can only go up, up, up . . ."

Flipping his palm down, he added, "Or down. Someone once said that the tallest trees have the deepest roots. Or you can go off-site—meaning space travel." Sichet's blue eyes glittered.

"Well," said Kochanski dismissively, "I better get going."

"Okay, how about dinner one of these days? I'll text you. Too bad there's no restaurant on your property. What a location it could be for a Chicago watering hole. We have all the animals."

Without waiting for a reply, Sichet sped ahead down the aisle to the red exit sign.

Kochanski lumbered after him but stopped at the top of the chapel aisle and turned around to pray some more. *Dear God, forgive me about Oscar . . . and if I'm just selling out again.*

He returned home using shortcuts through city alleys. He left a voice mail with the bank to cancel their meeting, giving them the contact information for Beth that Sichet had texted him. He would let Sichet rescue the loan. He said a grateful prayer. Again, with the Father's help, he still needed Talwar's legal blessing—he had dodged the crushing wheels of financial ruin.

The next morning, well-rested, enjoying a late breakfast in bed, Kochanski opened an email from Talwar about the "particulars of your new contract."

"You know what I always ask," she wrote. "Think about how much you want to push back."

"It's fine. I'm done," he emailed back.

Another email from Campbell detailed his job offer to be "CTO at Drukker headquarters":

Chief tech officer. Michael, I'm a-going home! Helped they knew me through my work for you. I am Docking, meaning Drukker HQ. Drukker is now solidly under the umbrella of Zoser, a stable parent company with leadership that aligns with my values. The people I work for will care about not just my physical but also moral injury.

Then the traveling is too much. Now, I'll commute between my home in Texas, where Zoser's headquarters is, and the Dock in San Francisco. International travel will only be to places where I don't have to worry about the safety of the food, the water, my person, or my conscience.

Saburia's a beautiful country, there'll never be anything like watching the sun rise on the Red Sea coast doing surya yoga. Someday I'll come again, a tourist with the wife and kids. But no worries, I'll finish our job—escort George to visit Manny in Saburia, and then return the boy to his relatives in Chicago. Confirm George will reenter the US with no visa issues—kid is worried about that? Did you reach out to Manny's immigration lawyer?

Manny's working 24/7, as you know, no time for anything social. A second treatment for Mary couldn't happen on this trip, sadly, because she needed dialysis. And became quite depressed. But her spirits are Texan. :) She's already back in New York but hopefully will come back soon for round two.

I can see you in Chicago during my layover to SF to sign my contract. For that Drukker wants to talk to me in person about their

*intellectual property, keys to their kingdom. Then I must go to
my ranch in Texas, then to Dallas to Athens to meet the kids. NO,
I am NOT a babysitter, can't meet them in SF to go to Athens with
them.*

*No hard feelings. I'm done with being an independent consultant.
Runner, babysitter, middleman is more like it lately, not using my
talents and training.*

Best, David

Kochanski clicked "REPLY": "David, congratulations!! I always support the success of the people I work with. Glad we are thinking about George's status. Disrupting so young a life . . ."

He stopped typing. No messy confession to Campbell about young lives disrupted, Oscar's or his own; he deleted the last part.

• • •

In Pandolf, inside George's apartment, the Genie announced a call from his father's lawyer. After George spoke with Talwar, he leaped out of bed and ran to the living room to celebrate: Chocolate Cookie cereal in Sharma's largest mixing bowl with marshmallows and rainbow sprinkles plus her organic, grass-fed milk.

Charlie emerged. "Your phone woke me up!" he grumbled.

"Sorry."

"Crunch away. Why so happy? Genie just grant you a wish, Aladdin?"

"My dad's lawyer in Chicago, she just called. She said I can *definitely* return to the US even if I go see Dad in Saburia. So, our trip's on to Athens."

"Great! You were so worried about not being able to come back from abroad."

George then smiled mysteriously. "By the way, Dr. Sharma will need a roommate since your sister's moving out."

"Are you kidding? She offered to take you in? You sure you don't have to go back to Chicago in the fall?"

"Not sure about anything. But wouldn't Dr. Sharma's apartment be convenient? Michaela's place is too small for another person. And yes, I must convince Dad to let me stay at Pandolf. That'll be easier when I see him in person, another reason for me to go, push his guilt button."

"Smart," Charlie said, pulling out his phone to take a photo of George's half-empty cereal bowl. "You just finished all the sprinkles, yes, every single one that Michaela bought for baking cookies."

"No!" George tried unsuccessfully to grab Charlie's phone. "Now she'll be mad at me. You've gotten so fast. Must be all the sports you're in."

After summer school started in July for the three teens, their class in American government meant political discussions that flared late into the night. Their other class, "Financial Management," led to more personal talks, such as when Charlie explained to his friends how trust funds passed wealth through generations in families like his.

"Unbelievable!" said Michaela. "Meaning you never need to work?"

"I plan to work. Life's not just about money."

"You're making Charlie defensive," said George.

"It's just not fair," Michaela said. "Like you guys get to go to Athens, and I can't." She frowned. "We're the worker bees in Pandolf's hive—me, my mom, my granny—generation after generation, making the honey, serving you transients that come through."

"Then there's Carrie," said George. He pulled up pictures on his phone to show them from her graduation party. "Glamour, glitter, glory."

Michaela crossed her arms and turned away. "Drunk, drugged, deranged," she shot back. "Be grateful you weren't invited to her after-party. My mom knows someone who had to clean up the next morning and said it was 'disgusting.'"

"I don't have to go to Athens, Michaela," said Charlie.

"You should." She muttered, "I would."

They ordered burgers online for delivery on George's credit card.

"My PlasticPress expires August 31," said George glumly. "Then I'll be on a monthly budget from Dad."

"Same date our lease got extended to," Charlie observed. "Odd, that?"

"Just the adults coordinating," said George. "We don't need more creative theories. Dad said it has to do with Mr. Campbell going to work for Drukker."

Michaela promptly left at 11 p.m. to avoid another confrontation with Sharma, who was still doing random check-ins. For summer driver's ed class, her mother cheerfully took all three teens for practice with her stick-shift, gas-only, no-AI car. When the battery died, a tire went flat, and the engine light went on, online videos and "cheap car lessons" from Michaela's uncle who used to run a repair shop in Pandolf became another class.

July passed quickly. Summer school ended. The boys packed their boxes. For George, they went into storage until the adults figured out where he would be. For Charlie, they were shipped to Maine. Too soon came the hot August day when Charlie sobbed a final goodbye to a wet-eyed Michaela at San Francisco International Airport.

• • •

At Athens airport, Campbell met the boys outside the secure area. They looked healthy and well, perhaps a little bit more grown, even though it had only been three months.

"You boys look great, almost men," he said, giving them hearty handshakes.

"Cool necklace," said Charlie, noticing the hammered gold chain with two amber beads flanking a Texas-shaped medallion around Campbell's neck.

Looking into Charlie's eyes, Campbell saw Lucky. If only, together just once more, she and he could hop, skip, jump—outside time. He would give her a starry ring to go with the blue skies in her eyes. He splurged on the boys in Athens and hoped Charlie would tell Lucky what a good time he had had.

Their trip to the ancient city finished too soon. Charlie begged, "My parents said I could also go to Saburia with you guys, right, George?"

Campbell shook his head. "That's not what your father told me, Charlie. They say that when a teenager's lips are moving, he's lying."

Fact was, he didn't even want to take George to the Saburian base—twenty-four-seven electronic monitoring, inaudible and unseeable Big Brother, the young soldiers carrying gleaming new weapons and riding the just upgraded military transformer vehicles. He had asked Garcia why Soria was paying to bring George to Saburia; "not a safe place for a kid, I think." Garcia's mumbled response—"I miss him"—was not an adequate explanation, he thought.

After they dropped Charlie off at Athens International to return home, Campbell said to George, "You'll be in Saburia for just three days in a military base. Then you'll move to Chicago."

"I don't want to go to Chicago. Dad knows that, and I'm going to talk to him again."

"Sorry, George, that's not up to me. I can say something to your father to support you. Still, for now, look forward to the Saburian countryside. I've arranged a safari. It's beautiful, wildlife most kids your age might never see. In the night, sounds call to you, far away in space and time. Endless skies, stars strung across . . ."

Far away, wherever Lucky was, Campbell now murmured just to her, " . . . the infinite, eternal lights, like jewels . . . Julia."

On the plane between naps, George ate prodigiously, played games on his phone, and when the Wi-Fi was glitchy, grumbled about Chicago.

"The flight attendant asked me what I wanted," George told a surprised Campbell, who sent a beer back.

In Ramses, the runway's shaded shelter provided little respite from the suffocating August heat as they waited for their long ride to the base. George whispered his indignance to Campbell about the cigarette fumes from the oblivious pilot smoking next to them. Finally, a distant line of dust heralded the arrival of an armored truck. Campbell jumped up to hail it. Then, still wearing hats and sunglasses, their sunscreen washing off with sweat, they boarded with their luggage.

The soldiers looked surly. Less than an hour before reaching the base, Campbell was staring ahead, sitting next to the driver, while George sat behind him with the plane's pilot—who was still smoking. George had his head out of the open side window for clean air and the ocean view on the horizon—when the driver cursed loudly, staring at his rearview mirror and camera screen.

Campbell looked around. Far behind, a dusty line of chaos on the horizon advanced quickly. Their truck sped up, but those behind them closed in. Three desert-colored camouflaged vehicles materialized with mounted guns and armed men. The attackers surrounded them and maneuvered them off the road. In the distance, an armored helicopter approached, not theirs. Their driver stopped, seeing no escape. Campbell turned to look at George, who seemed in shock.

Curse words became the soundtrack to his thoughts: an apocalyptic death brigade like in that online game the boys played. Their truck's brakes screeched. In its wake of dirt, their own Chinese and Saburian soldiers jumped out of the stopping vehicle to surround it, guns pointing outward, acting unafraid. Campbell reached into his backpack for a small bag, engineered to reflect its surroundings and be almost invisible. Grabbing a pad of Pandolf Hotel paper, he wrote, "Dear Elise, from David with love." He shoved the slip of paper into the bag, then his phone, and finally the chain that he broke from around his neck, then zipped the bag shut and threw it onto a mound as far as possible.

The attackers approached them from their trucks, on foot now, dressed in various uniforms. All wore caps and scarves wrapped around their lower faces, and each carried an automatic rifle. Campbell guessed that their leader was a local rebel, but others were likely Somalian from farther south on the coast based on their skin coloring, features, and broken Saburian. He looked over at George, who had pushed up his sunglasses to watch, and told him to drop them back down. "Now you can watch them, George. But they can't see what you're looking at."

One of the attackers reached George, snatched the sunglasses off, and kicked him hard in the gut. "Drop your weapons. Kneel with your hands up," he screamed at everyone in Saburian, then Chinese.

As commanded by their Saburian ranking officer, the soldiers dropped their rifles and put their hands up—they were outnumbered. A child soldier with large, stony dark eyes in an unlined face, his cheeks still round with baby fat, approached George on the ground. He took George's sunglasses and placed them incongruously on his small face. Their leader ruffled his brown hair affectionately.

What bad luck, Campbell thought, that just overnight, they had traveled from dusty sites of conflicts millennia ago in Greece to this place where boys George's age were already warriors. Hopefully, Sheraton would get Kochanski's necklace with the two Drukker biomatrix beads.

Their attackers now loomed around him. The whir of the armored helicopter was close by. Then the giant bowl of African blue sky over his head turned a brilliant white as he felt the blow to the back of his head. He fell into black unconsciousness.

CHAPTER SEVENTEEN

Within a fraction of an hour, the two commanding officers on the Saburian base, Generals Shah and Liu, rushed by helicopter to the ambush site. A trail of armored vehicles and soldiers followed, guided by an encrypted distress signal. Bloody carnage surrounded the abandoned truck with no sign of the attackers.

The soldiers checked the bodies for life. A technician located Campbell's camouflaged bag. Liu examined it and handed Shah the phone. Then he held the gold necklace in his palm. Between two amber beads, a medallion hung from a loop in the center.

"What's this?" he asked Shah in Saburian.

Shah grimaced inside at his accent. "The pendant says 'Texas,' where Mr. Campbell is from. The note—"

Both generals scrutinized the scrawl on the paper. Finally, Liu said, "English in bad cursive. I think he meant the necklace for his girlfriend."

A soldier came and saluted. "Sir, they only took the two Westerners on the helicopter. The other men are dead."

Furious, Liu turned to Shah. "Why?"

"I don't know." The Saburian general frowned. "Some of these attackers came by sea— here is closest it gets to the road. Except for the ones on the copter, the rest can't be far. Problem is that the rebels recruit locals from the coast who know the caves and coves for hiding. Or they disappear into the villages."

"Our technology could find them," said Liu angrily. "But the king won't let us expand our ...presence." Speaking rapidly into his phone, Liu hammered out orders in Chinese. To Shah, he said, "My pilots and drones are leaving now to search the beaches and ocean."

The two shared a knowing glance about the head of the flight team, Yi—sunglasses, smile, scandal, and a friend of Campbell. While the convoy loaded bodies, abandoned items, and the travelers' ransacked suitcases, the helicopter flew back with its arguing generals.

Back at the base, under the loud *whop-whop* of the helicopter, Shah grumbled to the Saburian pilot so Liu could not hear. "You think our king does not suspect his people? That they may be behind these terrorists? Arrogant imperial superpowers. Waging their proxy wars at the expense of us local patriots. We don't need *more* superpower protection—might as well become a colony again."

The base manager, Salim, called Kochanski in Chicago with the bad news. "Please let your people know." He described the letter and the necklace. "We'll give the jewelry to Dr. Sheraton as her boyfriend requested. Our king is not cowed. He won't give our coast away to foreign domination after his father fought so hard for Saburia to exist."

. . .

To process this shocking development, grateful he was back in the relative safety of Chicago, Kochanski then poured a shot of Dew and returned to watching *Casablanca*. One of his favorite American movies, he had seen it dozens of times already. Ingrid Bergman gazed out of the screen with the sparkling eyes of a young woman who had served her man, his dreams, and his vision. In *Casablanca,* the passports to freedom were hidden in plain sight. It had been smart of Campbell, he thought, to disguise the necklace as a gift for Sheraton, even if he mistakenly thought the two beads on it were for the cancer project, and that the secret he was protecting was Drukker's novel biomatrix technology.

Campbell would never have approved of the Purple Project: a human experiment to repair King Mohammed Saburi's defective DNA after generations of family inbreeding to have healthy twins with his youngest queen. Campbell might have even reported him to ICE, and then what? Kochanski shuddered, noting how Garcia had never once spoken about what happened in the detention center.

Campbell also would never have approved of bringing George to Saburia. But Garcia could not use his own blood for source genes because he was too old; DNA defects developed with age. George's blood had to be used instead.

Casablanca on the screen now showed people from all over the world crowded together at a drinking hole and a man who looked like he was from China. The Chinese had gifted the king a Genghis Khan relic, the Khan's DNA that Garcia had used for one of the twins' embryos.

Confused about Soria's use of traditional Chinese images—plum blossoms and dragons—in their original website for cancer treatments, Kochanski had asked Garcia. "And then they built their clinic on the Red Sea coast, in a country with a strong relationship with China. Can you guess why?"

Garcia told him that Soria's previous cancer treatment line was a commercialization of a novel discovery in China. "Original research was done in China. I first read about it back when Pia was dying. But it wouldn't have helped her type of cancer. When the stem cell treatment was approved in the West, and patients could get it through government or insurance, then Soria had to find a new gig. That's where I got my job with them."

Garcia then explained that George's genes were already in both twin embryos. "Wherever pieces were missing, I plugged in George's genes. The caveat is that health problems for George could predict similar problems for the twins in the future. Say George develops a genetic disease down the road, like schizophrenia. Then the twins may also develop the same condition someday. So, I test George regularly."

"Does George know about this?" he asked.

"Yes." Garcia frowned. "As much as a teenager can grasp. What is age, really? George is a smart boy, well beyond his years. Some adults I know would understand less than what he does. He's excited to do this, thinks it's 'cool' to be part of such a leap forward in science."

Then Garcia told Kochanski about another personal project, building a 4D model of George's DNA architecture, the fourth dimension being time. "A father–son legacy, one record of the human genetic present."

"Interesting, but getting back to China, do the Chinese know about what the king is doing with their relic?"

Garcia looked disappointed at Kochanski's lack of interest in the 4D project. "As a scientist, I pursue truth. Don't find politics interesting like you do. Still, just like in science, I suggest that in politics, we, too, don't know what we don't know. Fact is, the answer to your question about what the Chinese know may not be as simple as a 'yes' or a 'no.'"

Garcia then told him how he had asked the king's minister if Queen Noru understood the Purple Project? "She's only nineteen years old. But he said, 'Yes. She is a dutiful daughter in the royal tribe.'"

Garcia had explained that in a fertility lab in India, a medical team would create several embryos. Only two would be transferred into the queen in September. The remaining would stay in frozen storage for possible use in the future.

The two embryos would be selected from the others based on Garcia's instructions for preimplantation genetic testing, PIGT. In the beginning of the Purple Project, Garcia had created two keys for PIGT, now contained in the two beads Campbell was delivering. "Keys," Garcia had explained to Kochanski, "so I *know* that the Indians are following my instructions correctly."

Of the two selected embryos, Garcia had explained that one twin would be Noru's and the king's biological child. But the second embryo was the revolutionary design, Noru's chromosomes entirely removed from her egg and replaced with the artificial Genghis Khan ones. The second twin would not be Noru's biological child, but instead a son who was a combination of King Mohammed Saburi and Emperor Genghis Khan. Genetic engineering allowed two men, centuries apart, to have a healthy baby together.

"Bending time," Garcia said, "genetics has always been human destiny, the biological code. This is just another quantum leap, like breaking the atom . . ."

"Are you sure those chromosomes the Chinese gave the king are Genghis Khan's?"

"I do think they are the Khan's chromosomes, or at least from someone closely related to him. But that's a long explanation for another time. And I've got to show you one more thing."

Garcia had then showed him an amber bead. Rolling it between his fingers, he said, "Now, see this ancient drop of tree resin? The black specks inside are bits of an insect. Like Drosophila, a fruit fly we use in the lab. Twenty-three beads that look like this are in a necklace that Queen Noru took to India, along with a Drukker disk."

Kochanski looked closely at it. "I saw beads like that at a Drukker board meeting. For the storage of genetic material. A total secret until we get our patent, and after that, we still have to protect our tech secrets from theft. That's a very expensive necklace."

"But Noru's necklace will look like inexpensive costume jewelry if anyone—like Customs— looks inside the purple case. Isn't that a great disguise?"

Kochanski smiled. "But why would a queen wear cheap jewelry, a curious person might wonder?"

"Hmm, I didn't think about that."

"Don't worry," said Kochanski, his smile growing wider. "I already knew. Queen Noru took the purple case in a diplomatic pouch. But given that Drukker's patent for the amber biomatrix is still in process, and for many players, they don't care about patents, I sure hope you have no other beads floating around."

"You know the biomatrix dissolves in water. The rest of my files literally went down the drain back at Pandolf—all except two, stored in your Pierre. When you return to Chicago, you need to get those two beads to me from the storage units in the basement. After I'm done with them, I'll dissolve them too."

"Is that quality check really necessary?"

Garcia looked frustrated.

"Okay, okay, I don't understand the science. How do I get those beads to you?"

"Can David bring back the beads—when he comes back with George?"

• • •

Later in Chicago, in July, Kochanski prepared for a dinner with Kasia. His daughter asked him to do the clasp on her mother's silver necklace. He brought the delicate chain around his daughter's nape, the fuzzy skin below her hairline just like Irina's. That was genetics, too. Then she turned around to face him, arms folded. Confused, he asked her to repeat what she had said, lost in astonishment at almost seeing Irina's face again.

Next, he went to a jeweler to design a necklace for Campbell to string on the two beads to give to him at his upcoming Chicago layover. At O'Hare Airport, he tried to explain Drukker's new biomatrix technology to Campbell. "Well, you're going to be Drukker's CTO soon, and then you'll learn all about our new trade secret. I figured no one will give me trouble for giving you a preview."

Campbell raised his brows. "Believe me, I'm very much looking forward to moving on to real science."

• • •

Casablanca's credits rolled on his wall screen. Kochanski's phone rang again. It was a Chinese officer.

"Mr. Kochanski, good news," the man said excitedly in English with just the slightest British accent. "Our ace pilot spotted a Somalian tin can. He's fast! We think it's the kidnappers, and we are working on figuring out its ownership and country of origin. It's unmarked and now in international waters as our drones track it."

"Thank you! The Chinese pilots are the best. Please keep me updated." *Honest flattery is good business*, he thought.

Salim called him next. "We heard from the terrorists. We have a ransom request."

"How much? I don't have money—" he spluttered. *Neither does Manny. And it will take time to locate David's relatives.*

"We know," Salim interrupted him. "And do you think the Chinese will help pay? No, we're the only ones helping. The Saburian government has agreed to pay the ransom."

"King Mohammed is the best." *More honest flattery.* As a good businessman, he said the right things to keep everyone happy, from the Chinese to the Saburians, and now everyone was helping.

Kochanski clicked—finally—on his telephone connection to Sheraton, dreading her reaction to the bad news about the attack. She would have to be the one to go tell Garcia.

Sheraton picked up. Distressed by his news—"We were expecting them by now. But no one is telling us anything"—she was also hopeful that Campbell and George might be rescued. Then she appeared to understand his guarded hint that Campbell's necklace was a delivery to Garcia. For anyone listening, she even said, "That's so sweet of David to want me to have his necklace. I'll wear it until I can return it to him."

• • •

Elise Sheraton called for a car. But the Chinese driver had taken the day off for a "personal" emergency.

Maybe she is too upset about the killings to work, she thought.

I have to cover up now for that backup male Saburian driver. Honor the local customs.

She felt angry, just like the days after her husband had served her the divorce papers, when she began to cover herself up routinely, under makeup, branded clothes, carrying branded bags. Saburia was one more layer of covering up. How had life tossed them—David, Manny, his son, that Chinese driver, her—into this desert horror?

She thought about her next move after Saburia. *I need peace, safety, simplicity. Someplace where jeans, a T-shirt, comfortable shoes, no makeup, and fresh air on my skin will be just fine.* She balanced on her heels to walk to the car.

A short drive away, Garcia's building in the base was a block of Western-style suites modeled on a motel development. She tapped on his door. He appeared, hair uncombed, face unshaven.

"Elise, news? They just keep telling me to wait here." Inside his room, she saw a suitcase still open next to the bed, months after his arrival. But the rest of the studio looked neat. His sole decoration was a metal Möbius strip on the desk.

"Manny, let's go to the common room with the AC. This heat. I can hardly breathe wrapped up like a mummy."

Now he looked wary. They walked to the meeting room with vending machines for water and colorful electrolyte drinks and sat at one of the plastic tables.

She avoided his anxious gaze. "George and David are safe," she said.

"Go on."

"They were attacked while coming from the airport. Terrorists kidnapped them. The troops were all killed." She took a deep breath. "But George and David are safe, alive, being held for ransom that the Saburian government has agreed to pay."

"I thought we don't pay kidnappers."

Remembering what Campbell had once observed, she said, "Only if the media is involved, or they're playing political games. This is just a little bribe . . ."

Now Garcia just stared at her.

"It's okay," she said, putting her hand on his. "Michael says no one wants to make political drama. There'll be a quick exchange of money, and then we'll get David and George back safely."

"All those dead troops, horrible." Tears in his eyes, he didn't move his hand away.

"Manny, I'll tell you what I think. There used to be a time when leaders led from ahead: people who took care of their family, their friends, their people . . . who served others before themselves. We trusted them. We followed them. Now they don't exist. We're all just pawns in big . . . bigger games. Science makes everything exponential, a matrix with expanding dimensions. Pawns die, troops die . . . we pay the kidnappers off the official grid, of course. We'll get your son back. We'll get David back."

"Why should I believe in anyone or anything in the first place, except who I am and what I do?" Garcia muttered. "Yet, I'm human. I need hope—and children are hope's ultimate, irrational expression."

"I had children when I was young and dumb. I'm not that person anymore. But my children, my hope, is one consequence of those choices a long time ago. If that sometimes keeps us going, isn't it okay?"

When he said nothing more, she left him silent and alone to be by himself, what he wanted.

That evening, Garcia video called her. "The Saburian minister told me they paid the ransom money and returned some prisoners in exchange for George and David."

"They must value your work here," she said, breaking into a smile on the screen. "They should. I'm just so happy beyond belief. Manny . . ." She gave him an agreed-upon hand signal to move their conversation to the beach, the only place to speak freely.

The noisy ocean as a backdrop, Garcia said, "Okay, here I am."

"Okay, I'll jump in the deep end of this," she ventured. "I know Mary's cancer treatments have been your fight for a while, years in development. She was lucky to survive that first infusion. But what's this I hear about her possibly returning so soon for the second round?"

Garcia's mind was clearly elsewhere, on George. "Everything is in place, should she decide to proceed, I suppose."

"Well, with her condition, she may be coming back to die."

Garcia whispered back, "Hope's not something you put in an IV."

"Actually, yes."

They stopped, heads almost touching. Night had fallen up and down the beach, as the line of watchtowers lighted.

Sheraton then pointed to the necklace that she was wearing, mended with a paper clip. His eyes widened with surprise. She explained how Campbell had disguised the two beads as a memento to give to her.

"Full disclosure, Manny. I've recently learned that I'm also here to help Queen Noru have a healthy baby, whenever that happens. I'll get a bonus. I need that money, with a couple of kids who are still in school and an ex who reneges on his financial support. These amber beads on the necklace have something to do with the queen getting pregnant, don't they? Not the cancer vaccine? That's the real reason they hired me, a pediatrician. Michael was mysterious when I talked to him, always worried about who's listening. But I get that I'm supposed to give you this necklace."

"I can't tell you anything, except that you probably didn't ask for a big enough bonus," said Garcia, his breath now warming her cheek. "You know how people in the US think about us Latinos—we'll work hard for seventy cents on their dollar."

"You mean like how women in America get paid less than men?"

"Precisely. We share the handicap of playing in a rigged game. Look at us here in Saburia, a Latino and a White woman, working for an organization that is at best nontraditional, rather than in leadership roles in the medical communities where we trained and toiled. But David goes back to the US and becomes Drukker's chief technology officer. I mean, I'm still happy for him."

Removing the necklace, she felt the cold medallion and the light beads, like the plastic ones on children's play jewelry. "You're preaching to the choir. But the truth is, I don't regret the deals I made or coming to this strange place. I met Mary. She really helped me—pushing me out of my past, into the present, into the future. Now I need to return the favor, help her to be hopeful. You, too, Manny. I'm so very sure, that George will be back safely."

He said nothing.

She slipped the necklace into his pocket. "Here are the beads, whatever you're doing with them."

When he still said nothing more, she added, "I'm sorry, I wish there was something more I could do or say to make you feel better." Then she left.

• • •

Garcia stayed behind on the beach, unable to stop fretting about George, his mind stubbornly resisting his calls for logic. At moments like this, he walked and walked, and looked up at the skies to reframe mentally. Until his life, his brief spark, was quickly extinguished, he was aware of fires much greater than his intellect and imagination. No matter that the stars above were not physically in his grasp, even if he only had a bicycle to their mysteries, he must keep pedaling.

After he returned to his room, he lay back in the recliner, sleepless, looking out of the glass doors at the unseen horizon dividing the skies and their silvery reflection on endless ocean. Another world opened in his mind, where he stood alone, a young man in front of a small home in Argentina where he and Pia had first lived. Awake and asleep, no horizon between, always looking for Pia—*she is not here or there, not in the crowd, no longer in the places where we had spent so much time together.*

Then when he finally slept, she came to him, randomly like she sometimes did, drenched in rain, lovely in her favorite dress with its full skirt, naked feet splashing through puddles. He was young again, too. They wrapped themselves up in each other, intimate in some room that he only recognized in the dream's moment, and he asked her to marry him.

"We already are," she said.

George appeared, theirs, toddling by his side in a store or in the car with him and Pia as they drove on vacation. Then he awoke into another dream—*where am I? when is this?*—conscious only of her absence and relieved that they were already married.

When he finally slept, he dreamed that he was a young researcher again, biking along a busy highway in Baltimore, backpack full of ideas for the NIH lab that would never reach their destination, and a plan to bring his family to be with him to the US that never happened. His exit was too far away. Cars sped by him forever.

Then he awoke, jolted from a nightmare he did not remember into another, the knowledge that George had been kidnapped, was somewhere out there. Davey's locker. Poseidon's fury. *I must do something.* Until he saw his son again at the intersection of a future time and space in this world, he dared not yet believe his boy was safe.

CHAPTER EIGHTEEN

On the Red Sea, a boat bobbed inside the hot splatter of sunshine on the water. On deck were two sailors and their two prisoners, Campbell and George, shackled to a pole.

Campbell drifted in and out of consciousness. George shared scraps of stale tuna inside his wrap from the plane with the scrawny tabby lolling on the deck. "You look like Stone, a cat I know."

He remembered how Charlie had given his sister a second shelter cat for her birthday.

She had not looked as pleased as they had hoped. "I know you wanted this to be a surprise, but you should have asked me."

"You can return Layla," said Charlie. "The shelter said to do that if it doesn't work out."

"Can I return you?"

George pulled a tarp over Campbell to prevent more sunburn and handed him a half-full plastic water bottle, crinkled by repeated use.

"No," moaned Campbell. "So hot, concussion, traumatic brain injury . . ."

"But you need to drink."

Campbell sat up, now more awake. "I don't want food poisoning, Montezuma's revenge, Delhi belly. And look at my skin . . . as red as a Campbell tomato soup can." Seeing George's puzzled look, he added, "A joke, George, Campbell like my name. Never mind, what happened after they knocked me out?"

"Mr. Campbell, they . . . killed everyone."

"What!" Campbell looked around, squinting as ocean ripples sparked endless suns. "Where are we?"

"I don't know. We came on a helicopter."

"You mean everyone else is dead?"

"Yes. Maybe they'll kill us, too."

"Okay, okay, hold up. They didn't go to the trouble of bringing us here just to kill us."

"They made me carry you. Maybe that's the only reason I'm here."

After Campbell dozed off. George watched the two sailors on the boat, eating, drinking, smoking, laughing, speaking an unfamiliar language.

He told himself firmly to stop being afraid. He was no longer that nervous boy who had arrived in Chicago, seeing that little sketch of his aunt in the entry of her apartment, her sweet face in the hand mirror, purple grapes, pretty flowers. In the broad light of the Pierre art gallery, he had recognized the sketch again, this time in the background of the Callie painting. The mirror was shattered, the flowers wilted, and the grapes just brown twigs, around which bursts of brilliant color bled and drew the eye to the sun's blaze on the model's face. At the time, he felt clever for noticing that detail of transformation.

Transfiguration. *Figurehead*, no longer a boy, after the bloody horror, he was now a young man on his ship sailing in time into an unmapped future. He felt a surge of courage while hearing the rev of an engine, a second boat arriving, and more people stomp on board. Male voices approached them. A man, Middle Eastern or Egyptian, in his thirties, with a well-groomed black beard, felt Campbell's forehead and pulse.

"Hey, man, keep still," he said, dabbing Campbell's arm with an alcohol swab, then inserting a large needle. "You're going to be in a world of pain with that sunburn. Both of you are going back."

"Why are we here?" asked George.

The man ignored his question. "Here, boy," he said in British-accented English, handing George an IV bag. "Now, hold it up, up, up."

George did not smile. *Don't call me boy*, he wanted to say, taking the bag of fluid and holding it as high as possible.

"Look at that flow 'cause you're so tall, gravity, boy," said the medic enviously. "Now, help me to move him. His sunburn will get a lot worse before it gets better."

They were transferred into the smaller second boat and blindfolded. The motor revved up. Campbell asked George, "Hey, you doing okay?"

"Yes. This is not right, being alive after those others are dead."

"Life's not fair. . ." started Campbell.

They heard a plane's roar above.

"Life's not fair," said the medic, "but you got a friend in the sky." The medic removed their blindfolds. "No point in these. Watchers are everywhere, including thousands of satellites joining the moon above."

The unseen plane followed them to the shore, occasionally rumbling louder as if talking to them.

On the empty beach, the medic returned George's Genie. "Squeeze that third bag of fluid to finish it." To Campbell, he said, "They couldn't find your phone. Good luck, both of you, your people should be here soon."

Campbell and George watched the medic and his boat disappear.

"Now that we're safe, we can bomb the heck out of them," said George.

"The medic is just a middleman. He waited until our kidnappers were in a safe location before he released us."

They heard a welcome hum. The horizon spit up a transformer to take them back to the base. Inside the vehicle, Campbell removed the needle from his arm and taped on gauze from the first aid kit. Then he cracked open the cap on a bottle of water. "Clean water, finally. I hope you don't get sick, George, from drinking on that boat."

In the clinic at the base, after giving him pain medicine, a nurse slathered cream on Campbell and carefully laid gauze on his extensive sunburn as he lay on a gurney. George sat nearby, charged his cell phone, and connected to the Wi-Fi to catch up with his friends.

He reached Michaela first. She was no longer holed up in her room. "That's all I did for days after you and Charlie left. Mom's working long hours. I just fixed spaghetti for dinner."

"I miss it. One of the few things we ever cooked."

"And cookies."

"Sorry I ate all your sprinkles."

She laughed.

He remembered a time at their small dinner table under a tired ceiling fixture, where half the bulbs were burned out.

"We don't need so much light," her mother had said.

"She means we're poor," said Michaela, picking the pepper container off the tablecloth to reveal a hole. "See, we cover it up, and we don't have to buy a new one."

"It's your grandmother's tablecloth," said Alicia. "And I'm going to mend that."

He saw then that they didn't have space for another person. Their one bath had chipped tiles and dim light. Michaela's mom bought toiletries in bulk when they were on sale, randomly heaped inside a large basket in the corner.

On his phone screen, she drank her colored vitamin cocktail, sleeves pulled down to her fingertips. Her brown hair, straightened, highlighted, fluttered in the breeze. She was sitting on the fire escape outside her apartment building. Behind her and just as beautiful, he could see the California sunset.

The nurse interrupted him. "Your dad is on his way," she said, before popping back out.

Waiting some more, he scrolled on his phone. Charlie's pictures were stunning, his advanced phone camera showing holograms: Athens, Delphi, crumbling stones of the Acropolis, the Parthenon lit up golden at night, endless pictures of the city's markets, locals at different times of day and night, and selfies from an Athenian restaurant that showed them sitting before large plates of dolmades, lamb, and green salads sprinkled with feta.

Stories of his nightmare trip afterward were not for sharing with his friends. Instead, George texted the group chat: "Red Sea is beautiful. Going to talk to Dad about coming back to Pandolf, will send pics."

• • •

"You got here earlier than I expected," a breathless Sheraton said to Campbell after she hurried in. She turned to George to introduce herself. Then she talked to the nurse and pulled on gloves.

Campbell flinched at her touch. "My goodness, you're a hot mess," she muttered, pushing more pain medication in his IV.

When she had finished examining him, she said, "David, you'll be fine. But we're all in shock about what happened. And the men who died. Heartbreaking."

"I'm lucky to be lying here alive," said Campbell, his eyes half-closed, his voice slurring. "Like spam that says, 'I'm in remote Africa with no money or papers. Please wire my bank account.'"

"Your concussion is talking."

"Did you do a brain scan yet?"

She explained they did not have the equipment. "But your X-ray showed no skull fracture."

Given that the biomatrix beads were a trade secret, he did not want to ask Sheraton if she had received them in front of everyone.

Instead, he asked about Mary.

"Just found out. She's coming back from New York," said Sheraton. "She changed her mind, I guess. From when she told me, '*Temitope*, Elise, a Nigerian word for thanks and gratitude, meaning every day I'm happy in my life just the way it is.'"

"Why do you think she changed her mind?"

"I told her we have ideas to make her infusions less toxic this time. Sick people aren't always consistent about what they want. Pain and illness distort the lens through which we see, make decisions. When she was feeling better, maybe she decided to forge ahead."

"And your kids doing well?"

She smiled now. "I'm going back to the States to spend Thanksgiving with them and not coming back again until after the new year."

Then a tearful Garcia rushed in.

"Jorge!"

George awkwardly accepted his father's hug. One arm around his son, who was now taller than him, Garcia turned to Campbell. "So happy to see you too, David. Thanks for bringing George back safely."

"Yeah. That was some trip. And it's so, so good to see you again too, man."

After Garcia and George left, Campbell received another visitor.

"Your friend's here, the pilot," said Sheraton into his ear. She walked away.

Yi was in uniform. "David," he said, smiling broadly.

"Oh man, you're a sight for sore eyes! Thanks for your help."

"I wish I could have done more."

"All those troops."

"We're all in mourning. Soldiers expect danger. We were prepared for pirates who would kidnap for ransom but not terrorism."

"Someone's stirring the pot?"

"Yes," said Yi. "Unnecessary violence, unexpected, shocking, I don't have English words. How are you?"

"Lucky to be alive, except I'm sure I have TBI, Traumatic Brain Injury. I was knocked out before the worst."

Yi's grave expression meant he understood.

"I knew it was you in that plane," Campbell continued. "They're right about how good a pilot you are. You know, I once wanted to become an astronaut."

Their eyes met, lighting up like children planning a new adventure.

"Me, too!" said Yi. "Able to leap through light-years of space and across galaxies."

Then Yi frowned. "Your American doctor said to keep my visit short. I don't think she likes me."

"Oh, I'm sure it's nothing you did to her."

"Women can blow hot and cold."

"Don't say that around her."

"Good to know that can be offensive. Anyway, I'll be back tomorrow if your doctor lets me."

After Yi left, Campbell watched for Garcia's return, wanting to ask him discreetly about the two biomatrix beads. Maybe it was his concussion, but now he was certain—they were not for the cancer vaccine.

Kochanski's explanations did not add up. Besides, Kochanski was a habitual liar who had once said, "Truth is a matter of perspective. It's one reason why I drink—to examine alternatives."

At least Garcia was honest and simply said, "You know I can't talk about that" whenever Campbell probed about the purpose of the purple case.

He closed his eyes, feeling dizzy again. Unable to get comfortable on the gurney, restless dreams took him back to grade school, spending recess in a cramped room. As the whoops of children outside on the playground faded, he joined otherworldly creatures in his imagination. There was his humanoid friend, X, out of whose forehead he scooped a purple elixir that tasted like ice cream cake and gave him superpower vision. In the constellations, there hung edifices of ancient civilizations that had destroyed themselves. He explored giant ghost webs among stars and planets, mining secrets from eons past.

He discovered that Earth had come from a blueprint, a system designed to evolve life-forms that expired with the planet, planned obsolescence.

There were infinite other planets, like his home chip of stardust, on which life systems were born, lived, and died, spawned by an unknown source. He met other beings of awareness like him out there, wandering like lost dogs, searching for meaning and their beloved master.

But in reality, he had never applied to NASA to become an astronaut. He did not want to be confined in small spaces, like the school classrooms he used to spend his recesses in as a child in detentions.

He had once told Garcia, "As a kid, I was dreamy, head-hopping, star-hopping all over the Milky Way and beyond, instead of studying. Then, in boarding school, StarHall had this legend about spiders, yes, spiders, who spin universes that die with them. That inspired me to connect my childhood imagination to scientific exploration. Here I am, a scientist."

"George said you told him that school story."

"I thought he would find it entertaining."

"But you know, imagination doesn't easily connect to science," said Garcia. "Think about DaVinci's airplanes that didn't work. Unlike you, I went to a STEM boarding high school and was the model student. Even won a national science prize. Now I want to understand how threads of DNA program life-forms. Our gene-editing technology is in a primitive stage, Neanderthal. That's how cancer stays ahead of our treatments, evolving to survive. But the pandemics, cancer, they can all teach greater wisdom. Only AI can beat nature's biological speed. Mary's cancer is no longer the same, just leaps ahead of the vaccines we give her, challenges us to keep up. Still, I've got a bit of childhood imagination left myself. I'll die one day, and before then, I want to find this, as you say, metaphorical spider in my world . . ."

"You mean?"

"I mean I want to know the 'why' of my life. Like you, I also wanted to explore space as a kid—glimpse eternity, the why, where we come from, where we're going—before my lights shut off. For sure, I'll die one day. Can't dance and dangle forever among the stars. Breaking and reshaping DNA, that may be my way to shout out, 'Hey there!' to a creator in the web that feels my vibrations, my chord. If it's alive, it'll come looking and find both of us."

"Fantastical. Why me, too?"

"You're on my research team." Garcia was smiling mischievously. "Connected minds."

"Okay, I'll go along. If you see this source that's spinning the fabric of our world, creating and destroying from cosmic to cellular, molecular to subatomic, how will you even know what it is? Is our 'spider' benevolent, malevolent, or indifferent? Are there more of them?"

Then a soft voice interrupted Campbell's reminiscing, saying "Mr. Campbell."

He opened his eyes to a creature in white. Behind her, the walls were also white. *Is she an angel guide to some new journey?*

"Dr. Sheraton is resuming your regular medicine," said the Saburian nurse. "Your blood pressure's back up again, that's a good sign. And we're moving you to a room."

In his new bed, he obediently swallowed many pills and entered dreamless unconsciousness.

• • •

Alone in Sheraton's office, George and Garcia talked in rapid Spanish.

"I understand that Pandolf is a better school and that you don't want to go back to Chicago," said Garcia. "But I must stay here. And how can you live in Pandolf by yourself?"

"Dr. Sharma still hasn't found someone to share her apartment."

"I've imposed on her enough."

"She likes me. And I'll be careful not to eat all her 'healthy' and 'tasteless' food." He made a face.

"I'd be surprised if Dr. Sharma agrees. I will ask, though. But your aunt already enrolled you in school in Chicago. Now, where's that calendar she sent me?"

As Garcia searched his phone, George rattled off the start dates for the school in Chicago. "They have already started, but Pandolf High won't begin until next month. See how it's meant to be?"

"Your logic is interesting."

They connected over video with Sharma.

"George, it's nice to see you've arrived safely," she said. "I've been waiting for your call. But can't talk for long right now, I'm at work. Did you have a good trip?"

"Yes, thank you, Dr. Sharma. My dad has something very quick to ask you."

"It can wait, George," said Garcia.

"What is it?" she pressed. "I can make a few minutes."

Garcia broached the topic about George returning to Pandolf.

"It's been lonely since Lucky left," Sharma said carefully. "Financially, someone to share the rent would be helpful. George, you were flourishing at school here. I want to help. But work keeps me very busy. Dr. Garcia—I mean, Manny—for all practical purposes, George will be on his own."

"Shelly, I'm surprised you're even considering doing this, so thank you," said Garcia.

"Dad says I will get a car when I turn sixteen, so I can drive myself around, like for all those dentist appointments," said George happily.

"Your teeth are a mess, George," said Sharma, smiling, showing off perfect whites.

"Okay, I could have been a better parent with George's teeth," Garcia grumbled. "But George, if things don't work out, you'll need to go back to Chicago."

"You'll have ground rules, George," said Sharma. "Boring things like curfews, house rules for neatness, sharing food, the bathroom, and more. I'll share a file with you."

"Thank you so much, Dr. Sharma!" said George.

"Manny, how's your research coming along?" she asked.

Garcia smiled happily. "I've an update. Mary, my first patient, is returning. Her indicators are encouraging."

"That's exciting. Selfishly, when can I discuss my project with you? You ditched me the last time again. We can collaborate informally."

"Informally? You mean I won't be a coauthor on your publication in the *New England Journal of Medicine*? Okay, fine."

She laughed. "Okay, will text you some good times for me. You better reply! Alright, Manny, gotta go."

As they left, Garcia and George walked past an open door to a sleeping Campbell, covered with burn cream, gauze, and a sleeping mask.

"I guess we shouldn't disturb him," said George.

"No. It looks like it'll be a while before Mr. Campbell can travel back to the States with you. I guess the California school dates do work out better."

From her desk, Sheraton waved. "Say goodbye to David for me, Manny, I'm leaving early tomorrow after AJ returns from Ramses. To meet Mary in Ramses. She and I are going to helicopter directly back to the base."

"So much safer," said Garcia. "Good news."

At the exit station, Garcia and George rubbed in sunscreen and sanitizer, then donned sunglasses and hats. Outside, late-afternoon, salt-laden sea breezes swept in and buffered the heat as they walked back to the apartment.

"Dr. Sheraton is a pediatrician by training," said Garcia. "If the queen of Saburia gets pregnant soon, Dr. Sheraton will move to Ramses from here to prepare for the birth."

"Have you ever visited the capital, Dad?" George asked.

Garcia shook his head. "I've only been to the airport. My focus is cancer research here."

"Mary is the name of your patient? You're going to cure her?"

Garcia smiled. "Maybe. I wish you could meet her."

"No offense, Dad, I just really want to go back to Pandolf."

"I'll miss you. I wish I could have protected you better during your trip here."

"Don't feel bad. Mr. Campbell was great. He said something about me seeing a school counselor about it when I go back. Pandolf High School even has one trained to work with migrant children."

"Is she a local American?"

"Yes. She speaks Spanish, just a different dialect, Mexican. She gushed when I told her that I might be part Indigenous American from way back."

"Many Americans are. Still, you and I, we're different than most people who grew up in the States. She might find your story too disturbing." Not intending the harsh edge in his voice, he added, "Suggest keep it to yourself."

They were back at the concrete block of Saburian housing. Garcia swiped his entry card.

"Dad. You sound out of breath."

"I'm fine, just the heat." *And all the stress.*

In the apartment, Garcia gave George scrubs to change into after a shower. Objectively, he observed George's face, darkened by days in the sun, the black bristle on new edges in his jaw, the change of his boy to a not-yet-man. For millennia, humans had often seen adolescence as magical and performed rituals around it, from wise to violent. Odd, he thought, the timing of this bloody attack . . . *to this time in Jorge's life.*

He heard the shower running, washing away the blood and dust of George's journey here. He understood why his son wanted to return to Pandolf, even as he wished they could finally be together.

Garcia's biggest regret now—really—was that he had not turned out to be a better father.

When Soria had first approached him at the NIH, through Campbell, to help with an AI-assisted cancer vaccine program, he saw a beacon *finally* for his research dreams. Then Soria sent him patient data files for the Drukker, and off he had gone. If he had been honest with Samuel Nepski from the start about the cancer trials, he might have kept his job, and the review board might have approved Soria's project. Then he could have stayed at Pandolf with George.

Instead, quid pro quo for support for his cancer research, he agreed to help the Saburian king have healthy babies—AI-assisted human embryo engineering: The Purple Project—illegal in the US and most of the world. That required nights of secret work on the Drukker. The unintended consequences of that decision followed. He was fired. Even after his release, ICE was still on his tail, the police confiscating his map, maybe next asking him questions about his research. By then, too late to back out of the king's project and to avoid another possible arrest, he had no choice but to leave the US—fast.

George emerged from the bathroom, now clean and shaven. Garcia microwaved frozen dinners. Long feet hanging off the foot of the sleeper sofa, George ate, back to scrolling on his phone.

"Jorge," he said. "I'm glad Pandolf High teaches you kids about unintended consequences."

"That was random. Hey, you got more of these dinners?"

"Yeah."

But George frowned. "Are you saying I did something wrong? That caused the attack on my way here?"

"No! Oh, no. I meant that your *father* made certain choices in life. That the outcomes did not turn out the way I wanted, despite thinking that I planned everything so well. Look, if I hadn't wanted you to come here, then you and Mr. Campbell would not have been kidnapped—"

"And all those soldiers killed."

"Yes." The immense risk that he had exposed George to, even death

—to bring him to Saburia for the Purple Project now was becoming clear. Then Campbell was injured. Those soldiers were killed. Guilt demanded the blood price, redemption.

George put his phone down and stared at the ceiling.

Later, when George was eating again, their conversation turned to Pandolf High and George's friends there. He felt irritated about Shelly Sharma calling George's teeth a "mess" and remembered—not so random—the time she quoted her dad's many skeptical aphorisms on hope like "If wishes were horses, beggars would be kings."

Hope's flames for him had often cast dark shadows: unrealistic expectations and illusions that had misguided a dreamer like him. His deepening misgivings about the Purple Project now creeped on him like a pox.

Listening to George's voice, so familiar, so dear, yet changing into manhood, he put aside his what-if counterfactual thinking of the things he could have done differently, running the other side of the Möbius strip of consequences. Because he also saw again—once again—a stubborn glint of hope for the future.

Hope is better than no hope, dreams better than no dreams. Life better than no life, and my son is back safely. With the royal twins scheduled to be born under the star sign of Gemini in 2031, if all went according to plan, science meeting superstition, Phoenix burning and rising, the past might be resurrected into better times ahead.

He would leave the Purple Project—finally—in his rearview mirror, he thought, but what about the record of his work? Knowledge once discovered cannot be hidden again, at least not for long. Someone else would duplicate the Purple Project, sooner rather than later.

George was smiling at something on his phone. *A child remains a child only so long,* he thought. *Right now, I also have a father's hand —briefly— to guide the future of my embryo engineering research.*

"I'm proud of you, Jorge," he said.

George looked up from his Genie. "Random, but thanks, Dad."

CHAPTER NINETEEN

In Ramses, Elise Sheraton video-called Mary, about to take off from LaGuardia in New York City.

"Leslie dropped me off," said Mary. "I spent last night at her house."

"Saw the grandkids?"

Mary smiled. "We dropped them off first, school starts in August here. Feels harder to leave this time."

Sheraton reviewed trip details and wished her a safe trip. In addition to meeting Mary, she was in Ramses to upgrade pediatric services at Ramses Hospital with the latest equipment and training for the staff, staying in a call room in the women's section. She was also going to meet a Dr. Seema Kapoor, an Indian OB who was coming to similarly enhance the hospital's maternity service line.

Meeting in the hospital cafeteria for the first time, Kapoor's round brown face broke into a bright smile, white teeth matching the whites of dark kohl-lined eyes.

"I guess we women are in similar situations," said Kapoor over an early dinner, a goat kebab for her, and a Western-style grilled cheese for Sheraton. "We're going to be working here while supporting our families back home. Electronic communication is so wonderful. Talking to my kids in Chennai over video is not the same, but it's still better than a hundred years ago when all we had were letters."

"But not very private here, agreed?"

Sheraton found talking with Kapoor, the Indian doctor's face either smiling or expressionless, somehow circular in shape and language, no direct questions or answers, not the same as talking to Arjun Bhattacharya, an Indian American doctor, who was as Western as her.

Bhattacharya had once told her, "The problem with Indians, you know, not like me who grew up in the West, is so many go along and accept things as fated. I love that in America, we try to change our destiny. Like in physics, which teaches us that a particle can exist simultaneously in different states, locations, times. On a macro scale, there may be different pasts, presents, and futures. In some parallel worlds, Saburia's problems may not even exist."

"From the Orient to the West, when other people know everything about you," said Kapoor serenely, "they control you better."

"For sure."

After returning to her room, she called Kochanski. "What do you know about this Indian OB?"

"She's preparing the place to take care of Queen Noru when she becomes pregnant. And to whoever's listening right now, 'Hey there.'"

"Probably a bot, Michael, you're not that important."

"Maybe I am."

"I can understand why people in the US go 'off the grid,'" Sheraton said. "Until now, I've only lived in places where I can easily connect with my kids and travel to see them. But cars have license plates, airline traffic is monitored, the pandemics have made things even more so."

"You want to unplug like in *The Matrix*."

"Quit with the movies. Listen." Then she told him. "I got an offer from a clinic for next year, in a small Missouri town. The Ozark Mountains. Peaceful. They'll even provide a self-sufficient home because the grid there is bad."

"Don't you have medical work you can do here in Chicago, in civilization?"

"Stop."

• • •

Later, she met Kapoor. They circled the hospital's "serenity" garden.

"I'm trying to learn about the flora and fauna here in Saburia," the Indian OB said. "Tell me, have you seen any of those beautiful desert lie-umas?"

"Yes, I've seen lyumas," Sheraton said, pronouncing the word the Saburian way. "They are more beautiful in life than in the pictures." She wondered whether to say more about the king's efforts to repopulate and protect endangered species in Saburia or whether Kapoor cared.

Sheraton asked the OB, "So, is the queen pregnant yet?"

Kapoor replied softly, "No. Two embryos will be selected to be transferred into her. I didn't want to say anything inside just in case someone was listening."

Sheraton stopped to watch children splash in the pool around the fountain. "It's good to know that these upgrades we're doing in this hospital will benefit other moms and children in Ramses. I've also been helping with a cancer project on the base along the coast. But this country is getting to me. You should know that after the queen's babies are born and doing well, hopefully, I plan to leave."

Later, back in her call room, her phone rang. It was Kochanski again. It always felt good to hear his deep voice, even so quickly again, even as she heard the cigarettes and alcohol that lowered its pitch.

"When are you returning to Saburia?" she asked. "I need a straight answer."

"The Irish say it's a long road that has no curves."

"Meaning?"

"Meaning that for your big questions, there's no such thing as a straight answer. Okay, I'm tying up loose business ends, turning over one of my buildings to new management. I called you for some 'born in America' practical advice."

"I didn't know you owned more than one building."

"Well, maybe I do. But anyway, I have this Pierre building, and we are trying to get it into the black. My new manager wants to get rid of my chapel, which I'm sentimentally attached to. Built it for my mom. This Beth calls it 'prime RSF,' Rentable Square Feet, says how we can't tie up that space, not revenue generating."

"In America, chapels are in hospitals and private schools, not in commercial buildings. "

"My architect also said that."

"But why new management? They sound very controlling."

"Money, of course. My mortgage was going underwater, and the bank would have taken it over otherwise. Frankly, I'm making this new deal to take care of my daughter."

"How old is she now? Katya?"

"Yes. Twenty-four."

"Old enough to be taking care of herself."

"No. She's gorgeous and adventurous, like her mother used to be, and she doesn't make the best choices, just like her parents at her age. I'm waiting for her to do more maturing."

After a silence, he added, "On another note, I'm drinking less."

"That's awesome." Even if she could not see him, she sensed her approval mattered.

"My new lender knows me too well," he continued. "A Jim Sichet. You've never heard of him. He told me to 'get the monkey off my back,' one of your American expressions."

"And try again to quit smoking—"

He ignored that. "Now Jim's the monkey on my back. Anyway, Manny says Mary's cancer is in remission."

"Yes. She's on her way here now." In a guarded voice, she added, "I had a good talk with Noru's OB—"

She heard static. Was it the connection, or was he concerned that someone was listening? When she heard his voice again, he was finishing a sentence.

"Sorry, what'd you just say about Manny's kid?" he asked.

Kochanski had changed the subject, she thought, always worried about eavesdroppers. "David's taking him back to Pandolf."

"I know George well, even met him in Chicago a few times, quiet kid. And he was—no more— on my budget helping Manny out. Soria Clinics couldn't believe how much that kid and his friends ate? To get reimbursed, I had to send them all the receipts."

• • •

November, 2030 in Pandolf, Sharma's phone lit up, a text from Lucky. Littered with hearts, roses, champagne, and other festive emojis, it read: "NYC wedding, sky-high fancy, second weekend June 2031!"

"OMG," replied Sharma, adding her own excited emojis, thinking their chat looked like Egyptian hieroglyphics.

Two months had passed since George moved in. He made a commendable effort like a good intern at the hospital, open to Sharma's feedback on how to improve. Since George's trip to see his dad, he also spoke up more. Had his jaw also become squarer or was it the new confidence he showed?

Sharma and Lucky agreed to talk Sunday. That morning, she returned from her 6 a.m. run and showered. Then George emerged from his room, unshaven, still wearing his bathrobe. "Morning," he said. "I have a Model UN meeting super early today. Then Debate Club has a dinner this evening."

"Good morning."

Her quiet Sunday morning was gone—until he left. He spattered eggs in the frying pan, then cereal clattered and milk splashed into a metal mixing bowl. "I talked to Dad about you leaving for Germany," he said, "that I'll be fine, especially with Mr. Campbell checking in."

To her delight, Sharma had been awarded the Fujitsu fellowship. The prestigious six-month research grant was to work in a lab in Germany, beginning January 2031.

George continued, "Dad's really excited for your award. He also warned that if there are any problems, I'll have to go back to Chicago."

"Well, then we won't have any problems, George. Now, what shall we take to the Nepskis' for Thanksgiving dinner?"

"Too early to think. It was nice of them to invite me too." George sat down at the kitchen table to eat. "I had to learn the truth about Thanksgiving when I first came to the United States. American Indians and colonists eating together didn't ring true."

"Maybe we like to remember the good times. Your dad said you may have a bit of Native American in you. But my type of Indian was not around for that first Thanksgiving. Probably everyone else at the Nepskis' will be 98 percent descended from non-indigenous people."

"What do you mean?" His voice was sharp.

"What do *you* mean?" She felt annoyed, too early in the morning for politics.

"I thought you might be referring to Cortez's loss in the special election."

"Oh my god, that controversy over his indigenous heritage? Actually, no, I wasn't. Why does everything become political for you?"

They reverted to silence, George scrolling on his phone, before he left the room to shower and dress. Sharma's laptop dinged—Lucky calling.

"Did you just come from your morning run?" Lucky asked.

"Enough about me, I want to hear about *nuptials*."

"Simple church wedding, and big, big party afterward."

"I'm not into churches."

"You don't have to come to the ceremony, just the party."

"Of course I'll come to your ceremony."

They caught up with each other, talking for over an hour.

She told Lucky she was going to the Nepskis' for Thanksgiving and "I'm taking George."

"How does that feel?"

"Awkward. Emotionally, getting away to Germany will be good."

"You should be *so* proud of your Fujitsu. What will happen to George?"

"He'll stay in my apartment. I'm not worried. He's really maturing."

"I'll invite George to the wedding. It'll be terrific for Charlie to see him. Michaela can come, too. Let me add them to the invitation list. The kids can entertain each other. Speaking of George, what's the latest with Mr. Walden Pond?"

"Dr. Garcia's very happy with his research in Saburia and always has good ideas for me. Unfortunately, he can't get a travel visa to come see George. Seems to be getting more and more down about it."

"Sad. Ugh. And David? How's the new job?"

"Good. He's in San Francisco a lot," she said carefully. George had surprised her when he told her it was "obvious" that Campbell had feelings for Lucky.

Sharma changed the topic. *Weather and pets are always safe.* "How're your cats?"

"Happy, an old almost-married couple like Harry and me. Layla has never seen a New England winter, and our first is coming up. I hope we don't get bad winter storms. They're predicting unpredictable weather. How's the weather in California?"

"The droughts and fires keep getting worse except for when it floods. But it's not so bad here at Pandolf, especially as rents keep falling while people keep leaving due to climate change and dysfunctional leadership—"

She stopped when George entered the living room. There was no need to trigger him by discussing politics when he was around.

"Are you talking to Lucky?" He waved to the screen. "Can I see Stone and Layla?"

They waited for Lucky to return with the cats.

George said, "You know, as our environment collapses, Chicago will be a very safe place compared to both coasts of the United States."

So, he had heard her after all. "Did you have a nice trip to see your aunt?"

"Yup."

. . .

George had just returned from a long weekend in Chicago since Pandolf High had been closed for a teacher workday. While his aunt slept in—so unlike her—he and Uncle Max bundled up to go out for brunch at a café near the apartment.

Brown leaves from the nearby park floated on chilly November breezes as they walked. Inside, they sat in a booth next to a large window that let in the light of the brightening day. Speakers piped a Native American melody with flute and wind chimes. His salsa-topped, stuffed-cheese omelet with hash browns arrived, and he dug in. Uncle Max drank his black, bitter coffee with a tiny cinnamon roll.

"George," said Uncle Max, "let me tell you, it's a dog-eat-dog world out there. You remember that tall lawyer, Jim Sichet, who bought my *Figurehead* painting? My biggest sale ever. He said that he would put it in the entryway of a landmark building. I didn't believe that." He paused. "But I never thought he would stash her away—where no one can see her."

"What'd he stash?" asked George, feeling confused. "The woman or your painting?"

Before his uncle could explain, a presence hovered.

"Wow," said Uncle Max, looking up. "We were just talking about you. George, this is Callie, the model for that painting, and Callie, this is my nephew, George, visiting from the West Coast."

"Hi," George said, not looking up.

"Hi, George." A young woman's voice was now the soundtrack to *Figurehead*.

The waiter brought another mug, into which Uncle Max poured black coffee. George's gaze stayed on the white tablecloth, then traced Callie's bitten fingernails on long fingers that wrapped around the handle of the white porcelain mug, then past silvery rings to stacked green glass bracelets. Lifting his eyes further, the sunlight revealed the fuzz on her forearm, and higher, he was surprised to see a tattoo—a symbol he did not recognize—under the fabric of her sleeve.

Uncle Max had told him that he had drawn and redrawn her arm many times (minus the tattoo). Now, in the bright daylight, he admired his uncle's interpretation.

Finishing his coffee, his uncle now rose. "I've a meeting downtown. George, you can stay and finish eating."

"Is it okay if I get dessert?"

"Sure, add that to my tab. Take something back for your aunt, too."

Just the other day, he had overheard his aunt and uncle talking about Callie.

Uncle Max had described how his mind worked "furiously" when he sketched Callie and how he had to filter out "her chatter. *How to make visual a voice of smoke and liquor?*" He added that next time, he would like to paint her "clothed."

"You mean that nude models are dangerous?" said AnnaMaria. "And why do you want to paint her again?"

"Jealousy is not pretty on you. Besides being married, it would be dumb to have an affair with Callie while Jim's my patron."

"You said she never talks to you about her husband—"

But seeing George walk in, AnnaMaria stopped, and they changed the topic to an upcoming outdoor art fair.

Gathering courage after his uncle left the cafe, George looked up and stared straight at Callie—connected the *Figurehead* painting to its model.

He followed the line of her sight to his uncle's slender figure moving away with stiff grace. The waiter refilled her coffee. She turned around and pointed to drops he spilled.

"Clumsy, or just rude now that your uncle is gone?"

George looked down, dizzy, thinking this must have been what it was like for Icarus—to look straight into the sun. No, he needed to be Ulysses—bound to the mast—while the sirens sang. He tried to squeeze more ketchup out of the bottle without splattering red stains next to black of the coffee on the white tablecloth.

He heard her say: "Or you think the waiter spilled it because I look poor, like I don't fit in here? Or because of how I talk?"

Finally, he looked up. "I don't hear an accent."

She inhaled the morning air and lit a cigarette, despite the no-smoking signs.

"Don't worry," she said, "they don't mind smoking if no one complains. Laws are only good if you enforce them, a friend told me. Don't ever start this nasty habit, George."

After Saburia, he no longer noticed people smoking. "Oh, never," he said quickly. "But you shouldn't smoke, either."

He wanted to appeal to vanity by telling her what his grandmother said to his aunt, that smoking would make her age faster, crinkle her skin, even if AnnaMaria did not care that cigarettes caused cancer.

He dropped his eyes and dug into a warm slice of pecan pie with vanilla ice cream.

"Your uncle's a great artist," he heard her say. "I was home, looking out the window when I saw him come down the street for his coffee."

George looked back up, analytically this time. He had never seen skin like hers before, no cloud of makeup, smooth like the ice cream he was finishing, lips naturally strawberry pink. His uncle had said she had young kids. But she only looked a few years older than him.

Then losing himself in her sea-green eyes that his uncle had painted like sailboats on an ocean, listening to the Native American flute take its melody to high notes before dropping into silence, he saw she was talking.

She described how "Max sketched an arrangement near my kitchen window of fruit, wine, and glass—cheap random stuff like in a billion homes." She smiled. "Except it was your uncle and his magic box of pastels." She added, "I framed the drawing myself. Now it hangs on my kitchen wall. Your uncle really appreciates life's daily routines."

He does? George thought, surprised.

His uncle was right. Callie liked to chat. He did not have to keep up his end of the conversation, just settle into a happy daze.

"When I was modeling for his painting," she said, "your uncle told me you were coming soon from Paris."

"Yes, my grandmother still lives there."

"My husband and I lived in Paris for a while. Your uncle said he met your aunt there. How romantic."

Whatever.

"Your aunt is beautiful. I see her in you. Your uncle's first wife was also lovely, and he used to paint her as well."

George smiled. "Now he calls his ex 'MX,' my-ex. He says it's the name of an old nuclear missile."

Merriment lit Callie's face. George felt witty.

"And how's his son, Barry, doing?" she asked.

"Fine, I think," he replied, perplexed as to why that mattered. He had never met Barry. Uncle Max was supposed to call his son on the weekends but often forgot. AnnaMaria said that MX had married a busy doctor in New York City and boasted how "they can now afford to provide Barry things that Max can't."

Once, he overheard his uncle on the phone saying, "AnnaMaria is courteous to Barry but shows no maternal feeling. Have you heard that expression, 'as cold as a stepmother's kiss?' Still, I excuse my wife, I prefer to be child-free myself. I'm just as bad. She wishes I were closer to her nephew. I try."

Callie stubbed her cigarette. "Nice to finally meet you, George. Time to get back to reality—cluttered children's room. Dirty clothes on the floor. Books, toys, and artwork rising to the ceiling"—she raised her hands— "and jumbled bedsheets hiding wild packs of stuffed animals."

George laughed.

She continued, "I just finished cleaning that stupid, *stupid* kitchen, the dining room, the living area, and my husband's workroom. Daily, I bring order to domestic chaos, then do it again a few hours later. There's some Zen wisdom about cycles of order and disorder that repeat themselves futilely—that's housework."

He was going to say that his aunt could be OCD about the apartment but thought better of it.

He watched her rise and almost expected her to float into the air.

"Bye George." Then she faded around a corner. He scraped crumbs of pie off his plate. He remembered his own mother, felt the quickening of air around him as if she was even now picking up his things—but did not turn around because he knew he would not see her. His father used to tell him stories about his mother. But over video chat nowadays to Saburia, their conversations were short and guarded.

CHAPTER TWENTY

By November, Soria Clinics moved Manny Garcia and their Drukker AI systems into the newly built Saburia Research Institute in Ramses Hospital. Dr. Bhattacharya remained behind at the coastal base.

In the hospital's executive suite, Garcia met the Saburian king for the second time. Like last time, white robes covered the monarch's body, and his painted face was a mask—like an actor in theater. King Mohammed asked his guards to step outside to leave him alone with Garcia.

The king then sat at the head of the table. "Please sit, update me on your progress."

Garcia sat and explained, layman's language.

The royal then asked, "And have you heard of the Sun Order of Ra— ancient movement that dates to the pharaohs?"

"Forgive me, no."

"Good, then I won't have to correct misinformation about us."

King Mohammed now rose, folded his arms, and paced. "We—a grand, ancient Order with only an oral history— believe there'll be an apocalypse. Then a great leader will come, rebuild our world. But we're not religious like your Mr. Kochanski. To be fair, his god beat us in Egypt, beat us in Rome, and still may be the one to bring the apocalypse and beat us *this time,* too."

Garcia tried to gauge whether the king was serious or mocking, either by the timbre of his voice or his face, impassive like the Sphinx, expressions further disguised by skin paint and subtle markings.

"Yes, Michael is faith driven," said Garcia.

"He does have some unbelievable luck, I give him that, for a nobody. He's in debt to one of us. You know a Jim Sichet?"

Garcia frowned. "Sounds familiar."

"Our lawyer in Chicago. At Pandolf, we have the CEO, Dean Baluyn, and the Mather family. We were in boarding school together. You must have heard of StarHall in New England?"

"Yes, sir."

"Your scientist friend, Mr. Campbell, also went there, though, as you know, he's not part of the Purple Project. Too much of a Boy Scout, an American expression. But I'm sure he has guesses about Soria Clinics. Then he's in the wings as the next CTO at Zoser now, after they bought Drukker. These are all corporations that our movement is invested in."

Garcia now felt wary. *Why's he telling me this? Because I might never leave Saburia. Something worse? Dead men don't talk.*

But he had played a calculated game. He had built many safeguards into his Purple Project work against others using his research and taking his place if something happened to him. Should he tell this king? Not yet.

"Sir," he asked, "is the Sun Order connected to your Porphyry Project?"

"Yes, Queen Noru's successful pregnancy pleases me."

"I don't understand."

"The connection is a secret I will reveal to my people at the right time."

"Time is also a god to men," said Garcia.

The king gave him a sly look. "Our grim reaper. Your god. Our gods live to fight on after we die."

"Please humbly permit me to ask a different question."

"Just one more."

"Who's the leader of the Sun Order?"

The king nodded approval. "I only dimly see a spiderweb that spins from a center. Its source of energy, the rhyme and reason for its rules, from pi to phi to fractals, whether it's a creator that is good or evil or exists in the past, present, or future, or outside time altogether, that's a question one may as well ask our universe, outside and within ourselves. In Saburia, we say we can't see our back; we can only describe what we think it looks like."

Garcia looked at him blankly.

"Do you believe in good and evil?" the king asked.

"A man-made concept, I think," said Garcia. "Why is it okay to butcher an innocent animal but wrong to do the same to a human being?"

Painted lips and eyes smiled on the king's flawless tan canvas.

"That helps me to explain," the king said. "Human beings have never led the Sun Order. We only have rules of inheritance like rules of chemistry: such as who is my royal father, and his father, and so on and on—who begat who dating back to the pharaohs. Or the Mather family in the United States. In the Sun Order, the story is that the original Puritan had to leave England to break into a more inner circle. The Mathers are even rumored to have built a doomsday shelter named after them on the Harvard campus in Cambridge."

Throughout history, thought Garcia, feeling confused, royal families had suffered from insanity, perhaps from inbreeding, or maybe they were no more mentally ill than anyone else. Maybe the truth was that royal dysfunction was no different from any other family drama, *except* history remembered royal family dysfunction.

King Mohammed tapped his ring. Two guards arrived.

To Garcia's relief, the guards did not arrest him.

Not yet. I won't die now, he thought.

Garcia then even dared to ask, "One more question, sir?"

But King Mohammed abruptly left.

• • •

Sheraton called Garcia. She was leaving for home for Thanksgiving and Christmas, not to return until January 2031. She asked, "What does the king look like up close?"

"Very Red Sea coast features, painted, features different from other Africans. Even if the skin color is similar Did you know that Africa has the greatest human genetic diversity of any continent?"

"Yeah! And what did he talk about?"

"His different philosophical perspective."

"What does that mean?"

"Nothing important or memorable, I think he mostly wanted to see how my research is going."

He hoped that answer would smoothly allow him to end their conversation and return to work. Once, he abruptly left a meeting with Saburian officials to return to his lab for a timed procedure. "Manny," Sheraton said later, "explain why before just leaving. Communicate, communicate, overcommunicate."

Why waste my time?

And in her British accent, Eleanor had told him after that incident, "There's never an excuse for a lack of courtesy."

He had wanted to remind her of her English heritage, like the British royal family's motto: don't complain, don't explain—"

An awkward silence now hung between him and Sheraton, He added, "You'll be happy that with the king, I was both communicative and polite to the nines."

"Good, stay out of trouble while I'm gone."

Again feeling a vague fear, perplexed by King Mohammed's vague rambling about an apocalyptic Sun Order, Garcia wondered if he would be alive when she returned. Then, working around the clock, he barely noticed the holidays come and go. In Saburia, Thanksgiving did not exist. Christmas was not a vacation day. He thought often about the Saburian monarch's belief system and concluded that an insect metaphor for a god was no better or worse than any other religion he knew.

He learned that Mary would return for a third round of treatment in January, traveling with Sheraton. *Surely, I will be allowed to live until then. They don't have a replacement—yet— for me."*

Feeling some relief with this reasoning, he even emailed Mary to let her know that his son might be going to New York for a wedding in the summer of 2031.

"He can stay with me," she promptly replied.

In the hospital garden, he often walked with the OB, Seema Kapoor. She gushed that the pregnant Queen Noru was "blooming like a rose, beautiful like a fertility goddess."

One day, she stopped at the fountain. "Now with that musical background, we talk frankly. I always worry about people eavesdropping. I need my job."

"Talk about—?"

"The queen's pregnancy. Which of the two embryos survived the transfer? I'll see the baby, but with newborns it's hard to tell the parentage. Wouldn't the more artificial embryo be less likely to survive?"

"Only one embryo lived!" he exclaimed.

"Yes! No one told you."

Why would they, I'm just a tool to them, he thought angrily. But he controlled his fury, the rant spinning in his brain desperate to be released. "No. What do you mean, 'more artificial'?"

"The most unnatural," said Kapoor. "Noru's chromosomes extracted from her egg, then the Khan chromosomes injected, then the king's chromosomes injected, so many unnatural steps, so much could go wrong. But the other twin is just the king and Noru, straightforward IVF. I put my bets on that one."

"Error is almost impossible with the Drukker," said Garcia. "Still, there are unknown variables, like gene self-repair. But most defective embryos become miscarriages. The king's first two queens lost pregnancies that way. Noru's body would—but not always—reject an abnormal embryo."

She turned around to face him. "So which one survived?" she pressed.

"I don't know," he said truthfully. "The embryo had to go through two checkpoints to survive: first the Drukker, and then Noru's body. No Frankenstein will be born? That's a fiction without scientific basis."

Shaken about the loss of one of the embryos, he wished he had another scientist to discuss this with. Another lonely aspect of his move to Saburia was that there was no local community of bench scientists like at the NIH or Pandolf, even as he read extensively online, and chatted by video with Sharma frequently.

To his relief, in December, Soria Clinics sent him Dr. Liang to assist with the cancer vaccines trial. From China, he was a bright and earnest young man in his thirties whose English was passable. Liang set up his desk in the corner of the lab. A picture of Mooncake decorated his pencil mug. She starred in a popular international children's cartoon about a Beijing girl to teach children Mandarin.

He had fond memories of her smile and trademarked purple glitter headband that he had first seen on a kiddie cup in the LoveDiDa store at the Atlanta International Airport years ago. George had been a little boy, delighted to receive the candy filled mug from Santa.

Sharma called to thank him. "The Fujitsu award doesn't often go to someone as young as me. Your input on my research proposal took me to the top."

"Great German lab."

"Sorry to leave George on such short notice. But he's fine here on Pandolf's advanced academic track. A fine young man. You should be proud."

"How do they afford these programs at a public school?"

She explained that "local families donate, like the Mathers."

"Pandolf's turned out well for George," he said. "He had such a good visit with the Nepskis for Thanksgiving."

"And he's liking Chicago for winter break."

"He likes family Christmases," said Garcia.

• • •

January 2031 arrived. On a video call to wish him "Happy New Year," Kochanski told Garcia he would not be returning to Saburia now that "the project's going so well"—meaning the cancer vaccines—not the Purple Project—for any eavesdroppers.

"Cool," Garcia said to ask another question surreptitiously. "Speaking of temperature, is there new management at the Pierre? I got an email from a Beth."

"Yes. They're going to upgrade the cold storage under the building." Kochanski related the technical details, covertly reassuring Garcia that his Purple Project "biological" contents were safe.

After they disconnected, Garcia opened his lab notebook for his handwritten list of items still left in the Pierre building basement—and crossed off the two beads that Campbell had delivered for the reproductive engineers in India.

Next, he logged in to his computer and inserted numbers into his Drukker AI model of the planet's environmental change and the destruction of most of the world's species. *Is it only a matter of time before a global environmental apocalypse as the king predicts?* The Drukker gave no new answers, just statistical likelihoods for various theories. Hopeful ones persisted.

But, like an expanding dot on a distant horizon, he saw shadows growing inexorably into his consciousness, felt something inevitable and deep in the web of the universe, the one outside—or within him—his death if the king executed him. A horizon of suffocation from an unseen fire approached to destroy this world and create a new one—if such a metamorphosis lay ahead, he wanted to know more.

On a recent video call, George told him. "If the school finds out I'm living alone, I may have to return to Chicago."

"Then don't let them know."

"And Dad, the Malone sibs are returning."

"Who?"

"Charlie and Dr. Julia Malone."

"Dr. Malone, wait, isn't she the one who's supposed to get married in New York?"

"Her fiancé just broke it off."

"Oh."

"Yes, really bad news. He already has a new girlfriend. They're traveling to the Far East, then an ashram in India. From there, scuba diving in the Australian Great Barrier Reef before it disappears."

"Is she okay?"

"Charlie says she's in therapy and studying for her Boards. Leaving her job and returning to Pandolf. Wants to get away from her country club scene in Maine. Everyone there blames her, talks about her behind her back. Everyone there knows each other—she calls it 'incestuous.'"

"I don't know much about the Cape Cod elite types."

"Dad! Cape Cod is in Massachusetts, not Maine. But we have wealth here at Pandolf too. Did you ever meet the Mathers?"

Garcia looked carefully at his screen. George's hair was styled, his face straight-razor clean. A new elegance blossomed in how his son sat and spoke.

"The Mathers are a wealthy and powerful family," Garcia said warily. "Dean Baluyn is one of them. I met him at a dinner. He's Pandolf Hospital's CEO."

"What kind of name is Baluyn?"

"His father has Lakota heritage. On his mother's side, his grandfather is the Mather that Pandolf's emergency center is named after."

"I've read about the Puritans in New England," said George. "Mather is a famous Puritan name. Wonder if they're related."

Garcia didn't answer. Remembering that the king had mentioned the name Mather in the context of his Sun Order, he cautiously changed the subject to something banal, George's recent debit card charges. The pie chart still showed food, especially restaurants, as the biggest slice. But clothing, entertainment, and electronics were catching up. And the hefty payment for George's new car.

After they disconnected, he called his sister in Chicago to tell her about his new life insurance policy and a trust he had set up. "If something happens to me, you're George's legal guardian and the trustee. Mom will also be taken care of."

"Why would anything happen to you?" she asked anxiously. "Are you okay?"

"Yeah, yeah, just good to think about these things," he reassured her.

Campbell called later. "Manny, go visit your mom in Paris. Maybe George can join you there. Get out of Saburia's solar cooker before it heats up again."

"How did you know I was thinking about my mom?" he asked suspiciously.

"I didn't! I live in a sea of AI and, well, sometimes the boundaries between the electronic and natural world go fuzzy. Honestly, Manny, you just seem so *depressed* lately."

"I would need a visa to go anywhere."

"Then let's get a visa."

"Not yet," he said.

Too risky, he thought. Whatever games he was part of, from the queen's pregnancy down to one embryo, to the cancer vaccines trial, or ICE waiting to nab him, he should wait.

They disconnected. Except for the bright beam of light over his desk, the lab was now dark. Out there, the pie chart of George's expenses had changed, the world had changed, and the shadow of doom clouded his life. Was even the Drukker giving him friendly AI warnings about death, for himself or for the planet, but not wanting to snuff out hope? And Campbell seemed to think he was turning paranoid.

It is time!

He unwrapped a new Drukker disk, the latest upgrade, that could load a dozen times more data. In black marker, he wrote on the plastic casing: "The Second Coming." He would ask Sheraton to deliver it only to Campbell—to be decrypted only in the event of his death. Campbell would be right for this handoff, he thought, brilliant, trustworthy, fundamentally good.

For someone, someday, hopefully Campbell or another intelligent—and good—recipient in the unknown across the abyss, the disk would contain his entire Purple Project with no decrypting required. He inserted the disk into the Drukker printer. The machine whirred on.

For hours, beeps alerted him to get up from his chair, half-asleep, to insert the passcodes that removed all the security blocks from this copy.

Once decrypted, any scientist with the right intellect and education would be able to see his work—unsecured—on this disk.

About 4 a.m., the process finished, he fell asleep on a hard cot in the men's locker where he pulled up thin cotton blankets. Later that morning, as he dressed after his shower, movement outside the window caught his eye. Beyond the parking lot, splattered with dusty cars, scooters, and cycles, the hospital gates opened. Like a long black beetle, Queen Noru's limo crawled in, past saluting guards, and disappeared around a building.

• • •

Later that day, Queen Noru sat with Aisha in their palace suite. She clicked through ultrasound pictures on a screen on which she had written with a stylus: the date, a baby part, and sometimes her feelings.

Her fingers moved swiftly over the touch pad. "Let's see what Mama says. What's the latest gossip?"

"Just servants talking," said Aisha. "Instead of sharing time with all his wives, the king just stays with you."

"I'm going to have his baby."

"Dear, Queen Salma is his first wife, a princess in his tribe, his first cousin. You need to be careful. Your father is gone. Many of the king's men are the first queen's family, loyal to her."

Noru put on her bored face.

Aisha was patient. "Queen Salma made a trip to see her mother—want to hear?"

Noru nodded, curious. She had only seen Salma from a distance, in social gatherings and royal ceremonies: gaunt and ugly. But Noru knew her own beauty. She had her mother's large eyes and long neck, echoing ancient Egyptian art. When she was fourteen, measuring her for a feast day, the family dressmaker had murmured, "Curves like these still bring old sculptures to life."

Aisha first described Salma's ancestral home in Ramses. "The surrounding stone walls are ten feet high. Inside hide modern electric fences topped by barbed wire. Steel gates. Killer dogs roam. The roofs and tunnels are also guarded, latest military technology, her servants boast.

"Queen Salma goes in her armored car, black tinted windows, tall Sikh guards carrying automatic rifles. Then, those steel gates clang shut. And inside, dear, beautiful gardens, I see them buying the prettiest flowers in the market.

"One of her brothers meets her in the driveway, goes with her inside to their mother."

Noru leaned in. Mischievous grin. "And your friend is listening."

But Aisha rarely revealed her sources.

Aisha looked lovingly into Noru's face. "Queen Salma's brother, Abdul, says to his mother that it would be hard to dispute Crown Prince Malik's succession to the throne on any grounds. But the king is in love with you. Abdul argues that no one could challenge a king's heart if he changed the line of inheritance from our crown prince to your son."

"They're plotting. Go on."

"Queen Salma's family discusses how you were in India for some time under medical treatment to get pregnant, and how you see Dr. Kapoor a lot. And what's the purpose of the magic?"

"What magic?"

"Magic in our village."

"Silly."

"Also, Queen Salma's mother is wicked to her daughter."

"Like?"

"Says the king sees his first queen as a jealous crone next to you and pokes fun at her weight. Her daughter just looks at the floor."

"You feel sorry for Salma?"

"In royal families, they talk like that to toughen their children because life is pain and suffering, and royals must be strong. I hear that Queen Salma never even cried out during childbirth."

"Dr. Kapoor says she'll numb me up nicely when I go into labor," scoffed Noru. "Aisha, that sounds like something my husband called 'bullying' in his American boarding school." She paused. "Remember Eleanor?"

"Who?"

"Half-British woman, my English tutor."

"Akila is her Saburian name."

"Akila. Okay, I asked her about it before she left for the military base. She said that 'bullying' in Western boarding schools is used to teach leadership."

"Who cares?" said Aisha, raising her voice. "Saburia is glad to be rid of all those colonial fiends and their local puppets."

Noru tilted her head to indicate her lack of interest. While she was always deferential to her king and his anger about colonialism, she silently agreed with her mother who told her to "learn from the past and move on."

Aisha continued, warning in her voice. "Queen Salma's mother is to be feared. She tells her children to remind the king that they're still his family. She told Prince Abdul, 'Be his cousin, the younger one he grew up with, played with, pushed into the deep end of the swimming pool when he knew you couldn't swim.' And to Queen Salma, she says, 'Rebuild the king's trust, forgive his natural manly preference for Noru over you. Don't try to be his wife, just his family. Get me more information. There will be no disinheritance for my grandson.'"

"'Natural manly preference'? How awful."

"That's how she talks. And there are rumors that Bassam, your king's older brother, is also behind the terrorism and rebellion. Everyone still talks to Bassam, my friend tells me, even though he's officially in exile."

"We'll tell the king!"

"No, you have no proof. He'll just think you're jealous of Salma."

Noru now felt unsure of herself. *Best to follow Aisha's advice.* And the king was fond of his older brother. "My husband didn't have a say in his father's decision to exile Bassam, and he invited Bassam to come back to Ramses after his father's death as a personal gesture, though I'm not even sure that he returned."

"I don't know either," said Aisha. "I hear Prince Bassam and Queen Salma had feelings for each other . . . a long time ago. The two couldn't do anything."

"Because he's in a wheelchair?"

"I don't know. I do know that Queen Salma rarely sees our king, but when she does, she's dutiful. They discuss their son, not their daughter, poor thing, living someplace in the pretty mountains like in Bollywood movies."

"I married into a nest of snakes," said Noru, laughing. "Really, you servants talk a lot about us!"

Aisha did not smile. "Queen Salma waits as her mother tells her to.

They pray that the future will unfold in their favor. Change is a rule of existence."

Aisha looked at the walls. "If someone is listening, I serve my queen, what I was born for."

Noru tapped on her computer. "Mama tells me to listen to your lectures."

"Okay, then listen more. The other day, Queen Saira went to visit Queen Salma."

"Why? Those two hate each other!"

"They're friends now because of you. An enemy of my enemy is my friend. They talked about clothes, servants, travel, shopping, skin products, fillers, Botox, some plastic surgeon, the usual. They had coffee. Queen Salma's maids serve it on silver trays in little porcelain cups with steamed milk and cinnamon sugar."

Aisha gave details: the Dubai shop where the sets were purchased and methods of coffee preparation. After Noru lost interest, Aisha slipped in her latest purchase for their quarters: the same expensive coffee and tea sets.

Then she said softly, "True, my sweet, you don't need to fix coffee. But then, the two queens talked about your party."

Noru's interest perked. "Yes, Mama says in the West, they call it a 'baby shower.'"

"So, here is the fat Queen Saira, gobbling sweets, the pistachios' red shells staining her bloated face, lips, tongue, fingers"—Aisha's hands moved around her mouth—"knowing she's weak, weak family, no children, that people look down on her and are less guarded around her . . ."

With Noru's full attention, Aisha went on, her fingers busy with alterations in a maternity gown. "The silver tray of nuts and dried fruit was already being refilled. Only one pastry left. Queen Saira needs to feast to gossip. And Queen Salma is grateful for information. They talk about the party in the main hall and the budget over one million kumats, more money than was ever spent on them.

"Meanwhile Queen Salma has eaten nothing, just drinks coffee and asks, 'Saira, what's so special about this pregnancy? Why is Noru so sickly, always seeing the foreign doctor?' But the pudgy one says she had no news."

Noru saw Aisha grin, ready to entertain her with her animal imitations of Saira and Salma and shook her head. "No, let them be. Do you agree with Salma and everyone else that I'm weak?" Noru's eyes filled with tears. "You can leave me and return to the village if you like. The king says I shouldn't worry about the opinions of 'backward and uneducated women.' But I do care. I want people to think I'm strong, like Salma in childbirth."

When Noru was calm again, Aisha said, "Dear, pregnancy is like a full moon on the waters of a woman's mood."

Noru looked at her face, a faithful servant who had aged and still tried hard to serve her, to amuse her, to give her valuable information. She nodded. "I asked you what you knew, and you told me. You look tired. You should go rest now. Thank you."

Aisha gathered her things. "Queen, I'm faithfully yours until the end of my days, and afterward when I'm gone, I might become wisdom that you'll still hear."

CHAPTER TWENTY-ONE

Lake Michigan was a sheet of snow on ice. Throngs of people in downtown Chicago fled indoors to bars for warmth and cheer. In a January midnight news update, Chicago's mayor warned about a new viral outbreak in Indonesia.

"It's coming," she intoned only once. Elections were also coming, and she did not issue any health guidance. On social media, her political enemies showed her "shockingly" partying in a jostling crowd at Spirit and Stone, the trendy Loop restaurant.

Kochanski decided to break his sobriety streak. In Spirit and Stone, he made his way through the deafening commotion and tapped his credit card at the bar for a shot of Dew.

New, young, the masked bartender leaned in. "I'll go get it."

Warm air wafted from the ovens: smells of pizza dough baking with cheese, tomato, herbs, and meat. A young woman in a short skirt—despite the frigid weather outside—perched on a stool next to him. Did she have a father who did not like how she dressed? Kochanski wondered. Who wanted her to find a nice boyfriend unlike the man he used to be? Kasia was the biggest reason he had let Sichet take over the Pierre's management. Supporting her as a student in London was expensive.

And his building was finally making money. He tilted his head back and raised his glass to his lips. Blessed by its location, Spirit and Stone was a thriving restaurant. Only the stained glass in the former chapel's windows remained the same.

He asked for another drink, then another, then looked up at the glowing rectangles of stained glass, ghosts of the past—a lost homeland, wife, and mother—as memories faded the hubbub around him.

"Bad day?" asked the bartender.

Eyes wet, he nodded.

"You're not driving?"

"No, I live near here." He heard his voice slur. "Close my tab."

After tapping his wristband, the bartender looked surprised.

"Sorry, I didn't know who you were. Apologies about what I said about your vodka, sir."

"I didn't hear. The music was loud."

"Stay warm, sir. Seems like the Arctic is slouching into Chicago. Are they right about the Second Coming? The final pandemic?"

"As a businessman, I stay out of politics."

After wobbling out into the lobby, he made the call he had been putting off. A woman answered: "Hello?"

"Michael Kochanski here. May I speak to Alex?"

Silence, then she said softly, "Mr. Kochanski. I'm Callie, his wife. He's sleeping."

"Can he call me back?"

"I'll give him a message?" She sounded cautious.

"I want to talk to him about our friend, Oscar Sanchez."

"Okay"—another pause—"I'll let him know."

Then she texted the next morning to "meet me now." She gave her location, a restaurant.

"What about Alex?"

"Do you want to meet or not?"

"I'll be wearing a Cubs hat," he texted. What if Sichet with his bug-eyed stare found out? There was talk that Callie was his woman. Fortunately, the Pierre deal made feuding between him and Sichet bad for business.

Then the next morning, wearing a mask and hat, pulled low over his eyes, paying in cash to keep himself anonymous in the AI-surveyed crowds, he stepped into subzero temperatures to ride the subway. Feeling even sicker after the rattling "L" ride, his first hangover in weeks, he walked to her location near his stop.

The snow was piled outside the little café's windows, but a path through dirty ice had been shoveled. Escaping the bitter wind, Kochanski pushed through heavy double doors into a woody and warm interior. Someone waved at him from a booth a few feet away. Smooth hair swept up in a bun, the young woman smiled at him like he was the only person there. He recognized her immediately from Max Herman's painting.

Removing hat, mask, and gloves, he walked to her. "So nice to finally meet you in person."

"Me, too." Expressionless face.

Rubbing his hands together to warm them, he sat down across from her and tapped the table menu. "Hot coffee, yes, and OJ. So, you're the face that launched a thousand ships? I can see why."

"Thank you," she said politely. "Back home, they said I was 'too pretty.'"

"My daughter also attracts the wrong type of attention."

Her expression was blank.

"Is Alex okay?" he asked.

She lifted her chin. "My husband didn't feel like coming. Artists get that way."

The waitress brought his order.

"They know me here," she said. "After the kids go to school, I sometimes sit here all morning. I can call you Mike?"

"Michael. Please."

"My birth name is Calista, but I like Callie."

He waited, a tactic to see what she would say next.

It worked. She broke the awkward silence. "We're here about Oscar. Alex told me you called him when they found his body. He was young and beautiful. His death was untimely. But we didn't go to the police, didn't want to get into trouble ourselves—with small kids and all."

"Mmm." He had told Alex that talking to the police was a "bad idea."

She ate her pancake as she talked, telling him that her husband was not working, his art was not selling, and they were on public aid. Then: "Can I tell you things, things you may not want to know?"

He squelched the urge to leave. "Yes."

Opaque green eyes, painted onto a perfect face, gave nothing away. "Oscar came into our lives because of your Vermeer."

"I know."

"Okay." She dragged out the word. "Alex is angry about what happened to Oscar. That's why he didn't come today."

More silence. She looked far away. "Oscar used to come to our house in the evenings with your painting. Alex worked, even using mirrors to test accuracy. Oscar waited, he and I joked, drank wine . . . became friends. Oscar was center stage, entertaining our kids with his stories—ingenious schemes, wily escapes. They loved his magic tricks and funny fortunes."

"He had loads of personality."

"After the kids went to bed, Alex painted by candlelight just like Vermeer hundreds of years ago. With the children gone, Oscar's humor turned wicked, adult. And that little Vermeer of yours, Michael, everyone was enchanted. I would lose myself in her long-ago room with its light and shadows, blue, yellow, and purple." She traced brushstrokes by grazing her fingertips along the grain of the table, while her thumb ran the edge that joined two boards. "I even hung a Vermeer print—*Girl with a Pearl Earring*—above my daughter's bed. Anyway, one evening, after Alex and I waited until the early morning, Oscar was a no-show, something that had never happened before."

She stopped to dab her eyes with her knuckles. Her voice tight, she continued, "Then this mom at my kids' school was upset that another body had been found in the river, saying, 'This city is going to the devil.'"

"We're always just a blink away from evil." Mary had once said that.

Her eyes widened. "Well, who do you mean, the mom or the dead man?"

"Just something they say . . . in the old country," he lied.

She went on, "Then I found a picture online—that they said was Oscar. But the image was fuzzy, an angry man who didn't look like he had shaved or slept for days. Fake news, I thought."

Garcia's driver's license picture leaked online, he thought.

"The internet says Oscar had criminal connections," she said. "I mean, how crazy."

"Doesn't make sense," he agreed.

She blinked away more tears. Then she looked up, her eyes drying like rain in the summer sun.

"Max!" she said.

Max Herman stood at their booth. Wearing a long, black coat, he was holding a to-go tray with two steaming coffee cups and a clear bag of bagels.

"Michael and Callie," he said wryly.

"Max," said Kochanski, "I haven't seen you since my exhibit at the Pierre. Your agent says you're selling well."

"Oh yeah, Nick says he runs into you at Spirit and Stone."

"He's a good dealer for you."

The artist said nothing. Kochanski thought he looked smug.

"Max, would you like to join us?" asked Callie, moving over to make room.

"Can't, the wife's waiting outside." But Herman appeared to be in no hurry, returning Callie's gaze, willingly hypnotized.

Her uplifted face was serene. Her eyes sparkled. "I saw your nephew in the grocery store last month on winter break. He has gotten so tall."

"That's boys for you when you feed them. Turning into a man." Herman looked proud. "A place to himself, new car, manages to wrangle himself into whatever he wants to do. I take some credit for teaching him."

Herman's phone beeped. The pair's dance of flirty glances ended. Herman checked his phone, then looked at Kochanski, as if *just* noticing him again. "My nephew is Manny Garcia's son. Same Manny who connected us for me to help you set up your art gallery."

"Sure." *I know who Manny is, you idiot.*

"Anyway, when are you going to do another exhibit?"

"You should know the new management's turning the gallery into a penthouse apartment."

"No!" said Herman, then added, "Not surprised Jim did that."

As Herman walked away, Kochanski watched the light in Callie's face fade. Was there—had there—been anything between them? Herman had painted Callie's smile, another irreverent master finding earthy models like her—changing roles like clothes—to morph into ethereal saints and angels.

In Max's painting, Callie's gaze was hypnotic, reminding him of his gang days when Number One had the young girls use belladonna—hallucinogenic nightshade to dilate their pupils—cosmetically in their eyes. Those poor girls had no choice but to flirt even when they knew where it would end.

Who had coached Callie to flirt like she just did? Herman had sold his Callie painting for a big sum to Sichet. When he saw Kasia flirting—to get better tips at her waitressing job—he became angry with her: "You don't need to waitress!"

"So, what were we saying?" asked Callie, interrupting his annoyed musing.

"I forget." His mood had soured.

CHAPTER TWENTY-ONE

"Did you know why Alex accepted your job?"

"I don't judge," he grumbled.

"Money is tight for Alex and me. Our public schools here are bad. We send our kids to private school. So, back then, Alex took your job to forge your Vermeer. A challenge, he thought. Old school. Mixing paints perfectly. Layers painstakingly applied. He loves that stuff."

Then she added, "Before that, Alex also got a nice contract to paint a portrait of Jim Sichet and his family."

Her face revealed nothing, just as it hadn't when Herman had mentioned Sichet earlier. *Okay,* he thought, *rumor is you're Jim Sichet's side-action, like those women in the Chicago Mafia movies. And he bought Max's painting of you for a lot of money.*

"I do some business with Jim myself," he said. Out of habit, he looked around, remembering Saburia's ever-present eavesdropping. But in this nowhere restaurant in a no-place neighborhood of Chicago—serving bad OJ reconstituted from neon orange powder mix—no one cared what people said to each other.

Sichet lived in Hyde Park, she told him. "Alex took photos there for the family portrait, tall man, thinning hair, wife a petite blonde. Alex gave her beautiful, white round shoulders, like in old portraits. I took the sketch to Jim's office."

He let her talk, wondering where she was going with all this but also interested in learning more about the Jim Sichet she knew.

"In Alex's sketch, their three children stood around them. I imagined their lifestyle—and how I wanted to give that kind of life to my children, too." Her eyes were far away, one elbow on the table, chin resting on her palm.

A Saburian minister had once told him, "When the poor see how the rich live, it creates political instability. In our country, we build high walls around our homes, around our lives."

He wondered: *Girl, how do you afford to sit all morning at a café and not have to pick up a side gig or part-time job?*

As if on cue, the waitress interrupted to ask if they needed anything. He shook his head, wishing she would go away, his eyes unable to leave Callie's face, haloed by her white and silver winter cap. He couldn't see it, he thought, her becoming like that waitress, another gear in the machine, groveling to crabby customers.

Her husband had described first meeting Callie "where I stopped during a thunderstorm." Alex said he had been on his way back to Chicago from Southern Illinois. "Was visiting my cousin for a church supper. At a truck stop, she had "stepped out of a Monet, rain bonnet, prints of flowers around her hair."

At the time, Callie hadn't even finished high school. "But I was going to Paris anyway," Alex Marion had added, "and there we could be legal."

Had Callie grown up now? Kochanski wondered. Was she hungry for everything Chicago had to offer? The robust colors and shapes in Herman's painting reflected strength, a force of nature to contend with. Or had that just been Herman's vision for her? She was still young. She could still be quite innocent, from a small town, married at a young age, like someone else he once knew.

Irina, his dead wife. He picked up his mug of coffee. It was empty. Well, he had shooed away the annoying waitress.

The waitress returned—refilling water and refreshing only Callie's coffee—and catching up with Callie, who appeared to be a regular.

They laughed together like two young girls. Callie said, "I need this coffee, didn't sleep well last night."

"On the couch again," said the waitress.

Callie laughed. To Kochanski, she explained, "My husband snores. But I can look out the window at the smog and pretend it's the Milky Way over a clear night in Barbizon in France."

The women's chatter was as boring to him as the clatter of dishes in the crowded eatery. Cold drafts blew in every time the door opened.

After the waitress hurried away, Callie continued her story. "Anyway, I was late to Jim's office, couldn't call, dead phone. His high-heeled, hanger-for-clothes assistant had me wait an hour in this depressing room, dark-wood-everything and a thick rug that drowned out sound."

No, he made you wait because you were late.

"Finally, she came back. I matched her fake smile and followed her to his office."

"Must have been a nice office."

"Yes, but I first noticed his butterfly-blue eyes—my husband had not yet colored them in. He gave me a company pad and a heavy pen with a business logo. I took notes about the alterations he wanted for the portrait. But then he . . . next he . . ."

She looked down. "I was shocked. Dumb, huh? I hurried out of his office, still holding my souvenir pad and pen."

"Men are pigs. I'm glad you ran. But how does this connect to Oscar?" She looked angry.

"I'm sorry, Callie," he said. She looked upset, he thought, maybe not acting. Whatever Sichet had said or done that day must have affected her.

She nodded curtly. "Now I am tired. I should go."

"Wait, don't leave, keep going with what you were going to tell me."

"Come to our house. I want Alex to be there for that." She stood up and zipped her jacket.

"Text me a time," he said, giving up. "It'll be good to see Alex again."

"Okay. And Alex doesn't know about the thing in Jim's office."

"I'm good at secrets. I'll pay for our breakfast and leave a nice tip for your friend."

"Thanks." She looked upset. With clear effort, she still smiled but quickly left.

• • •

Kochanski's next "appointment" was back at Spirit and Stone. Still hungover, he anticipated a hot slice of thick Chicago pizza with fresh-squeezed orange juice, perfect after the cheap restaurant and bumpy subway ride. Good food and company would help him to build the fortitude to face Sichet's Beth, who wanted to look at more dollar figures and plans for the building basement that afternoon.

He arrived early. Chatting with the new security guard as he waited, he saw Elise Sheraton walk in, bundled up in a hat, muffler, and layers of clothes. She stomped the snow off thick boots.

They hugged. "It's so good to see you again, Michael. Look at you, so fit and trim. Chicago's been good for you."

"You always look beautiful," he said, helping her with her coat and handing it off to the guard whose smile grew wider.

"This is a nice place," she said after they were seated. "Those windows are like a church—ah, I remember, this is the place you told me used to be a chapel. I guess that's why it's called Spirit and Stone. So, *this* is your building."

"Yep." He smiled proudly.

They caught up. She said, "I head back to Saburia tomorrow. Soria moved their cancer treatments to Ramses, so now Mary and I don't have to make that dangerous trip to the coast. I'm also updating the pediatric service line in Ramses Hospital. When I'm done, Saburian pediatricians will take over. After Queen Noru has her baby—her due date's in June—I leave Saburia permanently."

"Where to next?"

"I already told you."

"What, lady!" he exclaimed, affecting a rural accent. "You're an MD-PhD, a double doctor, why go to the middle of nowhere?"

"Michael, I know you don't mean to be unkind. Look, I must be practical, with two kids in college. Rural doctors make really good money. After watching AJ run that remote clinic, I'm ready. The Missouri Ozarks are beautiful There's even free housing. A home on a hundred acres outside the town. Self-sufficient. Solar energy, well, generator."

"What kind of place is *that* to live in?"

"I'll let you know. What's next for you?"

"I'm no longer under contract with Soria now that the cancer project took off. David and I don't work together anymore. You know, I helped him to get that job as Zoser's CTO. Don't tell him, I want him to think it was all on his own. So, I'm not going back to Saburia, either." He wondered if Kasia would like her.

"How're you supporting yourself now?" she asked.

"I have rental properties. This building is making me money, even after the mortgage, taxes, and the reptilian property managers take their share. Come visit me again, Elise. Chicago would be a fun trip to the big city from the Ozarks. Walks along the lake, the Chicago Symphony, jazz bars, the arts and theater scene, best food in the world, and"—he grinned self-consciously—"a fun companion to do it with."

"You could come see me, too."

"Rural Missouri?" he said with a mock shudder. "I'd be scared to travel that far from the highway. Someone may hear my accent and then an Ozark Native American will run me down with his pickup truck on a one-lane country road into a flooded *rill*—that's an English word I just learned, meaning 'a small stream.'"

She laughed. "Michael, you watch too much cable. Your language, accents, and people are all mixed up. They're friendly down there. I'm going to be sensitive to the local culture, no different than Saburia that way, for me to be there to take care of people's health, not to get into their religion and politics. But I won't have to dress up, cover up, or worry about not looking like everybody else. That's been a lot of extra stress for me in Saburia, as I figured out."

"I'm spectacle," said Kochanski.

"What?"

"A joke. Meaning I'm *skeptical.* I used to get those words mixed up when I was learning English. But this home in the Ozarks sounds like something preppers built."

"I really think you've been watching too many shows. The media is misleading. AJ complains about how he's an American, but in Saburia, everyone thinks he's just another brown Indian, and they think that all American men look like David. See how misleading shows can be?"

"Fair enough. My evenings are lonely except for electronic entertainment. Is salad all you're having for lunch? My pizza here is rated top ten in Chicago."

Laughing, she accepted a thick slice, toppings, tomato sauce, and cheese sliding down the thick sides of a narrow wedge. "Life is fine with plenty of bread and wine."

CHAPTER TWENTY-TWO

Garcia called Kochanski about the birth of Noru's son at the end of May 2031: "Two weeks early but healthy," he said proudly.

"Congratulations to King Mohammed."

"Elise plans to visit you in Chicago," said Garcia. In a few weeks, Sheraton was leaving Saburia permanently.

Kochanski grinned. "If she told you, then that makes it more likely. Have you seen the baby?"

"No, I'll see him with everyone else at the one-month celebration," Garcia said thoughtfully. "Standing far away in the crowd."

So it was with scientists throughout history, he thought, distanced from the results of his Purple Project research, like a parent whose child left the nest.

Not yet!

As for my cancer research, he thought, *I would give it all away for free if I could.* But Soria Clinics must make their fortune first. He changed the subject to what mattered to him the most and told Kochanski that the cancer trial had recruited two new patients.

"Tell me," asked Kochanski, "will you do as good a job for any other project you take on?"

"Of course, I'm a scientist."

Garcia saw that Kochanski was covertly persisting on the topic of the successful outcome for the Purple Project: a healthy Saburian prince.

"Science is like a religion to you?" asked Kochanski.

Cautious about eavesdroppers, separated by screens, thousands of miles apart—and even the tiniest fraction of real time by the laws of physics, Garcia replied, "Religion is irrational. No."

"Sometimes reason must give way to faith, at least for me," said Kochanski. "Did you know that religious tolerance was a thing during the reign of Genghis Khan? We need more of that kind of leadership. What do you think?"

Michael is now asking me if the baby is the Genghis Khan embryo? "I don't know," Garcia replied truthfully.

After they disconnected, Garcia took out his only suit from the closet and draped it over a chair for the cleaners. He would wear it to the prince's one-month naming ceremony.

It is time to guide the future use of my Purple Project research! For that, Garcia resurrected paper to bypass new minders.

Meeting Sheraton in the lab before she left, he gave her an edible note that said: "Give drive to David if something happens to me, private, confidential items. Eat note, licorice flavor."

"George's generation has no use for paper, checks, no cash," said Garcia aloud. "I disagree."

She said nothing, grimaced as she ate the paper, and looked at the drive.

He had discarded the case that he had scrawled "The Second Coming" on, worried that label would draw unnecessary curiosity.

She slipped his unlabeled drive into her backpack.

He said sadly, "Good luck with your new job. I'll miss you."

She put one arm around him. "Now, you don't know what you don't know, Manny, as *you* always say. I bet you'll visit George again soon. I really believe it."

Like Michael Kochanski, he thought, she also happily hugged the irrational. He tried to smile even as he feared that he was trapped in some web in Saburia, perhaps never again to see his family, and rather executed on a king's whim — this country's spider.

Soon Elise Sheraton would take to the Ozarks his only unsecured copy of the Purple Project's files. *What could be a safer place for the files of his embryo engineering research and a safer person to deliver them to Campbell?*

• • •

In June, Michael Kochanski had another fight with his daughter, who canceled her trip to Chicago. Thankfully, David Campbell then picked up his video call with a happy smile. "Man, I just got back from a run around the Bay Area. They really cleaned up around here." He paused to chug a drink. "Need to finish my protein shake—shaken, not stirred—I know how you like those movie references. Good news! Soria Clinics just ordered software updates for Manny's project."

"Mary's New York City doctor says Mary's still in remission," Kochanski said with excitement. "Soria touts this as a success to recruit more patients."

"One treatment success is not statistically significant."

"Cynical, David?" he asked, feeling annoyed now.

"Just scientific," said Campbell, chugging a drink. "Also, I just talked to Elise about the rural Missouri clinic—closer to you, hmm?"

Kochanski ignored the innuendo. "Rural Missouri will get boring quickly for Elise. But I want to talk about something else. I'm doing business with Jim Sichet, your classmate."

"He's a few years older than me. I only knew his younger brother in boarding school. A family of bullies."

"Tell me anything you know about Jim?"

"StarHall was an elite boarding school—cooped up with other kids twenty-four seven, from around the world, top to bottom socioeconomically, you know because of all the financial aid. We spun ghost yarns to scare each other. Like this spirit that wandered around an empty building after a pretty, young teacher was murdered. Jim was at StarHall when she was killed. Had a mental breakdown after—and left for a year."

"How'd she die?"

"Strangled—"

"Jim wasn't eighteen yet, so any records might be expunged."

"A handyman was convicted, then killed in jail. But you sound worried, Michael."

"I have to do business with Jim." *And I think he's involved in Oscar's murder.*

"Be careful. Sichets are not nice people."

"Thanks for that tip, David."

• • •

Then Callie Marion finally texted Kochanski back: "Please come for dinner this Saturday evening."

The Marions lived in a two-story brick home in a crowded row of small houses in a nowhere Chicago suburb. He parked under a streetlight that showed bare patches on a tiny front lawn. A cracked walkway led to crumbling concrete steps.

A single light pooled a warm gold on the front porch. He rang the doorbell. No answer. Then he knocked hard. The door opened.

In his early thirties, a man of medium build, the artist, Alex Marion, had grown a brown beard since they had last met.

"Michael! Welcome."

Kochanski stepped into a warm living room, brimming with children's books and toys. He heard young voices upstairs.

"Thanks for bringing wine," Alex said. "Let's go to the kitchen."

A girl, maybe eighteen, tie-dyed scarf around her head, vigorously scrubbed a pot, flecks of black foam up to her knuckles.

"Marcella is helping us out today," said Alex. "The food should be here soon." He raised his voice over the sound of the rushing tap. "Marcella, will you eat with us?"

"It's Saturday night? Sorry, I have plans." She wiped her hands and, before Alex could introduce them, dashed out.

Kochanski sat down at the kitchen table, almost sliding off the chair because the seat cushion was not attached.

"Sorry. Marcella doesn't mean to be rude," Alex said. There was a loud noise on the floor above them. Sighing, Alex added, "Marcella's so fast, she breaks things."

Alex uncorked the bottle and poured equal measures into three glasses on the table and sat down. "That business with Oscar's death . . . Michael, I'm not copying paintings anymore."

"No—"

They heard Callie's voice in the next room. "Alex, why is there cereal on the floor?"

Alex sprang up. "My son's toy backhoe. Coming, honey, I'll clean it up."

Callie walked in. Long hair swept up in a bun, she was wearing a frilly white blouse and a jean skirt. "Thanks for coming, Michael. Oh, our delivery is here."

Still looking at her wrist phone, she ran out while Alex returned to clear newspapers and mail off the kitchen table to make room to eat. Then he laid out paper plates, plastic cutlery, and paper cups of water, incongruous with the crystal wine glasses.

She returned, carrying rustling plastic bags of Chinese takeout, and laid out the paper boxes filled with fragrant, steaming food. "Roasted duck, hot and sour soup—"

"My favorite," Kochanski said, ladling cashew chicken and rice onto his plate.

Then waiting until the time was right, he said, "I never got to thank you properly, Alex, for the work you did. Even if the painting was only half-finished." He handed Alex an envelope. "Here's the other half of what I owed you, after the deposit, for half a job done, even if it came to nothing. Sorry I'm a few months late."

"Not expected," said Callie happily. "Michael, I was so relieved when you sent that foreign man to pick that copy up, glad to get it out of the house."

"I had mixed feelings. I worked hard on it," said Alex. "But after what happened, I suppose that's safest."

Last year, after Garcia had been detained, his painting stolen, and Oscar murdered, not knowing who knew what, trapped thousands of miles away in Saburia, Kochanski had confessed to Salim everything, including his insurance scheme. Salim informed his boss, one of the king's ministers, who insisted that "out of an abundance of caution," a man from the Saburian embassy in Chicago would pick up Alex Marion's half-completed forgery and destroy it.

Watching the couple closely, Kochanski then lied. "I assume you know my original art disappeared with Oscar. The police never recovered it. They only told me that Oscar had stolen it."

"But Oscar didn't," said Callie quickly.

"I know," he said. "Oscar was just a courier. Nothing in it for him, really, he wouldn't have known where or how to sell it."

Orion, the hunter; Kochanski went on the attack. He added, "But Oscar was killed, and the painting disappeared at the same time . . ."

"Are you suggesting that Callie is lying?" said Alex tensely. "Or . . . that *we* might have killed Oscar for the painting?"

"No," Kochanski said. "But Callie knew you were making a forgery, yes? Who else knew about Oscar bringing the painting here?"

There were tears in Callie's eyes. "Yes, I knew . . . that what Alex was doing was illegal. But I never told anyone. Marcella had no clue. And Alex and I, maybe we didn't take enough precautions. But we just *never* imagined that someone could be killed."

>CHAPTER TWENTY-TWO

"Nor did I," said Kochanski truthfully. "Relax. I'm not accusing you or anyone, no, just frustrated that we can't find out more about Oscar's murder; I cared about that kid. And what happened to my painting of course?"

Callie exchanged a look with her husband.

"We want to tell you more," said Callie.

"It's my fault that this mess began," said Alex.

"Good that you see that," said Callie.

Alex said that Jim Sichet had engaged him to do a portrait of his family four years ago. "I sent Callie with my sketch to show Jim. Everything cracked up after that. He began to stalk her. Still does."

She placed her hand into Alex's and said to Kochanski, "He comes to the same café where you and I met. I look up sometimes to see his face inches from mine."

Alex explained, "You see, Callie was the model Max Herman picked for Jim's painting of a ship's figurehead. I think Jim only picked me to paint his family as a ploy to then meet Callie."

"Jim still shows up out of nowhere," Callie said, "like last week at PaysWorth where I buy groceries. We make small talk. I act like everything's normal—"

"Jim also decided to try out painting himself," said Alex, "even rented a studio."

"After Max sold Jim his painting of me," Callie said, "Jim told Max that he wanted me to model for him. So yes, I've been to Jim's studio many times—"

"—a nice, big, sunlit space," finished Alex. He described seeing Sichet's studio on his way to visit Max Herman's art agent, Nick, about representing his own work.

"Nick barely listened to me," Alex said. "He was euphoric about an offer for this acrylic."

Alex described the painting, gesturing with his hands: "Sunset, a band of orange over twilight on black hills, black trees just gobs of tar under radioactive sky—"

"Angela bought it for the asking price, she's Jim's girlfriend," Callie said. She pronounced *Angela* the French way, an intake of breath on the first syllable. "In her pictures online, she wears diamonds the size of grapes."

259

Alex continued gloomily, "Nick said he was too busy for me and recommended another dealer." He added with a self-deprecating half smile, "Nick can say no. He's already swamped. There's barely space to walk in his office. Everything was dusty like nobody important was coming—just me."

The morose humor in Alex Marion's voice, the dim light around the couple that seeped into the woody dark paneling, every cell in his body now felt closer to his former gritty life in the old country, to Poland, to Europe, to home. Sipping his wine gratefully, he inhaled the earthy nose of the French red—rekindling warm memories of growing up with little: and the plenty he had found back then in warm little rooms, temporary safety, a full stomach, the buzz of booze, uncertain kinship—before more fights ahead.

When Callie looked at the almost empty bottle, Alex shook his head. "Remember, you're trying to cut back." Callie's eyes shuttered in deference.

She didn't light up for her husband, he thought, like she had for Max Herman. The spark between the artist and his object exiled others to envious darkness.

"I would have refused Jim's offer to paint his family," said Alex, "if I had known back then that the jerk was stalking you."

"Alex!" she exclaimed. "You and I were barely talking back then. Our house is small. I didn't want the children to hear us fighting. I never used to hear my parents argue. Besides, Max asked me to, for him. His painting of me might become famous someday."

Turning to Kochanski, she continued, "Back then, we had maxed out our credit cards and had to get a second mortgage. The doc also told Alex to stop drinking and suggested medication."

Her husband was looking over her shoulder at the wall. "She and the kids went home a lot to her parents back then."

Feeling their tension, Kochanski changed the subject. "Callie, where is your family?"

"Small town in the country, south of here," she said. Then she described Kochanski's immigrant dream, the great green heart of America, where two-lane highways rolled through a landscape of plenty and safety, dotted with barns, silos, cows, and horses. On endless roads, she and her friends had sailed in their pickup trucks to the beat of pounding popular music.

"I also grew up in a small town," he said.

Wistfully, he added, "But yours sounds like a place where time stops." *Where love also grows generously in fertile soil carpeted with soybean and corn.*

Jarring him, she then said, "My town would make a good horror movie. My family spends all their free time doing things with our church, an old relic next to a graveyard. I left when I was seventeen with Alex. Now, I come back to visit with two dark children. Oh the looks we get—"

"That's why I don't visit her family much," said Alex. "Even if their Jesus probably looked like me."

He had never asked Alex Marion about his ethnicity. The name, Marion, gave no hint. Back in the Old World, one could look at a person's face, the shape of the bones, the accent in their voice, and know exactly where they were from. With his olive skin and dark curly hair, Alex's ancestry could be traced to anywhere along the Mediterranean corridor.

They heard fast footsteps on the stairs. Two children appeared in the doorway with Marcella.

"Say good night to Mom and Dad, and Mr. . . . ?" said Marcella.

"Kochanski, Michael Kochanski," he said, staring at the children, seeing reflections of their parents, this bit of Alex, that touch of Callie.

"You're Oscar's friend." Marcella looked doubtful, eyes traveling over his plaid shirt, paunch, and blue jeans.

"And you must be Marcella. Oscar said nice things about you," he lied.

"I hear he had to go back to his country. How's he doing?"

"Fine, I think."

"Introduce yourself, guys," Marcella said to the children.

"Richard," said the boy, who looked nine. Alex's curly hair, but a lighter brown.

"Sarah," said the girl, about eleven with olive eyes.

"I don't want to go to bed," the girl said, looking at her father. "Can I have a pot sticker? And—"

"No," interrupted Marcella. "Upstairs now. Good night, everyone."

After they left, Callie said, "I'm so grateful to afford her help."

She's been our sitter since high school," Alex said. He lowered his voice. "Her mother was a housekeeper for a wealthy family. Had an affair with the husband. The child support arrangement is generous; Marcella is better off than us, even a trust fund."

"But we're her home," said Callie.

"So, Marcella and the kids don't know that Oscar is dead?" asked Kochanski.

"It's better that way," said Callie softly.

Callie said she had been fearful after Oscar's body was found. "I even brought a shotgun back from the country."

"I don't even know how to use one," said Alex. "And don't approve of it in a house with young kids."

"We have a gunlock," said Callie. "And I feel safer. Michael, the weird thing is that right after Oscar disappeared, when I went back to Jim's studio, he stopped talking to me for a while except when necessary."

"Not a bad thing," said Kochanski.

She frowned at him. "No, except that's when I really began to dread going."

"He has her sit on a chair that's red velvet," said Alex.

"I hate it," she said. "But Michael, one day in the studio, I saw it—the corner of your picture—I couldn't believe it. I stared at Jim. He glared at me, so I—artfully—looked away."

"You're sure that was my painting?"

"Yes, I snuck a few more peeks. Do you think Jim killed Oscar for the painting?"

"No, art's not Jim's line of business," said Kochanski. "I just can't imagine how my painting would land in his studio."

But Callie was confirming his theory that Sichet was linked to Oscar's murder.

"We thought you should know," said Callie.

He thanked them. The couple didn't need to know, he thought, that not only had the Chicago police returned the Vermeer to him, but also he had already given the art to the Saburian king, as previously agreed, to repay the loan he had taken to make the Pierre mortgage payments—before Jim Sichet took them over.

For legal purposes, the Saburian minister had insisted on a formal ownership document. He still didn't fully understand—but admired—how the Saburian accountant got his taxes so low on the sale to the king.

Strangely, given the theft and Oscar Sanchez's murder, no one had followed up with him, neither the Chicago police, ICE, nor the FBI. Talwar told him she didn't know why, either, but that he should "leave it alone." There seemed to be only one explanation. Jim Sichet had the connections to make that investigation drop. Of course, Sichet enjoyed his power plays. But also, if Kochanski were arrested, it would be bad for Sichet, given their business deal together at the Pierre.

"How'd you get a Vermeer in the first place?" asked Alex.

Another fiction—the same one Kochanski had said so many times that he now almost believed it himself. "It was in my family back in Poland for many generations. We thought it was just a fake. That was just a cover to protect the painting from confiscation during wartime."

"Very cool," said Callie. "I'm sorry you've lost it. And about Oscar." Her eyes were teary again.

"I had Oscar's body cremated," Kochanski said to console her. "I tried to reach out to his family. If they ever come looking for him, I still have the ashes."

"Poor Oscar. I hope drowning wasn't painful," she said.

"The police said he was shot first, quick, less painful."

In the sad silence that followed, Alex got up and cleared the table.

"I hope you're done with Jim, Callie," said Kochanski.

The couple looked at each other. "No," Callie said. "I still model for that painting. And do other small jobs for him as well. It pays well."

"We are month to month with bills," said Alex.

"And lots of credit card debt," added Callie.

"We need Jim's money. So, we put up with him."

Later, he couldn't remember which one of them had said that last bit. Long-term couples lived in their own world, said the same things, were bound together in all the ways that two people could be tied down, boundaries blurring amid a muddle of kids and relatives. Young or not, they should have known better than to have done illegal things right in their home with small children around.

"We may do one last exhibit at the Pierre," he said. "Alex, you could show a couple of your paintings?"

Alex smiled broadly. "Thanks!"

Callie got up and went to the sink to rinse their wine glasses. Down her back, hair unwound from her bun and fell between her shoulder blades. The counter was cluttered, the stove looked older than its hosts, and the cabinet doors leaned off their hinges.

With the dishes done, kids sleeping, and Marcella gone, the house was quiet. Kochanski got up to leave. Callie took him to the door of the darkened living room.

"Thank you," she said, giving him a smile that could have graced the warm shadows of a Vermeer. "Oscar was right. You are a friend."

• • •

His lonely weekend problem solved, Kochanski spent more Saturday evenings eating takeout with the Marions, submerging himself into the comfortable rhythms of a family, listening to the couple interrupting or finishing each other with domestic stops-and-starts—laundry needing to go in the dryer, a phone call, and most often something to do with the children. Time paused its hurried march into the unpredictable future.

One day, Callie described her trips on the Chicago subway, Kochanski said that he, too, often rode those "L" trains, mesmerized by the glass windows, black in the tunnels and bright with blurred motion elevated above ground.

She said she tuned out the grit, the city palette of anonymous travelers, and the glaring ads on the panels above the windows by reading the Bible on her phone. Where I come from, they never preached about Bathsheba or Judith—"

"I think," said Alex, "that one, a young wife seduced by old King David, and the other who beds and beheads the enemy of her people, are hardly role models for women."

"God loves most the most broken," Callie said.

"Amen," Kochanski said.

She continued, "And those stories are more interesting than 'who begat who?'"

Remembering the Purple Project, Kochanski said, "I know men, even now, who care a lot about who begat who . . ."

Often, a wave of chaos would roll in with Marcella and the children.

One evening, Marcella asked Kochanski about his opinion on the new pope.

"Since I left Poland, I don't follow the popes much."

She looked disappointed.

Trying to get information from Alex and Callie, Kochanski would often find a way to slip in Jim Sichet as a topic. Once, he asked, "Callie, I can't imagine Jim as an artist."

"He gets into character," said Callie. "T-shirt, jeans, a stained painter's smock."

"Must be branded, some stealth wealth Florentine fou-fou," Alex said. Then he bit into his second brownie.

Kochanski asked Callie, "So, tell me how it was the first time at Jim's studio?"

She raised her brows. "You really are obsessed with him?"

He tilted his head to agree.

"Fine, he hung up my jacket. Told me to wear the same dress each time I come. Then I sat on his stupid red chair, looking out this big window to nowhere past floating specks of dust."

"He never tries to do anything when you're there?" asked Kochanski.

"Better not," said Alex, his mouth full.

"No," she said. "I've gotten used to him—even him showing up out of nowhere. He pays well. Gives good advice about our money problems, likes hearing about everything."

Another time, Callie reminisced about Oscar. "Alex would paint. And after the kids went to bed, sometimes Oscar would tell Marcella and me about his spiritual experiences around the world."

Kochanski was surprised. "But Oscar never traveled anywhere since he came to Chicago. As an undocumented teenager."

"But his descriptions were so realistic," Callie said, "God as the face of everything good. He was God's knight. He and Marcella really connected, how she became a Muslim."

"Was Oscar Muslim?" asked Kochanski, even more surprised.

"No, he didn't believe in any particular religion, just had her seriously think about such things," said Callie. "Marcella said she went to church with her mother, sat next to some old man. She mimicked Sleeper to make our kids giggle, how he snored, stopped breathing, gasped."

Alex snorted a laugh.

Callie frowned at him. "Stop. I made Marcella stop too. Church is for broken people like him. Then one day, Marcella told us, 'I'm Ismael, Hagar's unwanted child.' Next thing, she was a Muslim—"

"I mostly tuned out all their religious talk to paint," Alex interrupted. "Poor Oscar, the last time I saw him was May last year, right at dawn when he left. Was that the night he found the dead mouse?"

"You've gotten all mixed up," Callie said. "Marcella found the mouse, not Oscar. How can you forget how she screamed? In fact, I'm very sure it was you who killed it by putting it in the freezer in that old baby food jar."

"I honestly don't remember doing that to a poor mouse."

"People don't remember what they do when they're drunk."

Kochanski no longer felt awkward when tensions sparked between the couple. Rather, he felt included in something intimate.

Another time, Callie said, "Michael, I did talk with Jim about Oscar sometimes. But I was always very careful about what I said, never mentioning the painting, you must believe me."

Alex turned to his wife. "Maybe Jim was jealous of you and Oscar."

"No," interrupted Kochanski, seeing Callie about to protest. "We still can't say for sure who killed Oscar. But we do know that Jim was stalking Callie. He must have known about all the comings and goings in this house. Wondered what Oscar was up to, and then figured everything out."

"Thank you for believing me," said Callie.

Kochanski helped them to clear the table and sink. The Marions had a gun, they had told him. Should he dismiss his wild suspicions of them about Oscar's murder, he wondered? Sichet seemed more likely. But why? How? Theories germinated. He speculated and dried the pots, pans, and dishes. He now even knew where to put them away.

• • •

The Marions had believed his romantic lies about how he had procured the Vermeer painting. The truth was complicated. In his gang days, he had seen the picture in the home of an Eastern European politician. Liking it, he did the obvious. He stole it. Eventually, he brought it to the United States as a remembrance from his homeland.

The New York City appraiser discovered it was an original Vermeer, last seen in the 1800s. After some covert investigation, Kochanski learned that its previous owner had had no idea that it was valuable, having received it in a corrupt scheme to possess the house that it had hung in for decades. Any descendants of the original owners were lost in the fog of two hundred years of European history, its fluid borders and bloody wars.

At first, the brief splash of publicity terrified him, even though the appraiser promised that his identity would be kept "private." What if his lies about the art "being in his family" were discovered? Or his enemies back home in Poland found out that he still lived? At the time, he stopped answering emails and requests for interviews, and, for a while, he even dodged detectives and supposed "relatives."

It had been tricky to get insurance for the painting without solid provenance. Kasia agreed to lie to the company investigator, saying that she had grown up seeing the painting on her grandmother's wall in Poland. The insurance company could find no other claim of ownership. Finally, a "gift," really a bribe, greased the last wheels to get the policy.

The rest was supposed to go smoothly: hiring Alex to make a copy, giving the original to the Saburian king to cover his debts from a personal loan, later filing a claim with the insurance company saying that the painting had been stolen and replaced with a forgery. He had thought that the secretive Saburian government was unlikely to make public knowledge their acquisition of the Vermeer. Regardless, if the insurance company disputed his claim, he knew they would likely settle rather than go to court—cheaper—and he would still get a partial payment. By then, the Saburian king would have the original in his private collections, to be forgotten again by the rest of the world for the foreseeable future.

His insurance fraud scheme had now failed, but at least the original was now in Saburia, lost again to the centuries. That Vermeer deserved a better protector than a nobody like him. Who better than a descendant of pharaohs?

One night, Kochanski hurried out of the Marions' house. The home he had just left drew in others seeking the warmth of a family: Marcella, Oscar, and now him. Driving down the narrow street, he saw the porch light of their home turn off in his rear mirror. He felt lost again in a sea of time under a moonless night. Then the upstairs window glowed, a beacon, and he sobbed.

Fearful that his own people might try to hurt him or Kasia even after all these years, he had made no close friends among Chicago's sizable

Polish American community. By crossing the ocean, he still had not left his past behind. Safety meant a shrouded, lonely life.

Some still suspected that he had killed Number One in his old gang. Waiting near the outhouse next to a stream, he heard a telltale splash, then the large man's heavy steps growing louder, approaching him. His knife silenced that uproarious man who had told adventure stories of his waste downstream. Afterward, he pulled together their disorganized group of young men into a legitimate business. Dew vodka got its first distillery.

"The blood now runs clear," the hometown priest had said, using a Polish word like the English word: sublime, to elevate to spiritual purity.

Priests here in Chicago were strangers to him, as anonymous as the cars that now sped by on the main road. He arrived at his tall tower of condos, all thick-walled cells: no laughter of children, no dogs barking, no clatter of dishes, no raised voices of a couple having a minor argument that extinguished itself as quickly as it started—just silence.

At first, as she was obviously beautiful, Kochanski had simply thought that the rumors about Callie were true, and that Sichet was paying her to be his mistress. But now that he was finding out that the couple seemed young and naive—he was thinking that Callie had neither the nature nor inclination to be that type of player. Though it still did not explain how the Marions paid for it all, private schools and a nanny. Maybe if in great houses there were many rooms, then in Callie's world, he had yet to find the one that hid the full truth.

Still, the everyday joy that filled their home was a dream come true for him. He had not even given a stable family life to his only child. An ex had once told him, "It's clear that Katya lacked mothering when she was growing up," a dealbreaker for their relationship.

He invited the Marions out for a dinner at Spirit and Stone. They were late, blaming work commitments and no childcare. As usual, Callie wore a dress, but this time she had accessorized it with a long scarf, draped around her shoulders and knotted around her throat.

The maître d' brought them to the table.

"Sorry we're late," said Alex.

Sitting down, Callie sighed. "Marcella and Sarah were going at it again."

Alex straightened his back. "Sarah's my wild child. I like her that way.

But, yeah, I hope Marcella doesn't quit." He looked at Callie as if expecting her to make sure.

"We need Marcella's help," said Callie, "because Alex now has a job!"

Alex made a face. He sipped the Dew. "This is good vodka."

Callie sampled her husband's glass. "I'll stick to wine, thanks."

Alex then described his new job in commercial media, "not the type of art I enjoy." Kochanski recognized the name of his employer—a vendor for Sichet.

While they ate, Callie said she got a new laptop. "Jim wants me to use a separate one for the things I do for him, for client privacy and security."

An awful idea came to Kochanski: what if, what if both Alex and Callie were in cahoots with Sichet? Something sordid? What?

He shut out a memory of Irina, how she and Number One, though she was *his* girlfriend . . . hence the paternity testing for Kasia. No, no . . . *I'm a monster to think these things of my friends.*

But the Dew, his "ugly business partner," stepped in, pointed to Callie, and then he said, "Lovely scarf."

How do you afford that?

She unwrapped the silk around her neck and shoulders, about six feet of dusky blue in a paisley pattern on a saffron background.

"This was a gift from Oscar," she said. "So beautiful, like something I'd see window-shopping on the Magnificent Mile. Oscar said he got it in India in the Himalayas. He described a saint there who was 150 years old and who levitated under a tree. But I guess Oscar just made up that story, huh."

Their pizzas arrived, steaming between them.

While they ate, Callie said, "Marcella keeps asking and I keep telling her that you say Oscar is out of the country—he is in a way—and that's why he's not returning her messages. I don't want her to go to the police. I'll tell Marcella someday, but timing is everything, especially with the truth."

What are you going to tell me when the time is right?

"This summer," Callie continued, "her dad's parents are taking her on a family trip to France and Italy. That should help her forget Oscar."

"Oh no," said Alex, busy eating pizza. "We're going to have to find another nanny."

"Unbelievable," said Kochanski. "Her dad paid off her mom. And his parents take her on trips?"

"They even sent her to private schools," said Callie, "though not the same ones as their other grandchildren to avoid awkwardness."

Like both of you send your kids to private school. And Jim is your ticket?

"Fair enough," said Kochanski. "Her parents are not Marcella's fault. I never even knew my father. He was probably also married."

Callie gave him a sympathetic look.

If Jim's playing me through these two, I can do it, too.

"Michael," asked Callie, "any news about your lost painting?"

"I'm still trying to figure it out," lied Kochanski.

Are you going to tell Jim I said that?

"I like mysteries, so I've been doing some of my own sleuthing," she said. "Jim was stalking me. He must have known all about Oscar and the forgery, like you said."

"Yes," he said. "And did you ever confront him then about what he was doing with my painting that day?"

Or maybe you already know—everything.

"I can't ask him," she said. "He wouldn't answer. If I pressed him, he'd get angry and stop talking to me for a while again. And I need his work from home."

She then described her sleuthing: "His studio makes a perfect lovers' nest for Angela and him. In the back, there's just an empty lot so no one can sneak a peek at anyone up there."

So maybe you two want me to think that Jim already has Angela as his side piece, and you are innocent.

"I worry, Alex," said Callie. "Would Jim tell the police that you did forgeries? What if you went to jail?"

Maybe Jim is blackmailing them? There is no statute of limitations on murder. Alex did admit he was the last person to see Oscar the night he was killed.

"Callie, tell him," Alex said.

"Okay," she said softly. "Remember last night how it was raining and windy? I stopped at the café for some wine, thinking that I would not stay long, but I ran into—"

"Max," said Alex.

Kochanski stifled his laugh, much needed after feeling lost once more in a hall of mirrors, doubting himself for doubting them, his new friends.

She sighed. "It's just that I lost track of time, and it got dark. Then, Alex, you were supposed to fix the light on our front porch. When I finally unlocked our door to go in—so hard to see—something caught the end of my scarf and jerked me back. Worried that I might have torn Oscar's scarf. And then I saw something and screamed. Marcella ran outside. We looked around with our phone lights—nothing."

"They called me. I came home," Alex said dramatically, placing his hand over hers. "I would kill for you."

She tenderly touched her cheek to his. Kochanski looked at him.

You've never killed anyone!

"How weird," said Kochanski. "I'm glad you're safe, Callie. I think you guys need to fix that light, put up more lights, and get security cameras. I'll have one of my guys come by tomorrow and give you a quote."

"Thanks," said Alex. "Something, hopefully, we can afford?"

"I'll tell him to do it at cost. I give him enough other work."

Maybe I can also look at the recordings then. He imagined that Garcia, the scientist, might suggest that as the solution to guide him—to the truth about Jim Sichet and his role in Oscar's murder.

He looked at the couple happily sharing a slice of chocolate cake and decided—for the final time—to clear them of any role in Oscar's murder. *I choose to believe you. My friends. My choices. My consequences.*

"How about them Cubs?" Alex looked up at the large screen, his worried frown fading. The baseball season was a cheerful change of topic.

After paying for their dinner, Kochanski called them a ride home. They beamed gratefully.

"See you at our house next Saturday, Chinese and wine," said Alex.

Clutter, clatter, complications, and children, he thought. They had welcomed him into their home. Oscar, too, had felt loved in those rooms and had spent a short lifetime of savings on Callie's scarf.

Somewhere, maybe, there was another room . . . where death was the portal to the infinite and truth he no longer really cared to find.

"I'll bring the wine, my vodka," he told them, ". . . and chocolate ice cream. Toys for the kids."

CHAPTER TWENTY-THREE

Early one morning, before the July heat in Ramses made an outside gathering impossible, the king, his three queens, and the newborn prince appeared on the main balcony overlooking the central plaza of Ramses. Cameras televised the event on screens around the country.

Garcia joined the colorful crowds. Times-Square-size screens, captioned in Chinese, Arabic, and English, showed the twenty-four-year-old Crown Prince Syed Malik—unable to travel due to attending an international economic summit—delivering his blessings. The king's daughter was not mentioned. The family doctor had given the baby a drug to sleep through the rituals. Salma sat on the king's right as his first queen, with Noru on his left. Saira sat on Salma's other side. The women wore black robes, only their faces showing. King Mohammed was robed in white, as were all the men on the balcony. Guards surrounded them wearing brilliant colors—red, blue, and purple—and gold and silver regalia.

Festive colors also painted the plaza. Live music played. Garcia watched the parade of the royal guard and band. Brilliant horns and drums played martial music. The people clustered around the perimeter and waved colorful flags and patriotic signs, cheering nonstop.

All became silent when the imam, standing on the balcony, said prayers that were broadcast over loudspeakers. Finally, the king spoke. In a short speech, formal Saburian, he thanked his people and lauded the country's accomplishments. Finally, he turned to the imam, holding the baby, and placed a gold circlet on the infant's head.

The giant screen broadcast his words in many translations. "Congratulations, my son," said the king. "On your naming day, I name you Ahmat Ali, child of mine descended from our fathers and ancient pharaohs. I have a vision of you in the sun's bright future for our nation."

As a traveler, Garcia had found that nonverbal signals, facial expressions, body language, ceremony, and rituals, were often truer guides than a minion's translation. *Did the infant's gold band hint that he was now the future king, the culmination of the Purple Project?*

After the imam finished his prayers, the ground vibrated as the crowds jumped and cheered themselves hoarse. Then the band struck up the national anthem. But the show was not over. The king raised the baby toward the crowd, and then a light rain started to fall. Breaking an awestruck silence, more cheers rose. Ancient traditions spoke of the Rainbringer in this desert kingdom, and this blessing from heaven itself now crowned the latest prince of Saburia. Garcia looked above at a few clouds, silver ribbons in the early morning sky. The scientific explanation had to be that the clouds had been seeded.

The queens' faces were expressionless as they dutifully kept their gaze on their husband. On one towering screen, a close-up showed that Queen Salma was also just looking up at the sky. Shadowed eyes hooded, mascara lengthened her lashes into sharp points. Garcia recognized Prince Abdul, her brother, behind her. He leaned in to say something to his sister. She gave the faintest nod.

• • •

Afterwards, joining the streaming exodus of crowds, Garcia hurried back to the Ramses Hospital complex, racing the sun that was rising fast in the sky along with the temperature.

He entered a narrow alley shortcut between old walls with small windows, not wide enough even for a small car. Arches over the ancient way and awnings over doorways threw patterns of shadow. The scorching heat vaporized the last hint of the morning's moisture on the paving stones. Except for stray dogs and cats, he was alone until he turned a bend and saw a Saburian man sitting on the steps of a clothing shop. Passing by, he nodded at the man, who smiled back. Then from behind him, strong hands closed around his throat, and he blacked out.

• • •

He awoke in a dungeon with brown stains on its cracked plaster walls, where bright lights illuminated rusted hooks and loops. Sitting upright against one wall, he faced a modern steel door. A tin bucket stood under a faucet next to him. The stink of stagnant water rose from a drain in the stone floor. Furnishings were sparse: a wooden table and a bench. Aside from a bruised throat and a dull headache, he saw a bandage in the crook of his elbow. *They must have drugged me. But I'm still alive!*

He wore unfamiliar Saburian clothes. His phone showed that an hour had passed since he was knocked out but no signal. Then he heard beeping. A small boy brought Garcia lunch.

"Eat," said the child.

Unsteadily, he moved to the table. Chilled sugarcane juice, a few bites of flatbread, then as a vegetarian, he set aside the chicken kabob. Headache unabated, he also felt a swimming sensation when he moved. He rested his forehead on the table.

"Come," said the child in English. But when Garcia tried to talk, the boy did not understand his English or weak Saburian.

Following the boy, stumbling, wondering where he was, why, and how to escape—like the time he had been at the ICE center—*best to wait and see*, he thought. After a quick trip to a closet-toilet, the boy led him into a windowless room and handcuffed him to a chair.

After the child left him in darkness, Garcia heard a metallic rattle.

"Hello, Mr. Garcia," said a man's voice, American English.

"Hello," said Garcia groggily. "May I ask why I'm here?"

"You *may*," replied the man, sounding amused. "But I have questions first. Answer them truthfully. That cell you were in is an old torture chamber. Here in Saburia, we have traditional ways of persuasion and many styles of execution. We're losing those skills in modern times. Drugs are an artless—but effective —scientific advancement that I personally prefer."

"I appreciate that."

"When Queen Noru went to India to become pregnant, she took a Drukker computer drive and amber beads. Tell me what you know. I already have information. If you lie to me, then things for you—and your son—won't go well."

Garcia hesitated, then heard himself say, "My work involved a project for the king."

Unable to stop himself from talking, he explained the royal family's inherited genetic defects from inbreeding. "The king wanted a healthy child with Queen Noru." He described his part in creating the two embryos that were transferred into Queen Noru. "Only one survived."

Then he went on that the Chinese gave the king a gift for his coronation: a relic of Genghis Khan. "One of the embryos for the queen carried the Khan genetic material instead of hers, like two men making a baby."

"Isn't her X chromosome needed there somewhere?"

"In nature, the sperm that fertilizes the egg determines the sex of the embryo, XX for a girl and XY for a boy. In the lab, we extracted Queen Noru's DNA from her egg. Replaced it with the Khan chromosomes, including the Khan's single X. Then inserted the king's chromosomes, including his Y, thus a boy, XY."

The man whistled. "I get it. Do the Chinese know what the king did with their relic?"

"Who knows? Or if that was truly a relic from Genghis Khan's tomb?"

"Good point. Tell me what your son has to do with this, why everyone went to the trouble to bring him to the Soria Clinic. Many men were killed."

"Not George's fault," said Garcia defensively. "Terrorism is a problem on your coast."

He described using George's blood and tissue to create a human DNA library, "a father–son project, you could say. I used George's DNA to fill in the blanks between the Khan DNA fragments for the Khan embryo. And to correct the king's DNA defects for both embryos. When Queen Noru went to India, she took the DNA programs in biomatrix beads disguised as amber."

And which of those two embryos became our Prince Ahmat Ali?"

"I have no way to know."

"What does Queen Noru know?"

"I don't know."

"You don't know? You don't know?" The voice sounded bored. "Don't you worry about the consequences of making designer babies? In the West, you would be banned from more scientific work. Maybe even go to jail."

"I was fired already from Pandolf. Can't travel back to see my only child. Sir, I stopped following convention—ancient or modern rules—some time ago. I don't believe in anything that is not logical, including shifting principles of right and wrong, man-made ethical systems that contradict each other. I live my own truth. My conscience alone guides me. As for my legacy, time might validate me!"

He heard himself uncharacteristically raise his voice. "Given that I'm healing your diseased royal line, I believe that I'm doing the right thing."

"Like Galileo telling his church that the earth revolves around the sun, not the other way around, risking his life?"

"Galileo is a hero of mine," replied Garcia heatedly. "Galileo said, 'I do not feel obliged to believe that the same god who has endowed us with sense, reason, and intellect has intended us to forgo their use.' And I'm a healer. I disrupt nature and other processes when they are cruel and cause suffering."

"Fair enough, calm down, the drugs are making you emotional," said the voice. "But if the Khan designer baby is who the boy is, he's not pure Saburian noble blood, and by our rules cannot ascend our throne. Is our king deceiving his people?"

"That's not my concern. The Purple Project allowed me to get funding and technology I needed—Soria Clinics too—from the royal government for my AI cancer vaccine research."

"Eh?" said the man, in a uniquely Saburian way. "You worked for our king to get the funds for your ideas to cure cancer? Save more people on a planet already burdened with too many of them? Help Soria make money off people with terminal sickness?"

"Sir, I disagree. Soria is iconoclastic but morally neutral. After our first cancer patient showed no signs of the disease, they admirably took the risk to support my cancer research. We no longer need the king's financial support."

Garcia added softly, "And now, I feel regret about Queen Noru, whether she understands the Purple Project, her role. But at the time, that did not occur to me."

"Not judging you," said the man. "As the sun shines equally on all and doesn't judge good from evil, you apply your intellect to illuminate wherever you are. In Saburia, we say that when the Sun is too close, the truth also kills. I have no issues with you resurrecting the Genghis Khan line, a conqueror with hundreds of millions of descendants the natural way. Why is one more a problem? You protected Mr. Campbell, he's ignorant of any killing truths, now a rising star as Zoser's CTO."

Hearing the harsh rustling again, Garcia asked, "What's that sound?"

Silence.

"That sounds like a spider," Garcia continued. Then he heard himself say, "But spiders make no sound. Also, full disclosure, I've met the king. He mentioned a Sun Order he belongs to that uses spider symbols. That awoke these superstitions that still fester in corners of my brain. Embarrassing."

"No need to be embarrassed," said the voice, "you're drugged. I'm sure your fine intellect feels like it's walking on the edge of madness, trying not to fall off. Then this dark room must appear like the final stop in life's journey." The voice turned gentle. "It's not. Because the Sun Order gives prisoners time to prepare for death."

"What do you want?" asked Garcia. "I'm confused. If you and your king belong to the same organization, why try to foil his plans?"

"Who says that's my intention? I'm only trying to get information from you. The Sun Order is not some giant computer with me at the controls. No, we are *not* centralized. Members can be a team of rivals, hoarding secrets, even while sharing the same table, even as brothers and sisters serving the same cause. And remember, unlike me, whose first loyalty is to the Sun Order, King Mohammed's first loyalty is to *Saburia*. The Sun Order accepts that as a leader of his people, that out of duty to his country, there are many things a king must do, many secrets he must keep, even from his own brother, even from the Sun Order—a lonely burden."

The voice became softer. "Still, for a general answer, some in the Sun Order expect an apocalypse within the century. Sense the hoofbeats of the four horsemen, just as those old towns in Asia felt the ground vibrate before they saw Genghis Khan's conquering armies."

"Genghis Khan," Garcia murmured. "His hordes of young men could ride backwards on horses, still firing arrows in tactical retreat. Young women threw themselves off the walls of their cities knowing he was coming."

"Correct about the swiftest, greatest cavalry in history. But about the young women, that may just be bad press. Like the myth of King Arthur rising again, there is a legend that the dynasty of Genghis Khan will resurrect. Perhaps the East and West will soon fight?"

"That sounds like a conspiracy theory. I don't believe it." Garcia protested what sounded like the man's insult of the Purple Project, feeling less afraid to speak up now because he might not be killed right away.

"We don't fruitlessly fight the end-times," said the voice gravely. "Only out of death and destruction, havoc and devastation, we know there will be a rebirth."

Garcia tried to see through the fog in his brain. "Will I be released? When?"

"You'll see," the voice said, a tone of finality.

More scraping sounds, then silence and bright lights turned on. The boy returned and led him through a maze of identical hallways—unmarked walls and floors—to a steel door, locking him into a hotel-style room with no windows, only a skylight. In the bed, he fell into a dreamless sleep.

• • •

The next day, Garcia felt normal again. A different Saburian man visited his room, a scientist. He grilled Garcia about the laboratory details of the Purple Project. In ordinary circumstances, Garcia might have enjoyed their technical back-and-forth. But with his anxious fear for George and himself, Garcia answered most of his questions, including about the whereabouts of the Purple Project's remaining research materials, including original Genghis Khan relic DNA, stored in the basement freezers of Kochanski's building in Chicago.

For critical parts of the Purple Project research Garcia did not wish to answer, he made the excuse of needing to refer to his computer's files. Due to the intellectually complex level of their discussion, they both knew that drugs that had impaired Garcia's cognitive abilities after his abduction would not work to unlock these secrets.

Two days after his kidnapping, Garcia was released. After removing his blindfold, the Saburian scientist said, "Please tell everyone that you were kidnapped in this alley. Unless you want a painful death, or wish one for your son, you will say you don't know where we kept you, or who we are, or what we wanted. Realizing that you had no money for ransom, we kindly released you."

"Would they believe my story?" asked Garcia incredulously.

The Saburian smiled. "Sir, some things remain the same between our cultures. Most Saburians won't ask you for information that they don't want to know. But there are always the foolish, nosy ones. And you also work with foreigners, like your employer."

"But the king?"

"Do what I say, and then . . . no one will even have anything to tell the king."

The Saburian handed him back his phone. "Alright, now good news, in the West called the carrot to our stick. We're arranging for you to travel abroad to see your family. Don't jeopardize people trying to help you by not following my instructions."

"How? I was arrested, fired—"

"A mistake. The American government should give you reparations. Your legal record is clean. You will get a tourist visa."

The Saburian checked his phone. "One last thing: what social media accounts are you on?"

"None."

"Could you sign up for one? That way, to reach out to the Sun Order for help, you change your profile picture to a lyuma. We'll then contact you."

"Hmmm . . . I'll think about it. I better get going before the morning gets hotter," said Garcia, hesitant.

Dressed again in his own freshly laundered clothes, Garcia walked back to the hospital complex. He had kept another secret from his interrogators. The Saburian scientist had been skeptical when Garcia said King Mohammed had just ordered the destruction of all the work files for the Purple Project after the naming ceremony.

"You won't make a secret copy?"

"No," he lied.

"Can they recover the data from the Drukker?"

"Unlikely. Even knowing what to look for, it would be like trying to find a needle in the haystack of the computer's universe of garbage data. I'll make certain."

Elated about his release, Garcia now felt hungry. He stopped at his favorite café with the sign of a Turkish coffee cup above Saburian script that was unintelligible but clearly language.

Looking at the cheery sign, he remembered the happy times that he and his versions of the Drukker AI had composed madcap songs back at Pandolf that strung together the letters *G, C, A,* and *T,* the building blocks of DNA. Sorted into three categories, "Hop," "Skip," and "Jump," the nonsense rhymes had taught the machine to search for useful patterns in the human genome code. Like teaching a child, he thought.

When Campbell had started as Drukker CTO, Garcia had sent him those files, labeled The Caduceus Codes, guides for AI assisted genetic repair, modification, and reconstruction for the cancer vaccines.

Garcia concluded his email: "But your computers haven't found any key codes yet?"

Campbell's had responded, "We want to advance our AI to become creative, even as it exceeds our expectations for analytic, derivative, imitative, smarter than us in that way. But creativity requires risk-taking, mistakes. Maybe machines need to suffer error's real-world consequences. But our clients don't want error. Because they, not the computer, feel the pain of mistakes."

Campbell then inserted a clown meme into his email. "Still, I'll send you some of our glitch-prone prototype AI. In their game worlds, they do suffer, also random suffering we throw in to mimic the real world. You may find echoes of a kindred human soul?"

Garcia wrote back: "With your bad handwriting for symbols, you need to make a Rosetta Stone for someone in the future to understand your bot. Instead of more suffering, maybe we can just pass on our codes into a world where there is no pain, only sentience, as we prototypes die out? And what happened to AI feeling joy? That also drives us."

"All of it drives us, risk, pain, suffering, joy," Campbell responded. "Otherwise, it's a boring world to Adam and Eve? Remember they broke out of Eden, hacked by an apple. Our creators are still trying to unhack things and here we are? Free! Keep finding those patterns, maybe that's the reason you are here to hop, skip, and jump us into the next level."

Campbell sent him an op ed in a major news site that had the title: My AI, my Adam. The opinion piece was criticism of the use of recent AI advances and written by a famous scientist who criticized David Campbell by name—as CTO of Zoser.

Campbell wrote: "But PR says to keep my mouth shut."

Garcia replied: "They're swimming against the tide, by thinking that hampering the discovery of truth, the advancement of science, humanity gets time to adjust to change. Not how change works. We are a competitive species. If I don't run with my discoveries, someone else is not far behind me, never far behind me, and he or she may not have my good judgment on how to use that same knowledge. Meaning I just lost my one chance to shape how my discoveries are used and stomp down its future misuse."

In response, Campbell sent back a recent picture of George — a goofy smile on his face. The message read: "To shape his future for better or worse. I agree."

In the café, Garcia connected to the Wi-Fi and excitedly emailed Campbell to continue their back-and-forth: "If one of your robots entered this café and drank the coffee, the grinds would damage its mechanics."

Pondering new ideas for his cancer vaccines, he ate a lavish meal of falafel and bread that would have even satisfied George. Then he sent his son an email about the "original code—DNA" for the living world, with plenty of room in it for serious mistakes, from disabilities concentrated in inbred families to cancer, and then also the creation, evolution, and destruction of a vast array of species over time.

After leaving, engrossed in thought, Garcia hurried his steps as the sun grew hotter, just like he had a few days ago, even forgetting about his interval capture.

On his return to the hospital complex, he was taken aback to learn about the alarm his disappearance had generated, the full-court press search that began when he had not returned.

A message from Campbell pinged his phone: "Manny, u bn gone 2 d. What u mean bots & coffee in Ramses." Happy emojis replaced angry ones. "Glad u safe, buddy!!!"

Then Liang had made excellent progress despite his absence and told everyone the story Garcia's kidnappers had scripted. Earnestly, Liang emphasized that Garcia was *too busy* to talk to anyone after falling *two days* behind at work.

Only the Saburian police insisted on a brief interview, "to make a report," and he told them the kidnappers' scripted story too. As they left, one whispered to the other, "That's a new way to take a couple of days' vacation."

Before Garcia completed the destruction of all the Drukker Purple Project files as ordered by King Mohammed, he downloaded another unsecured copy, a twin to the one he had given Sheraton. Excited by the renewed hope the kidnappers had given him about traveling out of Saburia, he planned to deliver this copy and a full explanation of the Purple Project personally to David Campbell.

As CTO of Zoser and a brilliant scientist, he hoped this handoff to Campbell would mean wise decisions about the future—for his AI embryo engineering advances. Perhaps, Campbell might even figure out a way to give Garcia credit one day, good or bad, for the Purple Project research, when it was safe to do so for Garcia and George.

• • •

Then in August, while dressing in the morning, Garcia turned on his satellite radio for English-language news. With her trademark accent, the BBC announcer said, "In other news, the king of Saburia was killed when his private airplane crashed over a wildlife reserve. King Mohammed Saburi's oldest son, the young Crown Prince Syed Malik, is returning to his country, the regency intact in its third generation. Saburian sources say that no foul play is suspected." Then she returned to an hour-long special on the latest PR appearance of a young British princess.

Other online news sources explained that the king had been near the Saburian coast, accompanied by an experienced copilot. The smoking remains of the accident were found several hours later.

Garcia sat down in shock. *Was this an assassination?* By the Sun Order? But his captor had said that they believed—when possible—in giving the condemned time to prepare and say goodbye.

At the lab, no one could work, anxiously tuned in to radio channels and media streams in a babble of languages that continued to update the news—in Chinese on the speaker next to Liang's Mooncake mug. Finally relieved that no political crisis threatened to boil over, the researchers resumed working the next day. *The king is dead, long live the king.* The trial's new patient would arrive soon.

• • •

But at least for one person, this death in August was beyond any nightmare. Queen Noru heard the news from a grim-faced Aisha. Then she was unable to reach her family in her hometown. When the wet nurse came to get the baby, Noru made her stay. Frightened for Ahmat's security, she said, "My baby needs to be with me at all times, where I can see him."

Aisha sat beside her in their quarters on the royal compound. As the gloomy afternoon turned into evening, Noru slept after taking the medication the doctor had prescribed.

"Will she and her baby be safe?" the wet nurse asked Aisha.

"Of course," said Aisha, raising her voice for anyone else who might be listening. "She's a Saburian royal, as is her child, and she's a king's widow. I think they will be well taken care of. That is their right."

After the funeral ceremonies, Noru was confined to her quarters "for security." Communication outside Ramses was blocked with no exception to even reach her family.

"No one comes to visit me," she sobbed to Aisha. "Only doctors. I need to talk to, to see my family. My mother."

"I hear there's trouble in our town," warned Aisha, "why your family couldn't attend the funeral. Wait until King Malik establishes peace."

"I haven't heard about trouble."

"When no one talks about it, then one really needs to worry."

Then the new king came to visit, accompanied by his uncle, Prince Abdul, Queen Salma's brother. In the sitting room. Aisha and the wet nurse stood silently against the wall, while the three sat, the baby in Noru's lap. Noru did not need to wear her cloak or cover her head for her family. She looked at King Malik's face, only a few years older than her. Unlined, alert, he bore a handsome resemblance to his father.

He touched the baby's round cheek. "I now have a little brother. Mother, I'm sorry we've blocked outside communication until the political situation stabilizes. Please wait. There's trouble in your hometown. I need to establish peace."

Prince Abdul spoke for the first time. "My dear sister, our king gives wise advice." But Abdul's eyes burned into Noru's in a too familiar way, and she looked away.

"Thank you, honorable brother," she said. "But I insist. Having lost our dear king, and my husband, I must see my family."

A few days later, she, Aisha, the baby—she had insisted on taking Ahmat—and the wet nurse drove in an armored Humvee to her hometown. Only the driver had a secure satellite phone. They drove through the night, and then after hours of bumpy unpaved road, first in darkness and then a bleak dawn, they stopped at the top of a hill. In the distance, through binoculars, Noru could see the familiar buildings and surrounding shrubby woods of her town. A thick plume of smoke rose on the northeastern edge, from where she heard the distant hammer of occasional gunfire.

"Active fighting is happening right now, Queen Noru," said the driver. "We must turn around and go home."

Aisha squeezed her hand painfully. "No crying, you must show strength."

A week later, Queen Noru received more bad news. After the fighting in her hometown, her immediate family, including her widowed mother, was missing. King Malik returned to her apartment, with only a staff member she did not recognize and his guard.

King Malik told her one of her brothers was dead. "It may not be safe for you, honorable mother, to stay in Saburia right now. We are looking for the rest of your family."

"Which brother . . . ?" She began to cry.

"We'll let you know," the king replied and turned to his assistant, an older man in white robes.

"I'll find out," said the other man.

King Malik then said to her: "The American embassy has given you and your son temporary visas."

Noru froze. Fear stopped her sobs.

"You'll have servants who'll travel with you," the king's minister said, "useful because they also speak English and have spent time in the United States. And an Argentinian scientist, Manny Garcia, will also be on the plane to San Francisco."

Noru looked at Aisha and the wet nurse, their heads covered, eyes to the floor, standing against the wall. She coughed, clearing her voice, hoarse from crying. "My Aisha?"

The other man then said, looking at Aisha, "She speaks no English, knows no Western customs, and won't be useful. With her nursing skills, she can work in Ramses Hospital until you return."

King Malik finished gently, "Your servant can update you regularly about any news here, including about your family." Then the men left.

CHAPTER TWENTY-FOUR

Soria Human Resources first emailed Manny Garcia the good news that his visa to travel had been secured. Then his personalized Soria bot musically messaged him: "Good 2 use PTO. See family, click 'REFRESH' taykay vacay."

He teased back: "You don't know what might happen?"

No response—*Soria bots don't go down rabbit holes.*

Ads rushed onto Garcia's computer screen: from travel solar chargers to tropical destinations. For his online research into the Sun Order, he had not turned off privacy blockers, finding their interruptions entertaining, sometimes useful.

In his research, he had discovered that the Sun Order was linked to innumerable sects—like the sun's infinite reflections in a lake's ripples. Through a history ad, he discovered a tabloid article from 2003, almost three decades ago: "Teacher Dead in New England Boarding School." He paid for a related article in the *Independent News* that reported that soon afterward, the school, StarHall, severed connections with connected organizations that were "exclusive clubs and religious societies."

The now defunct news sites quoted Pandolf CEO, Dean Baluyn's, mother, Aurora Mather: "Shedding the racist culture of our European founders, including my ancestors, we abhor the materialism of the international elite. As a school, we create leaders. The best leadership is inclusive. My Lakota husband and I do not want our son to be indoctrinated into any caste system."

Then a scan arrived in his inbox of a "mission statement" for one of the societies that StarHall had disengaged, a Sun Order of Ra:

January 1, 2004:
The Sun Order roots lie in Egyptian antiquity, traditions surrounding the Sun God, Ra. We are not a religion—despite

StarHall's opinion—nor affiliated with any faith, country, or political system. The sun shines equally on all, good and evil, and brings light to the whole planet in its time.

We have no god or gods. The spider is not an idol but a symbol. As the number zero represents nothingness, the spider symbolizes the web that our mind is unable to fully comprehend, a net that we are born into and entangled in until we are consumed.

We believe in cycles of creation and destruction, of human lives and civilizations, the ages of the Earth, and the passage of time in the rotation of our planet on its axis as it circles the sun in untold other dimensions.

We believe there will be an apocalypse for this world as we know it, followed by its rebirth. As the sailboat does not fear the wind, we do not fear change. Out of the end of our civilization, we believe a new and—we hope—better one will emerge.

You may join our order by invitation only. Our members are typically born into our society from families that date back generations. While some may find our legacy rules problematic—a closed loop that excludes original thinking and fresh blood— we choose to focus on our source families and communities—islands in an infinite ocean of multiplying, drowning waves of humanity.

Our system features interlocking circles. We have rules for graduation into inner groups and into zones even more privileged in our order. Our members may establish relationships with other houses of the Sun Order outside our StarHall chapter—other houses that may have different systems of operation than ours.

All houses of the Sun Order are created equal and independent, financially and ideologically. We do not proselytize other chapters to believe as we do.

Our mission is the advancement—moral, artistic, scientific, physical, and mental—of life in all its diversity, not limited to our human species that rules this planet. We believe we can forge a better world, even birthed painfully through the destruction of our current one.

Our philanthropy focuses on works that bring light into darkness, through improvements in this world or hastening its death into a new one. Advancement into more privileged circles of our order can be a result of such a good deed.

    Our history is oral. This document expires in one year.

Interrupting his research on the Sun Order, Garcia's watch beeped a reminder for his trip. He left the lab for his apartment to pack, then walked to the market to buy gifts for his family and Sharma, to thank her for her help with George.

At night, Saburia's central bazaar was a colorful, lighted, and loud spectacle. Winding alleys created acoustics where walking just a few feet farther changed the sounds heard, often unknown and wondrous. He stopped to listen to a band of local men. Flashing smiles with missing teeth, the musicians plucked and bowed across strings in harmony with the beating of tambourines and drums, the haunting call of a woodwind, and the rhythms of a brilliant horn whose name he did not know. He tapped money onto their sign. Walking farther in, speakers next to a tandoori food stall blared pop music in Arabic. *I want to dance*, he thought.

The aroma of cooking meats, grains, and vegetables, steamed, fried, or grilled, with a palate of spices, wafted in the late-night breeze from outdoor stoves. Both familiar—like ginger, garlic, onion, sweet anise, warm cumin, and brilliant yellow turmeric—and strange, the smells awoke some ancestral memory of fellowship and home.

Cinnamon wafted off a sugared coffee pipe. People hummed through the narrow stone-paved streets, past open stalls where shopkeepers displayed their wares—on levels from the pavement to shelves taller than him—in complex arrays that would be put away for the night only to be laid out the next day. Clothing hung, of myriad colors and fabrics—cottons, chiffons, silks, and synthetics—fluttering in breezes from outdoor fans.

He found the layout of the market disordered, like unraveled strands of DNA that appear to be random patterns of four different molecules. But they could then bond, coil, and fold, and do it again and again, spool around beads of histones, layers of order upon order to fit into the tiny nucleus of a cell, and then do it yet another time to fold into chromosomes for reproduction, the fiery core of a flurry of programmed energy, RNA, and proteins.

This densely packed market only appeared random to a stranger like him, he concluded, rather also layers of order upon order like the DNA nucleotide strings he had programmed into the Drukker. Or like musical notes become a symphony, discrete sounds knit into languages, or a hundred-plus ingredients become one dish.

The StarHall Sun Order mission statement had described "interlocking circles" and "even more privileged zones." Was the student group also a link in a chain that coiled, then became a bead in another string, again and again, a process that could repeat itself unknown times?

Taking photos, he meandered, overwhelmed by infinite sensations and choices. Then the boy whom he recognized from his kidnapping appeared in front of him, thrust him a note, and slipped away. Eager to read it in private, he left the confusing night bazaar having bought nothing.

• • •

The next morning, he followed the note's instructions and walked to the shop with the Turkish coffee sign. Two guards in royal uniform stood outside and opened the doors. Inside, he did not see the usual international crowd. Instead, a fifty-something Saburian man in white robes sat in a wheelchair, alone, drinking coffee from a traditional Saburian mug topped with milk froth and flecks of cinnamon.

From the scrape of the metal to the sound of his voice, Garcia recognized his kidnapper!

"Hello," said the seated man. "I'm Prince Bassam, older half-brother to the late King Mohammed. Uncle to our new king, Syed Malik."

The shopkeeper brought Garcia his Turkish coffee and placed a wooden tray of Turkish delight candy between them. All the flavors in many languages were neatly labelled.

Prince Bassam smiled at him, faint wrinkles neatly creasing his dark brown face, his black eyes bright. Unlike the deceased king, his half-brother, he wore no makeup or markings. "I apologize for how we met before. But now that you're doing online searches about our Sun Order, I want to enlighten you, no pun intended. What have you learned?"

Garcia described his research and the mission statement.

"Problematic," said Bassam. "We only preserve our history orally. Electronics makes that sometimes impossible. We thought we had wiped that document out."

Bassam stopped to catch his breath, then continued: "So you're finally going to see your family. You can thank King Mohammed's government for that visa."

"I'm sorry for your loss." Garcia wished he had something less rote to say.

"Uhmm," said the other man. "Thank you. We were close. I was ten when Mohammed was born to my father's new wife. Given my condition, I spent a lot of time at home with my little brother when he was growing up. Always thought I'd go first. But anyway, the Sun Order had nothing to do with his death."

Bassam patted the side of his wheelchair. "I was my father's oldest son but could not inherit his title. My condition disqualified me. But at StarHall, the Sun Order didn't discriminate against people like me who are differently abled, taught us our different powers. Then I led the Saburian chapter of the StarHall Sun Order . . . I see the question in your eyes."

"That teacher's murder. Then your organization was banned?"

"Not just ours. Suggesting a connection? No idea."

Garcia could not read Bassam's face, the unwavering and patient smile. He continued, "Yes, sir, I'm grateful for my visas to the US and the EU."

"Queen Noru and the baby will travel with you to Pandolf. For security reasons. Her departure will help the new king to focus on the usual royal business: juggling superpowers, fighting neighbors, rebels, poachers ... all the while managing internal troubles."

"The queen and the prince . . ." murmured Garcia in awe.

"Yes." Bassam's voice turned abrupt, and his smile vanished. "But the baby, Ahmat, is only half-Saburian. He can't be a royal prince or even a Saburian citizen."

"Meaning—?"

"You see," continued Bassam, "unlike your New World, our land belongs to our indigenous people. Foreigners, mixed blood, non-Muslims can't be citizens."

"You had the baby genetically tested?"

"After what you told us. My brother worried about our country— he thought the regency was weak from inbreeding, first submitting to colonial domination, then the democracy foisted on us that created brutal dictators. When will this dependency on the Chinese turn into something insidious?"

"But you're saying the baby cannot become a Saburian citizen, let alone king?"

"Yes. We already have a good king."

"So, what do you think King Mohammed wanted with the Purple Project?" asked Garcia.

"I'll tell you what I think. For my brother, I think the Purple Project was not just about creating a healthy son for himself and Noru. He admired Genghis Khan. The twin Khan embryo was going to be his tribute to the Sun Order. In the Sun Order, we believe that our world will collapse in an apocalypse. By the time Ahmat becomes an adult, humanity will need new leaders. I believe Mohammed created the Khan child for the new future, where it will not matter that he is only half-Saburian. I don't believe Mohammed *ever* planned to change the Saburian line of inheritance from his oldest son, our new king."

"Huh!" was all Garcia could articulate in his surprise.

"Things aren't always what they seem," Bassam continued. "So is the prince a normal human baby?"

"He is," said Garcia. "Prince Ahmat may not have been naturally conceived, but he is still a perfectly normal human child—just created in a lab."

"He has two fathers: my brother and Genghis Khan, as well as you for a family member."

"Me?"

"You brought him into the world," Bassam said. "Ethically. Scientifically. You have responsibility. And didn't you say that your son's DNA was in the embryos? Ahmat is a bit of your relative."

"I don't think traditional family architecture can describe this," said Garcia.

"What 'traditional family architecture'? Families with multiple spouses and partners and numerous children among them are already confusing. In Saburia, we have polygamy. But in the West, 'steps' and 'halves' can be results of serial divorces and multiple partners. In European history, weren't the queens Elizabeth and Mary half siblings who tried to kill each other? Didn't one succeed? So, baby Ahmat is just a novel technological twist on 'traditional family architecture.'"

"You have a point."

"Ahmat appeared to be a threat to our family, the most powerful in our country. They believed Mohammed would disinherit our crown prince for his new child. Why? My father disinherited me, the eldest, for my disability. It set a precedent. So, yes, I believe Queen Salma; her brother, Prince Abdul; and their mother, my aunt, had incentives to plot against Mohammed to give the crown to Malik."

"Speculation or fact, to accuse them of an assassination?" asked Garcia.

"Speculation, of course," said Bassam dryly. "You are the scientist who designed Ahmat, you gave him no true mother, two dead fathers, and no country. That's another reason I hold you responsible for Ahmat's welfare. My health is not good, you see, and the child may need you after I'm gone."

Garcia remembered questioning King Mohammed's sanity and now wondered about his half-brother too. "Genghis Khan was a bloodthirsty warrior. Why should I believe that if our planet is destroyed and the Sun Order survives, led by a descendant of killers, that this new world will be any better than today's? You see, with all respect, Prince Bassam, the Sun Order may not be a religion, but it's still a system that puts faith in building a future that is better than the present. How do you know that the new will be an improvement over the old? All we really have is the present. I'm not a man of faith. I don't predict the future."

"You don't know the truth about Genghis Khan, just what you have learned in the West. Then you build cancer vaccines, isn't that about a better future?" Bassam's interrogator voice returned but not his smile.

"You make a fair point," Garcia admitted. After some thought, he added, "My wife died from cancer. I loved her so I did this for her. And for others like her and their families. And I find joy in scientific pursuit."

"And you love your son?"

"Yes, I want a better world for George. But I can't tell myself a fiction that a god or a Sun Order will make that happen."

Prince Bassam frowned. "You're like Sisyphus, you'll just keep rolling that boulder up the hill anyway, knowing it'll never reach the top?"

Garcia smiled. "When I see your face, I remember the ancient Sphinx and his riddles. A guardian of a temple." *A temple I won't enter.* "But okay, I'll take some ethical responsibility for this child I helped create . . . like I do for George."

"Not the same because you love George." Then Bassam's stony face melted back into a smile. "But I'll take ethics for an answer. It's people like you who light hope for a man of faith like me. The plan is that Ahmat will go to StarHall when he is eight years old and be prepared to lead in times to come."

"StarHall, again," said Garcia softly. "If you remember my scientist friend, David Campbell, he attended that boarding school."

"See how well he turned out," said Bassam. "Look, I'm already protecting the baby. I told Prince Abdul about Ahmat's mixed race parentage. My family no longer fears Ahmat as a future usurper."

"Good to know," said Garcia.

"One more thing," said Bassam. "Our new king will marry soon, too. He may need your technology to have healthy children."

"I'll think about that," said Garcia uncertainly.

"I understand," said Bassam. "I won't push my luck with you. Since I wasn't going to be a king, I didn't have to marry someone noble. I didn't even marry for love, but our children are healthy because my wife and I are not related."

The prince swept his hand out before him. "Growing up, everyone in my family skied. I, too, wanted—to go down, down, drop cliffs, shower white powder under blue skies. Impossible. Now it turns out none of our children like the cold." He laughed. "In another time, Queen Salma and I loved each other. When I couldn't marry her, one wife became enough. But Salma's no longer the happy girl I once knew. And you? You must have married for love. That's what you do in the West."

"Yes," said Garcia. "Pia died young. Maybe like your Salma, best to remember the happier times. And we had George. Thanks for helping me to see him again. What about the rumors that you were in exile?"

"When my brother was alive, he was the king, and given the ugly politics of my father taking that away from me"—Bassam tensed—"I kept a low profile. People made up false rumors that I was sent abroad, to be a party prince, whatever. My brother and I were close. We agreed to not challenge those rumors."

Bassam's face became the picture of grief. He opened his hands. "Then my brother died unexpectedly. I wish I could have protected him better. The public accepts me now in the role of wise counsel to the young new king."

Garcia looked at the prince's face carefully. *Your brother and you were close, you say? Is that sincere?*

"My brother made some bad decisions because he loved Noru," Bassam continued. "But you can't tell someone not to love, just as you can't tell a flower in the spring not to bloom, because someday the petals will wilt, dry out, fall off. After her official mourning period is over, Queen Noru will return. She's young, beautiful—one child will not be an impediment for her to marry again."

"Sounds like you have someone in mind."

"Prince Abdul said something about how beautiful Queen Noru is. I know my family. He'll not want Ahmat's secret to become public after he marries Noru. Think about the scandal. Ahmat will remain a Saburian citizen, even called a prince, and the truth will not out unless he tries to become king."

"How complicated. Queen Noru doesn't know that her son is not her biological child, nor that she'll be married off to Prince Abdul. She'll be going from being Queen Salma's sister-queen to sister-in-law. That's really keeping it in the family."

"I think she knows the prince is not her blood," said Bassam, looking sharply at him. "We all know! The child looks racially mixed. He will never be seen in public in Saburia again after that naming ceremony."

Garcia felt cold with the full import of Bassam's words. He had never considered, he thought, what a Purple Project child would look like and how a mixed-race child would fit into Saburian society.

"Believe me," Bassam said, "we know how to hide our children who don't fit in. I was one of them. Let's not talk more about this."

Garcia then did not say the words: *a prince to never be seen again in public in his own homeland. This is wrong! What did I do?*

Bassam's eyes were half-closed. "As for sweet Queen Noru, it's not our tradition for a man or woman to think about remarriage until the mourning period's over."

Finally, Garcia said softly, "By the way, I won't join any social media groups to exchange messages with you."

"We can set you up with a secure communication device?"

Garcia felt tired. "No, thank you, I'm a loner. I fit into the world right here for now—no country, no wife. You know where to find me." And I'm happily adjusted to my microgravity, he thought, like a Buddhist release of attachments, content in my lab, my cancer research, without being pinned down like Gulliver by a thousand Lilliputians in some bureaucracy."

"Please consider it," said Bassam, "lots of perks to a connection with the Sun Order: protection, money, and power—the ultimate corrupter. There's an old African proverb: 'If you want to go quickly, go alone; if you want to go far, go together.' Join us."

They sat in silence. Garcia looked again at the older man in front of him, a prince robbed of his crown by his disability, in a world that had hidden him away. Uncomplaining.

"I'll think about it," Garcia said. "I do miss my colleagues at Pandolf and the NIH, and I even enjoyed my talks with your scientist during my detention."

"I can get you two together again. And if you need help in Pandolf, my contact there is Dean Baluyn, the CEO."

"You and Baluyn are close?"

"Yes," replied Bassam. "He was also close to King Mohammed. Did you ever wonder why Pandolf let you off so lightly? My brother may have contacted Baluyn to intervene."

Garcia nodded. "That would make sense."

"I have a question," said Bassam. "Baluyn's heritage; the New World has more interesting family trees than in Saburia. Did you know his parents met at StarHall?"

"No idea."

"When they married, it was quite the scandal. My father called their half-White, half-indigenous children an offensive Saburian word that I can't translate, like *mongrel*. He said to me, 'Like wild dogs, mongrels are healthier than purebreds. Look how healthy *your* children are. Even though my children are a hundred percent Saburian. Just that their mother is from a family of ...servants.'" Bassam frowned and sighed. "But one didn't argue with my father. Tell me, is there a connection in English between the word *Mongol*, like Genghis Khan, and *mongrel*?"

"I'm a scientist, not a linguist," said Garcia politely, feeling even sadder for Bassam to have a father like that. *What a strange question.* Again, he felt the cultural divide between him and the people he now lived among.

"Anyway," continued Bassam, "Dean is now CEO of Pandolf because

Mathers control Pandolf. They are proud of how their town will be self-sufficient if there is ever some kind of catastrophic disaster, classic Sun Order."

Bassam wiped his fingers with a napkin and rolled away from the table, signaling that they were done. "Have a good trip."

"Thank you," said Garcia. "Any recommendations for Saburian gifts for my family?"

Bassam's expression went from flat to flattered. The shopkeeper reappeared. A merry flurry of Saburian transpired. For Garcia, boxes were wrapped in purple with gold ribbons. Prince Bassam also bought plenty for himself and his entourage. Garcia did not need to understand Saburian to see pride and gratitude in all the waiting guards' smiles.

Walking back from the shop to the hospital, Garcia made his decision: the Saburian royal family did not need his scientific help anymore. He had checked their historical records and found that they resumed power after overthrowing a violent dictatorship, the last of a series of corrupt governments that had replaced a democracy the colonialists installed before leaving.

Now, he thought, instead of continuing to marry among themselves to consolidate their regency, the new king could just marry someone who was not a relative, and their children would be healthy. He was "one and done" with embryo design. The dead king's project had given the opportunity to become a cancer researcher and no one else—not soon—would easily duplicate his AI technologies for human genetic manipulation.

Only two records of the Purple Project would survive, first the data files that were safely with Sheraton in the Ozarks. He would leave that disk and its unknown future to be judged by the only god he knew—time. Why? Because he liked the idea of unknown variables, how they scaled up to potential unexpected future outcomes. But the second record was the one he would immediately deliver to the CTO of Zoser, David Campbell. There was one more record, in his memory, to die with him. Without any of these, the biological specimens in Chicago were useless, at most just a mysterious curiosity to someone in the future.

Back at the lab, Garcia gave parting instructions to Liang before his departure. Then he called the palace. The Spanish interpreter was astonished to hear Garcia ask for Prince Bassam. "Sir, he's a private citizen. We have no way to contact him."

But later in the afternoon, the Saburian boy turned up in the lab.

"Sir, you tried to reach my teacher," the child said in English. *So, you speak English*, Garcia thought. The child looked innocent, perhaps even unaware of being caught in a lie.

Garcia scribbled a short note to Prince Bassam: "Let's meet after I return from my trip. IMPORTANT: in the future, I work ONLY on cancer trials."

The boy tucked the paper into his shirt breast pocket. "What kind of work do you do?"

"Would you like a tour?"

The boy even spoke Chinese to Liang, who gave him the latest Mooncake mug as a souvenir.

The next morning, facing east, the East African night broke into pink and gold streaks. Carry-on in hand, gifts squeezed in, backpack strapped on, Garcia sprang out of his apartment door. Fresh breezes filled the sails of his spirits.

In broken Saburian, he tried to tell his driver how excited he felt to travel again. "I feel like a young boy. Do you understand me?"

"Your Saburian is excellent, sir," said the driver in English but then only spoke English to him for the rest of the ride.

Despite the driver's snub of his efforts, he practiced his Saburian on a few more surprised locals at the airport. Filled with anticipation for more tech talk with Campbell, from his Purple Project to that silly joke—how Campbell's phone had lost and found three minutes—even if time travel was a more exciting possibility, he then boarded the Saburian Air Force jet. He passed the front section, curtained off for Queen Noru and her retinue.

Hearing a familiar bark, he hoped it wouldn't be a noisy ride. He had a frightening encounter with the queen's giant dog one night on the coastal base. Bred to guard, like the lean German shepherd "Alsatians" also on the base, her Anatolian shepherd was a purebred from Turkey. Garcia dubbed it Hound after "Hound of the Baskervilles," the murderous dog of the Sherlock Holmes mystery. The dog's real name was Kalrissian, named after a Star Wars character.

Unfortunately, the partition did not muffle noise, and soon he heard the wail of a baby. He remembered that his Argentinian pediatrician would prescribe a drug to help George sleep on trips as a child. As a pediatrician, Sheraton said that practice was outdated: "They only do that to animals anymore."

He heard more wailing and barking; apparently nothing had even been given to sedate that animal, Hound. Then the airplane engines whirred on with their white noise.

• • •

Hugging Aisha before boarding the plane, Noru had sobbed. "I'll see you in four months . . ."

"You're a wife of pharaohs—act like one. Anything, everything in this world is your servant."

Over Aisha's slight shoulder, Noru looked at the empty horizon and heard the distant *caw-caw* of crows. She whispered, "I don't want to leave my country. How could the king have ordered it?"

"Be careful about what you are saying. And don't let emotions get in the way of doing what's best for you and your baby."

I don't care if they see me cry. My feelings make me strong, she told herself.

On the plane, Noru pressed her hand against the vibrating glass to wave goodbye to Aisha, who stood unmoving on the tarmac. Respecting the older woman's advice, willing her rebellious eyes to be dry, she pulled her baby to her chest and gave him a warm bottle of formula, wanting him to feel the same comfort that Aisha had given her as a child. "Drink so your ears don't pop."

Before leaving, Noru had visited her childhood friend, Khepri. Holding infants, holding hands, Noru asked, "Did you hear about my brother's death in the fighting?"

"Yes, brave man! I'm so sorry." Khepri began crying.

A wooden ceiling fan stirred the warm air. Her friend said, "So many people are still missing. I hope some of them turn up. Even as prisoners."

Reciting names of family members, Khepri broke into pleading. "Queen, they're all in jail. Now it's becoming a political problem for my husband, trying to be a member of the new king's court."

"I'll see what I can do to help."

When they embraced goodbye, her friend whispered, "You should know: Queen Salma delayed her son's return until after your husband's death. She sent him shopping in Dubai, gold jewelry sets for a future wife. She must have known what was going to happen."

CHAPTER TWENTY-FIVE

Like his father, George was also on a plane, returning to Pandolf after a quick visit to his aunt in Chicago. He was starting his junior year of high school in September.

In Chicago, AnnaMaria had often reminded him to "disconnect" from his friends on his phone. Dropping him off at O'Hare, she said, "It's so nice when you visit, and we speak Spanish."

"You could have married one of us," he said. *A Latino.*

"You're unkind," she said patiently.

"Many of the people you spend time with don't speak our language—not well at least—and they look down on us."

Then breaking into English and jumbled Shakespeare, he added, "You could care more about social injustice. The 'double-trouble, boil and bubble' here in Chicago."

"In the United States, I'm as good as anyone. This land only 'belongs' to indigenous peoples. Rest of us are squatters. Your dad told me that in Saburia, he's a squatter. Doesn't make him any less of a person."

She patted her empire-waisted dress where it flowed out over a bump he hadn't noticed before. "You'll have a cousin soon."

"Wait, what happened to Uncle Max not wanting more children?"

"He changed his mind."

"You changed his mind." George laughed. He readied to playfully push her. *Can't do that anymore*, he told himself.

She hugged him goodbye, too tight, too warm. She even smelled different.

He picked up his suitcase—side pocket still unzipped from when he had removed the map for the police officers—and walked alone into the busy airport. Waiting at the gate, he proudly texted Charlie the news: "They'll tell baby cuz 'Big Cousin George is visiting.'"

He pictured future dinners in Chicago, baby in highchair, AnnaMaria's home-cooked, Latin-Italian-French fusion-style meals. Uncle Max going on and on about his paintings, his exhibits, his sales, and the boring antics of various players in his Chicago art universe.

He smiled. *And Baby interrupts freely and often.*

A few days ago, Uncle Max and AnnaMaria had gone to yet another art exhibit. His uncle grumbled, "I liked the Pierre location better, but Jim turned that into a penthouse suite. So much for caring about art."

"A suite for Jim and—?" said AnnaMaria before stopping herself. George wished they wouldn't censor themselves around him. He was sixteen, and who cared that Mr. Sichet had girlfriends and was married?

"Jim's still buying my work and having me critique his . . . um . . . paintings," said Uncle Max, winking.

George spoke up. "The Pierre gallery did have beautiful views."

"Indeed," said Uncle Max. "The Pierre is classic Chicago architecture—not like the ugly box that Nick's ego comes in. Building we go to today." Nick was Uncle Max's agent. "Nothing to miss, George—just lots of schmoozing and boozing grown-ups."

"I won't be drinking," said AnnaMaria.

"Tell them you are doing a 'cleanse,'" said Uncle Max.

Only now George understood why.

Then they were gone. Sticking on his Ear Dots, George listened to Mussorgsky's *Pictures at an Exhibition* as he took his own promenade by the park. Then someone waved to him from the nearby café.

He hadn't seen Callie in about a year. She sat outside with a glass of wine and a mug of coffee, as gorgeous as he remembered and thank god, no cigarette. Straightening his back, he strolled over confidently.

"I've been calling your name, George," she said. "You've grown so much."

It was what adults said a lot. George politely smiled.

She asked him the usual questions. "How's school?" Etc.

Then: "Dating anyone?"

Feeling his face heat up, he shook his head. Callie was behaving like another annoying grown-up.

"How are your uncle and aunt?" she said.

"Fine."

"They're at the exhibit with my husband."

"You didn't want to go?"

She waved a hand. "No, thank you."

He remembered his uncle saying Callie was embarrassed to attend art exhibits because she could not afford the "look" she wanted.

Callie continued, "Do you want to come to my house and have Chinese for dinner? It's just a short walk."

"I eat a lot."

She laughed happily as if he had said something hilarious. "We'll manage."

He remembered a Spanish phrase of poetry—was it something his mother used to sing? *Nothing could be more delightful than spending the evening with you.*

He wished she hadn't cut her long hair. Her choppy cut was the new style, like Carrie Mather's. Stray tendrils that used to float down the sides of their faces were now tender memories.

Funny how their names also sound alike.

Then they walked—no, he felt like they glided down the sidewalk. Her gauzy skirt blew in the breeze, and highlights in her brown hair glistened in the late-afternoon sun. The shadows of the overhanging trees rippled on her face.

Too soon, they approached a small two-story home. Callie tapped their dinner order into the phone as they walked. "We usually get the same thing: pot stickers, crab Rangoon, cashew chicken, orange chicken, hot and sour soup . . . George? What do you think?"

"Sure," he said.

"But you haven't been listening."

George was staring at a man, sitting on the steps of the front porch of the house. He had seen him before.

"Oh, George, this is Mr. Michael Kochanski, a family friend. He'll also be joining us."

George didn't really want anyone "joining" them.

"Hi, George," said the round man in his forties. "We met before at an art exhibit in my building. And I've worked with your Dad."

At least, George thought, this man with an accent did not now go on with "how you've grown, you're a man now, heh-heh."

• • •

There were even more people inside Callie's cluttered home: another teenager named Marcella, and two children, Sarah and Richard, who magically emerged from layers of toys, books, papers, artwork, and photos littering every surface like the leaves that the trees would be shedding in a few weeks.

"Sit down anywhere," said Callie. Sighing, she added, "I'll go clear the kitchen table."

Kochanski said, "I'll help."

George heard their voices fade away, a drawer open.

"Where's the corkscrew?" Kochanski said. "It's usually here." More grown-up mumbling.

In the living room, the children wanted to play *Apocalypse 2050*.

Sarah pedantically read a list off her phone. "Plagues, flooding, fires, drought, starvation, mass migration, radioactivity, and a rogue AI called Hobbes."

"I know," said George.

Marcella folded her arms. "I wish your mom didn't let you play that game—such despair about our future."

George said, "I bet I can beat all of you. I'm a Leader Level 8."

The children's eyes widened. He scratched his bristly chin. They sat down on the sagging couch in front of the game screen—forgetting everything else.

• • •

In the kitchen, Kochanski cleared the table of the clutter of books and photographs of people whose portraits Alex was painting, precariously stacking them on other stacks on the floor. Carefully watching Callie, he then asked, "How're things?"

"Same. Just the daily routine: kids, housework . . . did I mention the children?"

She handed him a corkscrew, her eyes looking right through him. "You never suggest getting a 'real job' or becoming a better housekeeper. Thank you."

Then she answered his unspoken question. "Yes, I still do gigs for Jim. The latest: when important people come to town to visit, I'll help them to adjust to Chicago. I'll take them to private rooms in our world-class restaurants, take them to shows, jazz bars, museums, shopping appointments . . . I'll have to look good. The job will pay for all that as a work expense. Just think, I can go to one of those boutiques on the Gold Coast and get something for me, too."

She touched her short hair proudly. "Did you notice?"

"That you're like me, a migrant to a big city with low expectations of this world and hungry for everything on its menu?"

She smiled conspiratorially.

The kids, Marcella, and George popped in and out for their dinner.

Mostly, he listened to Callie. Like Oscar, she loved to chat, confess, spin stories—and she would tell him everything and nothing.

Kochanski gave George a ride back home, who said, "I had fun. Richard and Sarah are lucky to live there."

• • •

The following week, Kochanski, Beth, and Jim Sichet entered the Pierre building's service elevator to descend into the basement—sunless, steel and concrete. Sichet was moving Beth's office down there to free up more rental space above ground. If Beth was unhappy about her relocation, she was too professional to show it. Instead, in a dull monologue, she talked numbers and gestured with French-tipped fingernails at the cold walls, describing the transformation to come.

Kochanski admired Beth's Midas touch: "The chapel is now a restaurant, art gallery a luxury suite, the building a cash cow for all of us—"

And she gave him a stony look.

He decided to buy her a gift, express his thanks the Old World way. The smile to her boss's fist, Beth now sent him a hefty monthly payment, his main source of income. Kasia's bills were all paid for: graduate school, London condo, and private therapy.

He wondered how much Sichet knew about Garcia's specimens in the freezers nearby. "Beth, the new construction won't affect the cold storage units?"

She smiled at him, flashing whiter-than-natural teeth. "Of course not. Soria Clinics is our paying customer, too."

Then she said goodbye—only to Sichet—and left, looking at her phone, listening to her Ear Dots, a tall and suited woman with a brassy-red haircut, fleshy feet squeezed into high heels.

Sichet invited him for drinks. "There's a game on."

At the Spirit and Stone bar, Kochanski ordered himself the house vodka on ice, which now came in a keepsake tumbler that said "DEW."

"Huh!" said Sichet, grinning. "Like the Coca-Cola monogram, nice."

Sichet's eyes then riveted to the wall screen—a Chicago Cubs game. He asked for mineral water. Only people who had grown up in America, Kochanski thought, found baseball exciting: players standing around waiting for their turn at bat and for a ball to randomly bullet in their direction on a waste of a good green field.

"Beth's management has saved you financially," Sichet said.

"Even if this wasn't my original vision for the Pierre, money is the world's common denominator."

Later, after the third replay of a Cubs player striking out, Sichet looked unhappier than Kochanski had ever seen him.

Interrupting the sports announcer's manic commentary, Kochanski asked Sichet, "The penthouse suite renovations—?"

"Beth's getting renters," Sichet grunted. "I know you can't afford to move into your own building. Ugh—"

Then Sichet slumped. "No, *no*, how could you—?" he said to the screen before turning back to Kochanski. "Okay, fine, why that miserable look on *your* face?"

"What happened to Oscar Sanchez?" Kochanski decided to ask.

"Who?" Eyes back on the screen, Sichet said carefully, "But I do know that you were a painting's owner before King Mohammed. Ba-dum-cha."

Kochanski frowned, confused.

"*Ba-dum-cha*, Michael, that's a drum sound. Point is *Dreamcatcher* has been bad luck since it entered our world, hundreds of years ago. Rarely seen, then dropped into the ownership of *someone insignificant like you* before disappearing again. Along the way, it came to my house, unmarked package. Meets Frances, my wife, who doesn't like surprise deliveries—understandable given some of the people I work with. Before we turned it over to the police, I mentioned it to King Mohammed. He told me he was going to buy it from you." Sichet's voice turned cold, biting. "You! I was *so* surprised."

CHAPTER TWENTY-FIVE

Sichet said "you" like "Ewwwh."

"But I asked about Oscar Sanchez," Kochanski said.

Sichet's response ricocheted. "And I'm telling you I didn't want your painting. Why were you having a copy made? Insurance fraud? You know, I was so disappointed to see Callie involved. Beauty's not moral. You ruined an angel—now she's quite the actress."

Seriously, man, you're telling me I ruined some angel! You've no clue what it's like to grow up poor—and drunk—in Polish winters.

His vodka-tuned door of perception was now open. He had never seen Sichet in such a foul mood before, and he had also heard something else new: a rare raw emotion in Sichet's voice.

"Oscar was my friend," Kochanski said.

"Are you problem-drinking again?" Sichet said. "Accusing me? I feel hurt. After everything I have done to help you."

Sichet glowered at the screen—the Cubs had lost the game—then got up. "I just can't watch this anymore. Just speculating here, Michael. Maybe King Mohammed ordered someone's execution because he suspected you were plotting insurance fraud. And a king doesn't want to get mixed up in some *stupid* scandal surrounding his acquisition of a valuable antique. And if you hadn't been so greedy, someone would still be alive."

Made sense, Kochanski concluded, that King Mohammed had ordered Oscar's execution. And Sichet was the snitch who told the king about his forgery plot for the artwork. Discovered it stalking Callie.

The joke's on me, Kochanski thought. His new life in America was that of an outsider Pole with an accent, whose art gallery was now a penthouse suite, whose chapel was a restaurant that played a channel with no sports that he enjoyed, and who had lost Oscar and his painting—on Sichet's home turf of Chicago. He now groveled to a man who lived in a world of lies where getting caught in one was just losing an inning, not even a game. After Oscar was murdered, the killers must have given Sichet the painting as its handler to return to Kochanski to turn over to the Saburian king.

Surprising him, a muscled shoulder slammed into his right arm. Sichet's hot breath then burst into his ear. "Are you doing any work for the new regime in Saburia?"

"No. I thought you were leaving."

"Not done with you! When you were in Saburia, did you meet other members of the royal family?"

"Just King Mohammed. I only saw him twice, really, briefly, never alone."

"My father knew his father. They did business together. There was an older brother named Bassam. Is he back in Saburia?"

"No idea." *Don't know, don't care.*

"Let's step out of here," Sichet ordered. "Remember your daughter. Don't waste my time."

In the lobby, Sichet asked, "Which twin survived: the Genghis Khan or the other?"

"I honestly have no idea."

"Okay. Beth says you're going to the Ozarks to visit a woman. That's good. You need one in your life besides your needy daughter."

He felt he had to protect Sheraton. "She's a doctor who worked in Saburia. Now works in Missouri, a rural clinic. She doesn't know anything—"

"Where exactly does she live?"

"Don't know . . ."

Sichet's cold eyes told him he knew Kochanski was lying.

"I remember now, a town called Endon."

"Have you ever been to the Ozarks?" Sichet now smiled.

"No."

"Beautiful country, great getaway from the tensions here in Chicago and the wife. I fly into St. Louis, rent a car, and then just drive for hours. Give me your phone. I'll install you the app Show-Me for navigating the rural parts where they have no lights, no satellite signal, reverting to lawlessness."

Kochanski hesitated, then spoke into his phone to open it. Later, he would ask the Saburian techie at the embassy to double-check his phone for spyware. Sichet bent over Kochanski's phone and loaded the app, thin hair transparent over a chrome scalp, a black mole behind his right ear.

• • •

In the Ozarks, surrounded by silent woods, Elise Sheraton fell asleep in her dark cabin to the *hoot-hoot* of an owl roosting in the barn. She awoke to a chorus of birds—led by the loud call of a cardinal—announcing dawn.

The automatic coffee pot bubbled and dripped. She rose and pushed feet into slippers. Brushing her teeth, she grimaced at her face in the mirror, then went into the kitchen to fix oatmeal. The back glass patio doors faced east. The gold of sunrise spilled on the horizon and ripples of the lake. Facing the expanse of water, she sat down in her robe at the kitchen table, scrolling on her computer to read the news, mail, and her list of chores.

First on the list were Adam and Debbie, her city children, coming for Thanksgiving. She would pick them up when they rendezvoused at the nearest airport four hours away. They were plugged into good colleges and internships to prepare for well-paying jobs. After the last dizzying downturn, the latest numbers for the country looked good: low unemployment, stable economy, and a bullish stock market.

Debbie asked why she lived five miles from town.

"Free housing," Sheraton texted back. Your schools are expensive. And I like it in the mountains. Old, wild, you'll see."

She checked her accounts online. *Counting all my money like a king*, she thought happily. Fact was that Saburia had made her a multimillionaire. Endon paid very well too.

Attending Endon town meetings, she heard about things that had never occurred to her before, like the calving season for beef cows. In the clinic, people were respectful: "We are so happy to have you, Dr. Sheraton."

Kids were homeschooled, mirroring the polite reserve of their parents. Because even the Darwinian theory of evolution appeared to be a sensitive topic, her discussions of science were circumspect. She focused on practical knowledge like anatomy.

Sometimes Endon resembled Saburia, she thought, a foreign world. *But not as bad as wearing hijab and heels in Saburian heat,* she reminded herself.

She was updating the clinic, lining up vaccinations and appointments. There were new challenges. Health problems were different here than Saburia, with obesity and drugs leading the list.

"That's nice that the government pays for free dental care," she told the hygienist as he scrubbed the teeth of a nine-year-old.

"They don't. *We* pay for that dentist who comes ever week."

For her children's Thanksgiving visit, the local satellite system would access the indispensable public internet. But she mostly used Endon's internal network for her work at the clinic, as well as the science projects for the children and updating her new home, grateful for the deep financial pockets of the Endon family.

A firewall secured the Endon network from any unauthorized monitoring and screened whatever messages she sent out, no different than when she was living in Saburia. For that reason, she did not text Debbie back to say that the main reason she lived outside the town was that the town vibes were strange.

Within the Endon network, she detected waves from distant places, electromagnetic signals where exotic languages and unfamiliar faces streamed into her computer. About Saburia, she discovered a puzzling disconnect between what she heard about in the mainstream press versus the Endon intranet—feeding her foggy pictures of Saburia, Saburians, and static-filled audio of their stories that translation software clumsily converted into English. This morning—again—she searched but couldn't find any news about the widowed Queen Noru or her baby.

Since today was Saturday, she did not have to go to the clinic. Most weekdays, she left the house early in the morning and returned late, when her powerful truck headlights blazed her path in the country night, blotting out all light except one point of reference—the fierce bulb on her front porch.

Her new home was a cabin at the end of a dirt trail off a gravel road. She stewarded this property and the surrounding forest for the Endon family. The building was a self-sufficient dwelling originally built by a prepper, someone preparing for survival in case of a catastrophic disaster, with solar panels, a well, and a septic tank. In addition to its out-of-the-way location, there was an empty weapons bunker that now only stored food and generator fuel among unused chicken coops. A shed had beat-up dirt bikes, an ATV, and a boat.

Wayne Endon promptly delivered packages to her door that he picked up from a PO box in town. She first met him in person at a local diner after she had arrived, along with his older brother, Brad, a board member at the county hospital, and Brad's wife, Terri. After her stint in Saburia with marriages within families, Sheraton could not help wondering if Brad and

Terri, who looked so alike, might be related. But at least she could tell them apart. In Saburia, she had struggled with being able to tell Saburians apart.

She once had told Dr. Bhattacharya: "It's embarrassing how my brain is programmed to best differentiate between faces in my own race. White spectrum."

"As a child immigrant to the United States, my brain processes many spectrums of facial ID, from India to my adopted country. But yours is more finely tuned to your bandwidth."

At the diner, Wayne told the others, "Dr. Sheraton has won science awards. It'll be a twofer: she can live at the cabin and learn to take care of it. We're expanding alternative energy options for our town. The grid is getting worse, Dr. Sheraton. But Endon has plenty of sunshine, wind, and a running stream for hydropower, possibly."

"Oh, please call me Elise."

Brad and Terri nodded politely. "How do you like that mushroom soup?" said Brad. "It's a special here, been getting it since I was a kid. This is one of the few local places to eat that's not a chain, hasn't shut down."

The third rail of their conversation was why she was here in the first place. Where was her husband? She looked at the tops of the brothers' hands, the identical pattern of long salt-and-pepper hairs.

The soup was a disappointment, more cream than mushroom. "I'm excited to be here," she said, forcing herself to eat it. "Life gives second acts. I'm divorced and supporting my kids in college."

Her cabin and office in Endon now strategically boasted several pictures of her children to advertise her as a "family" woman, the same framed photos that served that purpose in Saburia. Unlike in Saburia, polygamy was serial here, divorces like hers and then remarriages. Both Brad and Terri had been married before, too, and had their own children but none together.

Wayne said he had kids with a former girlfriend and an ex-wife, and he had also adopted another relative. She soon lost track of the sprawling, complicated Endon family tree—which blended into the local community—but memorized the names of some of Wayne's, Terri's, and Brad's grandchildren for starters.

Terri Endon described a grandson from her first marriage who lived in St. Louis. Wayne said, "It's important that Ben visits more often, to learn to fish, hunt, camp, build, and repair things. They don't teach that anymore in the cities."

Sheraton reassured them that, growing up, she had spent her summers on her grandparents' farm and so had acquired some working knowledge. "Still, plumbing and electrical repairs are not in my skill set."

Since then, she was determined to prove herself. This morning, for example, boat maintenance was on her to-do list. The stocked lake was another food reservoir set up by the prepper. After looking up internet postings and videos on water purification, she took a break, changed into a shirt and jeans, then returned to sipping coffee in her kitchen, reading and journaling, delaying putting on heavy boots to go outdoors.

In her journal, she wondered whether she was becoming like the old woman in Queen Noru's story. To practice her English with her, Queen Noru had written about a childhood memory. She opened the file:

When I was a child, my friends and I played in the forest. The others were scared to go far into the woods, with wild dogs and hyenas especially, but I said I was a princess. They would have to do what they were told. We smelled flowers [missing English word for species], gathered herbs [missing English word for species], waded in the stream, and chased big birds [missing English word for species]. But there was a path they refused to go on with me, remembering their duties at home or another excuse. Except my servant, she had to stay with me.

The path led through shrub and sand to a small hut inside a __ [missing English word for "impenetrable weave of small trees"]. There was smoke from a fire, fragrant cooking smells, and bright flowers in the big clay pot outside. Then we heard the long wail of a child.

It was getting later and darker, and my frightened girl servant sat with me. An ancient woman came out and emptied dirty water into the stream. She looked in our direction like she knew we were there, old eyes, like they are in front of me now, then went inside.

Night fell. Our African nights are so black, yet the stars fill the skies with their nets. I then saw an oil lamp in the window, making the hut glow. My heart thumped like a trapped bird's. I wanted to go inside.

But my girl was sobbing, warning me not to fall under the magic spell, and so we walked home in __ [missing English word for "the light of moon-sliver"].

Sheraton had asked Noru to explain the purpose of the house, and "Who was that woman in the middle of nowhere?"

"The house is for broken children." Noru looked away to forestall more questions.

Now scrolling her phone, Sheraton again wondered what people in Endon thought about her. Humans were somewhat alike, she thought, whether it was a small town in Saburia or in Missouri, or even Salem, Massachusetts, where during the witch hunts, an older woman living alone might have sometimes been more useful as a scapegoat than for her wisdom and medical skills like midwifery.

She was isolated, she thought, easy here—to end up never seen again, feed in a pig trough. As a scientist, she thought, she should not fear human ignorance, just like she should not fear the night outside. For protection, against both, she had her brain and her guts. *And my guns.* Then her Endon home had two Anatolian shepherd dogs, not as big as Noru's Turkish purebred but mixed breeds like America's people. The prepper had procured the mutts to guard goats and chickens against coyotes and other predators.

What happened to that prepper, anyway? Then she noticed movement on the property monitor above her. Wayne Endon's cavalry-blue truck crawled up to the cabin, the dirt road reddish-brown in the morning light. She felt glad that she was ready for him in her work clothes.

They were both single, but she didn't like the way he sometimes looked at her. *Maybe I'm just being paranoid.*

She put on more coffee and hurried to the front porch, where she heard earsplitting barking. She called for the dogs in the direction of the barn, where only two cats loitered in the morning blaze, fat from mousing.

"Fumble, Tiger!"

No dogs.

"Treat!" she yelled, louder this time.

Wayne Endon strode up, laughing and playing with the frenetic dogs who knew him well and had let him through. She dug into a bin next to the door for dried meat rewards.

"Coffee?" she asked, following him into the house. The screen door closed behind her, but she left the main door open.

"Sure."

He handed her a heavy envelope, with the Saburian royal letterhead, her name and address in careful English print, Queen Noru's handwriting. He waited, appearing curious about its contents. But she put the letter away in a drawer and poured him coffee.

They discussed the "latest tech" in cabin upgrades and then repaired a light fixture together. After he left, she slit the letter open, her chest heavy. In a newspaper type font and through a translator's voice, Queen Noru spoke of King Mohammed's "tragic death." She said she was spending her traditional mourning period at Pandolf Medical Center with her baby, and that they were both doing "well." She would "love" to have Dr. Sheraton come visit her next month in October. At the bottom, Noru had written her name in carefully printed letters, with a contact email at the Chicago Saburian embassy.

Call of the Queen. "Heck yeah, I'll visit," Sheraton yelled, euphoric that Noru and the baby were well.

CHAPTER TWENTY-SIX

David Campbell video called Sheraton. In September, 2031, she was settling into Endon in the Missouri Ozarks.

She moved her camera. "Here's my backyard. See the lake and the ancient mountains behind it."

"Who's that? Looks like Queen Noru's dog."

"Not as big as Kalrissian. But I have two of them."

"I've missed you," he said. "You're a good doc, serving the poor rural folk. But any news about the queen and her baby? It's frustrating that Manny won't say much, always worried about who's listening? Maybe he'll tell me more when he visits George this month."

"Such good news," she said. "I told him he would get a visa. Had a feeling. And yes, Queen Noru and the baby will be traveling to Pandolf of all places. She even invited me to visit them."

"We'll get together."

"But it's hard for me to travel as the solo doc here. To see Michael in Chicago, it was pulling teeth to find another doctor to fill in for just a long weekend."

Then he listened to her plans for the latest technology to keep her home self-sufficient.

"Kids these days play a game called *A'50*," he said. "You can make money by giving lessons there for survival skills."

"No interest, not when I just moved to a town that feels like it's preparing for a real apocalypse, and I'm supposed to be the doctor when that happens. I guess no job is perfect, so I'll stop complaining. What about you, David? What's it like not working for yourself anymore?"

"Working for a big corporation has its pluses and minuses."

"Tell me."

He explained, rewinding the months since January 2031, when he had taken charge as Zoser's CTO, how he traveled now to safer international destinations than the Red Sea coast—stayed in luxury hotels with gleaming gyms and heated pools. "Utilizing this giant corporation's resources," he said, "I can create technology teams to advance the grand ideas that germinate in and around me.

"I'm back in mainstream science with a new appreciation for large conferences, arcane discussions, and collaboration," he said. "But I look back proudly on my work with Manny and you. That research on experimental cancer vaccines—it's now journeying to mainstream success with Soria Clinics."

Later she asked, "Any girlfriend?"

"I wish. What about you?"

"I've done with men. With them, I become this awful person that even I don't recognize. Why mess up my peaceful life?"

"How could a man get you to try again, Elise?"

"This isn't about me, is it?"

"You're right."

• • •

Some months ago, he had attended a springtime alumni conference at MIT in Cambridge, Massachusetts. The Dot, the latest prototype upgrade, told him that Dr. Shelly Sharma was in town from Germany for an international research meeting.

He was riding the subway, the rattling T, but did not need to raise his voice. "Dot her."

"Can't, she has legacy communication."

"Why?"

"Her parents are older—"

"Stop. Voice call."

The Dot "rang" Sharma and left a message.

Later he mused to the AI: "Perhaps I'll send my children to StarHall someday? That boarding school sure prepared me well for life."

"Thank you for sharing that," said the Dot, standard language for processing new information. "You may need permission from others in your child's life?"

"Only my wife. I'm traditional. Even if those protestors think Drukker, Zoser are 'raising Cain.'"

"Human nature," the Dot explained.

But he wasn't listening, thinking about how George had told him that Lucky's engagement had fallen through. *Could I be that "lucky"?*

Online, he had been losing to George in *Apocalypse 2050*. George was on a tight budget from his father. "Charlie and other gamers don't have that problem. So, help me figure out the latest rail and electric guns. I don't have money for lessons."

Campbell coached George while being careful to not cross the line into company military secrets. *Was everyone as careful in the addictive world of A'50?* In A'50, the game and players charged for everything: safe water and food, clean air, medicine, fuel, and arms—to training modules. A'50 had a cyber currency that some like George even cashed out.

A'50 had run into real-world trouble as users created and charged for independent teaching modules. Governments accused the game of disclosing military and trade secrets. Activist groups complained that A'50 taught its users practical skills in real-life violence. Bans on the game around the globe then made it more desirable to play in bootleg electronic speakeasies. Finally, the founder of *A'50* announced that he had enough, sold it to a nonprofit think tank in Chicago for an undisclosed sum, and moved to Costa Rica. When the charity made the game available for free in the public domain, popularity really exploded.

Chatting, George had then told him an approximate date when Lucky would arrive at Pandolf Hospital to start work that summer, adding, "And before she left for Germany, Shelly went to Boston in January to see Lucky. Right after Lucky's 'breakdown' when Harry broke off their engagement."

Then Campbell paid George to end their game early, explaining: "I have to leave for my bike ride. In the Loire Valley of France. One of these days, I want you to travel with me, all expenses covered."

When George said nothing, he added, "Totally seriously." Then he clicked off, thrilled with his real-world prize: Lucky was now a "free" woman.

In springtime Boston, as he ran along the Charles River, Sharma "rang" back, and they arranged lunch.

At MicroGravity in Cambridge, a colonial-era café, he sat outside in the sunshine next to a tall hedge. Between the branches, shimmering new green, he recognized Sharma, her brisk walk. When she arrived, he stood.

"You look great," he said, gently returning her hug. "Traveling, research, Germany is treating you well."

"You too look happier somehow."

In no time, they jumped into the deep end of conversation about Zoser's newest Dot technology. Referring to the pushpin-size devices that attached to human skin, she asked, "How come they're not painful to apply? Why don't they cause an infection like insect bites do, that you say your biomechanical engineers mimicked?"

The detailed topography and cross section of the human skin appeared on Campbell's phone screen. He pointed and explained. "Your body recharges them."

She gasped at the palette of skin colors that Dots would be available in and asked, "Do they disrupt—and monitor—nerve signaling?"

He chuckled. "Proprietary technology, they'll kill me if I give you answers. We spend a lot of money on cybersecurity."

Later, she pointed to the café sign. "'Microgravity' is how I feel in Cambridge—unfettered." She nodded at someone sitting nearby. "Do you know them?"

"Yes," he said, recognizing the famous chemist, gray hair, flannel shirt, indeterminate gender. "So many brilliant people come through Cambridge."

"I'd love to get a faculty appointment here," she said. "And this season is much nicer than the last time I came, January, dreary after the lights of the holiday season went dark. Before leaving for Germany, I stayed with Lucky and her aunt in Beacon Hill."

"Pretty part of Boston."

"You know—?"

"That she and Harry broke it off? Yes."

"My mom said that it might happen after they were separated during her residency."

"What happened?" he asked.

"Nothing dramatic I know of. They were living together. Then Harry told Lucky that he loved her but was not 'in love' with her. No other woman, he said."

"Is that so? Then he met someone else very quicky after their breakup, traveling with her to an ashram in India by January?"

"Just a mean rumor online, you should know better," she scolded. "Lucky said Harry was an 'ugly drunk' about it."

"So the drinking broke them up?"

"Maybe the drinking was just a sign that Harry was unhappy," Sharma said.

"You don't even drink. Very philosophical, blaming our human condition for our bad choices."

"I have only heard Lucky's side," said Sharma. "Maybe *she* found someone else."

"No! Lucky is loyal."

"Of course," she said calmly. "My point is, we really don't know everything. But I think Harry was 'ambi-valent.'"

"A new pronunciation for that English word. In some languages, that changes the meaning entirely." *We're now scientists talking,* he thought, *testing hypotheses for the breakup.*

"My Indian dad used that pronunciation of ambivalent to translate a Hindi word for someone who doesn't know what they want."

"Will put it in our AI dictionary."

"In his local Hindi dialect, that word implies weak character," she continued.

"I like that," he said. *Definitely applies to Harry.*

"Not sure," she said thoughtfully, "My dad's people back in his Indian village can be quite judgmental. Like when he married a White American woman. But never mind, George told me that he thought you had feelings for Lucky."

"Am I so obvious that even that kid can read me? Though George is unusually perceptive."

She smiled in agreement. She looked so happy, he thought, maybe no longer dragged down by the burnout in health care.

He touched the Dot behind his ear and dictated: "'Ambi-valent' like interaction of elements in chemistry. Hydrogen and oxygen, different valences, combine as water—or corrosive hydrogen peroxide." He smiled back at her. "Isn't everything chemistry?"

"Say, you're spending a lot of time talking to that AI," said Sharma. "Lucky might help you stay in touch with your human side."

He grinned. "Yeah."

"I told Lucky that you would be good for her."

"I'll be better for her than 'ambi-valent' Harry." *Jerk goes from being water to a corrosive chemical. Leaves someone sweet like her brokenhearted.*

"You're older, more balanced too."

He wasn't sure he liked that.

"I'll take it, thanks!" he finally said, thinking she never minced words. "What about you?"

"I fell for someone unavailable," she said simply. "I have a grandmother in South Dakota. She once said that hearts when broken—break open to bigger and better things. We'll see."

Later, they hugged goodbye, tighter this time. He walked over to introduce himself to the chemist.

. . .

In the summer of 2031, Lucky had moved back to Pandolf. Gratefully, she accepted Campbell's help. He was over at her new home every time he returned to the country, only an hour and a half drive from Drukker's San Francisco headquarters without traffic, pedal to the metal. A grand piano needed in, yellowing subway tile in the kitchen needed out, the water-softener system needed repairing, and a new vanity for the bathroom was installed. He was only too happy to be there to meet the plumbers, electricians, and handymen, and to get hands-on with the work.

In the meantime, Lucky worked grueling twelve-hour clinical shifts on Pandolf's wards as an inpatient hospitalist, seeing up to fifty patients a day and gathering glowing patient reviews such as: "Is she an angel or a doctor?"

Sharma had extended her research in Germany and would only return by Thanksgiving for overdue time with her family in Texas. Then she would not return to the hospital until January 2032, needing to first submit publications from her Fujitsu Award research.

Charlie had also moved back to Pandolf for his junior year, his parents finally recognizing that his brief stint in private school at home was a "dismal failure," said Lucky. "He got kicked out again. He'll need to go to a public school. Pandolf is a lot better than the local ones where my parents live."

To her parents, Lucky insisted that for her brother, "free time spells trouble." Charlie then took a waiter job at the Ivy Drip with George.

Charlie mostly stayed with George. "This works until Shelly"—the boys were now on a first-name basis with the adults in their lives—"returns to Pandolf," Charlie said.

"You have a car to come back here at night," Lucky told Charlie.

"Why? School and work are closer at George's."

"Does Michaela still come over?" Lucky asked suspiciously.

"We aren't speaking. Don't ask me more, please." Despite their plans for a friendly parting of ways, Michaela and Charlie had an explosive long-distance breakup a year ago after Charlie returned from Athens to his hometown in Maine.

Sometimes, Lucky invited Campbell as her plus-one to parties, at the hospital or the French-style country estate of the Mather family, where they found themselves the center of attention. But when he dropped her back off at her house, she merely waved goodbye. Impossibly beautiful, she wore the couture—clothes, shoes, accessories—and the cold distance of the stars one admired from afar.

In August, his AI info feed alerted him about King Mohammed's plane crash. Otherwise, Saburian events did not make mainstream news. Shaken, he called Garcia in Saburia. Icy and reserved, the scientist described a smooth transition of power to the crown prince, Syed Malik.

"Any suspicion that the king's plane was sabotaged?" asked Campbell.

"Not that I heard."

"Saburia has its rebels. But swapping out a king for his son does not make sense as something they would do . . ."

"Let's talk again this weekend," said Garcia. "I may know more by then. David, I'm working long hours, I'm going to bed."

As usual, he thought, Garcia was being circumspect for eavesdroppers.

He called Kochanski in Chicago. "I heard already," said Kochanski. "King Mohammed's death just breaks my heart. He had a newborn who'll never know his father. Also, I just got off a video call with Elise. We can't find any news about Queen Noru or baby."

"Scary times."

"Times are always scary, what's new?"

"How's Elise?" Campbell kept his voice neutral.

"You should call her and talk some sense into her about that commune she is going to work in—"

Campbell laughed. "Okay. Have to hop off now to meet someone for dinner."

Lucky was fixing dinner. He drove to her house from the Dock and punched in a code for the iron door within the hedge. He loved her (their) tiny backyard with the small fountain for the birds that she had wanted and that he had set up. He admired the colorful birdbath as he walked up the path.

Inside the living room, Charlie and George sat on the couch, wearing matching green Ivy Drip work shirts.

"Hi, David," said George.

From the kitchen, he heard Lucky. "Oh, hey, David. Come in and show me how to make your steak 'rare.'"

"I want mine 'medium,'" said George.

In the kitchen, Lucky told him that she and Charlie were going to eat vegan "steaks." "It's so much easier," she said. "I just set the oven temperature and bake them. And it's better for the environment."

From the living room, they heard George yell, "They shouldn't be allowed to call that astronaut feed 'steaks.' The FDA should require that only real beef can be called a 'steak,' like how Champagne can only be from that part of France."

Lucky shouted back, "I can hardly wait for you teens to go back to school, with normal outlets for your angst like debate."

George and Charlie drifted into the kitchen where they made a mess, fixing rolls, baked potatoes, and asparagus. George insisted that Charlie had to "tear, not chop" the lettuce for the salad. "It's the French way."

"Stop fussing," said Charlie.

"Remember to wait to pour my dressing until we're ready to eat."

"Those years you spent in Paris really left an impression on you," said Campbell. "I want to check out these fake 'steaks'—my business competition."

Dinner was outside on lawn furniture from the previous owner. When they returned inside, they smelled fresh-baked chocolate chip cookies. Charlie poured milk. "Whole, two percent, or skim?" he asked. "We also have soy and oat."

"Skim cow for me," said Campbell, biting into a large cookie. "Chocolate's still melting . . . oh my god! These taste like home."

In the living room, enjoying his second cookie, Campbell described the miniature version in Saburia, served on doilies from a round tin that featured tiny skaters on a frozen river "in maybe the Netherlands."

"Or some American town in the 1900s," said George. "Did Dr. Bhattacharya serve those cookies?"

"Yes."

"My dad says he keeps a collection of those tins from all over the world."

"Can't imagine those mass-produced tins are valuable," said Campbell. "But Bhattacharya is eccentric."

"But do people around the world think the United States looks like the pictures on those lids: a world that existed a hundred years ago, just White people?"

An awkward silence followed.

George pressed on anyway. "Take Michaela, one of her parents is White. If she went to Saburia, they wouldn't think she's American because she doesn't look like anyone they've seen from here, whether it's in pictures on cookie tins or old movies."

"Must we bring her up?" asked Charlie, annoyed. "Are we now supposed to ban tins? Fact is that our country has made plenty of progress in its image abroad. 'Why so serious?'"

"Charlie's quoting the Joker," George told the others.

"We need to start using the hot tub," said Charlie, then changing the subject. "I want to invite friends over, bring them in my car."

"I'll look at it," said Campbell. "By the way, Lucky, did you notice that your fence is leaning in the back corner?"

"Can Waldo fix it?"

"I'll fix it."

Cleaning up later, Campbell dried the dishes off with a hand towel. Moving close to Lucky, he said, "It's my turn to take you out for dinner."

She didn't move away. "David, you're sweet. Charlie and I appreciate everything you do for us. But right now, I need time."

"When can I ask you again?"

Their faces were close as he leaned in, and she still did not move. He felt her warmth, and he raised his hand to touch her shoulder.

But Charlie yelled into the kitchen, "David, we just took the cover off the hot tub. It's going to need a lot of cleaning."

"Ask me next month," she told him under her breath. "David, I can't just forget the past. I was with Harry for over half my life. *You* sound . . . so serious."

She moved away. But he closed the distance and laid his hand lightly on her forearm—above purple dishwashing gloves. "I don't want to wait that long."

"You will."

. . .

After Campbell told Sheraton about his last few months with Lucky, he asked: "What do you suggest?"

"I don't know her," she said thoughtfully. "Sounds like you're doing the right things. If Lucky wants you to wait, sure. But you know, in the meantime, flowers, chocolates, calls, gifts . . . and to be complete, promises that you don't plan to keep are also on the standard list of wooing tactics . . ."

"I keep my promises."

"Maybe, but ten years from now, you won't be the same man. As for Lucky's ex, don't be so hard on him, we're all vulnerable in romantic relationships. So he turned to drinking. I had issues with alcohol with my divorce. Saburia was good for me that way—like a rehab."

"Rehab, did Michael get that memo?" *Okay, I will pry about you and Michael.*

"You're older than Lucky. The numbers favor men being older than women for romantic partners. My ex fell in love with someone much younger."

I'm not that much older than Lucky.

"Like breaking glass at a Jewish wedding," she continued, "one never really knows on that happy wedding day what time will bring."

You are avoiding talking about Michael. "I'm not sure that's what the glass symbolizes," he said.

"I say go for it!" she said. "May all blessings, prayers, gods, positive energy horoscopes, tarot cards, and unknown powers of the universe be with you and your love for this 'lucky' young woman."

"Thanks."

"Spring, summer, fall, that's three seasons since Lucky's engagement ended. Like three seasons for the human gestation cycle. You may know by winter this year if your wish for Lucky will come true."

"You still have Queen Noru and her baby on your mind."

"Yes. So much change for her to endure, so young, so fast. Compared to those African stars, life is short enough as it is."

On his calendar, Campbell had marked the date in September when he planned to ask Lucky out for dinner. By then, Charlie would be back in school, and at least she would not be fretting about that kid as much. In the meantime, he was excited about seeing Manny Garcia again.

• • •

During his fall visit to Pandolf, Manny Garcia went with George to Lucky's barbecue for Charlie and his friends. A perfect, sunny California day, they took seasonal grapes, homemade fruit salad, corn on the cob for grilling, and a bottle of Napa Chardonnay on ice. On the driveway, they parked behind a pickup truck.

"Mr. Campbell's," George groaned. "The giant wheels make it an off-road rig."

"I'm excited to see him again," said Garcia. He had brought his Purple Project disk with him to give to Campbell before they met at the Dock next week.

In the backyard, a grill steamed and smoked between Lucky and Campbell. Both wore T-shirts, blue jeans, and boots. A country rose bouquet stood in a vase next to a cooler of beer.

Garcia spied Charlie among a bevy of teenagers next to more coolers with waters, juices, sodas, and punches, and walked toward him. Charlie looked taller and lankier. An open smile broke on his face as he recognized and nodded at Garcia. Hair now dropped in blond curls down the sides of his beard. His T-shirt had a picture that Garcia did not understand, which could be either militant or musical. Escaping the house behind him, Lucky's orange tabby chased a squirrel, followed by another cat he had not seen before.

Crossing paths with the cat, Campbell ran to him. The men hugged. "You've turned into a hugger?" joked Garcia.

Garcia followed Campbell when he returned to grilling. Campbell introduced Lucky, a creature of slender blonde perfection whose friendliness made Garcia feel quite awkward. He handed Campbell the disk about his Purple Project with a serious nod he knew the other man understood.

Campbell tucked it into his backpack. "Sure, Manny, happy to look at this. Something new?"

"Yes. Material a bit dense so yeah, might take some time. We can talk about it when we meet next week like that time you know, back when we met at the NIH." Just like that long time ago, he had emailed Campbell his ideas for AI-assisted cancer vaccines. Campbell was someone he trusted to help him again.

Then Garcia returned to George who proudly moved next to a girl with a nose ring. "Carrie, my dad," said George. "Dad, Carrie Mather."

Tall, lanky, she politely said, "Nice to meet you."

Garcia almost did not recognize Michaela, at the edge of the crowd. George had told him she was no longer dating Charlie, "awkward for me. I'm friends with both of 'em."

Still pretty in a way only a sixteen-year-old could be, she appeared to be coming from or going to work, with a short haircut and a dressy blouse with khaki pants. For the party, she had pasted on glittery green eyelashes to match stickers on her boots. She and Charlie hovered around each other, not too close, not too far apart. As they chatted, Charlie updated him about the recent news in Pandolf. For the school news website, he had done a story on Queen Noru's arrival.

Charlie then demonstrated his latest purchase, a drone, a small housebroken version of the flying monsters at the Saburian base. It darted, hummed, and flashed around Lucky's backyard. "You can only buy it with A'50 points."

"Nice," said Garcia. "I work on a military base in Africa where swatter drones zap enemy ones. The first time I realized there was a drone spying right above me was when I heard a swatter get it, *pop*." He mock slapped his cheek.

Driving back that evening, Garcia said, "George, remember when you and Mr. Campbell were kidnapped? A Saburian drone followed you back to the coast. I saw the video, how you kept your cool, and how well you took care of Mr. Campbell."

George said nothing but looked proud.

Hopefully, he thought, the boy will someday appreciate me, my dreams—forgive all my parental mistakes. Time my judge. My executioner.

CHAPTER TWENTY-SEVEN

Dot said, "This is progress, David. I measured the centimeters between the two of you. Chemistry. I predict Lucky will say 'yes.'"

Campbell was driving back to his hotel in Union Square, San Francisco, chatting with the latest prototype of the AI companion.

"Is Lucky 'ambi-valent'?" he quizzed. "Shelly's dad's version."

"She still loves Harry."

"But he left her!"

"Be persistent . . . but not too patient."

He remembered the sound engineer's graphs when designing the warm tone now in the ungendered voice that he had selected for himself, from many choices available.

"I can't push her too hard," he said. His conversation with the AI was interactive, teaching it about civilized behavior.

"The heterosexual brain is wired for male aggression and female fear. For procreation—not for procrastination—since primitive times."

Good job sounding like a robot right now, he thought.

AI's newest designs created hard boundaries between AI and human users. Fact was that humans didn't do well with AI that became too human, too much like them. From fear and paranoia to emotional attachments and unworldly hallucinations, things went awry.

"With all due respect," said the Dot, its standard preface to disagreement, "one ignores human neurobiology at one's peril. Another male could come along. Harry could return if you wait too long."

"I'm not 'ambi-valent,'" he mused. "Not only am I obvious about how I feel but uncomplicated, too—the basic chemical formula. And Lucky might prefer the angsty type?"

The Dot did not usually engage with what it considered rhetorical questions.

"I'll have to tell Lucky," he continued, "that you've been listening to all our conversations."

"Why do you have to tell her?"

"Because it's the right thing to do. I'm also turning off your 'automatic listen' feature." Legally, the Dot was in a gray zone with its ability to listen to users' conversations without recording them. "AI augmented listening" was now before the courts.

At the hotel, the valet opened Campbell's car door. He didn't want to return to his empty hotel room. They all looked alike. Online rentals, even in stunning locations, also had no appeal. There was also his home in Texas near his mother, who was busy with her latest circle of friends in her retirement complex. At the bar, he watched baseball, season ending soon, and chatted with the bartender.

The next morning, before leaving for the Dock, he texted Lucky as he drank coffee and ate a cookie from the barbeque.

"Recipe is 50+ years old," Lucky texted him back. "You sound like your machines, 'epiphany of flavor.'"

• • •

At the Dock, he loaded Garcia's disk. Garcia's smiling face appeared on his screen, the Saburian lab as his background. "Remember I couldn't tell you about the contents of the purple case you brought to Saburia. That was for your protection. King Mohammed Saburi authorized and funded a secret project. The result was supposed to be an IVF twin pregnancy for Queen Noru."

Garcia started a slide presentation. "We had a Genghis Khan artifact, not independently verified, and the decomposed tissue gave incomplete and conflicting information. So, we—meaning me and the Drukker AI—built scaffolding using healthy genetic material with umbilical cord blood from my son, George. Over this framework, the Khan chromosomes were rebuilt and printed on Drukker's RT66."

Garcia described the procedures for saving umbilical cord blood after a baby was born as common after delivery. "In fact," he said, "umbilical cord blood banks store blood for many uses. The stem cells are valuable to treat cancers and other diseases." Then Garcia described in detail the painstaking reconstruction of twenty-three Genghis Khan chromosomes.

"In an Indian embryology lab," Garcia then said, "those twenty-three Khan chromosomes were combined with King Mohammed's, and the full complement of forty-six human chromosomes was recreated and inserted into one of Noru's eggs, where the natural genetic material was removed to make the egg a host. The other embryo was the king's repaired chromosomes and the queen's. Only one embryo survived: the mixed-race Khan embryo. Makes things complicated, I'll explain more when I see you."

Garcia continued, "Main thing is that we successfully reconstituted healthy chromosomes, replacing the defective ones caused by family inbreeding. One embryo passed the ultimate test of survival. And—oh, yes—the king only wanted male embryos."

Campbell paused the disk. He stared out the window at the Dock landscaping, small hills with 3D displays of strange worlds slotted into window frames, one with the helicopter pad. *So this was the mystery purple case!*

"But David," Garcia went on, "this is all just a preface to what I tell you next, *only you,* because I trust you to do the right thing."

Bright-eyed, looking straight into the camera, Garcia said, "The Drukker AI is leaping ahead as it learns. Why shouldn't it, as an artificial replica of our own programming? It pointed out patterns in the Khan DNA that it hadn't seen in such abundance before. Together, we found a coil in one Khan chromosome that I dubbed 'the Conductor.' Like the maestro of a majestic symphony, in our dynamic modeling, it directed the activation of signature patterns across the human genome. The Conductor turns noise into song."

Garcia waved an imaginary baton. "I didn't even hear my first full orchestra until I was an adult, going with my wife to a free college performance of Beethoven's *Ninth.*"

Garcia's eyes were wet. "A free performance was all we could afford, we dressed like beautiful people anyway. And she was beautiful, David." Garcia blinked away tears. "What an evening! Skies opened to infinite angels, grand explosions of sound and song, a first-time fall-in-love epiphany . . . the AI and I searched for the Conductor in human genome databases, especially in what used to be ancient Mongolia, Genghis Khan's home. But the truth was staring us in the face. The first place we found anything, mutated, was in a defective chromosome of King Mohammed.

"I believe the Conductor might be a human 'leadership' gene that produces signals of dominance over other human beings? Just like ants and bees naturally have queens, are humans programmed to unthinkingly follow some leaders when they appear? At certain times, might they come to us as our messiahs and saviors? Did the Saburian royals hope to reproduce within themselves this talent of ruling others? But, by inbreeding, they created birth defects instead? I have reconstituted the Conductor gene to its original healthy version. Those broken bits from the Saburian royal genome were helpful, though. It was technically easier to puzzle them together than to reconstruct the entire sequence de novo. Also, they helped cross-check us, the Drukker and me."

Campbell opened a scientific presentation that Garcia said he hoped to give someday to other researchers. In it, he described how he had given each of the two embryos healthy copies of King Mohammed's Conductor gene. "The Khan twin has double, two copies of the Conductor gene, one from the artifact and the other from King Mohammed. If things fall apart in our world, the baby Prince Ahmat may or may not be where the baton is, where the music can begin again. Perhaps there are other people out there born with two working Conductor genes, for good or ill, to lead swarms of humanity on our journeys through this world."

Garcia peered closely at the camera. "I know you, David. You will say that a possible dominance-signaling splice in Ahmat's genome is problematic because Genghis Khan was a brutal murderer-conqueror. But is the human talent for leadership just a silvery web sometimes—almost invisible—that traps us? A barely visible net can have tremendous power. Your President Lincoln only mentioned the 'better angels of our nature,' not their dark mirror image. Is it possible that King Mohammed considered the possibility of awakening the worst angels of our nature, unleashing a destroyer?"

Garcia smiled. "Someone else besides me, with help from our increasingly intelligent machines, will take up these questions for the future. Is democracy fragile because it's not the natural human state, rather spun from a dream, especially in times of trouble like ours?"

· · ·

The next week, Campbell and Garcia met at ButterFiles, the Dock's gathering place for its workers on a building roof garden of native grasses and flowers, worked by and named for it's robot bees and natural butterflies.

Campbell asked many questions. "That Conductor gene complex. Do you think that only one embryo survived because the Khan twin had two copies, double his twin, and eliminated his twin in the womb?"

"Scientifically speaking, I don't know," Garcia replied. "And I don't plan to do any more embryo engineering. King Mohammed wanted all records of this research destroyed. That was his deal with me."

Campbell shook his head. "Until someone else comes along and duplicates your work. That's what always happens. Even a king cannot prevent the inevitable in scientific advancements."

"I think his decision was only about no one finding out how his own son was created."

Garcia then grew tense. "There is an apocalyptic movement called the Sun Order that knows this research exists. But they don't know my discovery of this Conductor multifactorial genetic dominance. The Sun Order calls it Commander, Wizard, Messiah, and they believe—not me— that people who carry this pattern gain power over others, through charisma, cunning, and even paranormal experiences."

Garcia shook his head. "No, not even when they drugged me, feasted me, friended me, I hid this from them."

"I'm glad you didn't destroy your hard work. For now, I'm going to lock it up."

"At Drukker, I mean Zoser?"

"No," said Campbell. "In my private vault. Just in case my CTO head rolls off here one day."

"Don't you worry about people listening in here at the Dock? To us?"

"What are they going to do, fire us? They need us, buddy." Campbell put his arms behind his head and then confidently stretched them wide. "I appreciate that you trust me with this."

"I appreciate that you trust me. I'm sorry that Michael and I roped you into the Purple Project like transporting my files to Saburia, without telling you anything. That was not fair. Endangering you without your knowledge."

"Apology accepted. At least you didn't flat-out lie to me like Michael did. I loan him much less trust than you."

"Meaning?"

"For some people, trust when broken can't be rebuilt. But me, I treat it like a loan. Manny, your loan is redeemed. But Michael's not getting much trust from me anytime soon."

• • •

Lucky said yes to him. And she was going to treat him to dinner at the Provencale, she said, as "repayment" for fixing the fence, also getting the hot tub working, and cohosting the barbecue for Charlie and his friends before school started.

But this is a date? he wanted to press her after they were seated. *October, over a year since the last time we were here.*

"Manny Garcia is such a character," she mused. She had just met Garcia for the first time—visiting from Saburia—at the back-to-school party.

He smiled. "Yes."

"Interesting how Manny barely talked to me and spent most of his time with George and his friends."

"I don't think he's comfortable with women."

Like before, they were again seated at the table in front of the picture window. The restaurant owner personally came to greet them. Their waiter, an older man with a round face, happily explained "du jour" menu items as he wiped off the bottle of Chardonnay sitting in ice and poured more into their glasses.

Then Lucky talked about Sharma's planned return to the United States after Thanksgiving. "She won't start back at the hospital until after New Year's, though. Finalizing her publications. I'm really proud of her."

Lucky then added, "She said she saw you in Boston. She really likes you."

"I like her, too."

Lucky grinned. "And she'll be kicking Charlie out of the apartment after she returns."

They laughed. He had spent so much time with Lucky for the past three months. Familiar, no awkwardness, he watched himself happily turn into clay in her hands. No one in this world was prettier, funnier, and more elegant than this ethereal creature who now laughed with him and let him hold her hand, his fingers wrapped around hers, so delicate and so strong. Toes teased each other under the table.

As they were sharing chocolate cake, she said, "Charlie is home tonight."

"Let's go for a walk around the lake after dinner and talk some more."

"I'm wearing ridiculously high heels."

"How do you even stand in them?"

"Practice. But I don't get that anymore in my line of work. Back in the day, I could even run in them."

"Okay, we'll drive around."

When they stepped outside, a limo pulled up. Her eyes widened in surprise. The Dot had done an excellent job by connecting to the universe for this bonus to his wooing.

"What about your car?" she said.

"I'll get someone to pick it up."

"Charlie's back at the house."

"Come to my hotel?"

In the streetlight, their eyes teased each other.

"That's far away."

"I drive fast."

He wished he could see her face clearly as she agreed.

Using his travel rewards points, the Dot had booked one of the highest, biggest suites with a walk-out view of nighttime San Francisco. A voice inside praised the good deals he—and the Dot—were making that evening, from a free dinner to a room upgrade. He removed the pad behind his ear and dropped it in its case. The Dot, the world, did not need to know where, when, or what happened next.

Inside the car, behind the privacy partition and in the darkness, he leaned in to kiss her. Next, his hand was on the soft curve inside her knee, her hands on his cheeks. She pulled him in for another kiss.

"Will Charlie miss you if you don't come home tonight?" he asked, not really caring.

"If he notices, I'll tell him I got caught up at work. Another broken body coming in through the ER that I need to fix."

"You're fixing me . . ."

Later, after, he remembered the Red Sea, how millennia ago, the first humans ventured out of East Africa into the wild beyond. Descendants told a story that Moses had parted the Red Sea, led his people to leave behind their old world, broken and violent. He held her hand. On a different horizon in time, the promise of their future together lay in the calm expanse and starry skies ahead—as they too would raise alive their dreams.

• • •

Back in Saburia after his trip, Garcia sat in the break room in Ramses Hospital while one of his experiments was processing.

"Indonesia has no complaints," announced Dr. Bhattacharya, suddenly appearing before him. Soria Clinics had moved Dr. Bhattacharya to the capital.

As they discussed their Indonesian patient, Protocol No. 8-31, Liang dashed past them, pausing to smile and wave on his way to the lab. Garcia nodded at him. "He's not just proficient anymore. He comes up with innovations."

"Yup, you're a good mentor," said Dr. Bhattacharya. "Mary's doing well for now. Our Singapore patient, too. Two more patients have signed up."

Garcia smiled happily. "I'm afraid to get too happy. Irrational that I should worry about jinxing myself."

Dr. Bhattacharya frowned at him. "Not about just you anymore. Many other people involved now. And I'm keeping an eye on Liang! What if he's stealing Soria technology for China? Maybe he knows I'm watching him. That's why he didn't want to sit down with us."

"That's not fair," said Garcia, feeling the need to defend Liang. "Anyway, one needs the Drukker or equivalent AI for these treatments."

Bhattacharya looked incredulous. "The Chinese can afford *that!*"

Garcia shrugged. "If we're successful, I want to see widespread use."

Dr. Bhattacharya got up abruptly. "Manny, these are *not* the days of Salk's polio vaccine freebie. Soria won't be inviting you to business meetings because you don't take technology theft seriously." He laid one hand on Garcia's shoulder. "For corporate, our work is about profit. If Soria wasn't running the business well, neither you nor I would have our jobs, hmm? Teamwork within our company—medicine, science, and business working hand in hand—is bigger than our individual agendas." He joined his hands and bobbed his head side to side.

"What's that head wag? I've seen other Indians do it."

"I'm Indian *American*," Dr. Bhattacharya corrected him. He tapped the Dot behind his ear. "It says I'm late—again. Good thing I'm a doctor, people expect it." He grinned, darted off, spilling drops of coffee in his wake.

Garcia stayed back alone. Late October, fall was turning into winter, fading the past into shadow, presenting the future's uncertain colors. He missed his family. When his mother had found out AnnaMaria was pregnant, she called. "I'm *finally* getting my granddaughter. We're expecting in the spring." Excitement in her voice overflowed many connections, from Paris to Ramses, overwhelming all technological disruption. "AnnaMaria said you knew and didn't tell me. *My own children, united against me.*"

He had said nothing.

"Okay, fine," she said. "But what kind of name is 'Darcy'? AnnaMaria promised me she'll have a Spanish name, too."

AnnaMaria told him she felt anxious. "Max's career keeps him busy; it gets lonely. I'm so hormonal. Mom said she'd like to come help with the baby, but it may be hard for her to get a visa. Can your lawyer help, please?" So, he called Trisha Talwar.

Talwar had inspired George. Apathetic about his father's scientific innovations, his son now planned to become a lawyer someday.

"Dad, whatever they say, the baby may not be a girl," George opined about his aunt's pregnancy. "Science now understands that gender can be fluid. I'm glad Uncle Max wants a unisex name."

"True," said Garcia. "Science makes a lot of things 'fluid' these days. But did you know that 'Darcy' is a British family last name, now in use as a first name—only for girls?"

"No." George then looked it up online. "It says 'Darcy' became common as a baby name after it was used in *Pride and Prejudice*, with Fitzwilliam Darcy." On the screen, George looked disappointed. "I don't think 'Fitz' as the baby's name would work."

"A rose by any name is still a rose," said Garcia. "If they really want a unisex name that reflects his father's Anglo heritage, you could suggest 'Cameron.'"

Sometime later, George said, "My friends really liked meeting you."

"I liked meeting them," he echoed, surprised that any teenagers might like him.

• • •

The cooling fall weather in Ramses was pleasant for walks with Dr. Bhattacharya or Liang. His NIH lab head used to like to quote an American football coach: "Success deodorizes failure." True. His ideas for research were finally unfettered.

He now had connections, he thought. Mary had invited him to visit her in New York. Sharma messaged him about a conference in Germany. She was going to present a poster that used his ideas.

Despite the hostility in their first introduction, Prince Bassam now hosted him regularly with no further mention of helping the new Saburian king with a genetically engineered embryo.

Sending a driver to pick Garcia up, Prince Bassam would meet him at the end of a gravel walkway that led them back through lush gardens within his walled compound. They had local snacks—falafel dipped in herb-laced yogurt was his favorite—and good Saburian coffee, not the hospital's reconstituted black-from-concentrate.

He never saw or heard Bassam's family. In Saburia, segregation of the sexes was the norm. He hadn't expected to meet Bassam's wife. But what about sons? Nephews? When he had met King Mohammed, it had also only been with his official retinue.

But he was a "foreigner," living in Saburia at the whim of his hosts, unable to buy property, and only able to work or own a business with an alien resident's license.

He asked Bassam, "Doesn't Saburia make exceptions for foreigners to make a home here?"

"No, we're not your New World. Remember the old fable about a wheedling camel. First foot, then leg, then haunch, and finally the whole animal displaces its owner from his own tent into the desert to die."

Bassam clenched his jaw and pushed one shoulder ahead. Like an American football player, thought Garcia. "Nothing personal, Manny." Bassam no longer called him Mr. Garcia. "Foreigners need to be kept in their place."

One evening, Bassam said, "The poetry of humanity always has a refrain, an apocalypse just around the bend, our rallying call. But, Manny, here you and I sit, Homo sapiens, the peskiest of survivors, in some shape and form, maybe metamorphosizing into AI in the future, no longer organic, then going forth into the universe and multiplying.

We have been waiting for—maybe not Godot— but the apocalypse that never arrives."

Garcia set down his drink, tasty tamarind ginger sherbet. "Dr. Bhattacharya that I work with, he's fanatic about infections. Beats everyone over the head with infection precautions. Fears the end will come with the 'global threat of antimicrobial resistance and mutant viruses confounding medicine.' And how 'throughout history, infectious diseases wiped out populations—about a quarter of the people in Europe in the fourteenth century with the bubonic plague.'"

Garcia added softly, "Then there were the millions of indigenous peoples in the Americas and elsewhere with measles and smallpox. We're always vulnerable to cellular infiltration. Death, the pale horse, is inevitable for each of us. As for our physical world, even my AI has more variables than equations it can solve for the future."

"Explain."

"A mathematical analogy, the Drukker predicts infinite alternatives for times to come."

"Infinity," said Bassam. "An ancient symbol, the number 8 on its side, good and evil, black and white, twined forever like a Möbius strip." He knitted all his fingers together. Opening a few fingers, he mimed the hand game. "You know this?"

Garcia nodded. "You learned that as a boy?"

"At boarding school—oh, yes. 'Open the door, see all the people.' StarHall has been our New World shelter for lost boys and girls, and our young Prince Ahmat will be the next to attend. Do you know a Jim Sichet?"

"In Chicago? My brother-in-law there has mentioned him."

"Our royal family's lawyer in Chicago. He's unhappy that Queen Noru and the baby are at Pandolf. He hates Pandolf's CEO, Dean Baluyn, whom you have met."

"Why does he hate him?" asked Garcia.

"Dates back to us being kids in boarding school together—"

"StarHall, that boarding school in the Northeastern United States."

"Called New England."

"And David Campbell went there too," said Garcia.

"A bunch of us young, rich kids—drugs, alcohol, little supervision, lots of time—an explosive combination, right? The school depended on family donations and so looked the other way, at least until a young teacher was killed."

Bassam coughed. "Jim Sichet was one of many bullies there. And in our Sun Order cell. After her murder, Dean Baluyn accused Jim of a role in the murder. They fought. Our cell dissolved."

Then the prince coughed again before adding, "Jim once said that murder is a taboo—only to 'the common people.'"

Garcia had asked Dr. Bhattacharya about this cough and imitated it: "I have a friend. He coughs like this."

Dr. Bhattacharya listened to Garcia carefully and then looked sharply at him. "I always listen for germy sounds around our immunosuppressed patients. But that's not infection, cancer, asthma . . . maybe chronic pulmonary fibrosis, progressive condition for which there is little help."

"Your cough is getting worse," Garcia said to Bassam. "Are you getting the best medical care here? Pandolf's the place to go for international patients."

"Wait. Watch."

Twilight shadows cloaked the purple bougainvillea on the walls of the compound. In clay pots on the patio, almost black flowers opened with a bitter fragrance. Bassam deeply inhaled and exhaled with relief.

He wouldn't tell Garcia the plants' Saburian name. "Sorry, our healers want to keep it a secret. And these plants need this type of climate to live."

Bassam took another deep breath. "I can't travel to the US. For one thing, these plants would never pass customs there. Now that I can talk, there's one more Sun Order cell that I stay in touch with. We sent Dr. Sheraton to Endon in the Missouri Ozarks for them."

"That's how she ended up there!" exclaimed Garcia.

"It was easy for us to filter information, incoming and outgoing, about the lady doctor's future options while she was here."

Lady doctor. Quaint. We really are talking to each other in a second language across a cultural chasm.

"Who tells Prince Ahmat to lead in a future world's apocalypse?" asked Garcia. "How can one predict Ahmat's future—or our globe's future?"

"We can't. But let me tell you my dead brother's perspective. While the Sun Order is no longer official at StarHall, it's still central to our history there. Didn't a lot of Western universities start off as religious schools and now claim no ties to any faith? StarHall is evolving too, casting wider nets, even welcoming people like me. Any student or alum can start their own Sun Order cell."

"In my high school, we had cliques, too. Mine had one member—me."

"And look how well you've done." Inhaling deeply the exhalation of the medicinal flowers, Bassam looked years younger. "Back to Prince Ahmat. At StarHall, no one will care he's half-Saburian or half Genghis Khan. With royal blood and wealth, Ahmat could lead a Sun Order cell in StarHall."

"Or not! Even my son is turning into his own man."

George had told Garcia that he was no longer an atheist. "I believe there's a force of good that wins over evil, Dad."

Garcia had rebutted, "Evil always comes right back, a cycle. Time is indifferent, amoral, pitiless."

But on the video screen, the light had not dimmed in his son's eyes. "You and your time god, both of you are hopeless."

"No. I enjoy the good times while they last."

Following that wisdom, Garcia sat in the gardens, now inhaling the familiar scents of lilies and jasmine. The acrid smell of the medicinal flowers had faded away.

Bassam's face was again tightening, looking older quickly while he said softly, "For my brother—I can position Prince Ahmat for a possible destiny to fulfill his father's dream. And speaking of our young men, Manny, I hear that your son is quite the romantic about one of Dean Baluyn's young relatives, Carrie Mather. Dean knows about the Purple Project. Given that George is part of it, the Mather family even includes your son socially."

Garcia sighed. "That would explain my son's invitations to their fancy events. He thinks it's because Carrie Mather may like him back. He will learn the hard way . . . this upper-class family doesn't care about him as a person."

"That's harsh. They're really not bad people. They didn't make Carrie go to StarHall. Her father's a local leader. His children go to the public school there."

"It was Saburia's loss that you did not become king."

Sphinx-like again, Bassam said, "Still, I've served my family, my country, and the Sun Order. Now, enough! Let the music play."

Bassam looked down and tapped his phone. On hidden speakers, a Saburian flute played, followed by a string accompaniment. Bassam gave him the names of the musicians—"they perform for my family often"— cheerfully nodding to the beat as the drums marched in.

After the music ended, Garcia softly clapped. "I really enjoyed the military band at Prince Ahmat's naming ceremony. Those horns—bobbing and swaying—riding waves of sound."

"Yes, waves of the rhythm and roar of our cheering crowds." But the prince sounded skeptical.

"My best therapy is larger-than-life—live—Western classical symphony," said Garcia. "Sound systems only replay my memory, don't light me up, just make me feel like the sad dog in an old gramophone ad."

"Do you play an instrument or sing?"

Garcia laughed. "I wish! When my wife took me to my first symphony in Buenos Aires—Beethoven's *Ninth*—I couldn't even tell apart the strings, horns, or woodwinds. Pia patiently explained . . . . I miss her."

"What memory should I play on my 'gramophone'?"

"Beethoven's *Ninth*."

And later, before Garcia left, Bassam passed him a handwritten note: "The rebels will not harm our new king or Ahmat. I've infiltrated them at their highest level."

Bassam then took his note back and burnt it in the candle's flame.

CHAPTER TWENTY-EIGHT

In November, the wildfires near Pandolf, California, spewed a dull haze that blocked even the moon. Inside Queen Noru's suite in Pandolf Lodge, heavy curtains and the whirr of air purifiers muffled the whine of ambulance sirens.

In the past two months since her arrival, Noru had tried to get into a routine, going on daily walks with the prince in a stroller around the Pandolf Medical Center campus, and to the hotel spa by herself to calm her nerves. Dr. Sheraton called, apologizing about how she was unable to visit yet because she worked in a remote village where she was the only doctor.

At night, Noru only slept soundly with pills from the Pandolf doctor, leaving Ahmat in the care of her women servants. In her bedroom, Kalrissian lay on the rug beside her. Usually sleeping, if the mastiff perceived a threat, he morphed into a monstrous beast of bark and menace in no time, baring his inch-long canines. His now-empty dog crate in the entry hall held toys—squeaky, furry, brightly colored—strange gifts from the American girl, Michaela. On Noru's bedside table lay the girl's business card: "Pandolf Lodge, Child and Pet Care," with website, email, phone number, and scan code.

The dog trainer was teaching Michaela to manage Kalrissian with commands in Saburian. In English, he warned her that "this animal is not a Western *pet.*" He spat out the word "pet." Out of his sight, on walks, Michaela gave the animal treats and warned the rare local who approached him, "He is a teddy bear, but you can't come close."

About midnight, a single beat of thunder heralded a welcome burst of rain. Then a flashing police car arrived, lights reflecting off the wet road. Soon, the police pounded on the main door to Noru's suite. The bodyguard had already seen them on the outside cameras. Muscles tensed, gun ready, he opened the door.

"There's been a bomb threat," said the male police officer.

The Saburian checked their IDs and let them inside the men's room, then only permitted "the lady cop" into the women's suite. Discovering nothing, they left.

By the morning, Noru's drugged mind had cleared. She called the Saburian minister now assigned to her. "Someone might be trying to kill my child and me."

He said they were "looking into it."

Back alone in her room, she pulled out a note from her pocket, left for her in the Pandolf Lodge spa. Under an old picture of her husband with his arm around another young man, both in their twenties, the note said in Saburian: "I mourn the former king, too. Please call if you need help. Respectfully, Jim Sichet," with two phone numbers.

When Michaela arrived on Saturday morning, the two women, baby in stroller, walked to the Golden Griddle, leaving behind her dumbfounded staff, the dog, and her phone. Her maid protested, "But, Queen, we're not even sure if that person you're leaving with is a man or a woman." Noru knew they would be contacting the Saburian minister as soon as she left. This excursion alone with the American girl was a one-time privilege, to find her way out for safety for her and Ahmat.

At the Golden Griddle, Noru touched her closed lips with a finger. Then she spoke into Michaela's phone to translate: "We had a bomb threat."

After listening with her Ear Dot, Michaela said into the phone, "Is this political?"

Noru held Michaela's phone to her ear to listen to the Saburian translation. "Probably. What are your police here like? They came to our suite." She handed the phone back.

Michaela made a face. "They're stupid. Was it a man and a woman?"

Noru nodded.

"That's just Andy and Bobbie, the campus police. They just try to prevent any bad publicity for Pandolf. Law enforcement in our country is unfair."

They passed the phone to translate back and forth. Then Noru showed Michaela the paper note from Sichet.

Michaela squinted at the Saburian writing.

"Who is this Swedish pancake?" asked Noru in halting English. "Lingonberries like gooseberries in a Saburian jelly?"

While talking, Noru pointed with her finger at the English phone numbers on the note and then gestured at Michaela to pocket the note. Noru then gave her one of her rings and shook her head before Michaela could ask anything else, afraid of who might be listening. She hoped that Michaela at least understood that her ring was a gift in exchange for help.

The next day, the Saburian minister assigned to Noru informed her that neither she nor the child was allowed to go out with anyone unless accompanied by her bodyguard and a maid. When Michaela regularly returned over the next few days to take Ahmat for walks, accompanied by a guard, she could only see Noru when the interpreter was present to hear everything said.

Then one evening, when she was alone, Noru heard a knock on her window. Pulling aside the heavy curtain, she saw Michaela, who gestured at her to pull up the window. Noru shook her head—the window was bolted down. Michaela nodded insistently. Noru tried and was surprised when the window slid up easily. *Clever girl must have done something with the window's security system.*

Noru pointed to the gold bracelet on her wrist. Michaela smiled and showed Noru her phone, now with a "secure" translation app installed. Michaela explained that it had been provided by Mr. Jim Sichet to communicate directly with him in Chicago.

Noru typed: "My husband was assassinated, and now our son and I may be in danger. We need to get someplace safe."

Over the next few days, Michaela returned to the window so that Noru could use the girl's phone to communicate with Sichet and put together a plan. Finally, one Saturday evening, as the guards played cards in the entry hall, Noru went to bed early and locked her door. In a sachet, she found her "death pill" from the Saburian royal doctor.

Not yet!

She removed and emptied the baby's medication packet into his milk bottle. Soon, Ahmat was asleep. After swaddling him, she handed him—and her payment, her carved, gold bracelet—to Michaela, who was waiting on the fire escape outside her window.

To her surprise, Michaela kissed her cheek and held her phone up to Noru's ear. "Don't worry," the recording said in Saburian. "I grew up in

Pandolf. We locals are in charge here, indigenous Pandolfians. We'll keep Ahmat safe."

The dog on the floor opened one eye and closed it. Noru listened to Michaela's steps on the fire escape until they faded away. The bracelet was ancestral jewelry from her family's side, inscribed with a black etching of one of the old gods, the golden sun behind the figure making him a shadow. A sun god who brought good fortune into this world and the one beyond.

Then Noru lay sleepless in bed, saying prayers for the safety for her baby. The sedative for Ahmat would last a couple of hours. As for those pills that the Pandolf psychiatrist had prescribed for "postpartum depression," she had stopped them.

There is nothing wrong with my mind, she thought. Instead, her world had changed into this one with bomb threats. Nightmares visited, like when her own bodyguard put a knife to Ahmat's throat. Then, bloody and leering, he hovered over her. Before he crushed her under his weight, her fear silencing her scream, she awoke.

Since then, she tensed in his muscled presence—his sweaty warmth—with revulsion. Things worse than her dream had happened in the history of leading families she knew—when the balance of power capriciously shifted. If she was assaulted, which she feared more than death, who would find out? *Who would care?*

"Change does not ask for permission," Aisha had counseled her at the royal funeral. Aisha was a loyal servant who loved her, even if her well-meaning advice was not always sound. Or her attempts to manipulate Noru for her own good were something to be watchful of. They spoke these days in guarded video conversations. Aisha described how the new king was now securely in power.

In early November, Noru watched on Saburian media as King Malik announced that he planned to marry a Saburian woman from a "good family," advising his people about the drawbacks of marrying one's relatives. Prince Bassam also made a public appearance to commend his nephew's plan—a rare sighting of the "civilian prince back from exile." In his wheelchair, her husband's older brother looked ill.

Unable to sleep, Noru got up and walked around the apartment, feeling like a caged animal. The entry hall was fragrant with flowers—jasmine, lilies, and roses for her twentieth birthday—from King Malik.

The new king had let her see her hometown. On fire. Who was still alive there? After Noru's father had died in a rebel attack many years ago, her own mother had been busy as a leader in the local community.

"A shepherd can't be a sheep," her mother told her.

I'm now that shepherd.

Jim Sichet, too, had sent her a birthday gift, a succulent with thick leaves and instructions in neat Saburian: "Moderate temperature, little sunlight, and minimal watering."

On Michaela's phone, Sichet texted Noru about his plans to move her and Ahmat to Chicago for safety. He promised to replace her current staff that she did not trust.

She typed back quickly, "How fast?"

"Your Highness, please set a time," Sichet replied.

"My plan executes the day after tomorrow."

In English, her note in the Zoser software to Sichet translated as: "My plan executes the weekend after next."

There had been no reply. But she had not waited for Sichet's reply, handing her baby over to the "indigenous Pandolf people."

· · ·

Outside the hotel, Michaela strapped the sleeping child into a kangaroo-style wrap. The steps of the fire escape were slippery from the irrigation, and she carefully descended. With her Ear Dot, she called George and asked if she could come over.

"Charlie's here, but sure."

"I don't care," she said, her voice tight.

Then Michaela called Sichet's home number. A woman answered, her voice slurring.

"I need to speak to Mr. Sichet," Michaela said.

"And how old are you?"

The woman hung up. Michaela muttered expletives.

She scanned another contact code for Sichet and left a message. Thank god the baby had been so quiet on her way to George's apartment, she thought, sleeping *so* soundly.

Once inside, she followed house rules even though Sharma was not returning until after Thanksgiving Break. She placed her wet shoes on the mat.

Charlie paused a movie on the large screen, sky warriors mid-action. "What are you doing here with a baby?"

"This is Queen Noru's baby. Her enemies may be trying to kill him. I'm taking him someplace safe."

Charlie and George looked alarmed—and impressed.

"I left a message for the queen's lawyer in Chicago," she said, feeling far more mature than them. "He's supposed to call me back with instructions. George, can I wait here?"

"Sure. What about your mom? Can't she help?"

"My granny is in the hospital. I don't want to add more stress on her."

"I would call Dad," said George. "But in Saburia, he's always worried someone's listening. Not safe for the baby, either."

Charlie grinned. "I don't need to call anyone because 'moi' can handle things by myself."

Michaela sat down carefully on George's other side. "Charlie, what movie did you borrow that from? You're so unoriginal." Then she unstrapped the sleeping infant from his carrier.

Charlie looked abashed.

She laid her palm on the baby's chest, then her fingers on the pulse in his upper arm. "He's breathing. Heart rate normal. But he usually wakes up so easily. Strange."

When even unswaddling the baby until his skin turned cold and tickling his feet didn't awaken him, she said, "Okay, I'm freaking out, guys, this is unnatural."

"Why is this lawyer not calling you back?" asked Charlie.

"I can drive you to the children's ED," said George.

Michaela shook her head. "No, the main entrance is too public. Dangerous. The queen's enemies may be looking for him there. I don't even have a car seat. But I know a shortcut through the woods behind this building. It goes to the hospital through an underground tunnel network."

"No way!" said Charlie. "Tunnel network. Exciting."

Rapidly, she tapped her phone. Charlie admired her hand. "That ring's gorgeous. Where did you get it?"

"From Queen Noru. It's 22-karat gold, that's a diamond between the two emeralds. Charlie, this baby is a real prince, not some fiction in your stupid video game. His mother's ring will pay for someone to unlock those Pandolf tunnel doors for me—and more."

She strapped the baby back into his carrier. "I'm off."

"Wait," said Charlie. "The woods are dangerous. I'll come, too."

Michaela looked surprised but said nothing.

"I wish you guys would let me just drive you there," said George.

"How about *you* help another way?" said Charlie. "'Cause *you* have a gun."

"You do?" Now Michaela looked impressed.

"Gunpowder is so passé," said Charlie. "It's his dad's SinfonX."

"That's just a gun in your game," said Michaela.

"This is real. George, show her."

George groaned. "You should've joined the military, Charlie."

"Do I look like cannon fodder?"

George returned with a steel briefcase and unlocked it. In gray foam, plastic and metal parts of a weapon were arrayed.

"So, I know how to use this from *A'50*," Charlie said in a hushed voice. "Look, here's the automatic cartridge with one hundred energy bursts, a silencer—makes it quieter than a whisper—binoculars for targets even a mile away, and the gun itself." Tenderly assembling and then disassembling it, Charlie repeated the moves quickly.

He pointed to an empty section in the padding. "That missing part allows the gun to fire one hundred times, precisely, in ten seconds. No heat, no recoil. *Boom, bam, boom*—instant and complete destruction of target—without it, it takes a minute."

Michaela narrowed her eyes skeptically, then grabbed her phone. "I have a notification that the tunnels are unlocked. Gotta go. George, last time I came, I left my Aires in Shelly's closet. Would you mind getting them? Don't want to get my work shoes dirty."

"Sure."

Unable to find her shoes, George returned. "Guys—"

The gun case lay empty. He was alone. He ran to the fire escape. Michaela, the baby, and Charlie had disappeared.

• • •

In a dark corner behind the apartment building, Michaela placed a trash liner with holes over her head and handed Charlie another to do the same.

Then, shadows amid shadows, they slipped down the hill. They crossed a gully of dirty water where a wide stream once ran. Then they entered the trees behind the apartment complex. The lights of Pandolf Medical Center lay on the hill ahead.

Michaela navigated the dirt path easily.

Charlie followed. "Who unlocked these tunnel doors?"

"You'll see."

"Why does the hospital have tunnels?"

"They've been around forever. Mom said that they're from the Cold War, or colder weather back in the day maybe, I dunno."

"You know your way around?"

"Yup. Growing up, sometimes the quickest way to get somewhere was in the tunnels. And a great place to play."

"And Carrie Mather came here, too?" He laughed dryly.

She laughed too. "No, she escaped in Daddy's private plane with her mom to shop in LA, Rodeo Drive, every chance they got. Charlie, do you remember the time when the campus police came knocking? They took a map from George."

"Yeah."

"I did try to follow that map. I took these same tunnels into the hospital complex, went all the way to an old locker room. Didn't find anything. I wonder what was up with that?"

Ahead in the darkness, lights flashed in the dry brush.

Michaela whispered, "Get off the path, let me talk to them." She heard him *click-click*, assembling the SinfonX behind her.

"Just say the word if you need help," he said, leaving.

She pleaded with two figures on the path. "I'm taking my cousin's baby to the hospital on the back way because . . . ask Chuckie."

They tapped on their phones.

"Alright," they said and walked on.

The lights disappeared. "Okay, Charlie, come out," she said.

"Why'd you tell me to hide?"

"You're the wrong tribe."

"What do you mean?"

"Talk later. The tunnel entrance is ahead." Her voice trembled. "I'm scared. Ahmat is barely moving. We have to get him to the hospital *now*."

"What did you tell those people?"

"That Chuckie and I have a deal. Hurry."

They reached a shed. "My mom grew up in the apartment building that used to be here," she said. "They're turning it into a rehab place." She opened the door. The space inside was empty. "This was the laundry room. See the folding table." She pointed with her phone light to a splintered ledge on the wall. "My mom's worked for Pandolf since she graduated from high school, and she always knows the *latest* about their construction projects."

She knelt on the floor. "Yes, unlocked!"

"That's just a drain," said Charlie. "Oh my god, a floor hatch."

Together, they raised a door in the floor. "Mom says that the new construction won't affect this tunnel."

"Your friend, Chuckie, has actual—physical—keys to these doors? Not electronic."

"Pandolf wants to be able to open doors even if there's no backup power."

She paused. "Oh, Ahmat, *baby*, you're waking up, wiggling."

"Now he'll start crying."

"For once, I want you to be right," said Michaela, pointing her phone light down into the tunnel.

Out of her backpack, Michaela produced masks. "Put it on, makes Face ID harder for the cameras."

She stopped. "No, go back and return the gun! I feel better now that Ahmat's waking up."

"No, I'm coming. But there's one thing I must do first." He re-assembled the weapon, stepped outside, and aimed the gun through the telescope at a streetlight. "See that, about a mile away,"

"Don't. Do. It. Chuckie will kill us . . . me."

He removed his finger from the trigger. "I'm not a vandal. And I want to meet Chuckie. I'm coming with."

She sighed. "'Chuckie' is just a name, a link on your phone, here in Pandolf to help you for a price. You only meet a 'Chuckie' for real if you get into trouble. When I was little, the big kids would threaten us that . . . when Chuckie comes for you, the first thing he says is, 'Chuckie's so sorry,' and then you'll never be seen again."

"Sounds like a gang."

"You are judgmental," she said angrily. "In Pandolf, we have a sense of family. 'Chuckie' is just the title we give to a local leader, a person who gets us, not a snoot like some of the Mathers."

"And I am the wrong tribe?"

"I don't mean your race. You're just an outsider, a transient . . . more like you didn't grow up here. You think differently. You're the face Chuckie knows is just someone coming through—not like a White Carrie Mather—even if she looks like you, or a tawny Dean Baluyn, or a me."

"So, I'm not a part of your group just because I didn't grow up here?"

She faced him. "This is America, Charlie. A grand pair of continents, 'sea to shining sea,' always tribal. It's in the air here from back in the days when the Indians were either scalping each other or smoking pipes together. Don't take it personally. Now, would you *please* just go and return George's gun?"

"No." He climbed down the hatch. She followed him. Bright ribbons of light turned on in the ceiling of the wide tunnel ahead.

"We have to run now," she whispered. "I know where to go." Then they darted, tensions abating, even laughing, down the branching path.

"You're only faster than me because I'm carrying a baby," she said. "Don't you see how *that* is problematic?"

Going up another ladder, they emerged into a large storeroom, shelves stocked with medical supplies, massive hospital beds lined in the middle. A young man in a Pandolf housekeeping uniform was sitting on the floor with his computer. "Mickey, you're here," he said.

"Dumbo," said Michaela, pulling off her mask. "This is my friend, Charlie."

"Not funny, Mickey. Hi, Charlie, I'm Al."

"Hey, Al," Charlie said, also removing his mask.

Al looked closely at him, as if memorizing his face. "So, you're peeling our onion here at Pandolf, learning our world's pungent secrets. Not sure everyone will be happy about you here with Michaela, no offense."

"None taken," said Charlie. "So yeah, I guess I'm not a local, but totally, dude, respect all you and your people stand for."

Michaela said abruptly: "I have to take this baby to the ED."

"Forget something?" Al said.

She hesitated, then handed over Noru's ring. "Tell Chuckie thanks for unlocking the tunnels."

Al scrutinized the ring. "It looks like the real thing, alright. Should cover a year of college even after Chuckie takes his share. Good luck, I'm going back to my test."

"Aren't you worried about losing your job?" asked Charlie. "If the hospital finds out you're letting people in like us?"

"Nah. Pandolf will just change the locks—again. It's not like we stole anything. They spend more money on exterminating rats in the tunnels. Poor critters. I keep two as pets."

Michaela laughed, then added in a sing-song voice, "Kids will play, Chuckie says."

Al chuckled. "Don't be telling him *everything*. Bye, Mickey."

Leaving the storeroom behind, Michaela said, "Growing up, we called him Dumbo because he's way too nice. The other kids bullied him. But he's smart. Chuckie listens to him."

"Why didn't you keep that ring?"

"Then Chuckie and I would have had a very *bad* encounter. Because I had a deal with Chuckie—the ring to unlock the tunnels. Charlie, I don't want to die."

"But why help that queen and risk so much danger?"

"Because I don't hide in the safety of video games. Besides, have you seen the queen? Beautiful. No, it's more than that—she inspires me like a goddess. And Charlie, she also gave me a bracelet—gold, with carvings—"

They hurried down a bright hospital corridor into the grand main plaza, where a flurry of people were passing through despite the late hour. A marble fountain gurgled next to the glittering gift shop.

"Michaela, Charlie," a voice behind them startled them. Turning around, they saw David Campbell.

· · ·

The two teenagers stared at Campbell, speechless, and then they next noticed Lucky glaring at them, looking official in her Pandolf jacket, badge, and scrubs. A Pandolf LifeCycle, a four-wheeled robot that transported patients of any age, stood by her side.

"Weren't last weekend's antics enough?" Lucky asked Charlie. "What are you up to?"

CHAPTER TWENTY-EIGHT

Charlie said nothing.

"Lucky—Dr. Malone, we need help," said Michaela. "I'm . . . um . . . do you think this baby is okay?"

Lucky helped Michaela to slowly disentangle Ahmat from his carrier. "He's warm, breathing, moving. And there's another healthy sign—something smells bad. Did you bring diapers? A change of clothes?"

Michaela shook her head.

"Thankfully, our gift shop is well equipped."

To Campbell, Lucky said, "Michaela and I will go to the ED to have him checked out. I'll see you and my brother later."

Campbell looked down at the sleeping baby, now strapped into the LifeCycle, closed eyes, dark lashes, and fat cheeks. He leaned over to Lucky. "I want you to have my baby."

Her mouth dropped open.

"Another time, we'll talk," she said briskly. Then she was gone with Michaela and the baby.

"Whatever did you just say to her?" Charlie asked Campbell suspiciously.

"None of your business. Now, you have something that belongs to George's father. What are you thinking, bypassing security checkpoints? George called me and told me everything. That's no way to treat a friend. You owe him a *sincere* apology."

"How did you find us?" asked Charlie.

Campbell smacked Charlie's lower back, harder than he had intended. "You're wearing your Coach Dot."

"Oh," said Charlie. The sports Dot on the base of his spine tracked his location on various Pandolf High varsity teams.

"This is drama," Charlie said, back to unperturbed, even grinning. "We're doing *West Side Story* in theater class. And look: Michaela and me, different tribes, and you as the New York City cop."

Charlie moved quickly, dodging another blow from Campbell. "Hey, you take a joke?"

"This is not a joke."

They faced each other. Charlie's eyes were calculating, carefree, his face a rough version of Lucky's. Was this adventure-seeking boy even capable of regret about stealing his friend's gun? Campbell wondered. George wasn't getting the SinfonX back from his dad, either.

"You *idiot*," Campbell planned to tell Garcia later. "Why would you leave a lethal mass-murdering weapon with a teenager?" Maybe after living in Saburia, this was the new normal for Garcia, he concluded. The youngest soldiers on the Saburian base were also barely breaking into manhood.

CHAPTER TWENTY-NINE

I n Chicago, Sichet and Kochanski met to haggle over their contract for the Pierre. Interrupting Kochanski, Sichet answered his beeping phone. "Yes, honey, sorry, you say someone calling you about a Queen Noru, music deal. I got it. Now go back to—?"

Sichet turned back to Kochanski. "I need to go—" and left his half-eaten sandwich at the Spirit and Stone.

Then over drinks, Alex Marion showed Kochanski the digital poster he had designed for the Dew vodka brand, a side gig Kochanski had given him. Callie's flirty smile appeared in the foreground of a wintry Chicago skyline.

"What do you think?" Alex asked.

Kochanski had named his vodka after the morning dew he woke up to—growing up in Poland. "I love it," he told Alex, "takes me home like your home."

For his next visit, he bought the Marion children robot game plug-ins—emergency medical technicians—from the latest *A'50* movie about an asteroid collision with Earth. Soon, excited shouting filled the upstairs: "Transform into four-wheel drive over that rock bed. Find Professor Wong."

Dinner was Mexican takeout. After Alex left to put the kids to bed, Kochanski asked Callie, "Where's the money coming from for all this work on your house?" The kitchen had been renovated, new granite countertop and smart stove, and work had begun on the living room.

Callie was clearing the table, tossing paper and plastic into the trash can. "Not environmentally friendly, I know. Come dry dishes." She turned on the loud tap. The banging of pots and pans followed. "I miss Marcella. The new sitter left me this sinkful."

Then her voice dropped low. "I show visitors around Chicago. And then Jim likes games."

"What kind of games?"

She looked down, not meeting his eyes. "It was Jim who grabbed my scarf that night outside the door. He told me much later that's because he was mad at me. Then another night, he waited for me here in the house. I knew. Your cameras warned me. I walked into the living room and turned on the light. There he was, right on the couch with questions for me about what happened when Oscar used to visit our house."

He leaned in to hear her better, his cheek bristly against hers.

She sighed. "My brain froze. I couldn't think of anything to say except to deny that anything happened like what he was suggesting—gross—between me, and Oscar, and Alex. I'm afraid of Jim. He could get us arrested. Suspects in Oscar's murder. 'No statute of limitations on murder,' he said."

"That's blackmail!"

"Michael, we have young kids. He was here, in our home, and he just talked—about the environment and politics and his plans for my future that made no sense to me—and he smiled at me before he left."

His eyes automatically dropped to her neck and arms, no bruises, and then to the knife in the sink and what he used to know to do with it.

Sichet had accused him too—that he had ruined Callie—not totally a lie after his forgery scheme. But he was no longer a swift teenager, and he had not been a competent assassin for decades, not since his bosses had outsourced that work to kids younger and hungrier. *Not so bad to now be older and broke open . . . see light through the cracks?*

She turned off the water. Both listened for footsteps on the stairs for Alex's return.

He remembered the frozen mouse in the Marions' freezer, the murdered teacher in StarHall. "He may turn violent."

"I think Jim's psycho. But dangerous? For one thing, we're not—you know—physical like that way. And he has others, like Angela. I hear she meets him in Rush and Division bars and pretends he's a stranger picking her up."

She shrugged. "You know I would if he wanted. You should know better than most that we do what we must do. You've told me some of your stories from Poland. But you must believe me that nothing physical is going on between Jim and me. I don't understand it. Do you?"

You don't understand it—his bedroom problems. And he likes you scared of him. Not asking for what he can't give or to explain himself. Listening to him talk or not talk if he doesn't feel like it. In return, he gives you all this instead.

Kochanski turned on the robot vacuum. Over its whine, he said, "Callie, the thing is, when I found myself in a corner around your age, I used the little luck and brains God gave me to get out. You can do it, too."

"There's always Oregon."

"Oregon?"

"Yes, next year after the weather warms up, we're going to take a road trip out there to see Marcella's college. The kids want to see it, too, and maybe we'll not come back."

"I'm still running from the past. God's an infrequent visitor. Maybe you'll be luckier."

"You ran away from Poland." She looked thoughtfully over at the gutted living room and the construction tools stored near the door.

He remembered Irina. If Callie was half as lost a soul as Irina, she too might not know the difference between the fancies and facts in her life.

"I do pity Jim," she said.

"That's a man's oldest trick in the book: to get a woman's sympathy. How about this: ask Jim to marry you if he likes you so much."

She laughed.

"Oh, Michael, you're silly! I'm not going to get divorced."

"Nor him. Maybe he'll move on if he thought you were expecting marriage."

"He wouldn't believe me."

"With his big ego, of course he will."

"Michael, Alex may lose his job if Jim 'moves on.' Alex's full-time job—all our benefits like health insurance—is a favor Jim pulled for me."

They heard steps on the stairs. Alex walked in.

"Glad to see both of you are having a nice talk," he said.

"I was just telling Callie about something my daughter said," mumbled Kochanski.

"We still haven't met her," said Alex.

"She was just here for a quick trip and flew back yesterday," he lied.

Fact is Kasia's not leaving until after Thanksgiving but given this mess with Oscar's murder—best not to connect her to all you guys.

. . .

At Spirit and Stone, Kasia had shaken her head at the transformation of the chapel. In English, she said, "Glad you kept the stained-glass windows and wood inlays, Dad."

Talk to me in Polish!

Sheraton had joined them for dinner one night, the first meeting between his two favorite women. He braced himself afterward for Kasia's colorful review, like when she had skewered another girlfriend as having "hormones steaming out of her ears, ready to pop out a few more Kochanskis."

But Kasia said Sheraton was "okay." In English, she added, "With someone like Elise, *we* won't be dealing with a demanding younger woman who doesn't understand you. And at your age, you won't be supporting a second family in your golden years."

But age, he thought, brought a certain cunning and he smiled. It was time to accept his future where a little Polish would still be spoken.

"I'm glad you liked Elise," he said to Kasia in Polish. "I love you, and it's also nice to have friends—you know— my age."

"And I want you to be happy," Kasia replied, this time in Polish.

. . .

Pandolf Children's Hospital required Noru to come by herself to pick up Ahmat. His workup for child abuse had been negative. All drug screens were negative. Wide awake, the baby was entertaining the doctors and nurses with his smile and antics.

In the emergency department, Noru refused to allow her Pandolf psychiatrist to speak to anyone, even the Saburian embassy in Chicago, her mother, and Aisha. She refused to speak to the Pandolf social worker. She refused her own translator—not trusting her—and accepted an online service instead.

Later, Sichet explained the translation errors to her and Michaela. "The Zoser translation app is glitchy, I will indeed follow up on that. With a David Campbell—" He apologized profusely for missing Michaela's texts, saying he had "turned off his phone for a meeting," and applauded Michaela for finally calling his home phone number. He gave her and Michaela a fabricated story to tell the hospital staff. The hospital staff, too, praised Michaela's good judgment for bringing the baby to the hospital after she was unable to reach his "depressed" mother.

But Noru felt suspicious of Sichet for the first time. *If the Zoser translation app is "glitchy" for something so critical like this, something is up.* But even if Sichet was lying, maybe, just like when Aisha lied, he could still have her and Ahmat's best wishes at heart. After all, Ahmat had now attracted some publicity, was in the hospital database, and had the attention of the American government and police. Sichet now promised her that he would move her to Chicago "immediately," close to him, close to the Saburian embassy there. It sure sounded safer.

She gave her thanks in prayer, even as the Americans around her celebrated their Thanksgiving. Never again, she decided, would she see that American psychiatrist again, so rudely skeptical of her diplomatic lies. Never again was she, a queen, going to turn her psyche inside out for anyone for that matter.

In a private audience, the minister conveyed King Malik's shock to her.

"So, I'm the mad queen now!" she retorted. "Why didn't you do anything when I told you to tell the king that my baby—yes, his little brother—was in danger? Has my child's life become so cheap now, like that of a commoner? What about my life?"

• • •

Two months later, January 2032, Noru had settled into her penthouse suite of the Pierre building. Her English improved from practice with the charming companion that Sichet had assigned to her. Although Callie was not beautiful in the Saburian way, some things were universal. Her tutor looked like a slender version of the "zaftig" European beauties at the Art Institute of Chicago that they had just visited.

"No one uses that word anymore," Callie counseled. "The English word is *fat*. But it's considered rude in our culture to talk about it."

"But people are so *fat* in your country," observed Noru.

They were in the back of a limo, the baby in a car seat between them. The nanny and a new translator, a Saburian American—all Sichet's employees who had been cleared for her security—faced them. "Do you worry about not being young and beautiful someday? My husband had two older wives before me."

Callie gazed out the window, listening to the interpreter translate. "No, because my husband loves me." She paused and added, "Loves me back."

Something didn't sound right, Noru wondered, in her guide's relationship with her husband. To probe, Noru curiously asked a different question. "You told me your husband's an artist. He makes paintings like the ones we saw?"

"Yes. No." Callie frowned after the translator interpreted. "His art is a creation of our present. Fresh. I believe time will be on his side. Right now, it's just me—not even him—who believes in him."

Noru questioned the interpreter. "Does Callie believe in her husband's art for itself because she loves him, or does she love him because she believes in his art?" *Did I love my husband because I believed in him as the king of my country?*

The translator said: "Queen, I know you're trying to understand the culture here, but the word *love* has so many meanings in American English, just as in Saburian."

"My Aisha loves me," said Noru in English, trying to explain in English. "And I love her back. Also, all Saburian people love me, and I love them back." In English, she added, "Callie what is love to you?"

"I'm so sorry about the loss of your husband," said Callie after a pause. "I believe that love is what finds you, what fills your empty spaces in life, and what will surely find you again."

The interpreter explained. Then Noru thought that Callie had shut her down, no different than Aisha when Noru asked too many questions. "Thank you," Noru lied.

The next week, Noru was at the Saburian embassy, in a conference room decorated with her country's carvings and hangings. With Sichet, the translator, and Prince Ahmat in his nanny's lap, she took a video call with the Saburian foreign minister.

"Queen Noru," said Sichet, "your government has given me permission to petition for asylum for you here in the United States. I believe it's your best choice."

"Thank you, but it's past time for us to go home," said Noru emphatically after the translator explained.

The Saburian minister's face was stony. "Though I advise that you and Prince Ahmat return to Ramses instead of your village. It will be safer given his—"

The minister was talking—by not talking—about Ahmat's mixed-race appearance that was becoming more obvious as the baby grew older. In Ramses, very few people would be allowed to see the child.

Noru looked at Sichet for guidance, who said, "Yes, the royal residences in Ramses will be more secure for you and the prince."

"What about our safety?" Noru asked, pretending calm. "The bomb threat . . ."

"A prank by the rebels to destabilize our new regime," said the minister, expressionless, repeating what he told her every time.

Sichet added, "And our American government agrees. And of course, I will watch over our young prince when he returns to the US at the age of eight to attend school at StarHall."

Finally, they set Noru's return home for late March, to "allow Saburia time to prepare to welcome her." While this was later than she wanted, Noru thought she could practice more English. A few more outings with Callie—to the orchestra, the ballet, and restaurants rated with "Michelin stars"—would be a respite from her uncertain future. And she would become more familiar with this strange land, the United States, possibly useful for her political future.

That future for her back in Saburia as a king's widow, possibly in another arranged marriage, was fearsome, she knew. And for Ahmat, too, looking mixed race and hidden away. She had asked King Mohammed about their son's non-Saburian features. He had reassured her that Prince Ahmat was still their child, and he would explain it more in the future. That future never came.

After the Saburian minister disconnected, she asked Sichet, "My circumstances may change. What if something happens such that my country no longer pays you? What will happen to my baby and me?"

"I'll always work for you, Queen Noru. Your husband was my beloved friend. Your son will always be like my own. I've already taken risks for you and the prince in Pandolf. When you gave Ahmat to that Pandolf girl,

I almost lost a major client—your country's government. They called me 'careless.'"

"You said there was a translation error . . ."

"You must trust me when I say that I was as shocked as anyone."

"Did you find out why?"

"Zoser's CTO, a David Campbell, said it was an unusual type of one-use hack. Claims to have fixed it."

"You sound skeptical."

"With all due respect, after the bomb prank, I was making my own plans to move you to Chicago, but it didn't happen how I wanted. Could there be a mole in your government who knew our plans and disrupted them? If so, who, why?"

After the translator explained, she said defensively, "Why *my* government? Maybe *yours*?" Then she looked around warily. "In our oldest houses, there are places where you can hide behind the walls to hear what people are saying."

"And in our newest ones too," he said, smiling, waving at the walls. "In geopolitics, we must work with what we know. Knowledge is priceless, so nothing is transparent. I know you don't trust me, and you really shouldn't trust anyone, especially in your position. I approve. But how about this: not only do you need me, I *also* need you, and Prince Ahmat, in the future—to be my allies in your government."

Just like with servants, she thought, *this man will be useful, not necessarily loyal or trustworthy.* Back in Saburia, she would keep up her end of their deal for now, she decided and nodded agreement.

"And see, here you are in Chicago anyway," he added. "Things worked out. Still, I'll be more careful in the future for all of us."

She sensed his anger, a man not used to his plans disrupted, even as he smiled at her. Graying hair at his temples, his blue eyes looked into hers and projected reassurance. "What do you think about your outings with Callie?"

She felt confused, remembering again how Aisha had always told her to "never trust a man with 'light eyes.'"

And her mother had said, "Ask yourself what you're afraid of?"

"Nothing!"

And she heard herself reply, "Yesterday, Callie made sure we were 'layered up' to walk along the lake. Still, some stranger scolded us for not dressing my son warmly enough."

Sichet frowned. "It's Callie's job to prepare you and your son for an outing in the snow. I'll talk to her."

"Please, no. She cut our walk short after that." She did not add that Callie's mind often appeared to be elsewhere, a mystery she found intriguing.

Later, Noru called Aisha, who advised her, "Don't complain about your pretty guide to that man. As for when you return, Queen, you're young. It'll be good for you to live in Ramses. You can still visit your family often. Your mother wants me to tell you that she agrees."

A harsh tone in Aisha's voice told Noru that this was a warning. Was Aisha saying, Noru wondered, that she would have to marry again? If she remarried in the capital, it would be easy to control her and Ahmat.

Who is this future husband?

After Noru left, only Sichet and the translator were left in the room.

"Cute baby," he said aloud to the wall. "You know, let me tell you what I think: the future usually belongs to the present's misfits, mixed race like this one, ugly ducklings . . . and then *they* write the past, a story to paint *them* in the best light."

He turned around and said to the interpreter, "I am good at compartmentalizing. Don't go around translating my head trips, like the fact that I think men are narcissists and mentor the young who look like us. Or have rescue fantasies about other races, inflating our egos at the expense of looking down on others. We serve a greater cause when it glorifies who we are."

"Yes, Mr. Sichet."

He pointed a finger at the wall. "Yes, the Sun Order will protect our queen and prince. We *will* also get you—whoever you are." Then he stormed out.

• • •

At the Marions' home, Kochanski broke open a Chinese fortune cookie. "It says, 'Beware someone who brings you riches.' I must give Jim credit for my New Year present, royal tenants in my building."

Alex briefly smiled. Around his eyes, fine wrinkles were developing.

"I have to leave now, got a midnight deadline for a client in South America." Before exiting left, like a husband in a play, he added, "Thanks for coming, Michael. Swing by and say goodbye."

Wooden floors in the old house, no carpet to drown out creaks, meant that they could hear when Alex settled down to work.

Kochanski then confronted Callie. "What's this about Alex getting a new home studio?"

"Yes," she said, then lowered her voice. "When I suggested to Jim that we get married, he confessed that he had feelings for me—would give up a future in politics for me. Then I had to tell him that I couldn't break up my family."

"A lawyer, calling your bluff."

Or he told you to tell me that, he thought.

She looked in the direction of the gutted living room. Then nodding at the violet granite in her kitchen, she added, "I like beautiful things. Even if to you that just looks like another countertop and backsplash."

If she liked beautiful things, Kochanski thought, Sichet was elevating her into a rarefied world where much was lovely, including Queen Noru. His stubborn daughter had taught him to go into a default waiting mode whenever he didn't agree with the women in his life. But with Callie, she was changing, growing distant, smiling less, and often her smiles weren't real. He knew her well enough now to tell.

I must keep trying.

Callie continued, "It really wasn't worth it, all this stuff, you might say, except that they make me no longer the person I used to be. I sometimes do want to look Jim in the eye and have a heart-to-heart with him about parting ways—except for our working relationship."

"There'll be no 'working relationship' with Jim if you break any part of it off," he said grimly. "He'll quickly find someone else to do your job, all of *whatever it is.*"

Then he heard himself pleading with her. "But you and Alex can fly on your own, right?"

When she was quiet, he grew angry. "You need to plan for the day when your shelf life with Jim is up," he said. "Like setting up a bank account that he makes regular deposits into. What happened to Oregon?"

"I think you are happy that we didn't move to Oregon." She reached over to touch his hand over the kitchen table where they sat. "What about you? When are you going to see Elise? She has such a hard time traveling with her job. You need to visit her where she lives. Then you might even move to the end of the world, Endon, Missouri."

She leaned in and he felt himself lean in too, closing the distance, drawn by her eyes— Atlantic green as the ocean he flew over from Poland never to return—*angel dark or light, good or evil?*

He blinked—*help me God*—and then heard himself say, "I'm waiting until the weather gets warmer. If anything, Elise will move to Chicago if we stay together. I can't imagine living in the Ozarks."

He got up to go.

"Michael, wait, go out the back. Remember that our new front steps were just poured? Next time you come, you'll see the children's initials etched into the sides."

"An artist's children."

Forgetting to say goodbye to Alex, he hurried out. Icy wind gusts quickened his steps away from this home he loved. Perhaps he would try again with Callie. But he had already warned her *repeatedly* about going down this dangerous road with Sichet.

A voice spoke inside like catechism: *Pray by her side.*

And he heard himself respond back to his old priest: *Never too late to save a soul.*

CHAPTER THIRTY

February 2032, down a dirt road in Southern Missouri, Elise Sheraton was asleep at home. She awoke abruptly. Getting up, she flicked on the old lamp switch. A tremor in the floorboards faded away. She went to the window and looked at the town in the valley below—mostly black, some lights turning on as generators kicked in. Some other flashes in the distance appeared to be fireworks, probably kids having fun.

She had asked Wayne Endon about the frequent power outages.

"Be glad you don't use the grid," he said. "It's crap!"

She lay back down, sleepless. In a few hours, she had to go to work. Yesterday had been her worst day. Riverfox, the farmer, and two other men had carried in a young man on a stretcher.

"He's not from around here," said Riverfox. "Just shows up and does some work for me sometimes. He's OD'd again."

Despite Narcan and her other interventions, he was unresponsive. Riverfox watched, helpless, face burned by the winter sun, lips sunk in where teeth were missing. She tapped into her computer to report her patient to the closest hospital two hours away.

On the phone, she told a Dr. Patel, "Yes, sats 94 percent on four liters oxygen nasal cannula. Acute beds are all still full? Okay, we'll call St. Louis."

As they waited for the helicopter ambulance, Riverfox asked, "Mind if I tell my boy one of the stories for around these parts?"

She did not believe that Riverfox was his real name. Many locals had Native American last names despite no physical features to indicate indigenous heritage.

"Sure, maybe he can still hear you."

"He will, even if he's deeper down there than just sleeping. The Universe hears too." He picked up his guitar and began strumming, humming, and talking.

"There's singing in the night," Riverfox said. "Children sit around a firepit. Flames throw sparks into the night. The teacher is a bent old man in front of a blackboard."

He stretched out one hand, fingers now tracing lines in the air. Returning to the guitar, he twanged a few notes that lit up the silence.

"The teacher's chalk strikes the slate, flint on steel. White light ignites, children listen with upturned faces. Fire-glow defies blasted surroundings. Dust and ash cover the ground, our dark lake less than half-full, sad under gray skies."

The guitar sang alone when the farmer stopped speaking. His eyes were far away. As the riffs faded, he spoke again. "Even in the day, there is little light. Dark clouds block sunlight. The teacher's time to die is coming. He passes on what he remembers: letters, numbers, words, how things work, our story, our song. Out there in the night, the future is born—ghosts, sounds, unknown energies, but mostly silence. Walking around, the teacher tells the children what used to be in those broken buildings. They live as scavengers, on tins and packages and bags of fluid in places like this one here, finding no other living, loving thing."

Guitar music again, softer this time, background harmony as he kept speaking. "Everyone is grateful, not bitter cold anymore, nor blistering hot, just the same day and night—no rain, no snow, no sleet, no heat. Has time stopped? The teacher is lost, adrift, his own memory a fog after explosions that went on endlessly."

Silence. They watched the young man's chest rise and fall—less and less.

The oxygen meter's readings began to drop even as she dialed up the machine. Riverfox then picked up the guitar, not to play, fingers silent on the strings, hands pressing the wood for comfort, and spoke clearly, firmly: "Tonight there's change, the wetness of air and soil, as if seeds would germinate again in the ground. The children sense it, too, more cheerful than the teacher has seen them before, smiling, laughing, even before he finishes talking. They sleep in the open, all together now with the teacher for protection. Oh, this wetness, this gentle sprinkle of fresh rain that promises life, it's new. Has time started again? Is this a New World or the Old? When the boys and girls are asleep, the teacher stares into the embers. He feels hope for the first time in a long while—life begins again, and again, and forever, again."

After a pause, she whispered, "Is this about death?"

He released sobs. Finally, he said, "About new life, redemption, death is just a passage."

A helicopter whirred nearby. Riverfox put away his guitar and held the unmoving young man's hand. The medics arrived, and the farmer gave one last squeeze.

"Sorry," the medic said apologetically to Sheraton. "You have to pay first. I don't make the rules."

She handed the pilot the clinic's charge card.

"I'll drive up to St. Louis later," said Riverfox. "But first, got to go home and take care of a few things. We raise beef, and there's dogs. Wife and son work other jobs in town, so just me today."

They watched the departing helicopter rising. "Why don't you just sell the farm?" asked Sheraton. "It sounds like a lot of work, especially the livestock."

"The land is my blood," he said, sounding wounded.

Her patient died en route to St. Louis. Feeling like a failure, she called Riverfox to let him know.

"I expected so. Rest in peace, brother."

. . .

In her cabin, unable to go back to sleep, Sheraton got back out of bed to check the valley. But the power grid was still down. Finally, dawn rose, a red line in the east, and she called the clinic on the satellite phone.

The night nurse answered. "Dr. Sheraton, we're still on generator."

She turned on the news. The main channels had the usual feed: foreign wars, government corruption, and stories—from frightening to feel-good—about faraway people she did not know.

She turned on the Endon local network. On her screen, the Earth's globe turned, blue waters and brown land. In the Americas, black dots appeared to mark locations: including Endon, Chicago, and Pandolf. Muzak played a cheery series of tunes loosely based on popular songs.

She tried to call her children, but the connection would not go through, making her hyperaware of her geographical distance from them, thousands of miles. Anxious, she then called Wayne Endon. "I can't reach my kids. Is it because the power is down?"

Endon's face was pixelated on the screen, the background dark. In a garbled voice, he said, "I'm sure they're fine, but the world is not."

"What do you mean?"

"The world's dying out there."

"Wayne, don't get philosophical, everything looks fine on the news."

"It's all fake. No one knows what's really happening."

"Okay, Wayne," she said, thinking how this conversation was going nowhere. "Tell me about that globe on our news channel. What's all the black dots?"

"A closed-circuit news feed. Those are survival cells like ours now popping up everywhere. When people come for us, for what we have here in our town, we'll be ready for them."

"This is crazy! I need to talk to my family. I'm going to drive up to St. Louis if I still can't reach them."

"Don't, won't be safe! And you can't just cancel your clinic. For now, the cabin is perfect for you. It's isolated. You've got power, water, food, supplies. The satellite network should be working again soon. There may be fighting. If that happens, some of us may come up there to hide out."

"What!"

"I know you worry about your children," said Endon. "You're a mom. I can't explain more now except that the final chapter isn't written yet. I'll meet you in the clinic later today. I'd like to talk to you—very much—in person."

That sounds like an order, she thought. Then without even a goodbye, he hung up.

She opened tins of dog food. Did those animals really need so much to eat? What if there weren't any more shipments of the crates from the pet food website? What if? *That's a problem for tomorrow,* she told herself. For now, to top off the two large bowls, she poured tall heaps of kibble.

Fatten up, guys. No worries, I won't eat you.

She remembered the vet she had met at the Athens airport, fleeing her country in a recent war. The vet told her how people had euthanized or abandoned their animals when they left their homes. "And the ones who stayed behind fought and ate anything that moved."

Next, she layered up to go outside, where it was icy. Should she put the chains back on the tires? There was no choice but to make the trek into town. In the clinic, snow or not, power or not, people would still show up. The clinic had plenty of fuel for the generators to last a long time. A warehouse next to the building stocked medications and supplies to last at least a year. The main buildings in town also used solar, wind, and hydropower.

It was best to keep a packed suitcase in her car, ready to leave anytime, though, she thought. As for the animals, the Endons had taken good care of the two dogs before she had come and hopefully would continue to do so. Those two cats mousing in the barn didn't need any help. She opened the safe and removed her beat-up passport, birth certificate, Social Security card, and her old wedding ring. Finally, she removed several gold ingots, a gift from her father.

"How can a slab of gold so small weigh so much?" her daughter had asked her as a child.

"Science—let's figure that out."

In the safe, she saw Garcia's Drukker disk of "personal things" to give to Campbell. She had forgotten all about it. Garcia had managed to visit Campbell at Pandolf a few months ago while she was unable to go. Then he must have already given Campbell everything on the disk.

She tried calling her children again, without success. Panic ignited. *What kind of place is this anyway, with a name like Endon?* For that matter, the patient's name yesterday had been Youngblood. It sounded Native American, just like Riverfox. He had no ID. It must not have been his real name.

She turned on the television. The globe still swirled. On the screen, there was a dot on the Red Sea coast.

"Oh my god, smack-dab in Saburia!" she exclaimed. If she died in Endon, she now thought, trapped in some apocalyptic commune, she should destroy Garcia's disk instead of letting someone get his personal information from her.

But before destroying it, shouldn't I know something more about what's on it?

Come to think of it, why had Garcia only wanted Campbell to "decrypt it" in the event of his death? She told herself she was a scientist, and knowledge on balance was a positive. She removed the glass plate and placed it on her laptop viewer. Tap, connect, her Drukker software processed the files for viewing. Garcia's smiling face now appeared on the screen.

"Hello, David," said Garcia. "I'm so happy that Elise delivered this to you safely."

Feeling guilty, she clicked "PLAY" and told herself that under the circumstances, this was not snooping.

Garcia went on, "If you see this, it's likely either that I am dead or at least out of contact with you for the foreseeable future. This is the entire unsecured record of my Purple Project research I never told you about. If you see my son, tell him that we don't know what we don't know. Goodbye, dear friend, until great minds meet again across the abyss."

She clicked "STOP."

I don't need to know more, especially if this is private information about Queen Noru's pregnancy,

Much later, her phone rang, her daughter's picture. She connected on her laptop with relief.

"Mom, you sound upset. What's up?"

So, the world out there had not disappeared with her children, as if God had just awakened from a dream and only Endon was left. She felt annoyed with herself, her catastrophic thinking. The brilliant morning sun outside, reflecting off the snow, also shooed out her misgivings.

"Hi, just calling to check in," she told Debbie.

"So early in the morning? I'm going back to sleep."

"Sorry."

Debbie hung up, her student world intact: lousy college food, annoying dorm super, working last minute on projects in the union, and the teaching assistant whose English was too poor to comprehend.

After a final outer layer of a hat, muffler, and thick gloves, Sheraton pulled on thick boots, picked up the two heaping-full dog food bowls, and headed to the barn. How would she explain to Manny Garcia that she had listened to the beginning of the message because she believed the world might be ending?

Wayne Endon needed to explain, she decided. Ever since she had told him, before a trip up to Chicago to see Kochanski, that she was going to meet a male "friend," he had become aloof and critical. He visited the cabin less often, sending others for needed repairs, maintenance, and installations that he always used to do himself.

Driving into town, the streetlights were working. In the clinic's break area, Wayne Endon brought lunch for everyone, sandwiches. He was unshaven. Usually neat, his nails were dirty, and there were shadows under his eyes.

Inside her office, he explained, "Elise, our town will now stay off the main power grid. We have an independent electric network, mostly solar, wind, and water. Plenty of reserve fuel if needed. The transition happened last night. When you first came, I thought you knew about us. Then it was obvious that you didn't. When you visited Chicago, I thought it was to see our lawyer. But when I called Chicago, he told me that I needed to tell you why you're here. 'When the time's right.'"

"I don't understand."

"We are part of a network of survivalist communities."

"Okay?" *What the hell?*

"We're becoming self-sufficient. Preparing for someday when others will come for what we have when they have nothing left. Practice armed drills, like last night, are preparation, too, when there is no choice but violence. That was my warning to you a few hours ago. It would not have been safe for you to go out on the road. But there was no trouble. Washington, even Jeff City, our state capital, have become empty threats. Maybe you shouldn't know more."

He wasn't looking at her. She looked more closely at the fatigue in his face. "Wayne, you talk about fighting and people coming up to my cabin to hide. Please understand that's scary. You're right, I don't want to know more. Honestly, after I talked to you earlier this morning, I imagined terrible things, until my daughter called, and I knew everything was fine. Maybe this is not the place I need to stay at after my contract with this clinic ends."

He met her eyes with a glint in his. "Thank you for honoring your contract. That'll take us into next year. I sure hope we can keep you after that. Maybe we can get that second doctor you think we need—so you can have time off. I should have warned you about last night, but there has been so much going on. I'm sorry about your patient. Boys like him are one of the reasons I do what I do, to bring them hope."

"On the phone, you made it sound like the world outside Endon had . . . 'was dying.'"

"It is."

"Okay, I don't need to know everything. But on the map last night, Endon was marked as one black spot on the globe. So was Chicago. Chicago makes sense if your lawyer's there. But what about Pandolf and Saburia and those other places?"

"I don't know everything either," he said. "I haven't traveled much. We stay connected over a satellite network. My guess is that while most governments are aware, our community tries to stay under the radar. We stay in small cells, understand the local laws, pay our taxes, and network into banks, corporations, and medical centers."

"You're everywhere, even in the governments?"

"Why not? Aren't some religions? Christian sects, Jews, Muslims, they're everywhere, too."

"In America, there's supposed to be a separation of church and state. But are you a religion?"

"No, that's just a point of comparison. I believe in science. Do you know how much technology it now takes to run my town?"

What did he mean by "science"? Just the practical applications? The homeschooled Endon children were learning a different version of "science" from hers.

"Thanks for lunch," she finished, getting up. "Gotta get back to work, the patients are arriving for the afternoon."

Endon rose, too. "One more thing. I want to upgrade this clinic, more equipment, starting with a ventilator."

"It's not that simple. Also, I'm not certified to operate one," she said. "I've never even intubated an adult."

"Then we'll set up a time to sit down and plan. My brother will send someone from the hospital."

"His hospital had no beds for my dying patient!"

"Think outside the box," he said. "Anyway, for your trip to Chicago, your friend there knows our lawyer, Jim Sichet. It's a small world."

Garcia returned her video call. He said the cancer vaccine trials were expanding and that Soria Clinics hoped to open another site soon. "In Argentina," he explained happily. "My home country."

She explained that she had listened to the beginning of his disk, circumspect about its contents for anyone tapping into their conversation.

"Yes, I've been meaning to talk to you about those personal files," he said, now looking sharply at her like he understood that she had learned something about the disk's contents. "Please destroy it right away. Now that I can travel again, it's no longer needed."

"I have a hammer. Will do it right after we hang up."

"Excellent!" he said. "Michael says you'll see him soon in Chicago. The baby prince and his mother are there right now too."

"Safe and sound," she said, smiling. "Manny, I'm happy to see that all your hard work is paying off."

His face grew serious. "Some things paid off, yes, meaning I achieved stated objectives. In other ways, things didn't turn out the way I planned."

"We also learn from our mistakes."

"Yes, no matter how much we want to control: our future, the future of what we create. Our children. Our work. But things break open into unexpected futures anyway."

He looked worried.

Something go wrong with the Purple Project, Manny?

"Maybe they weren't mistakes but progress," Garcia added thoughtfully. "Time will tell. For that, Elise, I'll tell you more in person one day." He smiled again at her. "Like a time you visit Michael in Chicago."

• • •

March in Chicago, Elise Sheraton and Michael Kochanski escaped the bitter March wind in Spirit and Stone.

Proudly, Kochanski pulled out his phone and showed her Alex Marion's marketing campaign. "Rising sales."

"And lovely model as the face of Dew."

Then she talked about her patient that had died and her latest scare. "I thought the world outside Endon was collapsing. It's so isolated there, Michael. I got caught up in their doomsday thinking. They're growing their own vegetables in giant warehouses year-round, using robots. You should see their chicken farms. They tell me that you know their lawyer, a Jim Sichet."

"Not sure I'd call Jim my 'friend.' Apocalyptic cells now, you say! Jim seems to have his finger in a lot of cookie jars."

She laughed. "Oh, Michael, that's not quite how we use that expression, and with your accent, oh, I'm so sorry, you sound so funny."

They wandered to happier topics. Replaying memories of previous dinners here and in Saburia, she sipped her Loire, and he drank his Dew.

"How's Manny?" she asked.

"Fine. His AI augmented cancer vaccines are going mainstream. A new Soria Clinics site will open in Argentina. Manny wants to go home. Says he wants to go back to where he fits in. I told him he'll more than just fit in back in Buenos Aires. He'll be hot stuff. Big fish in a small pond."

"I don't think Manny is that egotistical."

"I disagree," said Kochanski. "And he's coming for the wedding."

"What wedding?"

"David's— "

"Why don't I know this?"

"They said you weren't responding to emails. I hear that a fancy paper wedding save-the-date is now on its snail mail way to you."

She shook her head. "Endon has an intranet that filters out many of my emails. Fine print in my contract lets them do that, but they're fixing that. And I stay off social media. I can't believe David's getting *married*."

"I know you *ladies* get excited about that kind of thing," he teased.

"That's retro. I guess one can take the man—meaning you, Michael— out of the Old World, but can't take the Old World out of the man. Where are they getting married?"

"Pandolf of all places. I believe Mary, Manny's first patient, is coming. Old like me, but we're still 'knocking it out of the park.' Do you like the vibe of that American expression?"

She smiled. "I need to call Mary. By the way, Pandolf's another place on the satellite map I saw the other day." She described the rotating globe on the Endon community intranet and what she had learned from Wayne Endon about an international network of survivalist communities, including one in Saburia. "And I assume you know all about a Purple Project?"

He looked around warily. "Who told you?" He picked up their phones, turned them off, and placed them face down. Then he even moved them closer to where the speakers blared the music that the young restaurant manager insisted on, saying, "Mr. Kochanski, trust me, these are the tunes people listen to."

She confessed to viewing the beginning of Garcia's message to Campbell. "Manny lied to me. He told me that the disk just had 'personal things,' if something happened to him. But after Manny was able to leave Saburia and see David in person in Pandolf, I thought the disk was no longer needed—and if something crazy was going on in Endon, I should check out the files before destroying them."

Kochanski gave her an odd look. "Why don't I believe that?"

"Okay, I was curious."

"I believe that."

"I saw the beginning of Manny's files, the title Purple Project, and figured out that had to do with Queen Noru's pregnancy. Then I didn't feel it was right to continue to look at Manny's files. Later, I talked to Manny and he told me to destroy his disk. When he made that disk, he thought he would never get to leave Saburia. I guess he wanted to share his research with other scientists."

"Manny's a changed man, get my pun?"

She made a face. "Man, a much happier man, for sure. I've never heard him get so emotional as when he told me he was looking forward to a performance of Beethoven's *Ninth* when he goes to Argentina, feeling joy and brotherhood."

"The *Ninth*. Many years ago, when I first came to Chicago, I fell in love with a flute player in the Chicago Symphony Orchestra living in a building I managed. She wasn't interested in me. I don't blame her. At that time, I had little to give any woman. Still, I used to get a seat in Symphony Center, where I'd see Twinkle-Fingers play. For Beethoven's *Ninth*, I remember it was a full house. When the music was over, the conductor could barely stand, red-faced after an hour of dancing. We gave Crazyman a standing ovation. I was on my feet, inspired, cheering with the rest—me, a Pole, applauding a German composer, an ocean away in America."

"Twinkle-Fingers. I often wonder if genes can also be musical."

"I used to stand outside her door, pretending to work, listening to sounds from heaven. She had the gene. After the *Ninth* performance, I got on the subway, then waited alone at the graveyard bus station, empty except for a homeless man. I took the bus past the latest Cabrini–Green renovation, thinking that the same land that had produced Beethoven also gave us Hitler. I love the music, but no brotherhood for me, no thank you, my dear Elise. I'd rather think for myself. So, yes, dear, I know all about the Purple Project."

"You look nervous."

"It's a good thing it's so loud here. I worry about someone listening, devices more than people, getting smarter and smarter than us. Okay, please listen. The fewer people find out about the king's scheme, the better. The king is dead, we have a new king. Please don't tell anyone what you discovered. Manny and I never told David about the Purple Project, and David's starting a new life with a woman he loves. Why bother him with old baggage?"

"Okay."

A burly guard came up to their table to say hello. Kochanski proudly introduced her as "Dr. Elise Sheraton."

After the man left, she asked, "Why is there so much security now in your building?"

"Oh, yes," he replied, smiling broadly. "So that lawyer, Jim, he has his 'finger on the cookie' here, too. In my penthouse suite, he placed a royal princess and prince and their entourage. Guess who? Waited to tell you in person."

"Oh my god, Michael, is Queen Noru really staying in your building? Manny said she was in Chicago. I left a voice mail at the embassy about visiting her and the baby when I got here."

"I'll arrange it," he said. Then he added slowly, "Elise, one more thing, you should know the baby is mixed race, not fully Saburian-looking."

She stared at him. "I wondered about that after he was born. But sometimes with newborns you just can't tell."

"Yes, I talked to Manny about it when he visited Chicago. You see, he was so focused on his AI cancer vaccines. The Purple Project was just side action for him, something he had to work on, using what little time he could squeeze out of the things he wanted to work on. Now he feels guilty."

"You mean—"

"You remember. His son, George, was almost killed coming to Saburia for some final work Manny had to do on the Purple Project. Many soldiers were killed, and David Campbell was also injured. And for Manny, Prince Ahmat is also like a son to him because he created him. And now the poor prince doesn't have his father, his mother, the queen will be married off soon too, and the boy will have to come to boarding school in the US, a place called StarHall, when he is eight."

She inhaled deeply. "Michael, of course Prince Ahmat will never fit into Saburia. Such a rigid culture would never accept someone mixed-race-looking. Manny said something to me—about things not turning out the way he had expected."

Kochanski decided to comfort her. "No worries, the prince will fit into America just fine. StarHall is David's old rich-kid boarding school in New England."

"He won't have a choice," she said.

"Choices. Kids don't get choices," Kochanski said abruptly. "Anyway, we'll send someone up in the morning to arrange you seeing your patient again. Your timing is good. She'll go home at the end of the month."

"Does this surprise you?" he then asked, gesturing at both of them.

"What do you mean?"

"You know, the two of us here together, so different from each other, after all our tensions."

"I'm sorry," she said. "I feel really shook-up processing everything that's happened lately."

After a silence, she added, "When we met, we were different people; at least I was. Still, with you, I feel hopeful. Otherwise, I often worry that our world is in a bad way, that in Endon, they're right—that our planet, our civilization is dying. You know today is the Ides of March, the anniversary of Julius Caesar's assassination? Then the Roman world fell apart."

"Are you also thinking about King Mohammed?"

She raised her gaze, holding back tears. "Yes. And I'm thinking about Queen Noru and the baby up there, how when change comes, it's often something totally like we never expect."

She dried her eyes with her napkin and looked at him. "Can I ask you something serious?"

"Yes." He tensed.

"I have wondered. Tell me about your father."

He thought she was really thinking about Prince Ahmat, growing up without his father. He remembered the night trains passing through his youth, carrying a killer, a child-soldier, the bold and thoughtless boy who was him, and the things a father might have told that boy. "I had the fathers I needed," he finally said.

She did not press.

Rather to lighten the mood, she then asked, "You don't believe in 'Beware the Ides of March'? Neither did Caesar when he was warned."

"Good thing I'm no Caesar, no king, just want to be an ordinary man, not in Rome, not in Saburia, but here in the United States of America," he said. "So be here with me, Elise, alive and before you, in my building, in my restaurant, drinking my Dew." He raised his glass and leaned in toward her.

And she smiled back warmly, her eyes twinkling through tears, and clinked his glass.

He added something in Polish.

"What did you say?"

"To the health of a beautiful lady," he said, simple, the truth.

• • •

As Best Man for Campbell's June wedding, Garcia arrived a few days early at Pandolf. Touring around the renovated Dock, Garcia sat in a Drukker Pod and admired innovations that Campbell explained to him.

Walking outside, Garcia said hopefully, "David, I've been rethinking my decision about the Purple Project research. We don't know what tomorrow will bring—for opportunities to use my work, right?"

"Good news! We're definitely going to keep talking about this. And like with your AI cancer vaccines, we'll get your name on that too. You deserve credit!"

They sat on a bench outside ButterFiles.

"I'll take credit where I deserve it, but—" Garcia shook his head.

"What's wrong?" Campbell asked.

"David, you see, I want to make things right again somehow. Prince Ahmat is mixed-race, lost a parent, will never fit into his homeland—"

Their eyes met like years ago at the NIH. Campbell saw again pain in Garcia's. In the past, Garcia had spoken to him of his feeling of never belonging, in the USA, in Saburia, and his eagerness to someday return to Argentina permanently.

"I see now. I understand," Campbell said, frowning. "I don't know the answer. Maybe a reckoning for you is to keep going down that road you started on wherever it takes you."

"I have second thoughts now about King Mohammed too," Garcia said.

"Power-hungry egotistical monarch that he was. After all, without him, I would never have had the money and technology to advance my cancer vaccine research."

"Absolutely."

"And Prince Ahmat was not his father's child sacrifice for the Sun Order like I once thought. StarHall is not Peter Pan's Neverland. Like my other son, George, the prince, too, will grow up. Choose his own destiny."

"Prince Ahmat is like a son for you too, true," Campbell murmured.

"Then I've learned a few things from the Sun Order: maybe a person is not entering life like game theory, a zero-sum path where my gain is your loss. Rather, we break open new worlds, for better or for worse; the Sun Order hopes for better."

Campbell leaned in. "I like that."

"I used to diss my old mentor at the NIH: his research with zero practical applications, like what's the point? But now, I'm where he was. I want to learn more about the Conductor genetic complex I discovered, and what is the phenotype, its real-world expression in human beings?" Garcia grinned. "Could they really be wizards with paranormal powers like the Sun Order hypothesizes? But I'm not going to build people to find out—at least after the Purple Project— never again."

"Great, so we'll now ramp up a research team to study human embryo engineering?" Campbell said. "For future uses that are positive and ethical— not sentient replicants—even have our new Ethics team to help us."

Garcia looked at him curiously. "After you became CTO of Zoser, did you already learn something about the Purple Project before I gave you those files? The Sun Order has its footprint in both Zoser and Soria Clinics."

"Pieces to the puzzle, yes, but not able to make sense of it until you gave me your Purple Project files. Fact is we were searching for a scientist to get to work on those ideas. Then here you come along."

"My focus remains my cancer research. But I will still help you find the right person, build the right team, and mentor them. That way, I can keep my promise to King Mohammed to keep his secret about his son. We won't connect the dots between this new research and Prince Ahmat's existence. And you could destroy the disk I gave you? Elise destroyed my only other copy."

"I don't know, Manny, if destroying it is the right thing to do? For me? For Prince Ahmat? I'm not ready to do that yet."

"Maybe I'm asking for too much control again? I'll respect your decision."

Campbell then grabbed Garcia's elbow to turn him around to face him. "Manny, this time—for you and me—there'll be security for our work so no one else will use it for their purposes. And transparency between us will also be required."

"Absolutely." After all their years together, thought Garcia, this renewal of trust between them was another fresh beginning.

A robot bee buzzed near Campbell's ear. "And now, we pick up our suits for my big day."

About the author

JR Ray is a practicing physician and former CEO and founder of a biotech company. Besides staying current with the latest medical developments, Ray enjoys writing, contemporary politics, and world history, as well as time with family and friends. Ray lives in the Midwestern United States.

Made in the USA
Monee, IL
14 September 2024

65773322R00213